WHAT'S NEXT?
SHORT FICTION IN TIME *of* CHANGE

WHAT'S NEXT?

SHORT FICTION IN TIME *of* CHANGE

Edited by

SHARYN SKEETER

GREEN WRITERS PRESS | *Brattleboro, Vermont*

Green Writers Press is a Vermont-based publisher whose mission is to spread a message of hope and renewal through the words and images we publish. Throughout we will adhere to our commitment to preserving and protecting the natural resources of the earth. To that end, a percentage of our proceeds will be donated to environmental and social-activist groups. Green Writers Press gratefully acknowledges support from individual donors, friends, and readers to help support the environment and our publishing initiative.

Giving Voice to Writers & Artists Who Will Make the World a Better Place
Green Writers Press | Brattleboro, Vermont
www.greenwriterspress.com

ISBN: 978-1-950584-86-4

COVER:
ARCHIVAL PRINT, 19TH CENTURY STEEL ENGRAVING.

Dedicated to

Jacob Michael Tucker and Layla Adelaide Tucker

ACKNOWLEDGMENTS

THANKS TO Dede Cummings for her encouragement from the first discussion about this book through to its publication. I appreciate the work of Rose Alexandre-Leach and the editorial staff at Green Writers Press. Thanks to Dr. Amritjit Singh for his valuable advice. My continued admiration goes to the accomplished authors who contributed to this anthology. I'm grateful for Jason, Anna, and Alice and other family members and friends who listened to me as I progressed through this project. As always, *dhanyavaadaha* to Chuck.

CONTENTS

INTRODUCTION

We face the danger of global warming, when the atmosphere of the Earth itself turns against us. We face the danger of modern warfare, as nuclear weapons proliferate in some of the most unstable regions of the globe. We face the danger of weaponized microbes, such as airborne AIDS or Ebola, which can be transmitted by a simple cough or sneeze.

—MICHIO KAKU, *The Future of Humanity*

No WONDER WE ASK "What's Next?" We're in a tough run. Covid-19 pandemic, economic hardship, climate change with its catastrophic fires and floods, war and international upheaval, food and energy shortages, personal uncertainty in relationships, rising crime, political conflicts, immigration, cultural polarization, gender and racial issues, and fake news. We've had it all these past years—and it continues.

This is the question that the authors in this anthology pose, directly or indirectly, though not one of their stories predicts a definite answer. Each author, in his or her unique fiction, offers readers the opportunity to consider their own next options.

Conflicts resulting from changes in nature are featured in several stories. Claire Boyles's "Chickens" pits the natural world against human laws and, in this case, the moral choice between life and death. Toiya Kristen Finley's characters in her "Outer Rims" are trapped in a pandemic and suffer the consequences of authoritarian decisions on public and private good. "Mother, Mother, Mother, Mother, Earth" is Donna Miscolta's story of the interaction between the human nature of mother and daughter and their everyday responses to Mother Earth. Climate is also a factor in Anthony Lee Head's "Heading Out." With a Zen approach that change is inevitable, his ex-patriots in Mexico who face the challenge of financial effects of a storm must seek new lives.

Charles Johnson's story, "Night Shift," taking place during the pandemic, presents the dilemma of choosing the right action with personal risk. A hospital security guard faces the choice between family loyalty and the law. Another story of family decisions is Shannon Sanders's "The Good, Good Men." Who is right here? We see the mother left without personal agency by the sons who care about her welfare.

On the other hand, Maurice Carlos Ruffin's young special assistant in "Election" works through her relationship with a politician who is also her lover. Living with wounds both physical and emotional, American Indian veterans weigh their options in the country they fought for in Joseph Bruchac's "Vision."

Immigrants' relationships are further complicated by their cultural differences. In Chitra Banerjee Divakaruni's "Doors," the married couple's expectations of each other's roles are defined by their upbringing as first- and second-generation Indians in America. The not-yet-divorced wife in Vijay Lakshmi's "After the Fire" rummages through the ashes, gaining an understanding of her lost marriage. Egyptian tradition and American culture are at odds in "A Good Marriage" by Pauline Kaldas, when the immigrant wife takes on the role of an Americanized woman. Ye Chun's newly arrived Chinese woman in "Anchor Baby" cannot imagine America as a real place. Yet, it's where she gives birth believing her baby daughter will have a better life.

Jane Pek's contemporary Chinese-American woman blends six hundred years of myth, history, and fantasy in "Portrait of Two Young Ladies in White and Green Robes (Unidentified Artist, Circa Sixteenth Century)." "In the Event" by Meng Jin has characters trying to negotiate their lives with the backdrop of potential earthquakes, nuclear war, popular culture, and an incident at Chinaman's Vista.

In "The Special World," Tiphanie Yanique's college student stumbles into an experience of gender confusion and religion, while he attempts to reconcile his relationship with his father. In "A Beautiful Wedding in Nantucket," Anna Sequoia's narrator, of Russian-Polish Jewish heritage, responds to gender, status, and organized crime issues as presented by a German-Jewish family's wedding that she's invited to.

By holding onto the predictable definitions of race, the woman and man in my own story, "Office Break," are stifled in their ability to fulfill their love.

How do we humans navigate the present and imagine the future in a world dominated by technology? In the everyday lives of Tom Gammarino's college couple in "Future Studies," it can be a relationship breaker. Touch is restricted in Brenda Peynado's "Touches." Her human characters exist in a world of robots, avatars, and the likes of a Commission for Digital Humanization. Asako Serizawa's "Echolocation" intersects culture, science, technology, and philosophy to ask the question "What's going to happen to us?"

No doubt there have been times when we haven't known what to believe. The narrator in "Innocence" by Clarence Major believes he witnesses a murder. Does he really? What version of reality can we trust? In "Teardrop," Joanna Scott's narrator cannot verify that she has really seen a woman weeping in a painting.

So, what's next for us?

Perhaps, individually, as in "A Fabricated Life" by Pamela Painter, we will untangle our rigidly comfortable identities as we foster authentic love for ourselves and others. Perhaps, too, we will understand what George Saunders's "Sticks," tells us, collectively, that change happens—yes, often unpredictably—yet built upon our actions in the present.

The protagonist in Amina Gautier's "A Whole New World" doesn't know what to expect as she moves into the vibrant, cultural diversity of Miami, after being warned by her faculty colleagues that it would be a "culture shock," like "being in a completely different country." What will she find there? How will she belong?

The stories in this book offer questions and options to consider in shaping "What's Next."

Sharyn Skeeter
June 2022

WHAT'S NEXT?

SHORT FICTION IN TIME *of* CHANGE

Chickens

Claire Boyles

JUST BEFORE SMITH, that turncoat of an Agricultural Extension agent, showed up on my farm with the rest of them, me and Jerry stuffed my chickens into wax-covered produce boxes and threw them in the back of the truck. I had just shy of a dozen hens, plus Hitchcock, the rooster. We covered them with insulated blankets to keep the noise down, and we played it real cool while Smith and the other agents searched the place. Extension used to be all advice and suggestion, but they're armed now, the agents, so now it's more like monitoring and enforcement.

"I know you still have those birds, Gracie," Smith said, the toe of his boot kicking open a fresh piece of chicken shit. "I've never known you without chickens. Why not just cooperate?" Smith looked awful smug for a guy who had soaked through the armpits of his shirt. I swear I couldn't believe, right then, that I'd ever shared his bed.

Last month Congress banned outdoor poultry flocks on account of the bird flu, made keeping chickens a Class A felony worth ten years, minimum. An hour ago, my neighbor Fran called to warn us when Extension showed up at her house. Fran is a sweet white-haired lady who made a deathbed promise to my mother that she'd look after me, but mostly she just knits me a hat every Christmas. Fran's birds didn't have bird flu and neither did mine, but Extension was going house to house slaughtering any chicken that even maybe could have touched a wild bird. They didn't test them or anything. Raising chickens is regulated now. You need to lock them inside giant barns, install special ventilation and filters, pay for licenses and inspectors. Only millionaires can have chickens now.

I'm real attached to my chickens, the hens anyway. They're barred rocks, and they have the loveliest black-and-white patterns, not quite speckled but not quite striped either, with bright red heads and combs. Each one has its own shades and markings, which is something you couldn't tell unless you'd spent a lot of time with barred rocks the way I have. It's like what they say about snowflakes and fingerprints. Each one of my girls is only ever just like herself.

I named my top hen Montana because her markings are just like the section of Rocky Mountain range that I can see, on clear days, from all the way out here. That range looks just like a woman lying on her back, knees bent, ready to take a lover, the peaks of her face raised to the sky, joyful and laughing, her hair all swept behind her into a shallow valley. Montana has those same peaks and valleys etched right on her back, like God held her up and traced the pattern to get it exactly right. Sometimes I wonder whether God repeated beauty like that everywhere on purpose, like maybe he hoped humans would learn to see and reflect it, to find a way to copy it in the things we make ourselves. God is probably so disappointed.

"Hey buddy," Jerry said, looking at one of the agents. "Smith here, your big boss man, is having visions, thinks he's got some kind of psychic chicken second sight. You ought to make some kind of report about that."

Jerry was shirtless and the bottom of his pockets were hanging out under the frayed edges of his jean cutoffs, flapping against his legs. I hate those cutoffs. I tell him all the time those cutoffs are too short, but Jerry says he needs ventilation to keep his balls from getting swampy in the summertime, and I hate swampy balls, so there's that. He's six foot something, skeleton thin. He's got a bald spot on top but the rest of his hair is almost as long as his beard, which touches his chest even when he's staring straight ahead. Not a looker, but he sticks close by, so he'll do.

"Watch it, Jerry," Smith said. "I stay here long enough, I'll find those birds. This is an illegal chicken facility you're running. New rules say you build them a special shed or you don't raise them up anymore. It's for their own good. For the good of everybody. Can't be too careful with this bird flu thing."

"Jesus, Smith," I said. "Next you'll come tell me that you have to lock all the people up inside sheds. For their own good. To keep safe. Is that what you want?" I know my history; I believe the government is capable of that, maybe even eager. The worst part of it, I think, would be the vicious establishment of the human pecking order inside the shed itself.

Smith stared at me for a long time then, but he only shrugged, and he didn't find the birds.

"You better get these weeds taken care of, Grace," Smith said as he got in his truck, waving at my corral. That corral is a mess of puncture vine and Russian thistle since they took the water, with purple loosestrife blooms infesting the edges of my old irrigation ditch. "You know I have to report them."

"Spray them yourself if you want," I said. "The government is the only invasive weed I worry about these days."

I worried for a while after Smith drove off, a plume of red dirt rising off the road behind him, about calling the government an invasive weed. They say we still have free speech, but it's hard to tell for real anymore.

Me and Smith were sweethearts in high school and for a couple years after, but he ended up on the government side of the water grab a couple years ago, and that was the end of that. He's good-looking though. A lot better-looking than Jerry. Smith's looks are the only thing I know for sure about him anymore.

The water grab was hard to swallow because I was raised patriotic. My dad fought in Afghanistan and other places he wouldn't name. Growing up, I spent Memorial Day at cemeteries, not barbecues, thinking about how freedom ain't free. I touch my heart when I sing the national anthem. I remember at least half the 4-H pledge, too, and I take it serious, something about using my head and hands for the good of my country. I believed so much in democracy and liberty and such that the first time I heard someone say that the government was going to eminent-domain our water rights, I thought it was a dangerous rumor and I said so.

My acreage had so much water attached I could never use it up, on account of my great-great-grandfather was one of the first with enough imagination to replace the eastern Colorado scrub plains with sugar beets and feed corn. I could have turned my property into a private lake, learned to jet ski. I didn't, because corn was easy to grow and a whole lot quieter than a pissy little two-stroke engine, but I could have. Then drought, panic. Public opinion was firmly in favor of stealing my water rights. Everyone who didn't own water thought that folks who did, like me, were greedy, hoarding bastards.

Smith was in charge of the grunt crew installing locks on the irrigation headgates that day. Fran's farm and mine shared a junction box, and I took my cues from her—chin up, back straight, eyes on everything, unblinking. The director of Extension, supervising Smith's crew, seemed unsettled by our presence. We could see his eyes looking our way even though he didn't turn his head.

Fran turned to me, shielding her eyes from the sun with one hand. "You know this was coming? He tell you?" The men could all hear her. She meant Smith, and I could tell he knew it because he went as red as he had the first time he saw me shirtless back when we were both just sixteen.

"Seems like he should have," I said. Smith and I had woken up together that morning, swearing at Hitchcock's incessant crowing, but out in the field he wouldn't meet my eyes. It was like I was holding the scales of justice. On one side, I put the corsage he'd gotten me for our senior prom, the earrings I knew weren't real diamonds but sparkled like they were, the promises he'd whispered, as I sobbed in his arms at my mother's funeral, that he'd take care of me. At the time, I'd taken his stone-faced solemnity for strength, but there, as he helped the government steal my water, I put it on the other side of the scale—stone face, stone heart—and I knew he and I had lost any sense of balance.

Fran frowned. "It does seem that way. Unless, of course, this is his way of telling you something else, Gracie."

The director of Extension gave Smith a hard look. Smith stared into the junction box, and I was glad to realize he was seeing a warped reflection of himself down there, the water disturbed by the action of the lock installation.

Most farmers out here put up more of a fight than me and Fran, of course, but Extension, with the National Guard on their side, made short work of the standoff. In related news, nobody cares that I can't put crops in the ground without water, that my savings are near used up and my taxes are near due. Bacon grows in petri dishes now, corn comes husked and wrapped in clear plastic. People don't care about farmers unless it's Halloween and they're looking to visit a pumpkin patch.

Hiding these chickens is real founding fathers shit. Straight justified civil disobedience. Anyone paying attention knows that birds belong outside. Seagulls follow the plows. Eagles glide on the high winds. Geese in V-formation still migrate with the seasons. Besides, you have to be exposed to develop immunity. That virus might soar for miles on the prairie wind like seeds of milkweed, of blue flax, but so does the dust that scours our noses and ears, the sunshine that bleaches us clean. My girls and their line will outlive those shed birds by a thousand years. They won't have to be afraid of wind and sunshine, of seagulls and seeds.

I'm ashamed it took me two weeks after the headgate incident to kick Smith off my farm, because every time he touched me it felt like he was stealing something else, but I have appetites, if you know what I mean. One reason Jerry's here is that I can't abide having a cold spot in bed. For a long time, I've been hoping I'll start to love Jerry the same way I loved Smith. Jerry is a better man, softhearted, which is new for me and I like it. Jerry's kindness opens me all up inside, blows the stink right out of me. Jerry puts a bouquet on the breakfast table every morning, even when all he can find is milkweed or ditch sunflowers. He has strong opinions about the consumption of green leafy vegetables, makes us smoothies every morning and skillet greens for dinner. I never have to wonder whether Jerry's on my team, but I don't always know if I'm all the way on his.

Three of the hens smothered during that first Extension raid, but Hitchcock and Montana and the rest came out of it okay. I've been taking Fran eggs every day to thank her. That must be all she eats because every day I see her she's shrunk a little more. I still have my garden, but she won't take any vegetables. She says they give her the slipperies.

My girl Montana is the top of the pecking order and she keeps the other hens in line. We keep them hidden behind the barn now, one wing clipped, the wire fence hidden from sight by the pigweed and lamb's-quarters, the Indian cabbage and ditch sunflowers I've let grow. They're all twined together, those weeds, their branches linked up like kids playing Red Rover, a wall solid enough to keep the hens hidden in place. I like to watch the flock scratch around and gossip. Those girls have opinions about everything. For example, they don't much care for their new covert lifestyle. They prefer things free-range. They think Hitchcock, the rooster, is a real jackass. I happen to agree.

Hitchcock is always strutting around like he owns the place, jumping those poor girls whenever he feels like it, which is all the time. He's insatiable. He tore the feathers right off poor Betty's back when he mounted her, which I think is why she's gone all broody and refuses to leave the clutch she's nesting on in the barn. The crowing isn't as much a problem as you'd think because Jerry made his living selling no-crow rooster collars to the backyard chicken crowd. It's real humane, the collar, just wire and Velcro around the rooster's neck. I wouldn't say this to Jerry but it's not really no-crow either. Hitchcock crows all day and all night. The collar keeps him just quiet enough that the neighbors don't hear, and at night I put a bushel basket overtop of him. We've got boxes and boxes of no-crow rooster collars in my hayloft because there's nobody to sell them to now. We're using Hitchcock to start our breeding program, and then even-tually we'll need those collars for the little baby roosters our girls are going to hatch. We've already got a waiting list of people who want their own secret flock. Mostly they're last-minute preppers. They might be militia. Jerry's worried some of them might be government spies, but the truth about Jerry is that he's always been real paranoid.

One time we were driving through Nebraska, me and Jerry, and a cop pulled behind us in the lane. His lights weren't on or anything. Jerry got all worked up about a dime bag he'd stuffed in the ashtray before we left. He was mumbling some nonsense about redneck cops and the war on drugs. I wasn't speeding and I knew my taillights and blinkers and all the stupid stuff cops pull poor people over for were working. The only thing was my Colorado plates. Nebraska cops were still super pissed off about legal weed in Colorado back then. You had to be a little careful.

"We've got to get rid of this shit," Jerry said.

"Be cool," I told him. "We're fine."

I heard some rustling, and next thing I knew, Jerry had a mouthful of weed. He ate everything in the bag. I had to give him my Pepsi to keep him from choking on how dry it was. The cop got off the freeway two exits later.

Jerry's real sweet, but he's a lot to handle.

They're comin' for the damn chickens!" Jerry's eyes were all crazy, and he kept looking over his shoulder and waving his shotgun around. I have sometimes moaned about the plains, about no trees, no hills, no nothing but fields and ditches and shortgrass prairie between me and the Rockies, the summer noon so hot I might melt, spread invisible-thin across the land, become tiny and helpless in the vast, big-sky world, but anyway the good part of it is the view is unobstructed. You can see deer rustling five miles away. Behind Jerry, past the dry ditch, past the oil rigs, past Fran's house, I could see a line of red dirt plume rising, traffic on the road moving quick toward my farm.

I had the same feeling I got right before the first raid, like when I used to jump into the snowmelt rush of the South Platte in June. I couldn't fill my lungs. My arms were thrashing around but not doing anything specific. My blood felt thick and gummy, slowed way down while panic sped the rest of me up. The air, like the water, held me down, constrained me.

"Grace, this isn't a drill! Not a drill! Get to the bunker!" Jerry was shirtless again and barefoot, running across the corral all frantic, and then he must have stepped on a goathead or something because he started swearing and jumping up and down, staying in one spot but turning in a circle, holding the shotgun with one hand and grabbing at his foot with the other.

Jerry worked the goathead loose and started running toward me again. "Goddammit, Gracie, move!" he yelled. We had a plan for this contingency, and yes, we'd run a few drills. We'd built a chicken coop bunker out of pallets we stole from the feed store. We lined them with scraps of plywood and stuffed them with straw until we had real solid walls. We had ammo and jerky and bottled water and K-Y Jelly stored in there. We could hold off a raid for a good long time. I'm realistic, so I knew that if we drew guns on Extension, it probably wouldn't end well. Of course, I didn't really believe it would come to that.

The dust cloud was moving closer. Jerry was still yelling. I grabbed Montana and three or four other chickens by their legs, flipping them upside down. This is supposed to calm the birds, or at least trick them into holding still. My hens are a bunch of ingrates, so they flapped around, screeching, trying to get a piece of my hand, or a fingernail, with their beaks. Jerry caught the other hens and we got them into the barn coop. I ran for my .22 while Jerry chased after Hitchcock. A .22 is not much of a gun. It's embarrassing to bring a .22 to a standoff with the government, but I had to live with the insult to my vanity. I climbed into the coop with the hens and looked out the peephole.

"Goddammit, bird," Jerry said. He was half bent over, real apelike, trying to grab Hitchcock. "This is for your own damn good. This is for the good of *humanity*."

My dad would have known better than me and Jerry what to do. He was trained so well for combat he started to live for it, to seek it everywhere, create it when he couldn't find it. I was real mad at him when I was a girl, for re-enlisting all the time, for leaving me and Mom to grow the crops, manage the harvest, keep the woodpile stocked all winter. Now that I've had some time to think it through, I know he probably did it for our own good, because he knew deep down we weren't the enemy even though he treated us like we were most times. Still, I was real hateful to him the last time I saw him, just after my eighteenth birthday, when he flew home for Mom's funeral. He told me he had to go back, that he'd used up all his leave. I told him if I wanted to see him I'd just join the fucking jihad. I got the visit a few months later, the folded flag. It's up in barn storage, covered in a bunch of no-crow collars.

Jerry worked up a sweat chasing Hitchcock around. His forehead dripped and glistened, and the moisture set random chunks of his eyebrows against the grain. Hitchcock and Jerry were in a standoff, Hitchcock in full choked little crow, when Smith came through the barn door. I had a good view and a clear shot into that scene. I chewed some jerky and settled in for whatever was going to happen next.

Smith was dressed up fancy, and he had one hand behind his back. His brown wingtips were huge, like real-life fancy clown shoes. He had overstarched his button-down shirt, but it was blue and it made his green eyes look good, and his blazer was only a little worn in the elbows. He looked real handsome even though his mouth was gaping open all weird at Jerry. Smith couldn't see me.

He wouldn't have expected to find me in the chicken coop, wouldn't have recognized the bunker as a coop. I don't know if Smith saw Hitchcock because the rooster went frozen and still, but Smith and Hitchcock looked a lot alike in that moment. They both looked worried and their feet were planted in odd directions. The rooster's eye was moving, vigilant, watching the two men. Smith was keeping one eye on Jerry, taking the measure of things with the other.

"Grace around?" Smith asked.

Jerry pivoted his body between Smith and Hitchcock and pointed the shotgun at Smith. "I want to see your piece," Jerry said, real calm. "I want to know what you're holding."

Smith took a step back and put a hand up, but it was a one-handed surrender, like promising something with your fingers crossed. "Let's just calm down. I only came out to talk to Grace. I catch you at a bad time, Jerry?"

"Who else you got out there?" Jerry said, lunging the shotgun toward the door. Jerry's voice was like one of those old-timey crank sirens, getting louder, more shrill, by degrees. "You got the guard out there?"

Smith seemed genuinely confused. "Wha?" he said. "The guard? What guard?"

"The National fucking Guard!" Jerry hit full wail, hopping from one foot to the other. He looked like he was on drugs. It's possible he was on drugs. "I know you're too chickenshit to come alone!"

Hitchcock made his move from behind then, launching with a staccato, helicopter whoosh. His talons, the scaly genetic gift from his dinosaur ancestors, landed on Jerry's shoulder and he beat Jerry about the head with his wings, the triumphant battle crow reduced to a few pathetic squeaks by his no-crow collar. Jerry let out some real high-pitched whoops and shrieks. He twisted around trying to lose the rooster, finally leaping onto a stack of two hay bales. In the chaos, his gun went off and I saw the spray of blood when the bullet hit Smith, who after a little staggering collected himself enough to pull a gun of his own out of a concealed holster and fire two really impressive shots. He took out Hitchcock and Jerry both before he hit the ground, and then they were all three silent, motionless. Next to Smith, the loose dirt from the barn floor was swirling, floating paisley patterns on top of a seeping puddle of blood, and in the middle of that spread was a single white rose. I couldn't see Jerry.

I retched up my jerky. Montana and the other hens started right away to eat it, fighting each other for position around my gut's steamy offering. All except Betty, who stayed watchful on her nest, protecting the shell-encased embryos of an entire possible future. People think chickens are stupid, use "bird-brain" like it's some kind of insult, but my girls have an instinct for self-preservation. They come home to roost at night. They scatter when shadows appear in the sky, search for cover from chicken hawks and bald eagles. They go broody when they need to and sometimes when they don't, like they're getting in some maternity practice. Soon, there in the coop bunker, the vomit was gone and Montana sat in my lap, preening her feathers, while I breathed deep and regular, trying to calm down.

I was thinking I should make a call, but the only government-type person I'd halfway trust was lying dead on my barn floor. I assumed a massacre, of course. It's natural I thought that, seeing that I lost both my parents at a pretty tender age. I imagine that every age you lose a parent is tender, probably, no matter how old you are. It's a raw sort of feeling. It didn't occur to me that any of those boys were still alive until I heard the moaning.

"Grace?"

It was a thin whisper, was all. I could barely hear it. I checked to be sure my .22 was ready, and crawled out of the coop.

I went to check on Jerry first. I knelt next to him, not realizing right away that the cool, thick wet I felt wicking its way into my pant legs, spreading in all directions around my knees, was Jerry's blood. His breathing was ragged and shallow. I took the shotgun out of his hands, kissed his bald spot, and whispered, "I'm sorry, Jerry."

"My leg, Gracie."

Jerry was bleeding bad from a wound in his thigh, near his groin but, luckily, not into his delicates. I grabbed at a pile of oil-soaked rags near the old Farmall, and Jerry winced when I pushed down, trying to put some pressure on the wound. The oil wasn't perfect, probably, but those rags were all I had to stanch the bleeding.

"You all right, Jerry?"

"That bastard shot me."

"You shot first."

"Accident," Jerry said, and then he shuddered, and then he passed out. I made a tourniquet then, tight as I could. The blood slowed, but still it seeped and puddled into the folds of the oil rag, staining it further. I must have gotten a little lost in the image, because when I heard Smith call my name, I felt a chunk of time I could not quantify had fallen away from me.

"Grace," Smith whispered. I looked his way. One of his hands raised up off the floor and held still for a minute, like he was giving me a real casual wave hello. It confused me, that wave, like maybe he wasn't as hurt as he seemed, but when I got closer I could tell he was. His gun was still in his hand. He wasn't pointing it at me on purpose, but the angle made me nervous, so I gently reached over and took it from him.

"Smith?" I said. "What the hell are you doing here?"

Smith managed a weak smile. "Dying, I think."

"No."

"Maybe. I brought you a rose, Grace."

The rose was now fully immersed in a puddle of blood. When Smith picked it up and handed it to me, blood dripped off the tips and ran in warm, viscous rivulets down his hand and under the cuff of his fancy blazer.

"That's real nice of you, Smith."

"You want to have dinner sometime? "

"Sure, Smith, but first I'm going to get you and Jerry over to Fran's. She can help you."

"Fran was my piano teacher when I was a boy."

"Yes."

"I killed all her chickens. I didn't want to, Gracie. I know what you mean, that thing you said about sheds and people and fear. But I did it anyway. It was my job, and I did it."

"You sure did."

"Fran hates me now."

"Maybe." I hesitated for a minute. Smith wasn't wrong to worry that Fran might be holding a grudge, and I wondered if I should take him to the hospital instead. Jerry, too. Smith seemed sweet, repentant. He sounded like he was on my side, at least about the chickens. But what if he was just trying to soften me up so I'd show my hand? What if the rose was Smith's way of making sure I didn't best him on this chicken thing, a way to get me in bed before he took me to prison? Being caught with chickens was bad enough, but what would keep the police and Extension and God and everybody from thinking I was the one who shot them both? I'd just touched every gun in that barn. My fingerprints were everywhere.

I thought of all the questions, the police investigation, the ramped-up Extension enforcement, and I looked at my own girls, who had swarmed around Hitchcock and were working together to make a meal of him. Montana had torn open his back vent, and the girls were working on a full disembowelment, pulling on his intestines like gray-blue membrane-shiny maypole ribbons.

I was very fond of Smith, but I was not going to take any chances with the authorities. I took off my sweater, all the fabric I had, and piled it onto the bullet wound.

"Come on," I said. "Fran will know what to do."

"Fran was my piano teacher."

"Yes."

"Fran hates me."

"Probably."

I tried propping Smith up, having him lean on me but walk on his own power toward the truck, but it didn't work and he took me down with him. We landed all jumbled up together, my arm pinned under his ass, his left leg overtop of my right. It felt nice to be close to Smith, except it was alarming how light he felt, how loose and floppy his limbs were, the way the blood had started to soak into his wingtips. I am on the small side of average for a woman, but farm life has made it so that I can lift improbable things. I picked Smith up over my shoulders and carried him. He had parked me in, so I headed for his truck instead of mine. Letting him down turned out to be lots harder than picking him up. I tried to be gentle, but I stumbled when I opened the door and dropped him pretty hard into the passenger seat. He moaned some then. His keys were in his pocket, so I had to grope him some to get at them. He kept on moaning, his eyes turned up into his head like he was trying to read the fine print on his own brain.

I tried to move Jerry, too, but I had used myself all up. My arms and shoulders burned and shook. I just couldn't manage it. I propped him against a hay bale, kissed his cheek. He was still breathing.

"I'll be back, Jerry," I whispered, letting my lips move against the softness of Jerry's ear. "I'll send Fran."

Tears prickled the back of my eyes as I walked away from Jerry. I know I'm not the person I wish I was because even though me and Jerry had been together for a couple years, and even though he was always real nice to me and I cared about him a lot, I was happy it was Smith already in the truck.

Fran came out to meet us in her driveway. She had her white hair up in a bun held together by two lead pencils and was wearing a house apron that covered almost all of her, like a painting smock. Smith wasn't talking anymore, but he was bleeding a little slower than in the barn.

"Take him into the kitchen," Fran said, glancing over each shoulder at the road. "Keep him over the linoleum. I don't want him bleeding all over my rugs." Fran wasn't smiling but neither did she look particularly grim. It was hard to tell what she was thinking.

I laid Smith down, gentler this time, on Fran's floor. "You going to help him?" I asked.

"I'll look him over," she said, handing me an old towel, frayed at the edges, with holes where bleach had eaten through the terry cloth.

"Okay."

"Where's Jerry?"

"He's shot too. In the barn. Can you go?"

Fran nodded. "After I look to this one, I'll go." She pointed at Smith's truck. "You best go hose out that truck. Try and get the blood as close to the stock tanks as you can, in the tall grass behind the barn where we slaughter the beef cows. Then you get that truck inside that empty grain silo in the back pasture."

"Okay," I said. Fran's hair was impossibly neat, not a strand out of place. I wondered how she managed it with those pencils, thought I'd ask her sometime about her technique.

"Grace," she said. Her voice was sharp, like a slap. "You get that truck out of sight quick now. Quick, girl."

"Okay."

The earth swallowed Smith's blood, the grass covering everything. The silo smelled sweet, fermented, like cider. I walked back to the house. Fran came out with a bundle of linens. She threw her bundle and the towel I'd used in her burn barrel, doused them with diesel, and lit the whole thing up. I stood there for a minute, mesmerized by the flames and the fumes, trying to get my head to focus, to formulate some sort of plan. The fire was not part of a holiday, not a summer celebration. This is not the end. There was still the coop, and Jerry, and whatever was left of Hitchcock.

"Jerry?" I asked.

"He's okay. Got him bandaged up and comfortable. Needs the hospital soon, but that's not your biggest problem, girl."

"Smith is going to die?"

"Ha!" Fran laughed. It was musical, like someone hit the middle C. "Dead men tell no tales. Darling, your problem is that this one is going to live."

"Is he awake? Like is he talking right now?"

"No." Fran was holding her hands over the fire, even though it was plenty warm outside. "Does anyone know he was at your place?"

"Not sure. He brought me a rose, is all. Asked me to dinner."

Fran gave me a long stare, right in my eyes. "Did he see your birds?"

"Yes."

"Jerry shot first?"

"Yes."

Fran shook her head. "Gracie," she said, "you have to make some decisions."

"What should I do?" I asked. Fran, all sweet and white-haired on the outside, with her piano lessons and her knitting needles, just stared at me.

"You do what you want," she said, "but listen. I'm going to burn my slash pile tonight. You got anything needs burning, I can throw it on."

Fran was like Montana. Beautiful. Nurturing. Ruthless.

I shook my head and went inside. It wasn't the first time I'd thought of killing a man. I'd thought about it a lot the times my dad was home from war, whiskey-clumsy, talking down my mom and me. It didn't seem likely that I'd pull it off, though, especially not with Smith. Then again, Smith had stolen my water, come for my chickens. This shit now was just the after-that of both those things, an ending that was starting to feel heavy, inevitable. My dad told me once that no matter how much he believed in spreading democracy and just wars and retribution for terrorists, it still took everything he had to look at another human through the sight of his gun, a body with a beating heart, with people who loved and were loved by them, a life in progress, and pull the trigger.

"In the end, Gracie," he'd said, "you do it because you're scared shitless that they'll shoot you first."

Fran's kitchen smelled mostly like applesauce but also metallic, like Smith's blood. Smith's head was shaved, his clothes were rumpled, and a thin line of drool ran out of the corner of his mouth. On his blazer, stuck to the lapel, was a piece of chicken down. I didn't know if it came from Hitchcock or Montana, but the wispy tendrils were shivering as Smith's chest rose and fell. Next to him, on the floor, lay a wooden-handled kitchen cleaver.

I wanted to feed him. I wanted to bite him. I wanted to smash my boot in his nose.

I couldn't stop thinking of the day they came to take the water, years ago, when Smith just stood there, head shaved, gun drawn, pretending not to know me as the director of Extension locked my water away. I closed my eyes, trying to picture Smith the way I had loved him best, back when we were both just high school kids and everything was still real simple. At our senior prom, his rented tux fit him perfectly. He wore his hair long and his curls caught my fingers as I straddled him in the backseat of his mother's car. I can still picture the way the full moon gave a sheen to the vinyl upholstery, the oily flavor of Smith's Altoids coating my own tongue.

Back in Fran's kitchen, I needed my rage, but somehow I couldn't muster it. I closed all the windows. It helped to feel confined, penned in, to want for fresh air. I knelt next to Smith, the linoleum cool on my shins. I wrapped my left fingers around the knife handle, ran my right knuckles along the side of his cheek. He smiled a little in his sleep. I leaned in close, ran my tongue along the curved edge of his ear.

"What," I whispered, my lips moving against the soft fuzz on his skin, "did you mean with that rose?"

Smith shifted a little, laid his entire forearm along the length of my thigh. He didn't open his eyes, and he didn't answer my question. I thought of Jerry, the way he used to put my braids between his thumb and his forefinger, run his fingers up and down them, declare his love for them, for me. He did the same thing with loose chicken feathers when he listened to the radio. Jerry said repetitive actions helped him get in touch with himself. I felt the steady beat of Smith's life where his skin warmed mine, and I breathed again, deep and regular, trying to match my pulse to his, trying to get in touch with myself. I was not afraid to act in my own best interest, but I could no longer discern the correct action. My instincts had lost clarity, cut to static. I imagined murderer's prison, chicken-keeper's prison. I saw my fields parched, my coop empty, my nation as confused and chaotic as my own silly girl heart—aching for freedom that seeps ever away, watching liberty puddle outside itself. Like tears. Like blood.

VISION

Joseph Bruchac

*T*HIS PAST YEAR *has been a dream. Not a good one. I'm not talking about a vision quest, the kind our old people used to send us out on when we were just coming into manhood. Sitting on a hill, day after day, night after night, without eating or drinking. Shivering in the cold. Waiting for a messenger to come, give us a song, a talisman, show us the way to help our people. Our bodies starving, our spirits glowing with hope and anticipation.*

Nope, not that at all. Not even one of those pre-packaged ones led by some so-called shaman maybe Indian, maybe something else. There have been a lot of them out there for the last 50 years or more. Like that guy who packed his paying customers into a sweat lodge and wouldn't let anyone out, even though some of them died. If there is any justice in this twisted world he's locked up somewhere for life, sweating it out behind bars.

Jake paused and waited. A knock came on the door. He put down the notebook and the pen.

He walked over slowly, limping a little bit. But at least walking. When they were loading him into the chopper at Kandahar, that right leg of his was such a mess he was sure his marathon days were over. However, the prosthetic fit well. He could run a long way on it. But the deepest wounds you couldn't see.

He didn't have to open the door to know who it was. No one else knocked like that, just short of battering the door down with a ham-sized fist.

"Lewis," Jake said, then swung the door open.

"Hey hey hey," Lewis Bigtree said, grinning like a bear, "no mask today. Plus I got good news."

"Oh?"

"The number of white people in the U.S. fell for the first time since 1790, according to new data from the 2020 census."

"So?"

"So we're winning! Just wait long enough and—the rate they are going they'll surround themselves and wipe themselves out."

"Right. And what will be left for us after they crash the entire ecosystem of the planet?"

"Good point," Lewis said.

Then he began to sing—badly as usual—the old Floyd Westermann song from his 1969 album *Custer Died For Your Sins,* based on the book of the same name by Vine Deloria.

They didn't listen, they didn't listen
they didn't listen to me...

The first time they'd heard that song was on Uncle Phil's ancient 8-track. It was already thirty years old—actually both the 8-track and the record album—but it was new to them. They were ten years old then and Floyd Red Crow Westermann was mostly known to them as the sidekick of Chuck Norris on *Walker, Texas Ranger.* But as soon as that record started playing, the three of them were hypnotized. Forget Ricky Martin and the Backstreet Boys. Red Crow made them believers. From then on in all their favorite bands were Skins.

"Sit," Jake said, nodding toward the kitchen table. "Coffee's ready."

"The good stuff? Right out of a raccoon's rectum?"

"Civet," Jake replied. He'd always loved coffee and *kopi luwak* was regarded by some connoisseurs as the world's best. *Kopi luwak* was a coffee made from partially digested coffee cherries, which had been eaten and defecated by Asian palm civets. Jake shook his head. "I'll never buy another ounce of that again. The way they produce it now is by caging civets and force-feeding them coffee beans."

"Shit," Lewis said. "Literally."

"No shit," Jake replied. Then they both laughed—briefly.

"So, want to raid some civet farms?" Lewis asked. "Like that time when we were teens and we got into that roadside zoo to let the black bear loose?"

"Which ran once around the zoo, grabbed a bag of feed and then went back into its cage?" Jake said. "No, the days of the Indian Avengers are done."

That was what they'd called themselves back then. Jake and Lewis and Ely George. All three of them fourteen and big for their age, big enough to get themselves into sufficient trouble to end up spending time at a youth detention facility after stealing that meat truck. The sentence would have been longer if it hadn't been for the fact that they drove the truck straight to the rez, spray painted the words FREE FOOD—INDIAN AVENGERS on the side and then handed out all the meat in it out to the poorest families.

"Philanthropy," the judge had said, her tone sympathetic, "But nonetheless illegal. So . . . six months," and she'd banged her gavel.

Reading Jake's mind as usual, Lewis nodded. "Trees wasn't that bad, was it?"

Trees was what all the JDs called the Three Trees Youth Camp in the woods outside Ithaca, New York.

"No priests," Jake said. "Just murderers."

True and a loaded response. At least 20 of their fellow "campers" were inner city kids who'd been involved in—though not sentenced for—homicides, usually gang against gang.

Ironically, Jake and Lewis, and even skinny Ely, had gotten respect as soon as they arrived. Because they were Indians. Having realized that, they played up their role as Noble Redmen at every opportunity—speaking monosyllabically and never admitting they knew less about nature than the camp's amateur naturalist science teacher. On one of their first nature walks with the class, Mr. Alexander had asked Jake what the Indian name was for a red-flowered plant growing by the swamp. "Ah," Jake had said. "We do not speak of that one." "True, my brother," Ely had agreed. "Ungowa," Lewis added.

"Because none of us knew what the fuck that was," Lewis whispered a minute later as they hung back from the rest of the group which was now walking respectfully ahead them, duly impressed by their ancient Native American wisdom.

No priests. That "no priests" part referred both the past and the present. The past was the stories Ely's Uncle Phil had told them about the Catholic boarding schools. Worse than any prison, those places were where he and the kids of his generation had been forced to go. Brought back every time they tried to run away. Their dormitory had been upstairs in the old cavernous building and every night they'd waited in their beds, dreading the sound of that one priest coming up the stairs to choose one of them for his midnight masses.

The present was the ongoing discoveries of mass graves behind one after another of those Canadian Indian schools, graves of kids who were reported as runaways—who never got home. 215 at the former Kamloops Indian Residential School in British Columbia. 751 at the former grounds of the Marieval Indian Residential School in Saskatchewan. And still counting.

Lewis lowered himself carefully into the sturdiest of the three mismatched chairs arrayed around the plastic table they'd picked up from the curb. At 280 pounds, not every chair was able to stand his weight, especially cast-off ones. They'd found that chair on one of their first Free Furniture runs after Jacob got his apartment. About a week after Mali had kicked him out.

Not exactly kicked him out, since it was mutual. A parting with good cause. Jake's memory took him back to that morning when he had woken up with his hands around her neck. She hadn't been fighting back. Just looking up at him, quietly repeating his name. Which had brought him back to where they were, rather than that outpost looking over the rocky landscape that generations of western invaders had bled out on.

He had gotten out of bed. He didn't say he was sorry that time. Mali knew him well enough to know how sorry he was. And it was the third time. Strike Three.

At least he hadn't been screaming that last time, waking up her parents in the next room.

"It's not going to work," he'd said.

Mali had nodded as he put on the prosthesis, threw his few possessions into his duffel bag.

"You know I love you," he'd whispered.

"I've never doubted it," she'd said. It had almost made him smile . . . almost. She'd always been stronger than him. She'd be better off as a single mother.

"I'll do what I can," he said just before she shut the door.

"I know."

He had been there at the hospital when she gave birth to their daughter. Also named Mali by mutual agreement. And he had been seeing Mali Jr. whenever he could, sending $50 every week until the pandemic came and his job doing security at the Walmart went.

It hadn't been a bad gig. He'd gotten to wear a gun again. Needed after that slaughter of innocent people, mostly Mexican Americans in that Texas big box store where the customers were mostly browner-skinned than your average white supremacist—of whom there were far too many around the country. Most of them feeling empowered and inspired by the current administration in DC. The idea of having a well-trained former special forces man watching the door had appealed to both the customers and the management of Walkmart. Until there were no longer any customers coming.

Lewis picked up Jake's notebook. "Still working on the novel?" he asked.

"More or less." Jake tossed his pen onto the table and retrieved the notebook from Lewis's hand, stuck it onto the shelf of his packing crate bookcase next to a long line of similar notebooks. More or less? Actually more. Jake was good at writing. That was the one positive thing—aside being the idol of gangbangers—that had come out of Trees. It started when Mr. Burak, the English teacher, pointed at Jake as he was starting to get up and leave the room with the rest of the inmates-in-training as the majority of the juvenile detainees called themselves. Fully aware that a sentence at Trees was like on-the-job training for a life of crime and resultant incarceration.

"Stay," Mr. B., as everyone called him, said.

Jake stayed, wondering what he'd done wrong.

Mr. B looked at him. Perhaps only for a minute, but it felt to Jake like an hour. Then the teacher held up Jake's paper.

"You wrote this?"

Jake nodded.

"Didn't copy it from anywhere?"

Jake shook his head.

"You're not shitting me? And don't give me any of that 'we Indians cannot lie' crap. I went to college with a bunch of Navajos and I've seen that game you guys are playing. Seen it done twice as good as you and your two compadres play it. So, straight answer. You wrote this?"

"I wrote it," Jake said. "It's good, isn't it?"

Mr. B smiled. "Damn straight and I'm glad you know it. But don't go thinking you're Hemingway."

Jake shook his head. "Not Hemingway—Momaday."

Mr. B laughed—the way someone laughs when they are doing it in spite of themselves. Then he pulled something black out from a desk drawer.

"Here," he said, holding out the notebook. "Write anything and everything in this. You don't need to show it to me. It's yours. And keep reading. Same deal. Anything—everything."

"Thank you," Jake said.

And when he left Trees three months later, the nearly-filled notebook was in his bag.

Jake poured the just-made coffee—ground from Peaberry beans into their cups.

Lewis took a sip. "Kona"

Jake shook his head. "Tanzania Peaberry."

Lewis raised his cup. "Here's to Ely," he said. "Drinking coffee in heaven where there's no IEDs."

Jake clinked his cup against Lewis's. "Ely," he said.

They sat quietly drinking. Finally, his cup empty, Jake tapped the tabletop with his knuckles three times.

"So what's the what?" he asked.

"Can you still jump out a plane?"

"With or without a chute?"

"Your choice, as long as when you land you can still use a chainsaw or a shovel."

Jake reached down, grabbed his ankle, undid a strap, pulled and then plunked his foot on the table . . . without the accompanying leg.

"What about this?"

Lewis shook his head. "No problem as long as you can land and keep it on. They're desperate now. Every smoke-jumper in the country is out there. Not a single hotshot crew left to send. You show them your credentials—what the three of us did in our summers before we signed up for the sand dunes—and you'll get the job pronto, Tonto. I know you're in shape. How about it? You and me and Smoky the Bear."

"I'm thinking."

"I know. I can smell the feathers burning."

Jake stood up and went to the bookcase. He pulled out his most recent notebook, opened it to the entry from two days ago. Then he started to read what he'd written.

Looking toward the foothills, all I can see is the smoke. That and the glow in the atmosphere above it. The hills are ghosts. Their outlines are blurred, out of focus.

Don't breathe deep when you're coming through smoke. That's when Uncle Phil said to me when I was a little kid. One of the original hotshots from our eastern rez on the border. Trained as a paratrooper and then, after surviving Korea, twenty years from

Colorado to California as a smoke jumper working some of the worst forest fires back up till the mid-'80s. The air hot enough to sear his lungs. Voracious voice of the fire roaring like some hungry cannibal giant out of our old stories as he calmly worked his way with the chain saw, his crew around him with shovels feverishly making fire breaks. Eighty-foot pines turning into giant crackling Roman candles.

But what we have now makes those blazes almost look tame by comparison. Whole towns eaten like marshmallows on the end of a stick that got held too long over the fire by some careless camper kid.

Looking at it, it seems hopeless.

But as for us Indians, hopeless is nothing new. So, what else can we do? We know where we need to be.

He closed the journal, slid it back into his place on the shelf, sat down again, "You had a vision," Lewis said. He wasn't joking.

"We were with Ely," Jake said.

"Yup, his spirit's waiting for us out there."

Lewis's tone was almost that when they'd been doing their movie Indians thing—sort of like the phantom Lakota rider that kid Bear was seeing every episode on *Reservation Dogs*. Except Lewis was serious.

He held up his bear paw of a left hand, began to count off on his fingers, starting with the little one, counting in Abenaki.

"Pazokw, you can send real support money to the Malis. Nis, you can pay your back rent. Nas, you can buy a whole new coffee-making set up and beans from every tropical country in the world, Yao," he pointed with his chin at the urn on top of the bookcase—"we can save up enough to finally make that trip we promised to Ely and scatter his ashes in Hawai'i."

He held up his thumb and looked at it for a while before finishing off the count. "Nolan, bro, big number five, not only will be doing good, we might get to die out there in those northern California hills."

Jake stood up and took Lewis's hand.

"Sold," he said.

Doors

Chitra Banerjee Divakaruni

I T ALL STARTED when Raj came to live with them.
But no, not really. There had been signs of trouble even earlier. Maybe that was why Preeti's mother had kept warning her right up to the time of the marriage.

"It'll never work, I tell you," she had declared gloomily as she placed a neatly folded pile of shimmery *dupattas* in the suitcase Preeti would be taking back to Berkeley with her after the wedding. "Here you are, living in the U.S. since you were twelve. And Deepak—he's straight out of India. Just because you took a few classes together at the university, and you liked how he talks, doesn't mean that you can live with him."

"Please, Ma!" Preeti paused halfway through emptying out her makeup drawer. "We've been over this a hundred times. Don't you think it's time to stop, considering the fact the wedding's tomorrow?"

"It's never too late to stop yourself from ruining your life," her mother said. "What do you *really* know about how Indian men think? About what they expect from their women?"

"Now don't start on that again. You and Dad have had a happy enough marriage the last twenty-four years, haven't you?"

"Your father's not like the others...."

"Nor is Deepak."

"And besides, he's mellowed over the years. You should have seen him when we first got married."

"Well, I'm sure with all the training you've given me, I'll be able to mellow Deepak in no time!"

"*That's* your problem!" Preeti's mother flared. "Making a joke of everything, thinking the world will always let you have your own way. I wish I *had* trained you better, like my mother did me, to be obedient and adjusting and forgiving. You're going to need it."

"Is this the same mother who was always at me to marry a nice Indian boy! The one who introduced me to all her friends' sons whenever I came home from college!"

"They were all brought up here, like you." Her mother refused to be charmed. "Not with a set of prehistoric values."

"Mom! Deepak is the most enlightened man I know!" Preeti spoke lightly, trying to push down her rising anger because she knew her mother's concern came from love.

"I want you to know you always have a home with us." Preeti's mother lowered the lid of the suitcase with a sigh, as though she were closing up a coffin.

"Enough of all this doom and gloom!" Preeti had given her mother a determined hug, though deep down she felt a twinge of fear at her ominous tone. "Let's not argue anymore, OK? Deepak and I love each other. We'll manage just fine."

Deepak's Indian friends had also been concerned when he'd met them at the International House Cafe to share the good news.

"*Yaar*, are you sure you're doing the right thing?" one of them had asked, staring down at the wedding invitation Deepak had handed him. "She's been here so long it's almost like she was born in this country. And you know how these 'American' women are, always bossing you, always thinking about themselves...."

"It's no wonder we call them ABCDs—American-Born-Confused-*Desis*," quipped another friend as he took a swallow of beer.

"Preeti's different!" Deepak said angrily. "You know that—you've all met her many times. She's smart and serious and considerate. . . ."

"Me," said a third young man, adjusting his spectacles, "I'd go for an arranged marriage from back home any day, a pretty young girl from my parents' village, not too educated, brought up to treat a man right and not talk back. . . ."

"I can't believe you said that!" Deepak stood up so abruptly that his chair fell over with a with a crash. "Women aren't dolls or slaves. I *want* Preeti to make her own decisions. I'm proud that she's able to."

"Calm down, Deepak-*bhai*, we're only trying to help! We don't want you to end up with a broken marriage a few years down the road . . ." someone protested.

"Our marriage isn't going to break up. It's going to be stronger than any traditional marriage because it's based on mutual respect," Deepak had flung over his shoulder as he walked out of the café.

On the whole it seemed that Preeti and Deepak had been right. They had lived together amicably for the last three years, at first in a tiny student apartment in Berkeley and then, after Deepak got a job with a computer firm, in a condominium in Milpitas. Preeti, who was still working on her dissertation, hadn't been too enthusiastic about moving to the suburbs, but she'd given in when Deepak pointed out how difficult his commute had become. And it was true, like he said, that she only had to come to campus a couple times a week to teach. In return he left all the decorating to her, letting her fill the rooms with secondhand shelves crammed with books, comfortable old couches and cushions piled on the floor, a worn Persian rug and multicolored wall hangings woven by a women's art co-op to which her friend Cathy belonged. He himself would have preferred to buy, on the Sears Home Improvement Plan, a brand-new sofa set (complete with shiny oak-finish end tables) and curtains that matched the bedspreads, but he figured that the house was her domain.

When finally, having settled in, they gave a housewarming party, all their friends had to admit that Deepak and Preeti had a fine marriage. "Did you try some of those delicious *gulabjamuns* she fixed?" said one young man to another as they left. "Deepak sure lucked out, didn't he?"

"Yes, and did you hear how she got the Student of the Year award in her department? Pretty soon she'll land a cushy teaching job and start bringing in a fat paycheck as well!" replied the other, sighing enviously.

Preeti's Indian girlfriends were amazed at Deepak's helpfulness. "I can't believe it!" one exclaimed. "He actually knows where the kitchen is. That's more than my brothers do." "Did you see how he refilled her plate for her and brought her her drink?" said another. "And his talk—it's always, *Preeti-this* and *Preeti-that*. Maybe I *should* let my mother arrange my marriage with her sister-in-law's second cousin's son in Delhi, like she's been wanting to."

Even Cathy, who wasn't easily impressed, pulled Preeti aside just before she left. "I must admit I had my doubts in the beginning, though I didn't want to say anything—your mother was already being so negative. Just like her I thought he'd turn out to be terribly chauvinistic, like other men I've seen from the old countries. And of course I know how stubborn and closemouthed *you* are! But I think you've both adjusted wonderfully. At the risk of sounding clichéd, I'd say you're a perfectly matched couple!"

"What was Cathy saying?" Deepak asked later, after all the guests had left. They were at the sink, she washing, he drying.

"She thinks we're a perfectly matched couple!" Preeti's face glowed with pleasure as she rinsed a set of mugs. Cathy's comments meant a lot to her.

"Funny, that's what my friend Suresh said, too."

"Maybe they're right!"

"I think we should check it out—right now." Deepak dropped the towel and reached for her with a grin. "The dishes can wait till tomorrow."

•

None of the guests had known, of course, about the matter of doors.

Deepak liked to leave them open, and Preeti liked them closed.

Deepak had laughed about it at first, early in the marriage. "Are the pots and pans from the kitchen going to come and watch us making love?" he would joke when she meticulously shut the bedroom door at night although there were just the two of them in the house. Or, "Do you think I'm going to come in and attack you?" when she locked the bathroom door behind her with an audible click. He himself always bathed with the door open, song and steam pouring out of the bathroom with equal abandon.

But soon he realized that it was not a laughing matter with her. Preeti would shut the study door before settling down with her Ph.D. dissertation. When in the garden, she would make sure the gate was securely fastened as she weeded. If there had been a door to the kitchen, she would have closed it as she cooked.

Deepak was puzzled by all this door shutting. He had grown up in a large family, and although they had been affluent enough to possess three bedrooms—one for Father, one for Mother and his two sisters, and the third for the three boys —they had never observed boundaries. They had constantly spilled into each other's rooms, doors always left open for chance remarks and jokes.

He asked Preeti about it one night just before bed, when she came out of the bathroom where she always went to change into her nightie. She wasn't able to give him an answer.

"I don't know," she said, her brow wrinkled, folding and refolding her jeans. "I guess I'm just a private person. It's not like I'm shutting you out. I've just always done it this way. Maybe it has something to do with being an only child." Her eyes searched his face unhappily. "I know it's not what you're used to. Does it bother you?"

She seemed so troubled that Deepak felt a pang of guilt.

"No, no, I don't care, not at all," he rushed to say, giving her shoulders a squeeze. And really, he didn't mind, even though he didn't quite understand. People were different. He knew that. And he was more than ready to accept the unique needs of this exotic creature—Indian and yet not Indian—who had by some mysterious fortune become his wife.

So things went on smoothly—until Raj descended on them.

"Tomorrow!" Preeti was distraught, although she tried to hide it in the face of Deepak's obvious delight. Her mind raced over the list of things to be done—the guest bedroom dusted, the sheets washed, a special welcome dinner cooked (that would require a trip to the grocery and the Indian store), perhaps some flowers. . . . And her advisor was pressuring her to turn in the second chapter of her dissertation, which wasn't going well.

"Yes, tomorrow! His plane comes in at ten-thirty at night." Deepak waved the telegram excitedly. "Imagine, it's been five years since I've seen him! We used to be inseparable back home although he was so much younger. He was always in and out of our house, laughing and joking and playing pranks. You won't believe some of the escapades we got into! I know you'll just love him—everyone does. And see, he calls you *bhaviji*—sister-in-law—already." At the airport Raj was a lanky whirlwind, rushing from the gate to throw his arms around Deepak, kissing him loudly on both cheeks, oblivious to American stares. Preeti found his strong Bombay accent hard to follow as he breathlessly regaled them with news of old acquaintances that had Deepak throwing back his head in loud laughter. She watched him, thinking that she'd never seen him laugh like that before.

But the trouble really started after dinner.

"What a marvelous meal, *bhaviji!* I can see why Deepak is getting a potbelly!" Raj belched in appreciation as he pushed back his chair. "I know I'll sleep soundly tonight—my eyes are closing already. If you tell me where the bedsheets are, I'll bring them over and start making my bed while you're clearing the table."

"Thanks, Raj, but I made the bed already, upstairs in the guest room."

"The guest room? I'm not a guest, *bhavi!* I'm going to be with you for quite a while. You'd better save the guest bedroom for real guests. About six square feet of space—right here between the dining table and the sofa—is all I need. See, I'll just move the chairs a bit, like this." Seeing the look on Preeti's face, Deepak tried to intervene. "Come on, Raju—why not use the guest bed for tonight since it's made already? We can work out the long-term arrangements later."

"*Aare bhai,* you know how I hate all this formal-tormal business. I won't be able to sleep up there! Don't you remember what fun it was to spread a big sheet on the floor of the living room and spend the night, all us boys together, telling stories? Have you become an *amreekan* or what? Come along and help me carry the bedclothes down...."

Preeti stood frozen as his singsong voice faded beyond the bend of the stairs; then she made her own way upstairs silently. When Deepak came to bed an hour later, she was waiting for him.

"What! Not asleep yet? Don't you have an early class to teach tomorrow?"

"You have to leave for work early, too."

"Well, as a matter of fact I was thinking of taking a couple days off. You know—take Raju to San Francisco, maybe down to Carmel."

Preeti was surprised by the sudden surge of jealousy she felt. She tried to shake it off, to speak reasonably.

"I really don't think you should be neglecting your work—but that's your own business." She controlled her voice with an effort, not letting her displeasure color it. "What I do need to straighten out is this matter of sleeping downstairs. I need to use the dining area early in the morning, and I can't do it with him sleeping there." She shuddered silently as she pictured herself trying to enjoy her quiet morning tea and the newspaper with him sprawled on the floor nearby—snoring, in all probability. "By the way, just what did he mean by he's going to be here for a long time?"

"Well, he wants to stay here until he completes his Master's—maybe a year and a half—and I told him that was fine with us...."

"You *what*? Isn't this my house, too? Don't I get a say in who lives in it?"

"Fine, then. Go ahead and tell him that you don't want him here. Go ahead, wake him up and tell him tonight." There was an edge to Deepak's voice that Preeti hadn't heard before. Staring at the stony line of his lips, she suddenly realized, frightened, that they were having their first serious quarrel. Her mother's face, triumphant in its woefulness, rose in her mind. "You know that's not what I'm saying." She made her tone conciliatory. "I realize how much it means to you to have your old friend here, and I'll do my best to make him welcome. I'm just not used to having a long-term houseguest around, and it makes things harder when he insists on sleeping on the living-room floor." She offered him her most charming smile, desperately willing the stranger in his eyes—cold, defensive—to disappear.

It worked. He smiled back and pulled her to him, her own dear Deepak again, promising to get Raj to use the guest room, gently biting the nape of her neck in that delicious way that always sent shivers up her spine. And as she snuggled against him with a deep sigh of pleasure, curving her body to fit his, Preeti promised herself to do her very best to accept Raj.

It was harder than she had expected, though.

The concept of doors did not exist in Raj's universe, and he ignored their physical reality—so solid and reassuring to Preeti—whenever he could. He would burst into her closed study to tell her of the latest events in his computer lab, leaving the door ajar when he left. He would throw open the door to the garage where she did the laundry to offer help, usually just as she was folding her underwear. Even when she retreated to her little garden in search of privacy, there was no escape. From the porch, he gave solicitous advice on the drooping fuchsias.

"A little more fertilizer, don't you think, *bhavi*? Really, this bottled stuff is no good compared to the cow dung my family uses in their vegetable garden. I tell you, *phul gobis* THIS size." He would hold up his hands to indicate a largeness impossible for cauliflowers, while behind him the swinging screen door afforded free entry to hordes of insects. Perhaps to set her an example, he left his own bedroom door wide open so that the honest rumble of his snores assaulted Preeti on her way to the bathroom every morning.

"Cathy, Raj is driving me up the wall," she told her friend when they met for coffee after class.

"Tell him that!"

"I can't! Deepak would be terribly upset. It has to do with hospitality and losing face—I guess it's a cultural thing."

"Well, have you discussed it with Deepak?"

"I tried, once or twice. He doesn't listen. It's like he's a different person nowadays—he's even beginning to sound different."

"How?"

"His accent—it's a lot more Indian, like Raj's."

"Preeti, you've got to talk to him." Over the rim of her cup, Cathy's eyes were wide with concern. "I haven't ever seen you so depressed. There are craters, literally, under your eyes, and you look like you've lost weight. Surely if he knew how strongly Raj's habits bothered you, he'd do something about them."

Cathy was right, Preeti thought on the way back as the BART train's jogging rhythm soothed her into drowsiness. She needed to make more of an effort to communicate with Deepak. Maybe tonight. She was glad she had taken the time that morning, before she left for school, to fix a *bharta*, the grilled eggplant dish which was one of his favorites. When she got home, she'd make some *pulao* rice—the kind he liked, with lots of fried cashews—and after dinner when they went to bed she'd lay her head in the curve of his shoulder and hold him tight and tell him exactly how she felt. Maybe they'd even make love—it seemed like a terribly long time since they'd done that.

But when she opened the door to the house, she was assaulted by a loud burst of *filmi* music. Deepak and Raj sat side by side on the family-room couch, watching an Indian movie where a plump man wearing a hat and a bemused expression was serenading a haughty young woman. Both men yelled with laughter as the woman swung around, snatched the hat off her admirer's head, and stomped on it.

"*Vah,* look at those flashing eyes!" Raj exclaimed. "I tell you, none of our modern girls can match Nutan for style!" Noticing Preeti, he waved a cheery hand. "Oh, *bhavi,* there you are! Come join us. Deepu-*bhaiya* and I rented a couple of our favorite movies from the Indian video store...."

"Yes," Deepak added, "that was a great idea of Raj's. I never thought I'd have such a terrific time watching these old videos. They bring back some really fun memories."

"I bet they do! *Bhavi,* did you know your husband used to be a regular street-corner Romeo in his bachelor days? *Yaar,* remember that girl who used to live across from your house in Birla Mansions? How you used to sing *chand-ke-tukde*—that means piece of moon, *bhavi*—whenever she waited at the bus stop ...?"

"That's enough, Raju! You'll get me in trouble now," Deepak said, but he looked rather pleased. "Preeti, come sit with us and I'll explain the Hindi words to you." He moved closer to Raj to make space on the couch, and Preeti noted with a twist of the heart how he casually let an arm fall over Raj's shoulder.

"I have to warm up dinner," she said through stiff lips.

"Oh, don't bother!" Deepak said. "We stopped for *samosas* at that little restaurant next to the video store—what is it—"

"Nusrat Cuisine," Raj supplied helpfully. "We're stuffed."

"We brought you back a few," Deepak said. "They're on the counter."

Preeti walked to the kitchen. Her body seemed heavy and unwieldy, as though she were moving in deep water. Emotions she didn't want to examine churned through her, insidious currents waiting to pull her under. She picked up the brown bag printed with the restaurant's logo and, without opening it, threw it in the trash can. She wanted to throw out the *bharta,* too, but with an effort she put it in the refrigerator.

As she started up the steps, she heard Deepak call behind her, "Don't you want to watch the movie?"

"No. I have a lot of schoolwork to catch up on." She knew she sounded ungracious. A party pooper, in Raj's language.

"Well, if you're sure...."

"Do you think you could come upstairs soon?" She tried to make her voice bright and pleasant. "I wanted to talk to you about something."

"Sure thing. I'll be up in a bit."

This can't be happening to me, Preeti told herself as she stared into the bedroom mirror. In the dim light her face looked sallow, unwell. She tried to remember her past successes—standing on a university stage in Ohio receiving her B.A. degree from the college president, knowing that she was one of a handful of students with solid A's; opening an embossed envelope with trembling fingers to find that she'd been accepted at Berkeley; standing at a podium and hearing the roar of applause when she finished presenting a paper at a national conference. None of it seemed real. None of it seemed to have happened to the woman who looked back at her from the mirror, the skin of her face drawn tight over cheekbones that stuck out too sharply. All her life she had believed that she could do anything she set her mind to; it was what her mother had always said. Now as a sudden wave of giddiness struck her, she felt doubt for the first time. Then she drew her breath in fiercely. *I won't let him ruin my life,* she said. For a moment it wasn't clear to her if it was Raj she was referring to, or Deepak.

She changed into the lacy pink nightdress Deepak had bought her for their first anniversary. She sprayed perfume on her wrists and practiced, in the mirror, the words she would say. *Think positive,* she told herself. *Losing your temper will achieve nothing.*

It was a couple of hours before Deepak opened the door of the bedroom. He was humming a Hindi song under his breath.

"You still awake?" He sounded surprised.

"Remember, I wanted to talk to you about something." *Calmly, calmly.* But her voice trembled, thin and high. Accusing.

"Sorry," Deepak said, a little shamefaced. "The movie was so good—I forgot all about the time." Then he gave a great yawn. "Maybe we can talk tomorrow?"

"No! I have to tell you now." Preeti spoke quickly, before she lost her nerve. "I can't live with Raj in the house anymore. He's driving me crazy. He's . . ."

"What d'you mean, he's driving you crazy?" Deepak's voice was suddenly testy. "He's only trying to be friendly, poor chap. I should think you'd be able to open up a bit more to him. After all, we're the closest thing he has to family in this strange country."

"Even family members sometimes need time and space away from each other. In my family no one ever intruded. . . ."

"Well, maybe they should have," Deepak interrupted in a hard tone that made Preeti stare at him. "Maybe then you'd be a little more flexible now."

After this, Preeti took to locking herself up in the bedroom with her work in the evenings while downstairs Deepak and Raj talked over the old days as the stereo blared out the Kishore Kumar songs they'd grown up on. Often she fell asleep over her books and woke to the sound of Deepak's irritated knocks on the door.

"I just don't understand you nowadays!" he would exclaim with annoyance. "Why must you lock the bedroom door when you're reading? Isn't that being a bit paranoid? Maybe you should see someone about it."

Preeti would turn away in silence, thinking, *It can't be forever, he can't stay with us forever, I can put up with it until he leaves, and then everything will be perfect again.*

And so things might have continued had it not been for one fateful afternoon.

It was the end of the semester, and Preeti was lying on her bed, eyes closed. That morning her advisor had called her into his office to tell her that her dissertation lacked originality and depth. He suggested that she restructure the entire argument. His final comment kept resounding in her brain: "I don't know what's been wrong with you for the past few months—you've consistently produced second-rate work. And you used to be one of my sharpest students! I still remember that article on Marlowe, so innovative....Maybe you need a break—a semester away from school?"

"Not from school—it's a semester away from home that I need," she whispered now as the door banged downstairs and Raj's eager voice floated up to her.

"*Bhavi, bhavi,* where *are* you? Have I got great news for you!"

Preeti put her pillow over her head, willing him away like she tried to do with the dull, throbbing headaches that came to her so often nowadays. But he was at the bedroom door, knocking.

"Open up, *bhavi!* I have something to show you—I aced the Math final—I was the only one in the entire class. . . ."

"Not now, Raj, please, I'm very tired. Dinner's in the kitchen—do you think you could help yourself?"

"What's wrong? You have a headache? Wait a minute, I'll bring you some of my tiger balm—excellent for headaches."

She heard his footsteps recede, then return.

"Thanks, Raj," she called out to forestall any more conversation. "Just leave it outside. I don't feel like getting up for it right now."

"Oh, you don't have to get up. I'll bring it in to you." And before she could refuse, Raj had opened the door—how could she have forgotten to lock it?—and walked in.

Shocked, speechless, Preeti watched Raj. Holding a squat green bottle in his extended hand, he seemed to advance in slow motion across the suddenly enormous expanse of the bedroom that had been her last sanctuary. His lips moved, but she couldn't hear him through the red haze that was spreading across her eyes.

A voice pierced the haze, screaming at him to *get out, get out right now.* A hand snatched the bottle and hurled it against the wall where it shattered and fell in emerald fragments. Dimly she recognized the voice, the hand. They were hers. And then she was alone in the sudden silence.

•

The bedroom was as neat and tranquil as ever when Deepak walked in. Only a very keen eye would have noted the pale stain against the far wall.

"Are you OK? Raju mentioned something about you not feeling well." And then, as his glance fell on the packed suitcase by which Preeti was standing, "What's this?"

"I'm leaving," she said, her voice very calm. "I'm going to move in for a while with Cathy. . . ."

She watched, eyes expressionless, as Deepak swore softly and violently.

"You can't leave, What would people say? Besides, you're my wife. You belong in my home."

She looked at him a long moment. Somewhere in the back of her mind was a thought. *Mother, you were right.* Oddly, it caused her no sorrow.

"It's Raju, isn't it? You just can't stand him, can you, although he's tried and tried, poor fellow." Deepak's voice was bitter. "Very well, I'll get him out of your way. For good."

She listened silently to his footsteps fading down the stairs. A long, low murmur of voices came from the living room. Then she heard sounds of packing from the guest room. She realized that she was still standing and moved to sit on the bed. Her limbs felt stiff and wooden, and she had trouble bending her knees. Sometime later—she couldn't tell how much—from outside her bedroom door, Raj thanked her and wished her luck in the hushed voice people reserve for the very ill. The front door banged behind the men.

She was still sitting on the bed when Deepak returned and told her that Raj would be staying at a motel till he found a room on campus.

"Hope you're happy, now that you have the house all to yourself," he ended acidly. And then, "I'm going to sleep in the guest room."

From the master bedroom, Preeti could hear his awkward bed-making efforts, the muffled sound of pillows thrown on the floor, the creaking bedsprings. A part of her cried out to go to him, to apologize and offer to have Raj back. To fashion her curves to his warm body and let his lips—so familiar, so reassuring—soothe her into sleep.

Instead, for the first time, she lay down alone in the big bed they'd bought together the week before their marriage. She closed her eyes and tried to recall the happiness of that day, but there was only a black square filled with snow and static, as when, while watching a video, one comes across a portion of the tape that has been erased by accident. She lay there, feeling the night cover her slowly, layer by cold, clean layer. And when the door finally clicked shut, she did not know whether it was in the guest room or deep inside her own being.

OUTER RIMS

Toiya Kristen Finley

out'er rims, *n.* ***1*.** areas of continents flooded in 2014 by rising sea levels due to climate change; the resulting regions.

WHY SHE BROUGHT THE KIDS one last time would be the question always troubling her, never finding its reasonable answer. She told herself she wanted them to see the shore before the world changed again. After all, no one regretted last chances unless they weren't taken. Six years earlier, she'd thought of visiting NYC, the bistro where she met her husband, to honor his memory. But she fussed over the budget. Her last chance passed her by, after half of New York City had eventually been submerged by the encroaching Atlantic.

She wouldn't rob her children of one last stay at the place they spent summers with their father. Branden and Shannon were more excited about the world changing than losing the shoreline. *Where will the land be next year? One day, the whole world'll be underwater!* they said, but they could imagine such things because they would be far from there when the storm's eye came roaring up from the gulf.

Shannon's head lolled against the door crushing her afro puffs, and her neck bent down on her shoulder. Yet she could sleep anywhere at any time, even during the biggest move of her life, and dozed in the back. Branden popped gum in the front passenger seat. He leaned his chin on his sharp knee and looked out the window at the highway. Normally, she would tell him to keep his shoes off the seat, but he was relaxed when he talked about things she thought should unnerve an eleven-year-old boy.

"Where's everybody gonna live?"

"Good question. Maybe they'll stay with family or friends like us before they find their own place."

"Everything's gonna get crowded real fast," he said. "The country keeps getting smaller and smaller. One day, there won't be room left."

"Well, when that time comes, maybe we'll live on the moon," she said.

He twirled the bubble gum around his tongue and smiled and went back to the view outside. "All those trees'll be gone." No sadness. No longing. Just a fact.

They were minutes away from the shore when she saw a figure laboring with a sedan on the shoulder of the road. The car slowed and she pulled over. Branden spun away from the window. Under those long, straight lashes, his eyes bulged with disbelief. "But he's a stranger!"

She violated every rule she'd given her children about people they didn't know. "He's having car trouble. I'm sure he's trying to get out of here, too."

She lowered the front passenger's window. Branden slinked down in the seat. "You need help?"

A young man emerged from under the hood. In the humidity and car's heat, sweat sealed his hair to his forehead. Trees shadowed him, but the redness around his pupils made the blue look like marbles protruding from his eyes. He glanced away from her and down the road, as if he couldn't believe she'd pulled over, either. "There's a parts place off exit six. If you could take me, I'd be much obliged."

Branden pouted and rolled up the window.

"Act right," she said.

"Ma'am, I really, really appreciate this," the young man said from the backseat. "Especially with the flooding coming."

"Where you headed?" she said.

"I don't know. Midwest somewhere, I guess. I'm tired of hangin' around the outer rims. Who knows when the next bad storm's comin'."

"I heard that." Her son wouldn't stop staring at the young man. "Turn around, Branden," she said under her breath.

In the rearview mirror, the young man closed his eyes. He leaned back and angled his face toward the roof, maybe to pray. With eyes wide, his lips parted.

"Mom," Branden said, "he's shivering."

The young man complained of a headache. He scratched his chest until his arms weakened and fell at his sides. But the guilt hadn't come to her yet. She'd take him to a hospital. If she hadn't picked him up, he'd be lying on the side of the highway. The worst that could happen, he'd be admitted; they'd make sure he was evacuated as a patient. But he could be discharged before then. It could be simple heat exhaustion. He'd walk out of the ER in a few hours and be on his way.

Guilt didn't catch up with her until she saw the white tent in the hospital parking lot and the officers directing traffic. A policeman wearing a surgical mask stopped her. He grabbed his walkie-talkie when he saw the young man in the back.

"Can I get you to park over here, ma'am?" Park away from the ER, where doctors in blue suits and large square hoods waited with pens and clipboards.

She nodded at the policeman. Her son sat up. He put his feet on the floor.

"I'm sorry," she said.

2. an area at the edges of a greater part or whole: He banished the thought to the outer rims of his mind.

This woman beyond Cantor's hood respirator did her best to force a polite smile. She rubbed her left thumb with the cracked nail of her right index finger. A bit of dirt clung to the cuticle. Dr. Cantor would rather have a child sitting in front of her, or at least a teenager. She could tell them she was a disease detective who got to wear moon gear, watch them grin or giggle in respect, and downplay the impending rage of water and sickness. But this was her first time wearing the level-4 suit. This woman, with her teeth set firmly against her lips, felt the threat of the hood and the mask.

Cantor felt pushed to find any hint or clue before these people were forced to evacuate, mixing with another population. And already the disease was spreading. This illness that looked like malaria and blossomed in the warm climate. This illness with seemingly airborne transmission and no mosquito bites. The woman in front of her tried to keep her stare on the table, but she'd glance at Cantor's rubber gloves. Crease her eyebrows at the hood and respirator protecting Cantor from the air she breathed.

She thought of all the ways she could make this woman less uneasy, help her drop her guard in this atmosphere. Make her more relaxed so they'd have some flow to the conversation, a greater chance to suss out an answer in an insignificant detail she wouldn't share otherwise. The only way she could consider them connecting was as black women with so few of them living here now. But they weren't sisters talking over coffee. From the stiffness in her shoulders and the frantic tapping of her heel to the floor, the woman made it clear that Cantor was not on her side.

"I'm . . . sorry we've made you wait," Dr. Cantor said. "Lots going on." The left corner of her mouth crinkled up, but she didn't know if the woman could see it.

"It hasn't been a fun few hours, I'll admit." She leaned in and raised her eyebrows with her voice. Cocked her chin.

"It's all right. I can hear you fine." It was Cantor who sounded hollow.

The woman leaned back, but her shoulders were still stiff.

Cantor glanced over the pages on the clipboard. "Ms. Burrell, you're from Portland, Tennessee, correct?"

"Yes. We're planning to go up to Ohio."

Cantor grinned like a fool. Burrell's eyelashes fluttered and her eyebrows frowned.

"My aunt lived in Clarksville," Cantor said. "I don't run into many people from the area. I used to spend summers there. My mom put me and my brothers on the 9-Rail."

"9-Rail?" Burrell shook her head. She managed her first real smile. Of fondness. "Haven't thought about the 9-Rail since it went underwater."

"Yeah. Guess you can tell I haven't been home in years."

"Where was home?"

"Alabama. Mobile," Cantor said. "Yeah . . . Went to school in Milwaukee and decided to stay. But Clarksville, I don't think I've been there in fifteen years."

"You wouldn't recognize it. It turned into a real city almost overnight."

Cantor laughed. "Man, I loved my aunt, but being trapped in that podunk town?" Burrell laughed with her.

"I'll miss it," Burrell said.

And Cantor composed herself. "Where'd you meet Don Jackson?"

"Is he . . . ?"

"He has a very high fever."

Burrell unclasped her hands and pushed herself forward. "We were on our way back from the shore. His car broke down. I just wanted to help him out, especially with everything going down. I didn't want him to get stuck or worse."

"When did you notice he was sick?"

She shrugged. She looked down, grinded her lips together like she was having a conversation with herself. "He was working under the hood, you know? And it was hot. He was sweating, and his face was red, but . . . I don't know. He was in the car maybe ten minutes? He seemed really tired."

"Did he tell you how he was feeling?"

"He said he felt really hot and he was getting a headache. He really couldn't say much."

"And how are you feeling?"

"Fine, considering. Can you tell me anything? When can I get my kids out of here?"

The clipboard fell against the desk. Cantor couldn't look at her head-on. Her eyes darted back and forth, back and forth, seeking the response that would give Burrell some comfort knowing she and her children would be okay. Burrell stared, demanded an answer from her. "I understand how difficult the circumstances are, but you'll have to stay for observation." And that was the most Cantor would force herself to say. She wouldn't let this woman know that her good deed could leave her whole family dead in a day.

Only Dr. Alagiah was in the makeshift lab. When the disease first manifested malaria symptoms, he'd kept his team optimistic. But as it proved itself to be contagious, the lab became haunted. A place they wished they could avoid. A place for work in silence as the weather reports hung over their heads.

Dr. Alagiah's expressions, even behind the protective hood, were clear. "We've received . . . We need to . . ." He dropped his head.

"Dr. Alagiah?" Cantor said.

He closed his eyes. "We got word we're to pack."

When his eyes opened, Cantor found the filtering around her face insufficient. She choked on the fresh air. "We have no idea—"

"We don't get more time. This didn't come from the CDC."

"We're going to *abandon* them?"

Dr. Alagiah cupped her left elbow in his palm. His arm stayed steady, but the rest of him shook. "They're hoping . . . it'll be the end of the disease. It's spreading too quickly in this heat—"

"With everybody evacuating, they're assuming everyone who's infected is here . . . or dead already."

He was still shaking. "But we'll have more time after the storms."

She threw the clipboard to the asphalt.

•   •   •   •

Already, the exposed had been pushed deeper into the hospital. Precautionary measures, they'd been told, to protect non-infected patients. No windows here. A vast, cavernous waiting area with the TVs turned off. To conserve power, they were told, in case there were difficulties during the evacuation.

Cantor and her colleagues collected some samples to take with them. Maybe the blood would reveal answers after the flood, once the disease had been drowned in this outer rim. And the CDC would have a point of attack should it rise again and make its way north. These people were helpful, all things considered. They'd laugh at themselves for being afraid of the needle or picking the worst time to be stuck in a hospital. But when they looked at Cantor, she could feel them screaming, *Please, please let me go now. I'm not sick.*

And at what point would they realize no one would come for them? The doctors and nurses would no longer check on them. The disease detectives would be gone, too. What then? As they realized they'd be left to go under?

Her colleagues didn't make eye contact as they worked as quickly and methodically as they could. They sweated behind their hoods. They said as little as possible. Cantor began to entertain a thought pricking her conscience—*what will happen will happen.* She could ignore it at first. Kept it at bay with rationalizations about her job and the nature of the disease. But these people . . . She saw the moment when they realized they were alone. When they freed themselves from this room, but all transportation was gone. When the tidal waves rose up to devour them. Worst-case scenario, she told herself, she at least tried to do something. She wondered if she were being selfish, but she didn't let that bother her for long.

Her daughter draped across her knee asleep and her son sitting next to her vacant-eyed and kicking the wall beneath his chair, she watched Cantor approach her with detached weariness.

"Ms. Burrell, may I speak with you alone?"

• • • •

3. OUTCASTS; forgotten or unseen persons.

Did he ask about them? He'd meant to. But he couldn't remember. Now he was sure he was awake, because he wasn't shaking like this a minute ago. He came in and out, in and out, until being asleep was like consciousness. Then he'd open his eyes and find he'd been to another world and just returned to this bed. When the pain from the headache let him turn his head, he saw all the people in the room like him, stuck in hospital beds, infected with the same damn thing. But they'd multiplied. There was more sobbing. More vomiting. Did he ask about them? Did he find out if they were okay? She had been so kind to give him a lift. Were they still here? Did they get away from the storm, or had the storm passed? The CDC people, he didn't see any now. They were never not around, giving him their "Don, how're you doing?" even in his sleep. Perhaps he'd asked one of them about that family in his dreams. He would ask now if he could find anyone. At one point, when he could recall being awake, the CDC angels swarmed the room. Their bulbous heads peered into him. Their vacuum-hose wings swooshed even when they stood still. They poked him with their plastic blue skin, asked him lots of questions. He didn't remember a mosquito bite. He didn't feel any, anyway. He was thankful for that. Mosquito-bite itches drove him crazy, and his arms were jelly now. He wondered if some other insect had done this. Mites seemed to be running up and down his arms, his legs, his chest, under his skin when he was in the backseat. And the little boy was angry with him for getting in the car. They were on their way out of that place, and then he came along with his bugs. Did the insects jump off him and onto that little girl? To their mother? To the boy? A woman whimpered and moaned across the room. He listened to his own bed twitch as his limbs rumbled and threatened to snap at the elbows and knees. He wished they would. Then he couldn't feel them anymore. He wanted to apologize. He really should apologize. He killed them. The blues said the family was still here. They were being checked on and poked up, too. If he didn't make them sick, he'd forced the storm on them. Perhaps this was the storm raging in his bones. Like old people used to say they could tell a storm was coming by the creakiness in their joints. He wished it would hurry. He waited for the waters. In this bed he was alone. But if he was going to die, he wanted the sea to pick him up and carry him out where he could drown with everyone else.

• • • •

4. ANATHEMA; the accursed. [2014-15]

He pushed his sister's head off his shoulder. She slapped his arm. Her eyes were still closed. "Quit it."

"You're hot," he said.

"I'm not, Branden," she said.

"You're heavy."

Mom talked with adults in the chairs near the corner. Three men and a woman. They were strangers. He didn't understand why she trusted them all of a sudden.

"When we leaving?" his sister asked. She put her elbow on the armrest and used her hand for a pillow.

"Be right back, Shannon."

Mom and the adults shook and nodded their heads at each other. All talked at the same time. Their arms swirled and chopped at the air. Their fingers pointed to interrupt.

". . . if we're sick? We get outta here We'll just make everybody sick and spread it—"

"But there's no reason to know that we are. We won't make it if we don't leave—"

"Go to the media. There's got to be a reporter following a storm here."

"You're crazy," Mom said. "I'm sure they're outside somewhere, on high ground."

"Why'd you tell us if you don't expect us to do anything?"

"I'm confused about the options," Mom said.

"Only one option we—"

"Mom?"

A shock spread through all five of them. Like the worst secret in the world got told and everybody was gonna get in trouble for it. They were scared. Adults. In a panic.

Mom jumped from her seat and grabbed his hand. "I need you to go wait with Shannon." Her eyes were shiny. The little lines around her mouth got deeper.

"Is that man dead?"

"I don't know."

"Are we sick?"

She didn't say anything for a moment. "I don't know."

Branden tried to free his hand from hers. She shuddered and let him go. "Please, just wait with your sister. Don't tell her. Don't tell anybody."

His chest itched. The itch crawled all over his stomach and his arms. He scratched, but he knew it wouldn't go away. Whatever that man had, whatever those weird doctors asked him about, he had it, too. He wanted to get away from here. But did he want to give the rest of the world *this*? It jumped onto him from that man. And it would jump from him to person to person to person until everybody on the planet died.

"You know you're not supposed to be in grown-ups' business," Shannon said.

"Stay away from me!" he said.

Shannon rolled her eyes. She crossed her arms and looked at Mom. "I'm sorry," Branden said. He sat next to Shannon, but he pulled his arms and legs close to his body.

All the adults came together. Branden watched them get angry and sad. Some of them cried. They hugged. Then they tore pieces of paper and handed them around. They all wrote on the bits of paper and handed them to an old Latino man. They talked some more, and the next thing Branden knew, Mom got him and Shannon and told them to stay with the other kids no matter what.

The quiet boredom in the room was gone. Branden immediately wanted it back. The men picked up couches. They ran toward the exits with them and rammed them into the doors. Shannon wrapped her arms around Branden's neck. Kids cried for their parents. They huddled into each other and screamed with each *bang*. Adults shouted directions at each other. They told their children to stop yelling because everything was going to be okay.

Hot breath and tears slid under his collar. Hair got in his mouth as kids held onto him and rubbed their faces on his shirt. The sickness hopped from person to person, and it wouldn't matter if they got out of the building or not, if they got away from the storm. Mom watched them bust the doors open. She rubbed her chin when the chains fell, staring out with that same look she had when the man in the backseat started to shiver.

The adults grabbed tables and chairs and pounded through the doors. They pulled their kids from the pack crying in the corner and threw them over their shoulders or ran so hard, they dragged them across the floor.

"Mom!" Shannon said.

She turned to them and frowned. "Hurry! Stay with me."

Outside the waiting room, furniture crashed through windows. The hallways burst in shards. Mom pressed Branden and Shannon to her sides, hunched over them and kept them near the back of the group. "Shouldn't have told them. Shouldn't have told them," she said to herself.

Parents pushed their kids through the windows. But their clothes and skin snagged on the glass. Some pounded on the walls until the walls turned red. "Don't look don't look don't look don't look!" Mom said, and they fell to their knees at the sound of heavy boots.

"Don't make me go through the window!" Shannon screamed, and she cried.

Men with thudding voices yelled in the halls. They said they'd shoot. They said to get down. They said to move back in the room, and Branden heard their fists hit cheeks and chins.

"Were they gonna shoot us anyway?" he said.

"Just get down," Mom said. "Just stay here."

"Were they?" Branden said.

"I don't know."

"We're not sick. They have to let us go," Shannon said. "Make them, Mom."

"We *are* sick. We're gonna kill people. But I don't wanna stay. Should we stay?"

"Mom—" Shannon said, but Mom was staring down the hall at the men with guns. She mouthed something to herself. Her lips moved faster than the words could make sense.

She pressed them to the floor. Then she bowed her head, too. With his eyes tight to the floor, not seeing anything, he heard Mom say, "I thought it was important; that's all. You didn't need to see it. *We* wouldn't have changed. . . . We make it out of here, you take care of you. Can't be any other way."

He thought the adults had figured it out. He thought Mom told them what they should do. He wanted her to say, *We're sick, but we can still live.* But he lied to himself. He wondered why *you take care of you* couldn't keep her from giving that man a ride.

Branden shivered again. He wasn't sure if the sickness made him do it, or Mom's fear rubbing up against him. But the cold and wet tickled his scalp, and he knew it was the wind bringing the rain through the broken windows.

Futures Studies

Tom Gammarino

I T ' S   F I V E   W E E K S into Val's first semester at the University of Hawai'i and he's sitting in his awesome-sounding-but-actually-kind-of-boring English class, The Rhetoric of Videogames, streaming a podcast with his cochlear implants while the teacher, this overzealous Ph.D. candidate in a retro tweed jacket with elbow pads, gives a sermon on the seven types of ambiguity (or something). The class started out interesting enough—on the first day they staged Plato's allegory of the cave with flashlights in the darkened classroom—but then they started talking about postmodernism and reading *The Life and Times of Tristram Shandy, Gentleman,* and Val lost the thread.

But now the teacher has just written the word "remediation" on the board and asked if any of them knows what it means. No hands have shot up, and Val feels just inspired enough to pause the really interesting discussion about neuromorphic computing he's been listening to and pick the thread back up:

"Isn't that like when you adapt something to a new medium?"

"Precisely. Any examples spring to mind?"

"Loads. Like how about Star *Trek* being a TV show, then a cartoon, comic books, board games, RPGs, videogames...."

Some palm trees outside the window seem roused by his answer.

"Excellent," the teacher says. "Anyone else have an example?"

"*Lord of the Rings!*" this girl proffers from the far end of the seminar table. She's hapa like Val, wears tortoiseshell glasses, and participates altogether too much. In point of fact, she's sort of annoying, but she catches Val staring at her sometimes anyway, because she looks more than a little like an age-projection of his childhood friend-cum-pen-pal, Hana. She's not Hana, though. Her name is Maya.

"Great," the teacher says. "It started as a novel, of course, but how have you seen it remediated?"

"As a film," she says.

"*Three* films," the teacher corrects her.

She shrugs.

"You're not a fan, I take it?"

"It's my favorite novel of all time," she says. "I just never felt I needed to partake in the Hollywoodification of it."

Val is moved to interject. "Why not? Those movies are tours de force." More than once he'd shown up raccoon-eyed to high school because he'd stayed up way too late finishing the whole trilogy.

"I don't need to watch them," she says. "Frodo's been trekking through my head since I was ten."

"You read the novel when you were ten?" Val's sure she's lying. She has to be.

He tried reading it when he was fifteen, but much as he loved the films, he couldn't really get into the books. The prose was so ponderous, and it was just so damned long.

"More than once," she says, and Val notices her lips, which could only be described as pillowy.

"*De gustibus non est disputandum,*" the teacher says. "Any other examples? Something less obvious perhaps?"

And the class moves on. But it's clear to Val that he and Maya have some unfinished business between them.

He catches up with her on the outside stairs after class.

"Maya?"

"Yeah?"

They've never spoken one-on-one before. In fact, except for a couple of professors, he's not sure he's spoken to *anyone* one-on-one since he got here.

"Look, I'm willing to make a deal with you," Val says.

"Oh? And what might that be?"

"I'll read the novel if you watch the movies."

"You've never read it?"

"No. I mean, I tried, but I didn't get very far. I generally prefer science fiction to fantasy. I like to think it's the nonfiction of the future. I do love the Peter Jackson movies though."

She pokes her tongue around the inside of her cheeks for a few moments.

"And why should I care whether you read it or not?"

"Because if it's your favorite novel of all time, shouldn't you want to be like a missionary for it? Spread the good news?"

She looks skeptical. "Is that why you're pushing the films on me?"

"What other motive could I possibly have?"

Val might even believe what he just said, that this is all about art and has nothing to do with her tousled hair, her ponds-for-eyes, the chocolate chip of a beauty mark on her cheek. "I have them all on my laptop if you ever want to watch," he adds.

Her face contorts and she looks at her phone while he taps his foot and studies some birds on a wire. At length she says, "What the hell," and it's as if she just told him his biopsy came back negative.

"Awesome! How's Saturday?"

"This weekend's pretty bad, actually. My auntie's visiting from Arizona."

"Well"—he consults the time on his phone, as if he doesn't already know it—"you doing anything now?"

"What, like now now?"

"I live just over in the dorms. I have a single." In general, freshmen get roommates, but Val didn't want one, and his parents have enough money—and enough experience with the law—that rules look infinitely pliable to them.

She nods and smiles. "I guess I could do that."

And Val has to press his luck: "It's only 10:30. We could make it a marathon if you want and watch all three. I mean, if you're not busy. I have some Hot Pockets we could eat. The total running time is just a little over nine hours, I think."

"Let's take it slow," she says.

"Totally," Val says, and he reminds himself that while computer processing power may double every eighteen months, not everything is a computer—at least not yet.

Nevertheless, three hours later Val and Maya are lying on his bed, attaining escape velocity from Val's solitary past. Granted, Val was preoccupied with Maya's ache-inducing suchness throughout the movie, but while he could perhaps have *imagined* her leaning into him with dilating lips and beckoning eyes, he would never have predicted the actual occurrence of that event here in three-dimensional meatspace. Val has never kissed anyone before, but he has no time for terror; he needs to perform. Fortunately, having seen many thousands of kisses in his life—in movies, city streets, shameful dreams—he finds that, for the most part, his mirror neurons know how to do this. But he is learning too: he never realized, for instance, how kissing is so much more than just a mouth thing, how their eyes and, especially, their noses are involved in ways they themselves probably don't understand. Maya's hands are wrapped around his back, his are running through her hair, and after a time he feels a powerful compulsion to do *more* than just kiss her, but he doesn't know the rules of engagement and doesn't want to presume. He will content himself to follow her lead.

"I'll have to go soon," she says.

"Just a couple more minutes," he pleads.

And then, for another forty minutes, they just stare at each other, separated by a few inches at most. He doesn't believe his face has ever been so near to another one, not even his mother's. He's so close he can focus in on only one little bit at a time, and he finds all of these human frailties there—blemishes, dead skin, a stray eyelash—but somehow they only make her the lovelier to him. At irregular intervals, they change the angles of their heads, and they smile a lot, and Maya bites her bottom lip sometimes, which reliably stiffens his hard-on, but mostly they are just looking at each other, memorizing the other's face in a sort of unforced ritual that feels so natural and fulfilling that they can't have been the first humans ever to have done it. It's a wonder there isn't a name for it.

Then Maya declares that she really does have to go.

So they hug for twenty-five more minutes, and then she ever so gently tears herself away.

But she leaves a piece of her there with Val, lodged right in the part of his brain that thought it knew anything about anything.

Falling in love is the last thing Val's first month of college has prepared him for. For that matter, it is the last thing the past twelve years of his life have prepared him for. Having gone to an exclusive private school on the Upper East Side, where his able-bodied peers treated him like a cipher at the best of times even as he got an A on every test he ever took, Val learned not to place too much stock in relationships. Early on, he found some relief in retreating to his bedroom after school and abusing the stuffed monkey with stuffed cochlear implants that his audiologist had given him. He hurled insults at it ("You're so stupid," "You never should have been born," etc.), stabbed it with scissors until the stuffing came out, used matches from the junk drawer to set fire to its face and the place where its balls would have been if it had any, until one day he came home to find the monkey was gone; presumably his mother had thrown it out, though they never talked about it.

At least he'd had Hana's letters to look forward to, but year by year her replies came more slowly, and with fewer words in them, until eventually the interval between letters grew to forever. Fortunately, by this point in his adolescence, Val had learned to take some of the edge off his loneliness with books. He especially liked the science fiction novels of Arthur C. Clarke, which he read on repeat. Compared with the precious, sentimental crap he had to read for English class, science fiction excited him with its infinitely expansive scope and its refusal to over-esteem *Homo sapiens* or flatter that species' capricious inner life. As one of Vonnegut's characters put it in a passage Val underlined twice and drew an exclamation point beside:

"The hell with the talented sparrowfarts who write delicately of one small piece of one mere lifetime, when the issues are galaxies, eons, and trillions of souls yet to be born."

By high school, Val's love of science fiction was resolving to a new love of science fact, in particular where it touched on computers, which Val took to be the engines of the future, if not yet its gods. By the end of his freshman year, he had taught himself three separate programming languages and read up on Boolean set theory, artificial intelligence, and machine learning. In his sophomore year, the dean, likely intimidated by Val's combination of off-the-charts intelligence and plain weirdness, allowed him to enroll in Intro to Comp Sci, an elective usually reserved for juniors and seniors. Val used the class to begin designing *TheOdicy,* a "god game" in which players governed a community of one hundred people, making sure to balance every member's well-being even as terrible, random accidents—dismemberment by lawnmower, sudden-onset blindness, AIDS from a toilet seat—befall them. He finished only a handful of modules that year but enjoyed every second, which cemented his feeling that comp sci might be his passion and calling in life. He was especially taken with the possibilities of virtual reality, which looked to be becoming more of a thing. Because of his implants, he was already able to have audio transmitted directly from a computer to his auditory nerve via Bluetooth—no need for speakers or headphones—and he saw no reason why someday soon he couldn't have images transmitted directly to his optic nerves as well. Eventually, he felt sure, humans would fulfill the cyberpunk dream of plugging in their nervous systems altogether, allowing for full immersion in augmented and alternate realities. No doubt that day was coming, but having chanced on an old book in the library called *The Age of Spiritual Machines* in his junior year, and then having followed the transhumanist trail through dozens of other books, Val soon came to believe that "day" would last about a nanosecond before we whooshed into whatever was next.

Unfortunately, Val appears to be the only person at the University of Hawai'i with a deep understanding of the future. In the end his parents had agreed to send him here only on condition that he do his graduate work at a "real" school (his father has a BA from Princeton, his mother from Stanford; both have JDs from Yale, which was where they met), and while he'd found the insinuation that UH *wasn't* a real school unbelievably arrogant at the time, his experience so far was making him wonder.

On the jittery first day of class, after the students had gone around the table introducing themselves, the sixty-something, washed-up hippy of a prof, Dr. Harmon, had had the naivete and gall to say to Val, "So you'll be our resident transhumanist this semester—there's always one." Val had done his best to humor the ignoramus, but inside he was stewing in his own bitter juices. Harmon then went on to write "Futures Studies" on the board, to circle the last 's' in the first word, and to pontificate, unpersuasively and for much too long, about how the future is "open and multiple"—as if every "choice" were *not* the result of a causal concatenation of events going all the way back to the Big Bang; as if there were some possible past in which Val's parents did not take him out of Hawai'i when he was five or in which a recessive mutation on connexin 26 did not make him profoundly deaf. It was patently offensive.

And if the dinosaur of a prof wasn't bad enough, the syllabus revealed that the assigned reading was going to be almost entirely about alternatives to capitalism and the possibility of self-rule for Hawai'i. Granted the class was entitled "Introduction to Political Futures," and these might not be uninteresting topics in their own right, but Val was fairly certain they'd be moot within a couple of election cycles at most. He made a point of staying after class one day in the third week to try and convince Harmon to assign some essays by real futurists like Vernor Vinge, Ray Kurzweil, and Nick Bostrom, and though Harmon didn't do that, he did try pandering to Val by assigning an essay called "The Cyborg Manifesto," published in 1985. The essay, admittedly, led to one of the better group discussions they'd had thus far—Mike, the thirty-something anarchist with the bare, sour-smelling feet, had especially strong opinions about it—but Harmon clearly expected Val to be electrified, and he simply wasn't. Donna Haraway, the author, presents the cyborg—part biological, part mechanical—as a way to deconstruct simplistic binaries like self/other, male/female, right/wrong, God/man, culture/nature, and civilized/primitive. Val was all for that. The problem was: Haraway used the cyborg as a mere *metaphor* for what flesh-and-blood humans might become, and Val thought that was a failure of the imagination. But as usual, Val was alone. That is, until, with a little help from J.R.R. Tolkien and Peter Jackson, he suddenly wasn't anymore.

By the time Val and Maya finish *The Lord of the Rings* trilogy a week after beginning it, they are so preoccupied with exploring each other's corporeal, mortal bodies, not to mention that most ancient of information-copying technologies, that by rights they have to start the trilogy all over again.

Is it any wonder that The Rhetoric of Videogames thereupon becomes Val's favorite class of all time? That he understands the Romantic poetry they are made to read for homework far better than he would have otherwise? That *The Lord of the Rings* becomes his favorite novel and the movies Maya's favorite movies? That he begins to see this glow around everything?

Falling in love has been a stroke of incredible luck for Val. His brain is gushing with beautiful drugs. Never mind that his grades have begun to tank and he hasn't made a lick of progress in *TheOdicy* lately; Maya is clearly the best thing that has ever happened to him.

Except that maybe she isn't. Maybe she's the worst thing. The fucked-up truth is: Val's not sure. In embracing his humanity, he worries that he might be betraying his transhumanity. After all, none of this is supposed to happen. None of it fits with any obvious extrapolation from the past. No girl ever desired him before, not in this way. He can't begin to understand what Maya sees in him. She is so *cute*. She isn't normal in the pejorative sense—she loves horror movies, plays electric bass, and has enough scars on her legs to attest to her having grown up skating in a skatepark—but she does have a generally positive outlook on the future, and, Singularity excepted, Val can't find any good reason why she shouldn't. Could it be that Harmon is right? That the future—the futures, rather—really are "open and multiple"?

Val can actually feel his mind dividing against itself. He's so happy that he's *miserable*. But also: he's so *happy* that he's miserable. He hides the misery from Maya, but she gets glimpses of it when she finds him brooding after sex, when he visibly flinches as he tells her how he's never felt these feelings before, and when, one muggy afternoon, he shakes off her hand on the front steps of Hamilton Library.

"What the fuck?" she says.

"That's a Futures Studies professor," he says, pointing his chin toward the tall dude with the soul patch who is posting flyers for some protest or other on the bulletin board beneath the monkeypod tree.

"So?"

"So he already gives me a hard enough time about the Singularity without knowing that I'm in a relationship. It wouldn't help my case."

Dr. Payne is the youngest and least clueless member of the Futures Studies faculty. Harmon introduced them in the hall one day and they chatted for a few minutes. Payne was cool, at least by comparison with Harmon. Soul patch aside, he also knew a thing or two about the Singularity. Granted, he was skeptical of the "hard takeoff" or "FOOM" scenario (i.e., recursive, runaway self-improvement) and wary of AI's conceivable indifference to humanity as it pursued its own evolutionary ends (as if evolution had "ends"), but he was at least a techno-optimist of sorts. In particular, he advocated for arcological cities on the ocean and the exponential growth of spirulina, an algae, to keep pace with population growth.

Val has told Maya all about the Singularity, and she has listened nonjudgmentally. She takes a different stance toward it, however. "Whatever's going to happen is going to happen," she says. "Just be yourself and don't worry about it." There is wisdom in that, to be sure, but Val for one doesn't want to be blindsided. Their relationship is still young enough that they don't talk about the future much, but when they eventually do, the Singularity is going to be a huge stumbling block. He knows this.

"Shit," he says under his breath. "He saw us."

Dr. Payne approaches them. "Hello, Val. Out recharging your batteries?"

They have a running joke—not very funny—about how Val is looking more and more like a cyborg by the day. Payne might be a bit more sensitive if Val told him about his fully implanted implants, but Val doesn't see any other reason why he should. He hasn't told Maya about them either.

"Actually," Val says, "I was just taking in some last-minute memories of human bodies before they become redundant."

Payne chuckles. "What a waste that would be," he says, turning his attention to Maya and extending a hand. "Doctor Payne," he says. "Not half as diabolical as I sound. Equally at home with Professor Pleasure."

Maya makes a face like *Who is this cornball?* but she shakes the hand anyway. "Maya Davis."

"Major?"

"Bio."

"Planning to be a doctor?"

"A pediatrician."

"Well then you two will have plenty to discuss, won't you? Here." He hands the couple a flyer.

"What's this?" Val asks.

"I'm organizing a rally against nuclear weapons. We'll have a booth at the sustainability fair. Come on by."

"Will do," Val says.

"A pleasure to meet you, Maya," says Payne, taking his leave.

Once he's out of earshot, Val snipes, "As if some rally in the middle of the Pacific is going to bring an end to the nuclear age."

Maya nods, but with pursed lips. "It's cool he's trying, though, yeah? Engaging with the real world instead of keeping his head in the clouds?"

"What's that supposed to mean?" Val asks.

"It's just that so many professors—"

"You think my head's in the clouds?" He can't believe it. After all he's taught her, she's still a skeptic, still an infidel.

She sighs. "Val, we're having a decent day so far. Can you

maybe just take a couple of deep breaths and let this go before you get all worked up again?"

She's so smart she can read the future like this sometimes.

He does his best to hold back the avalanche of his thoughts: he takes the deep breaths, swallows what he can of his pride, forces a smile. "Gi melin," he says—Elvish for "I love you" (they haven't said it in English yet, but Elvish feels more sacred to them anyway).

"Gi melin," she replies, and she returns the smile too.

And then Val is compelled to remind her that the Singularity is fundamentally a *good* thing, that the posthumans of the future will be all-around better than the humans of the present. "Isn't that exciting?"

"Whatever," she says. "Let's go get some coffee. I'm tired."

So they go to Paradise Palms, the little cafeteria across from the library, and they drink coffee, which makes Val think about caffeine and its effects on the brain. Then he looks in Maya's eyes and thinks about love and its effects on the brain, and wonders if a drug is a drug is a drug.

Foom! Their love grows exponentially. The Singularity doesn't come, but there's a new iPhone. For some reason Val can't understand, Maya stays with him, and he wants her to, though her very existence continually erodes the core of who he thought he was. With the exception of The Rhetoric of Videogames (A+), his first-semester grades are mediocre. Embarrassingly enough, he got a B in Futures Studies and a B-in Computer Science. In theory, he is deeply interested in the latter; in practice he is distracted, troubled, confused. Maya keeps inviting him over to her house to meet her family, but he keeps resisting. It feels like some sort of symbolic point of no return, and he's not ready for that. He's not ready for anything anymore. He's not even ready for the Singularity and that's what he came to college for. At least he has Dr. Payne this semester instead of that Luddite Harmon.

Val's relationship with Maya is, as far as he can tell from literature and movies, utterly normal. To wit: They text each other variations on "I love you" about twenty times a day (though Val continues to balk at the Rubicon of that exact formulation).

They develop pet names for each other. He calls her his "Middle-earthworm." She calls him her "Valium."

Though they don't have any classes in common this semester—they may never again—they've taken to studying together most evenings down at Glazers Coffee, a ten-minute walk away, when they can find seats. Otherwise, it's UH's Sinclair Library.

Saturday nights Maya usually stays with Val in the dorms, where they go at it like orcs and then spoon until morning. And they spend literally every day of Christmas break together. Val's parents wanted him to come home for the holiday, but he declined. On Christmas Eve, she strokes his hair while his eyes water. He tells her how alone and unlovable he's felt his whole life. She tells him how it's in part that vulnerability and sensitivity that attract her to him. "I like fixing people," she says.

They go the movies at least once a week. They like to go to matinees at Dole Cannery because then they can go across the street after and splurge on comics at Other Realms. Val didn't get Maya into comics; she came to him that way. Their tastes run toward different genres, though. He still goes in for superhero stuff by and large; for obvious reasons, he has a natural affinity for mutants, aliens, and the technologically enhanced, whereas Maya tends to prefer sword-and-sorcery stuff and anything to do with animals or children. They complement each other, one might say, though the old Val would have said that he reads *toward* reality whereas Maya reads away from it.

She takes Val to a classy restaurant in Waikiki for his birthday. They eat sushi and then walk along the beach beneath a Death-Star moon. Maya looks prettier to Val by the day. She lets her toenails grow too long, though, a good centimeter past the tips of her toes, like claws. He can't decide whether to tell her this or not.

They talk about taking a trip one of these weekends to Kaua'i where he's never been. He even floats the possibility of her coming home with him this summer to New York, where she's never been. Val wonders if his parents would like her. He also wonders if he cares.

Then one night in late January, having found no seats at Glazers, they are attempting to study together in the library. It isn't really working, so they declare a break and go outside. They take a stroll around the campus and end up lying under a svelte coconut tree in the darkling evening, searching out constellations. The only one Maya can point to is Orion, which Val finds kind of lame—her ignorance, that is, not the constellation. She doesn't even know about the nebula at the center of Orion's Belt. And she's a science major, albeit a different science. Val has always liked outer space. Even in light-polluted New York City, he spent many an evening of his childhood peering out his window through a telescope. Since he has begun seeing himself through Maya's eyes, however, he does wonder if it isn't a little sad or pitiful that he tends to prefer other worlds to this one, be they videogames, far-away planets, or The Future.

Maya puts her head on his chest and purrs, tickles his skinny thigh with a blade of grass. "Hey, do you know what today is?"

"Wednesday?"

"It's our four-month anniversary. It was four months ago today that you invited me over to watch *The Fellowship of the Ring.*"

It annoys him, her noticing this, for some reason. "Okay, but that's sort of an arbitrary thing to celebrate, isn't it?"

"Not so arbitrary. It's a third of a year."

"I guess."

"What's wrong?" She's always asking him this lately. Actually, he's always asking it of himself too.

"I just hate to be so conventional about things," he says. "Can't we make an effort to be more, like, *organic?*"

"Making an effort to be organic sounds pretty inorganic to me," she says.

Touché

She lifts her head from his chest and perches it on her arm instead. "And anyway, who's being inorganic? I just happened to notice that it's been four months since we started dating, so I expressed it. What could be more organic than that?"

"Are we 'dating'?" he asks. Somehow they've never exactly named it before, this thing they're doing, this relationship they're having. Indeed, Val has taken pains to avoid naming it, because names are not innocent, they're the vectors of expectations, and he knows he can't promise anything.

"I *think* we are," she says. "Would you prefer to call it something else?"

Of course they're dating. He's being an asshole. He knows this, but he can't seem to help it. His loyalties are divided. "I don't know," he says. "To tell you the truth, I'm feeling confused about pretty much everything lately."

"Did I do something?" she asks.

"I honestly don't know. In theory, I'm happy. I guess I'm just feeling . . . impinged upon or something."

"I'm *impinging* upon you?"

"It's just, I don't seem to know who I am anymore. Or what I want. Take this conversation, for example."

"What about it?"

"I guess I just never thought I'd be the sort of person who says things like this. It's all so . . . pre-posthuman."

She sighs. "Do you think we should take a break for a bit?"

He knows she's being sensible—he could benefit from some space probably, for soul-searching and whatnot—but that part of him that believed he would never have a girlfriend, and the rationalizing part that says he doesn't want one anyway because sexual reproduction is soon to be a thing of the past and yadda yadda, those parts of him find it hard to let her go, even for a bit. "I'm sorry," he says. "I love you, Maya. Of course I do, but . . ." He's getting all blubbery and disgusting. He is not supposed to be someone who ever says things like this. He hates himself and regrets being born.

"I love you, too," she says, acknowledging with a fleeting smile that this is the first time they're using these ritualized words in their proper order, "but if we're going to be in a real relationship eventually, I want us both to be a hundred percent. You're obviously not there yet. Which is *fine*. You shouldn't have to rush it. Anyway, we always knew we were going to have to deal with this sooner or later. You can't very well hold on to me and your Singularity."

"*Your* Singularity"—just what his mother had said. Maybe they're right; maybe it is just his Singularity after all.

"If we take a break," he asks, "are you going to see other people?"

"I doubt it."

"But you might?"

"I'm not interested in anyone else right now, if that's what you're asking. I can't say what will or won't happen, of course. Life is full of calculated risks."

"I can't stand the thought of losing you," he pleads.

"You'll never *lose* me," she says. "You're my friend, you've got my phone number, and I'm not going anywhere."

Val's face scrunches up against his will. She kisses him on the forehead and then stands up and goes somewhere he isn't. He doesn't say anything to stop her. This will haunt him for years.

He stays there under that tree for another hour at least, gazing up at the stars until he, too, loses sight of the constellations. Amid those myriad points of light, all he can see is darkness.

A WHOLE NEW WORLD

Amina Gautier

NO ONE IS GOING TO MISS YOU. After four years of teaching in the English Department at De Chantal, a Catholic university on the Northside of Chicago, you're leaving the Midwest for a major research institution in South Florida. For the past three months you've kept this news to yourself, keeping your lips sealed as you waited for the contract to be negotiated, the paperwork to be processed, your fall courses to be scheduled, and the whole thing to become official. You wait until the last day of finals at the end of the spring quarter. With teaching done and nothing but grades to turn in, your almost-former fellow faculty gather to shake off the school year. You attend the end of the year party to deliver the news and say your goodbyes in person.

The party's in full swing when you arrive. The conference room isn't big enough for all of the department's tenure-track faculty, admins, and adjuncts, so everyone attends in shifts, rotating in and out. As your colleagues crowd around the cold cuts, crudités, and cubes of cheese, you make the rounds to say farewell.

Even though you've been on sabbatical all year and you haven't seen anyone in ages, no one asks how you've been or says long time no see.

To your news, they say, "Nadia, it's all so sudden!" Which is true. You weren't even on the job market when you were recruited and made an offer you couldn't refuse. (Don't reveal the offer. Nobody likes a sore winner.) None of your colleagues offer congratulations or wish you well. No one lifts their glass of wine and toasts. No one asks a thing about your new tenure clock or teaching load. Curiosity trumps academic social etiquette. How you will dispose of your property is what they are dying to know. "What will you do with your condo?" they ask. "Are you to going to sell it? Or are you renting it out?"

"Neither," you tell them. You're keeping it. You don't have time to put your place on the market, get it sold, go apartment hunting in a new city, design new courses and syllabi, and pack up your life and move everything you own in a mere six weeks. Even if time were not an issue, you wouldn't sell or rent your condo. True, it's nothing fancy, but it's nice, you like it, and it's all yours. There's no doorman, elevator, game room, gym, or indoor pool in the building, but from your place you can walk to a movie theatre, a playhouse, a comic book store, a public library, and the lake. There are supermarkets in both directions, restaurants everywhere you turn, and a lovely wine shop three blocks away. If you don't want to walk, several buses run down your street and the CTA red Line is just up ahead. Aside from some books, clothes, and shoes, you'll be leaving your condo just like it is. You'll return to it during semester breaks and university holidays when you're off from teaching. No need to sell it or have to deal with property managers and finicky tenants.

Your colleagues look at you like you're speaking another language. They cock their heads to the side, squint, and ask you to repeat yourself. They're not sure they've heard you right. "So you're just going to *leave* your condo?" they ask, unable to mask their accusatory confusion. It's as if you've left a dog tied to a post outside of a supermarket or placed a baby in a basket out on someone's doorstep and gone your merry way.

Baffled, they shake their heads and take bracing drinks from their glasses of wine. "I don't know how you can do it," they say. "I know I could never afford that." They expect you to behave the way they would, but you are not them and they are not you.

"And what about Miami?" they ask.

You say, "I'll probably just sublet or get a short-term lease and rent some furniture."

That's not what they mean. They clarify, asking, "Do you think you'll like it there?"

You shrug and say, "Sure, why not?" You've seen *Miami Vice*, *The Golden Girls*, and *Eve*. What's not to like? You say, "I'm actually looking forward to taking my talents to South Beach."

Only two of your colleagues catch the LeBron James quote. One jokes about the town not being big enough for both you and King James. The other predicts you'll score cheap season tickets since Lebron's leaving the Heat and heading back to the Cavs at the season's end.

Everyone else wants to warn you. "Prepare yourself," your colleagues caution. "It's nothing like here."

You assume they're referring to the beach culture, predicting that it will be hard for you to focus on research when everyone else is off sunning on the sand. Reassure them. "Don't worry," you say. "I won't become a beach bum."

But that's not what they mean. "Miami takes some getting used to," they say. "Really, it's a whole new world."

An image of Disney's Jasmine and Aladdin seated on a magic carpet and flying high above the city of Agrabah comes to mind. Assure them you can handle it. Academia keeps you on the move. For years you've followed dissertation fellowships, postdoctoral fellowships, and tenure-track positions wherever they've led. Each time it's been a whole new world, a whole new place to which you've had to become accustomed, a whole new city whose ways you've had to learn.

Speaking in hushed tones, lowering their voices to whispers, clutching the stems of their wineglasses, and holding their small plates close to their chests, they let you in on a secret.

"Almost no one speaks English," they reveal. "It's a total culture shock." They say, "It's like being in a completely different country."

They say, "The one time I went I thought the pilot had taken us too far out."

They say, "It's not like it used to be twenty years ago."

They say, "I almost forgot I was still in America."

They don't have to spell it out—you hear them loud and clear. What they mean but will never come out and say is that Miami isn't white enough for them. A majority Latino city with seventy percent of its population classified as Hispanic, there are too many black, brown, and indio Latinos running around the city, and running the city, to suit them. It makes them uncomfortable to be in a place that's not predominantly white. They don't know how to be a minority. They like their Hispanics fumbling through phrases of broken English, not speaking three or more languages with ease. They like their Latinos picking fruit, bagging groceries, and driving taxis, not treating patients, managing condos and hotels, and approving or denying reverse mortgage loans.

They don't imagine they are offending you. If anything, they believe that they're preparing you for the culture shock that you are sure to feel; they assume that their misgivings are yours. How quickly they forget that Latinos come in all colors—even black—and that you can still be Latino without looking like Jennifer Lopez or the guy from *Saved by the Bell*. They know that you're African American, but they've forgotten that you're also Puerto Rican. Here, in the Midwest, you pass without intending to all because of what others fail to see. At home in your native New York, it only takes one glance for people to know what you are. In Brooklyn, there are so many ways to be Puerto Rican that no one ever bats an eye at your special blend, but in Chicago, no one recognizes you're Boricua unless you show up for salsa nights at Sangria's or The Cubby Bear. Hopefully, when you get to Miami, you won't have to carry pictures of your abuelo and tíos everywhere you go just to show that you belong.

Two months later, in August, when you leave for Miami and fly over a city whose condos and casitas nestle alongside one another, the culture shock commences. It begins in the airport.

As soon as you land, get your bags, hop into a taxi, and the driver asks for your destination and nothing else, you know it's true—you really have come to a whole new world. In Chicago, all the taxi drivers are nosier than a bochinchera hanging outside her window all day, bothering you with intrusive small talk about where you're from and why you're here when all you want is to get to your destination. In Miami, the drivers mind their business and allow you to ride in peace.

There are seven staff working in the condo building where you are renting an apartment, a Colombiana property manager from Medellín, two Cuban housekeepers who are old enough to be your abuela, and two maintenance men: one Cuban, the other Colombian. At the front desk, two older men, one Cuban and one African American, take turns signing in guests and recording package deliveries. It takes three months before you even notice that only the property manager and front desk men speak English.

It turns out that your former colleagues were right, after all. Miami *does* take some getting used to. In the Publix supermarket, there is more than one kind of sofrito, so now you have to choose. Goya or Badia? Either way, you can leave your pilón in the cupboard—you don't have to pound garlic, onion, green pepper, and cilantro to make your own. You no longer have to buy masa to make your own empanadas. In Miami, empanadas are everywhere—in the bakery section of the Publix, in the airport's food court at Versailles or La Carreta—they're even sold on the university's campus in a food truck near the building where you teach.

It's not all dulce de leche, though. Some of the ubiquitous empanadas don't measure up. The chicken ones are drier than what you're used to; they're missing that good Boricua sauce that spills out on the first bite. When you go to dinner at Lario's, singer Gloria Estefan's South Beach restaurant, your arroz con pollo is served to you in a skillet, the rice wet and soupy, with not an aceituna in sight. What's worse is that when you order arroz con pollo elsewhere, it comes slathered with a horrible thick white cream across its top. Even though Cuba and Puerto Rico are two wings of the same bird, you'll just have to fly alone in this case and stick to what you know. These problems take some getting used to, but these problems are your biggest ones, problems which you can easily tolerate in a city that offers maduros as an accompaniment for almost anything you order, problems you can put up with from a city that awakens the flavors on your tongue that have been napping for so long.

Hardly the whole new world your former colleagues predicted, Miami's more like a place you've almost been to before whose ways you remember. Force of habit makes you acknowledge the viejas you see standing outside the Metrorail station all morning hawking *The Watchtower* and you've always known better than to leave an occupied room without first saying buen día before you go. Maybe your Spanish isn't perfect. Maybe it's rustier than an iron nail and as broken as a shard of pottery. Maybe it's as unfinished as the poem it's always writing in your heart, but it's enough to make yourself understood, get your point across, and move through the city without difficulty. It's true that you hardly ever hear English once you leave campus at the end of the day, but you don't feel like you're in another country. No, you don't feel like you're in a foreign land at all. You're in the country beneath this country, the land beneath this land. You know exactly where you are.

HEADING OUT

Anthony Lee Head

Scientists and astronomers call them black holes. They are stars that have shone too brightly for too long. They use themselves up and burn themselves out, eventually leaving a darkness so dense that no light can penetrate it. When that happens, the brilliant place that once filled up a part of the sky can no longer be found.

IT HAD BEEN A FEW WEEKS since Bad-Ass Bertha passed through Paradise Beach. Before going on her way, the hurricane had decimated the town and taken down all the electrical lines along the coast. The plan issued by the Palacio Municipal was to have power restored to the big resort hotels first and then later concentrate on the neighborhoods.

Someone obviously decided that turning the resort lights back on would keep the tourist money flowing. Or maybe somebody in the government had been slipped some pesos to do it this way. Regardless, after the sun went down, the beach was pitch black. As I walked onto the sand, the only lights to be seen were from passing ships out in deep water.

I had brought along a candle and managed to find an unbroken glass while rummaging around in the ruins of my bar. I put the candle inside, lit it, and sat down on the sand where Poppa's Bar and Grill had once stood. The small flame didn't help a lot, but I wouldn't need any light to say goodbye. There wasn't much left of my place but a few scattered boards here and there. About half of the roof remained, supported by a beam that would fall with the first good push. Most of the deck had been buried in the sand. The rest of the building was strewn over the beach and carried inland. Out in the surf, one of my beer coolers floated with the tide.

In the old days, I could have built another bar in a few weeks without any problem. That's how it was done when I first washed ashore on Paradise Beach. A few local guys would construct some cinder block walls and cover the whole thing with woven palm leaves. Life was simple back then. Not anymore. Things had changed.

The storm had barely passed out to sea when the government started arranging to bulldoze over any memory of my place. By the time I was able to get down to the beach and assess the damage, I found a city inspector already posting a sign on the wreckage declaring my business abandoned.

"Señor I haven't abandoned anything," I said. "This is my place, and I have had this spot on the beach for the last 12 years."

He was short and stocky with a stomach that hung well out over the belt pushed low on his hips. His face was covered in perspiration from the effort of walking on the beach. With a bored expression, he looked up from his clipboard to glance at what was left of my bar after the storm had knocked it down like one of the three little pigs' straw houses.

"There is nothing here now. If you want to start another business, you must apply for a construction permit." He handed me my official notice and headed down the beach toward where Handsome Harry's Café once stood.

I had worried about this moment for some time. Even before the storm, the local authorities began enforcing new rules for building on the beach. Construction could only be done by pre-authorized companies, the owners of which were generally connected by family ties to local politicians. The prices they were charging were way beyond what I could pay to rebuild. Even with whatever the insurance company would pay, I just wasn't wealthy enough to get back on the sand.

It didn't matter. Even if I could afford to build a new bar, the city was never going to give me a business permit. I wasn't wanted anymore. Guys in suits were calling the shots now. Drug cartel lawyers and foreign investment bankers had begun taking notice of Paradise Beach long ago. Those types are always on the lookout for a place where money can be laundered and hidden in plain sight. This little slice of heaven looked pretty good to them.

It started quietly with the funneling of cash to local officials, cops, and hotel syndicates. Bit by bit, the bad boys had been laying claim to the town. Nobody seemed to notice. The Mexicans knew better than to say anything, and the tourists didn't care who owned the beach as long as the margaritas were cold. As for the expats, well, there was always another beach out there somewhere.

The hurricane had finally given the big-money folks a real chance to dig in on a large scale. Once the local politicians were paid off, the devastated beachfront was up for grabs, and plans for the transformation of Paradise Beach into another Cancun went into high gear.

Little places like Poppa's Bar and Grill would eventually be replaced by steel-and-chrome monstrosities complete with stone pizza ovens and giant-screen TVs. Multistory condo hotels would keep the tourists close by to sip drinks out of a spigot and swim inside a roped-off 'private' section of the ocean.

I figured Paradise Beach had a glorious future as a world-class resort town for the beautiful and rich, and it was clear I was not invited to be part of it. The people who ran things now had decided riffraff like me should be cleared off the new beach.

Oh sure, I might be able to find a job as a bartender somewhere in town. I could probably find work at one of the big hotels. I'd end up wearing a white shirt and bow tie while serving overpriced pre-mixed margaritas to dot-com millionaires. "Would you like salt on the rim, Mr. Smith? That will be another fifteen dollars, please."

Or maybe I could start over. I could set up shop back on the side streets of one of the outlying neighborhoods where rent was still affordable, hoping my old customers would search me out. But why bother? Even that wouldn't last long.

It wasn't my town anymore. Civilization had come to Paradise Beach, and like a young Huck Finn, I knew from experience I wouldn't fit in. It was time to get back on the Margarita Road.

As it turned out, I wasn't alone either in the choice to go or in deciding to spend my last evening sitting on the sand. My friend Chaz had similar ideas.

Chaz had been swimming against the tide for a while. A few years back, he had grown bored with sailing boats down from Florida for other people to enjoy. Later, the steady work of piloting party catamarans up and down the beach had allowed him to stay in Mexico on a permanent basis. Eventually he grew frustrated with trying to live off of shitty wages and a few tips.

Unfortunately, with Paradise Beach's growing status as an upscale vacation destination, there wasn't a real need for a sailor with Chaz's skills. Tourists didn't want much more than a sunset cruise just offshore for an hour or two. Even inexperienced local boys could handle that chore with a little training. Chaz told me he could have made some decent money if he was willing to run boats up from Belize at night with no questions asked, but that wasn't his style. "I'm desperate, not crazy," he said.

It had become clear that Chaz wasn't going to make a living on the water in Paradise Beach anymore. When I suggested he find something other than boats to make money, he dismissed it out of hand. "Sailing is what I do. I'd go crazy if I had to give it up for long. Besides, even if I could find work, it's time to go somewhere else. This place belongs to other people now."

I understood. Even before the hurricane had wiped the beach out, the wanderers who first settled in on this edge of the Caribbean were leaving. Those who stayed on were slowly being overwhelmed by new arrivals.

The beach had been filling up with North American retirees and upscale tourists for a while. They were joined by kids with too much money and attitude from Paris, Buenos Aires, and

Mexico City. Crowding the beach clubs during the day and packing the bars at night, they were well off, rude, and demanding. This was their town now. It wouldn't be long before the taco stands and fishing boats were crowded out by Diesel stores and Sunglass Huts. Strolling mariachis would soon be replaced by recorded hip-hop blaring through gigantic speakers.

People like Chaz and I were dinosaurs. Things were changing, and if we couldn't accept that, we needed to move on. Since neither of us was very good at adapting to the world we once left behind, we had each decided it was time to go. When we discovered the other was also leaving, we agreed to meet on the beach in the wee hours of the morning to say our goodbyes to the little bay that had been our home.

"Over here!" I yelled to Chaz when I saw him coming down the dark beach with a flashlight in hand. He made his way to where I sat and plopped down beside me. He had not come empty-handed. From his backpack, he pulled a bottle of very pricey, very old Cuban rum.

"Figured we ought to celebrate . . . or something," he said as he twisted the cap off the bottle. He took a swallow and handed it to me.

I hesitated. "Are you sure you want to drink this tonight? Shouldn't you save it for a special occasion?"

"Well, I had been planning on keeping it until the day Heidi Klum showed up and wanted a private sailing lesson." Chaz grinned. "Since she never did, this seems as good a time as any."

I tilted the bottle, and the rum flowed into my mouth. The taste was sharp at first, followed by a soft memory. Thank goodness the folks back in the U.S. had been saved from this insidious caribe-communist plot for decades. Maybe someday that would change. Maybe not.

Chaz took out a cigarette and lit it from the candle. He looked sad as he glanced around at the broken boards sticking out of the sand. It was all that was left of my bar. "Man," he said morosely. There wasn't much else to say.

"So tell me, where are you headed?" I asked, handing him back the rum bottle.

Chaz smiled again. "Querencia," he said.

"Where the hell is that?" I'd never heard of it.

Instead of answering, he asked me a question. "Have you ever seen a bullfight?"

I said I had, many years ago, and didn't care much for it.

"Yeah, you Americans like your beef killed in secret so that it magically appears in plastic at the grocery."

I ignored that. "What does that have to do with where you're going next?"

He didn't seem to hear my question but went on about bull-fighting. "When the bull first goes into the bullring, he is the king of everything he sees. He is the most powerful and skillful creature there. The bull knows this, the horses in the ring know this, and the men in those funny clothes certainly know it. They are all afraid of the bull. As well they should be. Then the attack begins. First, it's just guys waving brightly colored capes and flags. The bull charges again and again. He knows he can catch these puny little things, except it turns out he can't. Those fluttering pieces of color somehow stay just beyond his reach. He can never quite get to them."

Chaz stretched out his hand toward the sea and quickly closed it on nothing, as if he had missed whatever he was reaching for.

"Now the bull really starts to hurt. Men stick him with spear points from up high on horses. Others throw sharp darts into his back. It's all pain, blood, and confusion. Then the matador comes out. For an instant, the bull begins to feel better. He should be able to kill this one guy, but he can't. He's too tired by now. He has lost too much blood. To the bull's amazement, he finds the man has become his equal. He is uncertain, maybe even fearful, for the first time in his life. He needs to get away—to find a safe spot so he can get his strength back."

I was beginning to see what all this had to do with Chaz and me. "The bull wants to go home," I said.

Chaz nodded in agreement. "Just for the moment. Just to catch his breath."

"But he can't," I said. "He is stuck in the bullring."

"Yes, he is. And he is not leaving there alive. By now, even the bull instinctively knows this. That doesn't mean he's giving up.

He just needs to find a spot where he can feel safe for a minute. Maybe it's back up against the wall of the ring where he feels protected. Maybe it's the point furthest from the matador. It's different for every bull. Wherever it is, it's the place where he can gather strength before heading back into the fight. That spot is called his querencia."

Chaz and I sat quietly for a moment.

"So where is it?" I looked and saw him smiling in the glow of the candlelight. "Where's your querencia?"

"France," he said.

I was surprised. Over the decade I had known Chaz, I had heard him tell wild stories of sailing throughout the Caribbean and of years spent in Australia, the South Pacific, and a dozen other places. I had never heard him mention France. He told me about it now.

"When I was sixteen, I ran away from Belfast. I was tired of it all. Tired of the British soldiers, tired of the IRA drumbeat, and tired of being poor and hopeless. And I was really tired of being smacked around by my old man. I lied about my age and got a job on the first freighter heading away from Ireland. It took me over to Le Havre in France. I was seasick as hell and puked my guts out the whole way." He chuckled at the mental image of his younger self.

"When we docked, I headed inland. I didn't have a clue. I spoke no French and only had a few coins in my pocket. I was just trying to get as far away as possible from my miserable life. I started hitchhiking south. I would beg for food and sleep on the side of the road and then every day stand next to the highway with my thumb out. After a couple of days of hitching rides, a bloke dropped me off at the seaside in Nice. I had never seen a beach like that. There wasn't any sand. It was all rocks. Little round, smooth stones. Out in front was the Mediterranean, all blue and dark and just the most beautiful thing I had ever seen. It was sunset when I got there, and I stretched out on those little stones and fell asleep. I guess I must have been tired. I woke up with the sunrise and started my new life."

He sighed softly at the memory. "That's where I got my first job on a sailboat. That's where I was really born. I'm going back there."

"Do you think you're going to find that 16-year-old kid again?"

He leaned back and looked up at the stars. "No. That boy is long gone. There's no use in even looking for him. But it was my starting point once for a new life. I figure, why not try it again? Maybe I'll get just as lucky the second time around."

I lifted the rum bottle in a salute to him. "Querencia," I said.

Chaz nodded in return. "And you? Where's your safe place?"

I was afraid he was going to ask me that. "I don't know. I don't even know what's next. Cuba's possible. I know a guy who says he can arrange something for me. There's a beach club in Thailand where I can work if I want. And there's always New Orleans. I love the French Quarter. Maybe none of them. Maybe all of them. I do know I'm starting in Key West. Then I'll see what happens."

"Key West? What's in Key West?" Chaz asked.

I reached under my shirt and picked the gold sand dollar off my chest where it hung from a chain around my neck. I rubbed it between my fingers "Somebody special."

Chaz raised his eyebrows. "Really? The woman from Chicago? What's her name? Lynn?"

"Yeah, that's the one. We've been in touch. She called me a few days ago. She filed for divorce and put her house up for sale. She is ready to start her new life, she says. We are going to meet up in Florida and see what happens next. I think the Keys are her querencia."

"Are they yours?"

I shrugged. "I haven't figured that out yet."

"There's no place you call home?"

"I don't know. Maybe I'm still just chasing colored flags." We sat silently on the beach for a time, finishing off the rum and listening to the sea's night sounds. Eventually, the first rays of the rising sun showed in the eastern sky.

Chaz stretched his arms out as if embracing the whole scene. "Time for me to go, amigo. I have a plane to catch this morning. What about you?"

"I still have a few hours," I said. "I'm heading out tonight." He looked me in the eye. "Stay in touch. Drop an e-mail or something from time to time. Maybe we'll cross paths again."

"For sure."

We stood and hugged. Chaz stepped away and looked around the beach, its sand now glowing pink in the dawn. "It was fun, wasn't it?"

Then he was gone.

Sitting back down to finish watching the sunrise, I saw the small birds begin to run on the sand. In a short time, groups of pelicans began to fly low over the shallows, looking for breakfast. They had been good company for many years, and I hoped their new neighbors would treat them well.

I thought of how Chaz had asked me about finding a home. I wasn't sure I knew what home was, let alone how to go about finding one. Once, back in the hills north of San Francisco, a bald, robe-wearing Buddhist monk named Harold told me that understanding life started with the knowledge that nothing lasts forever. "It's always changing," he said. "Time is a stream rushing by. You can never stop it. All you have is this exact moment."

It's the same lesson that living on the beach has taught me. I've watched driftwood get stuck in the sand, only to be pulled back out to sea and carried by the currents to another beach or island. I often wondered: where does the idea of home fit in with all that?

One thing I knew for certain: I had always been drawn to the edge of the world—near an ocean where the sun rises or disappears, where the rules are a lot less rigid, and where the open water and endless sky can make a person feel free. For a long time, Paradise Beach had been like that, and if I had to keep traveling to find another place as special, it was a journey I was willing to take. Having the company of somebody I loved on that journey just might make it the closest thing to home I'd ever know. I hoped to find out.

A short time later, I heard the sound of trucks pulling up on the beach behind me. Out of the corner of my eye, I saw a bulldozer roll onto the sand. I stood and slowly walked up to the frontage road where my jeep was parked next to a recently created sand dune.

I was giving my jeep to Jorge as a farewell gift. It wasn't in great shape or worth very much, but if he could keep it running, it would be a help to his family. I was heading for his house, and he would drive me to the airport later that afternoon.

I stood for a moment, looking back out over the beach. The water was as calm and motionless as I had ever seen it. It must have been mornings like this that made the first sailors want to set out to sea to find something more. "Vaya con Dios," I whispered to the birds in flight above me. After a final glance out to the horizon, I stamped my feet to knock the sand off, climbed in the jeep, and drove away. I was back on the Margarita Road.

In the Event

Meng Jin

IN THE EVENT OF AN EARTHQUAKE, I texted Tony, we'll meet at the corner of Chinaman's Vista, across from the café with the rainbow flag.

Jen had asked about our earthquake plan. We didn't have one. We were new to the city, if it could be called that. Tony described it to friends back home as a huge village. But very densely populated, I added, and not very agrarian. We had come here escaping separate failures on the opposite coast. Already the escape was working. In this huge urban village, under the dry bright sky, we were beginning to regard our former ambitions as varieties of regional disease, belonging to different climates, different times.

"Firstly," Jen said, "you need a predetermined meeting point. In case you're not together and cell service is clogged. Which it's likely to be. Because, you know, disasters."

Jen was the kind of person who said things like *firstly* and *because, disasters.* She was a local local, born and raised and stayed. Tony had met Jen a few years ago at an electronic music festival back east and introduced us, thinking we'd get along. She had been traveling for work. Somehow we stayed in touch. We shared interests: she worked as a tech consultant but composed music as a hobby; I made electronic folk songs with acoustic sounds.

"The ideal meeting place," Jen explained, "is outside, walkable from both your workplaces, and likely free of obstacles."

"Obstacles?"

"Collapsed buildings, downed power lines, blah blah hazmat, you know."

Chinaman's Vista was the first meeting place that came to mind. It was a big grassy field far from the water, on high ground. Cypress trees lined its edges. In their shade, you could sit and watch the well-behaved dogs of well-behaved owners let loose to run around. We had walked past it a number of times on our way from this place or that—the grocery store, the pharmacy, the taquería—and commented on its charm with surprise, forgetting we'd come across it before. In the event of a significant earthquake, and the aftershocks that typically follow significant earthquakes, I imagined we would be safe there—from falling debris at least—as we searched through the faces of worried strangers for each other.

Other forces could separate or kill us: landslides, tsunamis, nuclear war. I was aware that we lived on the side of a sparsely vegetated hill, that we were four miles from the ocean, a mile from the bay. To my alarmed texts Tony responded that if North Korea was going to bomb us, this region would be a good target: reachable by missile, home to the richest and fastest-growing industry in the world. Probably they would go for one of the cities south of us, he typed, where the headquarters of the big tech companies were based.

nuclear blast wind can travel at > 300 m/s, Tony wrote. Tony knew things like this.

He clarified: **meters per second**
which gives us
I watched Tony's avatar think.
approx 3 mins to find shelter after detonation
More likely we'd get some kind of warning x hours before the bomb struck. Jen had a car. She could pick us up, we'd drive north as fast as we could. Jen's aunt who lived an hour over

the bridge had a legit basement, concrete reinforced during the Cold War.

I thought about the active volcano one state away, which, if it erupted, could cover the city in ash. One very large state away, Tony reminded me. But the ash that remained in the air might be so thick it obscured the sun, plunging this usually temperate coast into winter. I thought about the rising ocean, the expanding downtown at sea-level, built on landfill. Tony worked in the expanding downtown. Was Tony a strong swimmer? I asked with two question marks. His response:

don't worry 'lil chenchen
if i die i'll die

I was listening to an audiobook, on 1.65x speed, about a techno-dystopic future Earth under threat of annihilation from alien attack. The question was whether humans would kill each other first or survive long enough to be shredded in the fast-approaching weaponized supermassive black hole. Another question was whether humans would abandon life on Earth and attempt to continue civilization on spacecraft. Of course there were not enough spacecraft for everyone.

When I started listening, it was at normal 1.0 speed. Each time I returned I switched the speed dial up by 0.05x. It was a gripping book, full of devices for sustaining mystery despite the obvious conclusion. I couldn't wait for the world to end.

Tony and I were fundamentally different. What I mean is we sat in the world differently—he settling into the back cushions, noting with objective precision the grime or glamour of his surroundings, while I hovered, nervous, at the edge of my seat. Often, I felt—more often now—I couldn't even make it to the edge. Instead I flitted from one space to another, calculating if I would fit, considering the cosmic feeling of unwelcome that emanated from wherever I chose to go.

On the surface Tony and I looked very much the same. We were more or less the same percentile in height and weight, and we both had thin, blank faces, their resting expressions betraying slight confusion and surprise. Our bodies were constructed narrowly of long brittle bones, and our skin, pale in previous gray winters, now tanned easily to the same dusty brown. We weren't only both Chinese; our families came from the same rural-industrial province south of Shanghai, recently known for small-goods manufacturing. But in a long reversal of fortunes, his family, business people who had fled to Hong Kong and then South Carolina, were now lower-middle-class second-generation immigrants, while my parents, born from starving peasant stock, had stayed in China through its boom and immigrated much later to the States as members of the highly educated elite.

Tony's family was huge. I guess mine was too, but I didn't know any of them. In this hemisphere I had my parents, and that was it.

A couple years ago I did Thanksgiving with Tony's family. It was my first time visiting the house where he'd grown up. It was also the first time I had left my parents to celebrate a holiday alone. I tried not to guess what they were eating—Chinese takeout or leftover Chinese takeout. Even when I was around, my parents spent most of their time sitting in separate rooms, working.

"Chenchen!" his mother had cried as she embraced me, "We're so happy you could join us."

My arms rose belatedly, swiping the sides of her shoulders as she pulled away.

She said my name like an American. The rest of the family did too—in fact every member of Tony's family spoke with varied degrees of Southern drawl. It was very disorienting. In normal circumstances Tony's English was incredibly bland, neutered of history like my own, but now I heard in it long-drawn diphthongs, wholesome curls of twang. Both his sisters had come. As had his three uncles and two aunts with their families, and two full sets of grandparents, his mom's mom recently remarried after his grandpa's death. I had never been in a room with so many Chinese people at once, but if I closed my eyes and just listened to the chatter, my brain populated the scene with white people wearing bandanas and jeans.

Which was accurate, except for the white people part.

The turkey had been deep fried in an enormous vat of oil. We had stuffing and cranberry sauce and ranch-flavored mashed potatoes (a Zhang family tradition), pecan and sweet potato and ginger pie. We drank beer cocktails (Bud Light and lemonade). No one regretted the lack of rice or soy sauce, or said with a disappointed sigh that we should have just ordered roast duck from Hunan Garden. It was loud. I shouted small talk and halfway introduced myself to various relatives, as bursts of yelling and laughter erupted throughout the room. Jokes were told—jokes! I had never heard people who looked like my parents making so many jokes—plates clinked, drinks sloshed, moving chairs and shoes scuffed the floor with a pleasing busy beat.

In the middle of all this I was struck suddenly by a wave of mourning, though I wasn't sure for what. The sounds of a childhood I'd never had, the large family I'd never really know? Perhaps it was the drink—I think the beer-ade was spiked with vodka—but I felt somehow that I was losing Tony then, that by letting myself know him in this way I had opened a door through which he might one day slip away.

In the corner of the living room, the pitch of the conversation changed. Tony's teenage cousin Harriet was yelling at her mother while Tony's mom sat at her side loudly shaking her head. Slowly the other voices in the room quieted until the tacit attention of every person was focused on this exchange. Others began to participate, some angry—"Don't you dare speak to your mother like this"—some conciliatory—"How about some pecan pie?"—some anxious—Harriet's little sister tugging on her skirt. Harriet pushed her chair back angrily from the table. A vase fell over, dumping flowers and gray water into the stuffing. Harriet stormed from the room.

For a moment it was quiet. In my pocket my phone buzzed. By the time I took it out the air had turned loud and festive again, this happens every year, Tony had texted. I looked at him, he shrugged with resigned amusement. Around me I heard casual remarks of a similar nature: comments on Harriet's personality and love life—apparently she had just broken up with a boyfriend—and nostalgic reminiscences of the year Tofu the dog had peed under the table in fright. It was like a switch had been flipped. In an instant the tension was diffused, injury and grievance transformed into commotion and fond collective memory. I saw then how Tony's upbringing had prepared him for reality in a way that mine had not. His big family was a tiny world. It reflected the real world with uncanny accuracy—its little charms and injustices, its pettinesses and usefulnesses—and so, real-worldly forces struck him with less intensity, without the paralyzing urgency of assault. He did not need to survive living like I did, he could simply live.

I woke up to Tony's phone in my face.
r u OK? his mom had texted. Followed by:
R U OK????
pls respond my dear son
call ASAP love mom (followed by heart emojis and, inexplicably, an ice cream cone)

His father and siblings and aunts and cousins and childhood friends had flooded his phone with similar messages. He scrolled through the unending ribbon of notifications sprinkled with news alerts. I turned on my phone. It gave a weak buzz. Jen had texted us at 4:08 A.M.:
did you guys feel the earthquake? i ran outside and left the door open and now i cant find prick
*pickle

Pickle was Jen's cat.

A lamp had fallen over in the living room. We had gotten it at a garage sale and put it on a stool to simulate a tall floor lamp. Now it was splayed across the floor, shade bent, glass bulb dangling but miraculously still intact. When we lifted it we saw a dent in the floorboards. The crooked metal frame of the lamp could no longer support itself and so we laid it on its side like a reclining nude. There were other reclining forms too. Tony had put toy action figures amongst my plants and books; all but Wolverine had fallen on their faces or backs. He sent a photo of a downed Obi-Wan Kenobi to his best nerd friends back home.

He seemed strangely elated. That he would be able to say, Look, this happened to us too, and without any real cost.

Later, while Tony was at work, I pored over earthquake preparedness maps on the internet. Tony's office was in a converted warehouse with large glass windows on the edge of the expanding downtown. On the map, this area was marked in red, which meant it was a liquefaction zone. I didn't know what liquefaction meant but it didn't sound good. Around lunchtime Tony sent me a YouTube video showing a tray of vibrating sand, on which a rubber ball bobbed in and out as if through waves in a sea. He'd forgotten about the earthquake already, his caption said: SO COOL. I messaged back: when the big one hits, you're the rubber ball.

That afternoon, I couldn't stop seeing his human body, tossed in and out through the rubble of skyscrapers. I reminded myself that Tony had a stable psyche. He was the kind of person you could trust not to lose his mind, not in a disruptive way, at least. But I didn't know if he had a strong enough instinct for self-preservation. Clearly, he didn't have a good memory for danger. And he wasn't resourceful, at least not with physical things like food and shelter. His imagination was better for fantasy than for worst case scenarios.

I messaged:
if you feel shaking, move away from the windows, get under a sturdy desk and hold onto a leg. if there is no desk or table nearby crouch by an interior wall, whatever you do, cover your neck and head AT ALL TIMES
He sent me a sideways heart. I watched his avatar think and type for many moments.
I'm SERIOUS, I wrote.
Finally he wrote back:
umm what if my desk is by the window
. . .
should I get under the desk or go to an interior wall
I typed: get under your desk and push it to an interior wall while covering your head and neck. I imagined the rubber ball. I imagined the floor undulating, dissolving into sand. I typed: hold onto any solid thing you can.

·

I couldn't focus on work. I had recorded myself singing a series of slow glissandos in E minor, which I was trying to distort over a cello droning C. It was supposed to be the spooky intro before the drop of an irregular beat. The song was about failure's various forms, the wild floating quality of it. I wanted to show Tony I understood what he had gone through back east, at least in its primal movement and shape, that despite the insane specificity of his suffering he was not alone.

Now all I could hear were the vibrations of sand, the movements of people and buildings falling.

I went to the hardware store. I bought earthquake-proof cabinet latches and L-bars to bolt our furniture to the walls. According to a YouTube video called "Seeing with earthquake eyes," it was best to keep the bed at least fifteen feet from a window or glass or mirror—anything that could shatter into sharp shards over your soft sleeping neck. Our bed was directly beneath the largest window in the apartment, which looked out into a dark shaft between buildings. The room was small; I drew many diagrams but could not find a way to rearrange the furniture. Fifteen feet from the window would put our bed in the unit next door. I bought no-shatter seals to tape over the windows. I assembled the necessary things for an emergency earthquake kit: bottled water, instant ramen, gummy vitamins. Flashlight, batteries, wrench, and a cheap backpack to hold everything. I copied our most important contacts from my phone and laminated two wallet-sized emergency contact cards in case cell service or electricity went down.

I bought a whistle for Tony. It blew at high C, a pitch of urgency and alarm. I knew he would never wear it. I'd make him tie the whistle to the leg of his desk. If the sand-and-ball video was accurate, and a big earthquake struck during business hours, there was a chance Tony would end up buried in a pile of rubble. I imagined him alive, curled under the frame of his desk. In this scenario, the desk would have absorbed most of the impact and created a small space for him to breathe and crouch. He would be thirsty, hungry, afraid. I imagined his dry lips around the whistle, and the dispirited emergency crews layers of rubble above him, leaping up, shouting, "Someone's down there! Someone's down there!"

Suddenly I remembered I had forgotten to text Jen back.
did u look in the dryer? or that box in the garage?
everything ok over here thanks just one broken lamp
It'd taken me five hours to text Jen yet now I was worried about her lack of instant response.
did u find pickel? let me know i can come over and help you look
maybe she's stuck in a tree??
tony can print out some flyers at his office let me know!!!
I was halfway through enlarging a photo of Pickle I'd dug up from Google photos when my phone buzzed.
found pickle this morning in bed almost sat on her she was under the covers barely made a bump
She sent me a photo. Pickle was sitting on a pillow, fur fluffed, looking like a super grouch.

My office had no windows. It was partially underground, the garage-adjacent storage room that came with our apartment. We had discarded everything when we moved so we had nothing to store. The room had one outlet and was just big enough for my recording equipment and a piano. It was soundproof and the internet signal was weak. The recordings I made in there had a muffled amplified quality, like listening to a loud fight through a door.

The building where Tony and I rented was old, built in the late nineteenth century, a dozen years before the big earthquake of 1904. It had survived that one, but still by modern building codes it was what city regulators called a soft story property. According to records at City Hall, it had been seismically retrofitted by mandate five years ago. I saw evidence of these precautions in the garage: extra beams and girding along the foundations, the boilers and water tanks bolted to the walls. I couldn't find my storage/work room on any of the blueprints. Tony thought I was hypocritical to keep working there, given my new preoccupation with safety. I liked the idea of making music in a place that didn't technically exist, even if it wasn't up to code.

Or maybe it was. I imagined, in fact, that the storage rooms had been secret bunkers—why else was there a power outlet. I felt at once safe and sober inside it, this womb of concrete, accompanied by the energies of another age of panic. Now I filled the remaining space with ten gallons of water—enough for two people for five days—boxes of Shin noodles and canned vegetable soup, saltine crackers, tins of spam, canned tuna for Tony (who no longer ate land animals), a small camping stove I found on sale. I moved our sleeping bags and our winter coats down.

My office, my bunker. More and more it seemed like a good place to sit out a disaster. If we ran out of bottled water, the most vital resource, there stood the bolted water heaters, just a few steps away.

"Holy shit," Tony said when he came home from work. "Have you seen the news?"

I pursed my lips. I didn't read the news anymore. The sight of the new president's face made me physically ill. Instead I buried myself in old librettos and scores, spent whole days listening to the kind of music that made every feeling cell in my brain vibrate with forgetting: the Ring Cycle, Queen's albums in chronological order, Glenn Gould huffing and purring through the Goldberg Variations.

Tony did the opposite. Once upon a time he had been a consumer of all those nonfiction tomes vying for the Pulitzer Prize, big books about social and historical issues. He used to send me articles that took multiple hours to read—I'd wondered when he ever did work. Now he only sent me tweets.

He waved his phone in my face.

Taking up the entire screen was a photograph of what appeared to be hell. Hell, as it appeared in medieval paintings and Hollywood films. Hills and trees burning so red they appeared liquid, the sky pulsing with black smoke. A highway cut through the center of this scene, and on the highway, impossibly, were cars, fleeing and entering the inferno at top speed.

"This is Loma," Tony said.

"Loma?"

"It's an hour from here? We were there last month?"

"We were?"

"That brewery with the chocolate? Jen drove?"

"Oh. Yeah. Wow."

According to the photograph's caption, the whole state was on fire. Tony's voice was incredulous, alarmed.

"Have you gone outside today?"

I hadn't.

We walked to Chinaman's Vista, where there was a view of the city. Tony held my hand and I was grateful for it. The air was smoky; it smelled like everyone was having a barbecue. If I closed my eyes I could imagine I was in my grandmother's village in Zhejiang, those hours before dinner when families started firing up their wood-burning stoves.

"People are wearing those masks," Tony said. "Look—like we're in fucking Beijing."

Tony had never been to Beijing. I had. The smog wasn't half as bad as this.

We sat on a bench in Chinaman's Vista and looked at the sky. The sun was setting. Behind the gauze of smoke it was a brilliant salmon orange, its light so diffused you could stare straight at it without hurting your eyes. The sky was pink and purple, textured with plumes of color. It was the most beautiful sunset I had ever seen. Around us the light cast upon the trees and grass and purple bougainvillea an otherworldly yellow glow, more nostalgic than any Instagram filter. I looked at Tony, whose face had relaxed in the strange beauty of the scene, and it was like stumbling upon a memory of him—his warm dry hand clasping mine, the two of us looking and seeing the same thing.

Tony's failure had to do with the new president. He had been working on the opposing candidate's campaign, building what was to be a revolutionary technology for civic engagement. They weren't only supposed to win. *They* were the ones who were supposed to go down in history for changing the way politics used the internet.

My failure had to do with Tony. I had failed to save him, after.

Tony had quit his lucrative job to work seven days a week for fifteen months and a quarter of the pay. The week leading up to the election, he had slept ten hours total, five of them at head-quarters, face-down on his desk. He didn't sleep for a month after, though not for lack of time. If there was ever a time for Tony to go insane, that would have been it.

Instead he shut down. His engines cooled, his fans stopped whirring, his lights blinked off. He completed the motions of living but his gestures were vacant, his eyes hollow. It was like all the emotions insisting and contradicting inside him had short-circuited some processing mechanism. In happier times, Tony had joked about his desire to become an android. "Aren't we already androids?" I asked, indicating the eponymous smart-phone attached to his hand. Tony shook his head in exasperation. "Cyborgs," he said. "You're thinking of cyborgs." He explained that cyborgs were living organisms with robotic enhancements. Whereas androids were robots made to be indistinguishable from the alive. Tony had always believed computers superior to humans—they didn't need to feel.

In this time I learned many things about Tony and myself, two people I thought I already knew very well. At our weakest, I realized, humans have no recourse against our basest desires. For some this might have meant gorging in sex and drink, or worse—inflicting violence upon others or themselves. For Tony it meant becoming a machine.

Because of the wildfire smoke, we were warned to go outside as little as possible. This turned out to be a boon for my productiv-ity. I shut myself in my bunker and worked.

I woke to orange-hued cityscapes. In the mornings I drank tea and listened to my audiobook. Earth was being shredded, infinitely, as it entered the supermassive black hole, while what remained of humanity sped away on a light-speed ship. "It's strangely beautiful," one character said as she looked back at the scene from space. "No, it's terrible," another said. The first replied: "Maybe beauty is terrible." I thought the author didn't really understand beauty or humans, but he did understand terror and time, and maybe that was enough. I imagined how music might sound on other planets, where the sky wasn't blue and grass wasn't green and water didn't reflect when it was clear. I descended to my bunker and worked for the rest of the day. I stopped going upstairs for lunch, not wanting to interrupt my flow. I ate dry packets of ramen, crumbling noodle squares and picking out the pieces like potato chips. When I forgot to bring down a thermos of tea I drank the bottled water.

Fires were closing in on the city from all directions; fire would eat these provisions up. The city was surrounded on three sides by water—that still left one entry by land. It was dry and getting hotter by the day. I thought the city should keep a ship with emergency provisions anchored in the bay. I thought that if a real disaster struck, I could find it in myself to loot the grocery store a few blocks away.

In the evenings, Tony took me upstairs and asked about my work day. In the past he had wanted to hear bits of what I was working on; now he nodded and said, "That sounds nice." I didn't mind. I didn't want to share this new project with him— with anyone—until it was done. We sat on the couch and he showed me pictures of the devastation laying waste to the land. I saw sooty silhouettes of firefighters and drones panning grid-work streets of ash. I saw a woman in a charred doorway, an apparition of color in the black and gray remains of her home.

Once Jen came over to make margaritas. She put on one of Tony's Spotify playlists. "I'm sorry," she said, "I really need to unwind." She knew I didn't like listening to music while other noises were happening. My brain processed the various sounds into separate channels, pulling my consciousness into multiple tracks and dividing my present self. For Jen, overstimulation was a path to relaxation. She crushed ice and talked about the hurricanes ravaging the other coast, the floods and landslides in Asia and South America, the islands in the Pacific already swallowed by the rising sea.

Jen's speech, though impassioned, had an automatic qual-ity to it, an unloading with a mechanical beat. I sipped my margarita and tried to converge her rant with the deep house throbbing from the Sonos: it sounded like a robot throwing up. Tony came home from work and took my margarita. Together they moved from climate change to the other human horrors I'd neglected from the news—ethnic cleansings, mass shootings, trucks mowing down pedestrians. They listed the newest obscenities of the new president, their voices growing louder and faster as they volleyed headlines and tweets. In the far corner of the couch, I hugged my knees. More and more it seemed to me that the world Jen and Tony lived in was one hysterical work of poorly written fiction—a bad doomsday novel—and that what was really real was the world of my music. More and more I could only trust those daytime hours when my presence coincided completely with every sound I made and heard.

I was making a new album. I was making it for me but also for Tony, to show him it was still possible, in these times, to maintain a sense of self.

My last album had come out a year earlier. I had been on tour in Europe promoting it when the election came and went. At the time I had justified the scheduling: Tony would want to celebrate with his team anyways, I would just get in the way. Perhaps I had been grateful for an excuse. On the campaign, Tony had been lit with a blind passion I'd never been able to summon for tangible things. I'd understood it—how else could you will yourself to work that much?—I'd even lauded it, I'd wanted his candidate to win too. Still, the pettiest part of me couldn't help resenting his work like a mistress resents a wife. I imagined the election night victory party as the climax of a fever dream, after which Tony would step out, cleansed, and be returned to me.

Of course nothing turned out how I'd imagined.

My own show had to go on.

I remember calling Tony over Google Voice backstage between shows, at coffee shops, in the bathroom of the hotel room I shared with Amy the percussionist—wherever I had wifi. I remember doing mental math whenever I looked at a clock—what time was it in America, was Tony awake? The answer, I learned, was yes. Tony was always awake. Often he was drunk. He picked up the phone but did not have much to say. I pressed my ear against the screen and listened to him breathe.

I remember Amy turning her phone to me: "Isn't this your boyfriend?" We were on a train from Brussels to Amsterdam. I saw Tony's weeping face, beside another weeping face I knew: Jen's. I zoomed out. Jen's arms were wrapped around Tony's waist; Tony's arm hugged her shoulder. The photograph was in a listicle published by a major American daily showing the losing candidate's supporters on election night, watching the results come in. I remembered that Jen had flown in to join Tony at the victory arena, in order to be "a witness to history." The photo-list showed the diversity of the supporters: women in head-scarves, disabled people, gay couples. Tony and Jen killed two birds in one stone: Asian America, and an ostensibly mixed-race couple. Jen was half-Chinese but she looked exotic-white—Italian, or Greek.

That night I'd called Tony. "How are you?" I'd asked as usual, and then: "I was thinking maybe I should just come back. Should I come back? I hate this tour." There was a long silence. Finally Tony said, "Why?" In his voice a mutter of cosmic emptiness.

I have one memory of sobbing under bright white lights, some terrible noise cracking into speakers turned too high. This might have been a dream.

For a long time after, I was estranged from music. What feelings normally mediated themselves in soundscapes, a well I could plumb for composition, hit me with their full blunt force.

Now I was trying to re-enter music by making it in a new way, the way I imagined a sculptor makes a sculpture, to work with sound as if it were a physical material. Music was undoubtedly my medium: I had perfect pitch, a nice singing voice, and I liked the monasticism and repetition of practice. According to my grandmother, I had sung the melodies of nursery songs a whole year before I learned to speak. But I had the temperament of a conceptual artist, not a musician. Specifically, I was not a performer. I hated every aspect of performing: the lights, the stage, the singular attention. Most of all I could not square with the irreproducibility of performance—you had one chance, and then the work disappeared—which, to be successful, required a kind of faith. The greatest performers practiced and practiced, controlling themselves with utmost discipline, and when they stepped onto the stage, gave themselves over to time. This was also why I couldn't just compose. I wanted to control every aspect of a piece, from its conception to realization: I did not like giving up the interpretation of my notes and rests to a conductor and other musicians.

I wanted to resolve this contradiction by making music in a way that folded performance theoretically into composition. Every sound and silence in this album would be a performance. I would compose a work and perform it for myself, just once. From this material I would build my songs. If the recording didn't turn out, I abandoned the mistakes or used them. I didn't think about who the music was for. Certainly not for a group of people to enjoy with dance, as my previous album had been—I, too, had been preparing for celebration. My new listener sat in an ambient room, alone, shed of distractions, and simply let the sounds come in.

In the morning, Tony showed me a video of three husky puppies doing something adorable. "Look," he said, pointing up and out the window. From the skywell we could see a sliver of blue.

We got up and confirmed that the smoke had lifted. Tony reported from Twitter that the nearest fire had indeed been tamed. "Huzzah!" I said. I walked outside to wait with him for his Uberpool to work. The sun was shining, the air was fresh, the colors of this relentlessly cheerful coast restored. I kissed him on the cheek goodbye.

I watched his car drive away and couldn't bear the thought of going back inside. My legs itched. I wanted—theoretically—to run. I put in earbuds and turned on my audiobook. I walked around the neighborhood, looking happily at the bright houses and healthy people and energetic pooping dogs.

In the audiobook, things had also taken a happy turn. The lady protagonist, who had escaped Earth on a light-speed ship, found herself reunited in a distant galaxy with the man who'd proved his unfailing love by secretly gifting her an actual star. This reunion despite the fact that eight hundred years had passed (hibernation now allowed humans to jump centuries of time) and that when they had last seen each other, the man's brain was being extracted from his body in order to be launched into outer space (it was later intercepted by aliens who reconstructed his body from the genetic material). She had discovered his love in that final moment, when it was too late to stop the surgery—aside from then the two had barely spoken. Now he was finally to be rewarded for his devotion and patience. I thought the author had an exciting imagination when it came to technology but a shitty imagination for love. Somehow I found the endurance of this love story more unbelievable than the leaps in space and time.

That afternoon I tried to work but didn't get very much done, **dinner out?** I texted Tony. For the first time in a long time I wanted to feel like I lived in a city. I wanted to shower and put on mascara and pants that had a zipper.

Tony had a work event. I texted Jen. **sry have a date!** she wrote back, followed by a winking emoji that somehow seemed to say: *ooh-la-la.*

I decided to go out to dinner alone. I listened to my audiobook over a plate of fancy pizza, shoveling down the hot dough as I turned up the speed on my book. By the time I finished the panna cotta, the universe was imploding, every living and non-living thing barreling toward the end of its existence. I looked at my empty plate as the closing credits came on to a string cadenza in D-minor. I took out my earbuds and looked around the restaurant, at the redwood bar where I was sitting, the wait-staff in black aprons, the patrons in wool sneakers and thin down vests, the Sputnik lamps hanging above us all. Would I miss any of this? Yes, I thought, and then, just as fervently—I don't know.

Outside, the sky was fading to pale navy, a tint of yellow on the horizon where the sun had set. A cloudless, unspectacular dusk. I walked to dissipate the unknowing feeling and found myself at Chinaman's Vista, which was louder than I had ever heard it, everyone taking advantage of the newly particulate-free outdoors. I weaved through the clumps of people, looking at and through them, separate and invisible, like a visitor at a museum. That was when I saw, under a cypress tree, a woman who looked exactly like Jen, wearing Jen's gold loafers and pink bomber jacket. Jen was with a man. She was kissing the man. The man looked exactly like Tony.

I was breathing quickly. Staring. I wanted to run away but my feet were as glued as my eyes. Tony kissed Jen differently than he kissed me. He grabbed her lower back with two hands and seemed to lift her up slightly, while curling his neck to her upwardly lifted face. Because Jen was shorter than him. This made sense. I, on the other hand, was just about Tony's height.

I blinked and shook my head. Jen wasn't shorter than Tony. She was taller than us both. Jen and Tony stopped kissing and started to walk toward me, and I saw that it wasn't Tony, it was some other Asian guy who only kind of looked like Tony, but really not at all. Horrified, I turned and walked with intentionality to a plaque ahead on the path. I stared intently at the words and thought how the guy wasn't Tony and the girl probably wasn't even Jen, how messed up that I saw a white-ish girl with an East Asian guy and immediately thought Jen and Tony.

"Chenchen!"

It *was* Jen. I looked up with relief and dread. Jen stood on the other side of the plaque with her date, waving energetically.

"This is Kevin," she said. She turned to Kevin. "Chenchen's the friend I was telling you about, the composer-musician-*artiste*. She just moved to the city."

"Hey," I said. I looked at the plaque. "Did you know," I said, "Chinaman's Vista used to be a mining camp? For, uh, Chinese miners. They lived in these barrack-like houses. Then they were killed in some riots and maybe buried here, because, you know, this place has good fengshui." I paused. I'd made up the part about fengshui. The words on the plaque said *mass graves*. "This was back in the—1800s."

"Oh, like the Gold Rush?" Kevin said. His voice was deep, hovering around a low F. Tony spoke in the vicinity of B-flat. I looked up at him. He was much taller than Tony.

"Yeah," I said.

I stood there for a long time after they left, reading and re-reading the historical landmark plaque, wishing I could forget what it said. Chinaman's Vista, I thought, was a misleading name. The view was of cascading expensive houses, pruned and prim. The historic Chinese population, preferring squalor and cheap rents, had long relocated to other side of town. Besides me and probably Kevin and half of Jen, there weren't many living Chinese people here.

What was wrong with me? Why didn't I want to be a witness to history, to any kind of time passing?

The temperature skyrocketed. Tony and I kicked off our blankets in sleep. We opened the windows and the air outside was hot too. Heat radiated from the highway below in waves. The cars trailed plumes of scorching dust.

Tony texted me halfway through the day to say it was literally the hottest it had ever been. I clicked the link he sent and saw a heat map of the city. It was 105 degrees in our neighborhood, 101 at Tony's work. We didn't have an air conditioner. We didn't, after all my disaster prep, even have a fan. Tony's work didn't have AC either. Nobody in the city did, I realized when I left the house, searching for a cool café. Every business had its doors wide open. Puny ceiling fans spun as fast as they could but only pushed around hot air. It was usually so fucking temperate here, the weather so predictably perfect. I walked past melting incredulous faces: women in leather boots, tech bros carrying Patagonia sweaters with dismay.

My phone buzzed. Jen had sent a photo of what looked like an empty grocery store shelf. It buzzed again.

the fan aisle at Target!!

just saw a lady attacking another lady for the last $200 tower fan #endofdays?

That weekend, I took Tony to the mall. Tony had been sleeping poorly, exasperated by my body heat. He was sweaty and irritable and I felt somehow responsible. I felt, I think, guilty. Since the incident at Chinaman's Vista I'd been extra nice to Tony.

The AC in the mall wasn't cold enough. A lot of people had had the same idea. "Still better than being outside," I said hopefully as we stepped onto the crowded escalator. Tony grunted his assent. We walked around Bloomingdale's. I pointed at the mannequins wearing wool peacoats and knitted vests and laughed. Summer in the city was supposed to be cold, because of the ocean fog. Tony said, "Ha-ha." We got ice cream. We got iced tea. We got texts from PG&E saying that power was out on our block due to the grid overheating, would be fixed by 8 P.M. We weren't planning to be back until after sunset anyways, I said. I looked over Tony's shoulder at his phone. He was scrolling through Instagram, wistfully it seemed, through photographs of Jen and other girls in bikinis—they had gone to the beach. "But you don't like the beach," I said. Tony shrugged. "I don't like the mall either." I asked if he wanted to go to the beach. He said no.

We ate salads for dinner and charged our phones. This, at last, seemed to make Tony happy. "In case the power is still out later," he said. We sat in the food court and charged our phones until the mall closed.

The apartment was a cacophony of red blinking eyes. The appliances had all restarted when the power came back on. Now they beeped and hummed and buzzed, imploring us to reset their times. Outside the wide-open windows, cars honked and revved their engines. So many sounds not meant to be simultaneous pressed simultaneously onto me. In an instant the cheerfulness I'd mustered for our wretched day deflated. I found myself breathing fast and loud, tears welling against my will. Tony sat me down and put his noise-canceling headphones over my ears. "I can still hear everything!" I shouted. I could hear, I wanted to say, the staticky G-sharp hiss of the headset's noise-canceling mechanism. Tony was suddenly contrite. He handed me a glass of ice water and shushed me tenderly. He walked around the apartment, resetting all our machines.

We took a cold shower. Tony looked as exhausted as I felt. We kept the lights off and went directly to bed. Traffic on the highway had slowed to a rhythmic whoosh. I wanted to hug

Tony but it was too hot. I took his hand and released it. Our palms were sweaty and gross.

I was just falling asleep when I heard a faint beep. I nudged Tony. "What was that?" He rolled away from me. I turned over and closed my eyes.

It beeped again, then after some moments again.

It was a high C, a note of shrill finality. I counted the beats between: about 20 at 60 bpm. I counted to twenty, hoping to lull myself to sleep. But the anticipation of the coming beep was too much. My heart rate rose, I counted faster, unable to maintain a consistent rhythm, so now it was 22 beats, then 25, then 27.

Finally I sat up, said loudly: "Tony, Tony, do you hear the beeping?"

"Huh?" He rubbed his eyes. It beeped again, louder, as if to back me up. Tony got up and poked at the alarm clock, which he hadn't reset because it ran on batteries. He pulled the batteries out and threw them to the floor. He lay down, I thanked him, and then—*beep*.

I sat on the bed, clamping my pillow over my ears, and watched Tony lumber about the dark bedroom, drunk with exhaustion, finding every hidden gadget and extracting its batteries, taking down even the smoke detector. Each time it seemed he had finally identified the source there sounded another beep. It was a short sound, it insisted then disappeared: even my impeccable hearing could not locate from where exactly it came. It sounded as if from all around us, from the air. Tony fell on the bed defeated. He said, "Can we just try to sleep?" We clamped our eyes shut, forced ourselves to breathe deeply, but the air was agitated and awake. My mind drifted and ebbed, imitating the movements of sleep while bringing nothing like rest. I couldn't help thinking that the source of the sound was neither human nor human-made. I couldn't help imagining the aliens in my audiobook preparing to annihilate our world. "Doomsday clock," I said, half-aloud. I was thinking or dreaming of setting up my equipment to record the beeps. I was thinking or dreaming of unrolling the sleeping bags in my bunker, where it'd be silent and I could sleep. "Counting down."

"I'm sorry," Tony said.

"It's okay," I said, but it wasn't, not really, and Tony knew it. He grabbed my hand and squeezed it hard. Between the cosmic beeps his lips smacked open as if to speak, as if searching for the right words to fix me. Finally he said, "I kissed Jen," and I said, "I know."

Then, "What?"

Then, "When?"

My eyes were wide open.

"Last November."

High C sounded, followed by ten silent beats.

"You were in Germany."

Another high C. Twenty beats. Another high C.

"I'm sorry," Tony said again. "Say something, please?" He tightened his hand. I tried to squeeze back to say I'd heard, I was awake. I failed. I listened to the pulses of silence, the inevitable mechanical beeps.

"Tell me what you're thinking?"

I was thinking we would need a new disaster meet-up spot. I was wondering if there was any place in this city, this world, where we'd be safe.

NIGHT SHIFT

Charles Johnson

YOU GO TO WORK AT THE HOSPITAL AT 10 P.M., as you always do, but you're feeling like a lot of people who don't want to leave home during the pandemic. Doctors and nurses, health care providers, people in grocery stores, teachers, and security guards like you—you all are supposed to be "essential" workers. The people on the front lines every day (and night) because certain goods and services can't end without society collapsing entirely, although some days it seems to you at this dangerous hour in history, when Americans are killing and tearing each other apart, that this sea change has happened *already*.

As a young black man, you were of course always at risk from the moment you were born. But even *that* abnormal wasn't normal anymore. After months of the worst pandemic in a century, you've witnessed the devastating toll it's taking on the doctors and hospital staff all around you. It's like they're fighting a war with never enough supplies, or a battle they feel they lose every time someone on a ventilator dies, which is daily, or when one of their coworkers contemplates suicide, or collapses on the floor right in front of them from fatigue. On top of that, there is always the danger of being contaminated by this devilish, mutating, poorly understood, highly politicized plague themselves and bringing it back home to their spouses, children, or aging parents.

That isn't something you have to worry about. You're twenty-five, but you figure you don't have a family. Not really. Not since your mother died fifteen years ago, right here in this hospital after a surgery she was too weak to recover from. That left your older brother Jamal and you to somehow cross America's racial minefield of dangers on your own. And you don't talk. You don't want to think about him being "family." You've been practicing social distancing with him since the day he started carrying a gun, selling drugs, and running with a gang called the Cobras when you were still in your teens. You didn't like them. The Cobras used to beat you up before Jamal was jumped into that gang. Him being a Cobra, and so angry, cynical and fighting all the time, always opinionated and pissed off, broke your mother's heart, and you never knew your father. He just wasn't around. Your mother had tried her best to put you both on the right path. Blackness, she said, was not a curse or condemnation. But you had to be careful in a society structured by an infinite number of ways for its citizens to fail, make mistakes, blunders, or be defined as criminals, wrong in some way, or involved in something illegal. She always told you to strive to be more, to be better, to just be *human*, and to see obstacles as opportunities— to stand for *some*thing, she said, because if you don't stand for something, it's likely you'll fall for *any*thing.

So you always tried to do better. To avoid the landmines that Jamal stepped on. Like him, you didn't finish high school, but you earned your G.E.D., and you quietly do your best on your job here at the hospital. You didn't want to become a casualty or just another statistic. You were wired, you feel, differently from him, and feared if you tried to help your brother, he might drag you down with him. You haven't seen him in—what?— maybe ten years, and that was all right. You learned you could do just fine by yourself, if need be. You try to read as much and as widely as you can, and sometimes you take online courses, even though your budget on a security guard's salary gets too tight sometimes and ever so often you get behind on your bills.

Before walking into the hospital, you loop your plain, black cloth mask over your ears, then push through the doors leading to the Emergency Room waiting area, which is near the corridor that leads to the locker room for those who work security. As soon as you step inside you know something is wrong. One of the other security guards, Jim Sawyer, always stands inside the entrance at this hour, taking note of everyone who comes in or leaves. But not tonight. And then you hear a smear of loud voices in the waiting room. A dozen angry young people, bloodied, bandaged and moaning, scarred and scared, wounded and willful, some dressed entirely in black, are demanding medical attention. Behind them, you see the receptionist, Kimisha Thompson, who you like and maybe more than like, because she's always good-natured, kind, has a beautiful, bow-shaped smile that lights up her eyes behind her glasses, never burdens anyone with her personal baggage, and will listen as long as you want to keep talking. But tonight she seems overwhelmed when you squeeze through this rowdy, unruly crowd, none of them wearing masks or social distancing, and ask her what all this is about.

She's wearing a white mask sprinkled with red hearts. That makes you smile because it so fits her personality. It keeps slipping up toward her nose and ever so often she has to tug it back down toward her chin with her thumb and forefinger. Through the cloth, you hear her say, "There was a protest downtown. Don't ask me about what they were protesting this time, I don't remember. But when it got dark, some people started looting. Some attacked the police. One cop was shot and they took him to Harborview. Lucas," her voice, tremulous, sounds exhausted, "We're really short-handed tonight. The doctors are doing triage. Right now we don't have enough ventilators or beds. Five of the security guards, one of them was Jim, tested positive for COVID when they showed up for work, and they're being quarantined at home. Your supervisor has been trying to reach you all day, but he kept getting a message that service to your phone was disconnected."

You nod slowly. That was one of the bills you fell behind on. You can tell this is going to be a very long night. What you don't know yet is that it might be your last night.

"Okay," you say, "I'll come back to take Jim's place as soon as I can."

Kimisha holds up one hand covered by a blue vinyl glove. Above her mask, you can see her gentle eyes—dark brown pupils like chocolate drops—and pencil-thin eyebrows, but not her high cheekbones. Her silvery voice floats disembodied in the air. "No, one of the doctors—Dr. Chen—said they need someone right now in the recovery room in the east wing. That's where security is needed. You need to go there *now*."

"Are you going to be okay here by yourself?"

Her eyes crinkled. "I'll do my best. You go find Dr. Chen."

You hurry into the empty locker room, thinking of all the duties that awaited you at a hospital that is short-handed and under siege. You change into your gray, short-sleeved shirt, dark pants with gray stripes on the side, and strap on your duty belt with its keys, flashlight, radio, and a slot to hold your smartphone, then you pull on your turquoise latex gloves. But your mind is still chewing on what Kimisha told you. If the security staff was down five people tonight, who was going to do a floor-by-floor check of all the buildings every two hours? Who will be checking windows and doors? Who would make sure the security systems are functioning properly?

You wonder: Can *any*thing good come out of this ongoing catastrophe?

Dr. Chen, wearing a blood-splattered surgical gown, is waiting impatiently outside the recovery room when you arrive. You approach him cautiously because he always carries himself as if he's posing for a photo. Tonight, though, you can tell he's sacked and empty, running on the fumes. You place his age at sixty. Maybe sixty-five. For as long as you've known him, he's always been a perfectionist in an imperfect world, a physician strict about the right nutrition for his patients and the staff at the hospital, and he never trusts himself even to talk when he's tired, like now. When feeling numb after seeing ten patients die in a day from the virus, he balances his depleted energy by slowing down, breathing deeply, being ever more precise and mindful of even the minutest details, doing things "Tai Chi tyle," as he calls it, for his father taught him the 24-move Yang-style form when he was a boy. His motions as he waits for you are as slow as those of a man submerged in water, each posture or position he takes as he shifts his weight outside the recovery room flowing like the unconscious grace of actors in a Chinese opera.

You wonder for the briefest of moments what it would have been like to grow up with a wealthy, well-educated doctor as your father, someone teaching you survival skills that would stay with you for a lifetime.

"I just removed a bullet from the shoulder of a man in that room," he says. "I need you to call the police and keep him here until they arrive."

Yes, you think, that *is* the hospital's rule when someone comes in after being shot. You've had to call the police before to inform them about a shooting victim. Dr. Chen turns away, moving toward his next patient, and you step into the recovery room as if into a dream. The lights are dimmed so you squint to sharpen your vision, the room gradually snapping to shape, your gaze finally falling on a figure in a bed with chrome knobs and a metal railing. You step closer as he tries to lift his head to look at you. Your heart is fluttery in your chest, your palms feel wet as if your life is doubling back on you like a Moebius strip, because of course you know who this is, who it has to be in a country coming apart at its seams.

This is the night that was bound to come.

You find yourself standing speechless over this wounded man. Wounded tonight. Wounded so badly earlier in your lives. He recognizes you. You wish you could say the same for him. Ten years have passed since you saw him, and he is a mystery to you, looking as if he's aged two decades. He's stumbled into many racial landmines. He's been blown to pieces often. And now he's hooked up to IV tubes, wearing a polyester patient gown, and still groggy from his pre-surgery injection of mid-azolam. An angry, Saturday night knife scar stretches from just

below his left eye down his cheek to his chin. His skin is rough
from the hard alcohol-and-drug driven life he's been living with
the Cobras. His voice is flinty, fractured every now and then by
a chest-rattling cough.

"Can't stay here," he says, weakly. "He'p me leave."

You blink to refocus your eyes. It's been a long time since
you've seen an O.G. An original gangster. "You were shot . . . I
don't understand what happened . . ."

"You never will," he says, rolling his eyes. "That was always
your problem. You never get angry enough. When them pro-
testers started bustin' into stores, me and a couple of my boys
decided to liberate a little merchandise. You know, for repara-
tions. White people owe us *everything*. We *supposed* to be dead.
You know that, right? Some pig saw us. He shot at me and I
shot back. I told my boys to bring me here. I keep tabs on my
square, younger brother. Knew you worked security here. So
he'p me outside, okay?"

"Jamal . . . you shot a cop?"

"Yeah. He ain't the first. Probably won't be the last either.
Cops, they just another gang."

"You still runnin' with the Cobras?"

"That's right. They're my family."

"I thought *we* were family."

He gives a shrug, the corners of his mouth pulled down. "We
were, but diff'rent, like Momma always said. Aw 'ight? You
gonna he'p me or not"

"I can't let you go. I'll lose my job."

"Right. Your li'l job. And *I* could go to prison. I'm on parole,
man. They're lookin' for me. They'll put me *under* the jail. And
I can't do no more time. Just get me outside, let me hold that
cellphone of yours, and I'll call the brothers to pick me up. After
that, you'll never see me again."

You leave a silence, and lower your head, pinching the bridge
of your nose. Here was a landmine your mother never told you
that you would have to face. You imagine what might happen
when the police catch up with him. Suicide by cop.

"Don't make me do this. It's not right. It's crazy. In your condition, you won't get far!"

"Let me worry about that, okay? My boys will pick me up. Li'l brother," he laughs, raising his eyebrows, "welcome to the real world. There ain't no right or wrong."

You don't reply to that. Unlike Kimisha, he was never one to listen. For a second, you want to ask him what sent him to prison but decide you really don't want to know. It doesn't matter. He's family. And you can't abandon family, no matter what happens. Despite your differences, and regardless of the risk to yourself, you know you cannot deny his request. For better or worse, good or ill, you are bonded by blood.

He tries to rise from the bed. He can't do it alone. Before you can think, you're unhooking him from the IV tubes, lowering the railing on his bed and helping him to stand, moving slowly, calmly like Dr. Chen, focusing on each thing you do as if it will be the last thing you ever do. Awareness of death, you realize, makes every moment precious, a gift that must be managed carefully. Jamal holds onto you for support as you guide him to a wheelchair in a corner of the room, aware only of his pain and confusion, which somehow you accept, no matter how much you want him or this plague-wracked world to be otherwise. From the recovery room, it's a short distance to one of the service elevators only used by the staff. That takes you down and spits you out at an exit at the back of the hospital. You hope your supervisor is too busy to be at the screens that monitor all the entrances leading outside.

Jamal struggles out of the wheelchair, clumsy and Chaplinesque. He bends over briefly from dizziness, there on the loading dock. You give him a look that says, *GO*. And he smiles, barefoot and wraith-like in his gown, before limping off into the darkness. As you watch him disappear, a sadness washes over you as you surrender to the certainty that your life will always be interwoven with your brother's, contaminated by his, just as one day you likely will be infected by a virus so difficult to control but, unlike him, you know you'll survive all this as you did the racial minefields of your childhood. And move on with your life.

You walk back into the hospital to check on Kimisha and call 911.

A GOOD MARRIAGE

Pauline Kaldas

A MRA BENT INTO THE OVEN to reach for the casserole
bubbling with the white sauce escaping through the top
layer of bread crumbs. She underestimated the weight of the
ceramic dish filled to the brim with pasta, ground beef, and
sauce. Even though she had both oven mitts on, her right arm
tilted up to support the casserole fully and hit the top oven rack
right above where the glove stopped. The heat stung her skin,
corresponding to the sizzle of noise she made as she sucked
the pain of the burn through her teeth. Still, she continued to
lift the heavy load and place it on the stove top. She paused for
a moment and closed her eyes, allowing the pain to seep fully
through her skin. Slowly, she took the mitts off and turned on
the faucet, placing her arm beneath the stream of cold water to
let it cool the penetration of the heat.

A few minutes later, the casserole sat in the middle of the
dining room table, accompanied by a salad made with iceberg
lettuce, cucumbers, and radishes, along with a plate of fried
eggplant. She had tried to make salads with spinach or other
kinds of lettuce, adding mushrooms and tomatoes, but her
husband had rejected them. He had written down the name

of the lettuce he liked so she would get the correct one in the supermarket, adding that he did not like tomatoes. Amra did her best with the iceberg lettuce, adding olive oil and lime juice, but there was little flavor that she could muster out of it. Her serving of salad became smaller with each dinner, until she took only a single spoon.

Sometimes, when she went to the grocery store, she would purchase two ripe red tomatoes, and when she came home, even before emptying the shopping bags, she would wash and cut them into an awkward pattern of triangular shapes. She crumbled a good bit of feta cheese over them, adding olive oil, lime juice, a sprinkle of black pepper, and, sometimes, if she felt brave, a crushed garlic clove. The concoction satisfied a deep longing in her, and she ate the improvised salad with a small loaf of pita bread. The gas stove in their previous apartment had allowed her to toast the bread over the burner and, just when a flame caught the bread, she would turn it off and watch the fire die down slowly, leaving a darker charred edge. But this new house they had bought a year ago had an electric stove, and the same technique didn't work. She had tried once shortly after they moved, but the bread only stuck to the burner.

For the first two years of their married lives, they had lived in a small apartment in Cambridge, just one bedroom, a small living room, a single bathroom, and a square kitchen where everything was within easy reach. When she stood at the stove, it only took one step back to get something in the refrigerator or lean over to grab a spice from the cabinet. At first, she thought it was small, but placing herself in it, she found that it fit around her like the dresses she used to have made by the tailor who knew her figure so well that he no longer had to take her measurements. Her married life had begun in this apartment with her husband's promise that they would buy their own house soon and start their family.

The two years gave her time to adjust to her husband's habits and to this new world that would now shape her life. She learned to drive, found her way to the supermarket, and understood the arrangement of fruits, vegetables, meats, and cleaning supplies. She went to the mall and figured out the puzzle of this world's fashion to readjust her style. It was not as difficult as she had anticipated. Her education for twelve years at the Cairo American College had prepared her well, and she now realized that she had already stepped one foot into this world before arriving. She had learned the language to a fluent stage, and she was familiar with the movies, the TV shows, the fashion, and the current social issues.

Her father's ideas about education were peculiar. He had enrolled her in the most prestigious and expensive school in the country. But he had made it clear that he did not believe there was any need for a girl to receive a college education. For him, the goal of this prestigious education was making a good marriage that would honor the family and ensure that she had a husband who could take care of her. Her knowledge of the English language and her ability to carry a conversation about literature and current events, along with her attractive appearance, was meant to ensure that she would appeal to a well-educated man from a good family.

Once she graduated, she knew the suitors would begin to appear. She had watched the pattern with her older sister. Within a week, the families with eligible young men arrived at the house. Her sister was made to serve tea and petit fours that she claimed credit for making, although her mother oversaw the process like a hawk. Her sister played the part faithfully; however, she did insist on being given a choice. Her parents humored her, up to a point. After five suitors, they insisted she select one. "Any more than that and people will say you're spoiled and no one can please you." Her sister had clearly enjoyed being put on display, but she complied and chose the second suitor.

That night, Amra asked her why she had chosen that one.

Her sister shrugged and responded, "He is the best looking, he works for a foreign company that pays him in dollars, and he has a nice apartment in Heliopolis."

"Does he appeal to you?" Amra asked, her voice tentative. She was younger by five years, and she and her sister rarely discussed anything that mattered.

Without hesitation, her sister said, "He has everything I want."

While Amra's classmates prepared to attend the best colleges in Egypt or travel abroad to further their education, she knew that graduating from high school was the end for her. As a result, she could not answer her teacher's questions about what career she wanted to pursue. She was a good student, excelling in all her classes, but she had never thought about continuing her education. That door would close upon her graduation, and she knew better than to attempt to look beyond to what she could not have.

When she graduated, her father said, "Now it's time for you to continue your education with your mother. We don't want to be embarrassed like we were with your sister." Two months after her sister married, the husband came to their door unexpectedly. He asked to speak to Amra's father, and the straight line of his lips caused her mother to escort him directly to their salon, forgetting even to offer him something to drink.

Amra sat with her mother in the kitchen, watching her mumble and wring her hands. She got up to wash a cup in the sink, placed it back in the sink, and then got up again to wash it.

"What is it, ya mama?" Amra asked her.

Her mother did not seem to hear her, but she mumbled loud enough for Amra to hear, "ya lahwe, ya lahwe! What happened? It can't be the matter of children. All that has passed is two months. What did you do, my daughter?"

After about twenty minutes, they heard the men's voices and the door closing. Her mother rushed out from the kitchen to confront her husband, and Amra followed.

"What happened?" her mother asked, her breath escaping before her words.

"Your daughter can't cook or clean. The man can't eat at home and the house is full of dust. You will go there every day until she learns the duties of a wife. He promised not to say a word to anyone."

After graduating, Amra's days transformed from studying math, science, and literature to learning the intricacies of cooking, cleaning, and managing the household budget.

"These are the things you will have to do when you marry," her mother said as she handed her daughter the dust rag. Each morning, Amra and her mother went to the market to select the produce and the meat they would need for the day's meal. The earlier they went, the better their chances of finding the freshest vegetables and the best cuts of meat. Amra learned how to distinguish the good eggplant from the wrinkled ones that had been lying in the bin too long, how to get the seller to pull out the newer potatoes he kept tucked away for his favorite customers, and how to eye the meat so she knew if the butcher was tricking her with a poorer cut. When they returned home, the morning was spent preparing the afternoon meal—an elaborate dinner that usually consisted of at least three or four dishes. The latter part of the day was spent dusting, cleaning, and doing the laundry. At first, Amra felt overwhelmed by the tasks placed in front of her. Keeping up with the details of these household duties felt more taxing than deciphering her calculus homework.

At the beginning of each month, her mother sat her down to review the monthly budget. This was the only lesson that sparked Amra's interest. Every month, her mother received a household allowance from her father. With this money, her mother was expected to purchase not only food, but also other things needed for their home, as well as clothes and personal items.

"A smart woman knows how to handle money," her mother said. "And she knows how to plan ahead both for what is expected and what is not expected." Her mother explained how she set aside money for each of their household needs, anticipating things like the extra expenses around the holidays and clothes for special occasions. "But always, every month, no matter how tight things are, you put a little bit aside and you hide it and only you know where it is," her mother told Amra, looking straight into her eyes, as if trying to implant the words deeply into her.

"But why?" asked Amra.

"Because," her mother responded, and here she redirected her gaze at an obscure point in front of her that only she could detect. "You never know what the future might bring, and a woman should have her own money."

Within six months, Amra had begun to master many of her lessons, and often if her mother was a little tired, she went to the market alone. As she unloaded each item, her mother would tell her where she had made a good purchase and where she could have done better. Within a year, Amra did most of the cooking, her mother guiding her with only a few instructions. "Very good. Very good," her father said when Amra's mother gave her credit for the meal.

The days lingered, and Amra waited for the suitors to arrive. This was the final goal of her formal education and her mother's teaching—to make a good match and add to the status of her family. Amra knew that the news of an eligible young woman ready to marry traveled like a grapevine, but the suitors did not come quickly as they had for her sister. Amra was not in a rush, but she wondered if something was wrong with her. She dressed simply, wearing a skirt or pants with a loose shirt. Her black hair fell just below her shoulders, and she usually pulled it back into a high pony tail. She added little jewelry and avoided makeup, but she had been told she was attractive. Now, she looked in the mirror and wondered if she lacked something.

In the evening, she began to hear bits and pieces of her parents' whisperings: *too expensive—no money for marriage— finding an apartment—so many emigrating—she's almost twenty. Tayeb tayeb*, was her father's response, and she could imagine him patting her mother's hand to appease her and calm her concerns.

Apparently, there was a shortage of suitors. Since Sadat took over and implemented his new policies, prices had risen and it was becoming difficult to find a job and an apartment. Amra knew that more people were emigrating, going to Europe, Canada, or the States for something better. The choice of her life's mate would be completely random, whichever man happened to be here and have the means to get married.

Her mother started to tamper with her appearance. "Wear your hair loose," she said. "The ponytail makes you look so young. And a little eye makeup—you have such pretty eyes."

Amra tried, but when she left her hair loose, she felt as if it clouded her sight and she kept pushing it behind her ears. She knew her large brown eyes were her best feature, but she couldn't be bothered with the daily ritual of makeup; only on special occasions would she appease her mother and put some on. Another year passed slowly, and Amra continued to run the household, following her mother's instructions.

At dinner one night, Amra coughed, preparing her voice to speak. "I was thinking, ya Baba . . .

Her father's eyes rose from the plate to settle on her.

Amra swallowed, although there was no food in her mouth. The silence waited for her to speak. "Perhaps the American University . . . could I apply?" She felt the weight of her words descend, and, fearful of being crushed, she added, "I mean, just while I'm waiting."

Her father said nothing, and her mother's gaze remained absorbed on the fork in her hand. Amra looked toward the wall facing her, where she could see the path that her father had set for her clearly laid out, a path that persisted in its predictability. The meal finished in silence.

It was only a week later that Amra heard another whispered conversation between her parents:

But so far away, came her mother's muffled voice. *A good opportunity—she's twenty now—can't wait much longer,* her father affirmed.

Within a week, Amra found herself engaged to marry a man who spent one evening at their house talking mostly to her father. He arrived carrying a box of imported chocolates and a bottle of whiskey bought at the duty-free shop. His mother came with him, a petite woman whose husband had died several years ago. "An unexpected heart attack," she heard the woman say quietly to her mother. The man's name was Farid. He was a little taller than Amra, who, at five feet four inches, was one of the tallest women in her family. Farid was medium built, a bit stocky but not fat, his body exhibiting a belief in moderation. Amra noted a slight thinning of his hair, and later she learned he was thirty-five, fifteen years older than her. He greeted her politely, and then sat across from her father and directed the conversation toward him. After about twenty minutes, Amra brought in the tea and konafa she had prepared. Her mother had watched carefully as she made the sweet dessert, instructing her to make sure she put enough hazelnuts and almonds in it. "Nuts are cheap in America," her mother said. "You can find them everywhere. People can eat pistachios anytime. We don't want to look cheap."

She offered Farid the konafa and tea. "Thank you," he said, as he took the cup from her after directing her to put two spoons of sugar in it. Two spoons, thought Amra, every Egyptian seems to require two spoons of sugar in their cup of tea. Occasionally, a guest would sheepishly request three, confessing that they had a sweet tooth. If someone asked for only one, it would be followed with the explanation that they were dieting. Amra preferred her tea with no sugar, instead adding a bit of milk to cool the temperature and shift the texture of the brewing drink. As he sipped his tea, Farid turned his body slightly toward Amra and asked her some questions about how she had enjoyed Cairo American College and whether she had a Polaroid camera. "I work with cameras," he revealed, a sense of pride raising the pitch of his voice. But before Amra could ask exactly what he did with cameras, he turned again to direct himself toward her father.

Now, at the age of twenty-three, she stood in this kitchen with the electric oven, the burn on her arm fusing to her skin, wondering at the path of her life. The first two years living in their small apartment in America had held her attention with the newness of place. The changing seasons, purchasing her first warm coat and boots, learning her way around the supermarket, going to American movies, and becoming part of the social circle of other Egyptian immigrants. She adjusted easily, making good use of her Americanized education, catching the nuances of culture and language with little effort.

Farid had lived up to his predictable two spoons of sugar. Each day, he went to work, leaving at 7:00 A.M., and returning at 5:30 P.M., with the expectation of dinner at 6:00. On the weekends, he often took her on an outing, showing her different parts of the city or farther out to one of the towns bordering the ocean. They went to Gloucester, Salem, and Rockport. Each time they would take a walk, stop somewhere for lunch, and then return home. Amra watched the young people on the beach in their scant bathing suits, laughing and swimming. She knew that Farid did not know how to swim, so she never asked.

What she enjoyed most were the hours when he was at work. Cleaning the apartment and cooking a meal did not take as long in this country. There were vacuum cleaners, and the dust did not accumulate at the same rate as it did in Cairo. With so much food canned and frozen, she could make a meal in just an hour. Realizing that she had extra time, she began to venture out. The first day she left the house alone, she looked at herself in the mirror diligently to be sure she was acceptable to the outside world. She pulled her hair back into its ponytail, smoothed her eyebrows, and made sure her face was clear. She stepped gingerly outside and began walking, taking note of her direction. The space around her expanded and after a few minutes of focusing on the ground, she looked up and exhaled as if releasing every fear she had felt. Her afternoon walks became a daily ritual, taking in her surroundings, re-planting herself in this new place. She took note of the buildings, the people, and the shops, inhaling the possibilities of what this new world had to offer. She enjoyed those first years. Living in the apartment with its temporary feel and anticipation of moving suited her, keeping her on the cusp of change.

At dinner one evening, Amra cleared her throat, "Farid," she said. He looked up from his plate of rice and okra.

"I was thinking," she went on, "that maybe I could find work . . . a small job . . . to help a little."

He took two more bites of the okra then raised his eyes toward her. "Is there anything you need?"

She shook her head.

"We'll buy a house soon, and there will be children to fill your time."

When they bought the new house, the pattern of their days shifted. Their weekend outings stopped and they were more likely to be going to someone's house for dinner or inviting someone over. If they weren't socializing, Farid spent the week-end fixing something or taking her to a furniture store so she could fill up the new space.

The house opened up their inner world. Farid had insisted on three bedrooms—"for the children," he had said matter-of-factly. And there was a formal dining room so their guests could sit properly at a table, instead of filling their plates in the kitchen and scattering themselves about the small living room as they had done in their old apartment, some sitting on chairs and others on the floor. Amra preferred the haphazard quality of that apartment. There, she had found herself engaged in private talk with the women, sharing secrets and gossip outside of the men's world. Sitting at the dining table, the conversations turned stale, and no one seemed interested in what was being said. She felt her attention drifting from a set script they were all following. The kitchen was larger, but the additional space made her pause as she tried to remember where she had placed a certain pan or which cabinet held the rice. But it was the stove that irritated her. In Egypt, everyone had a gas stove, so she adjusted naturally to the one in their small apartment. Here, when she turned on the electric burner, it took a while for it to heat up, and when she turned it off, it remained hot. Her food often burned in those last minutes after she turned off the burner, thinking the heat was gone.

Amra felt her days roll and recognized the pattern, a parallel to the years she had spent after finishing school and living with her parents. The trips to the grocery store—weekly instead of the daily ones to the market; the cooking—now for Farid instead of her father; the social life limited to those who were similar—family in Egypt and other Egyptians here. America had held a promise of mystery, but once the newness of place faded, she discovered there was nothing really different here. She had tried offering Farid honey instead of sugar in his tea, but he had declined, saying it was too sweet. She tried putting the small pitcher of milk on the table, but he simply shook his head. Once, she had slipped an extra half spoon of sugar into his cup, but she noticed the slight squiggle of his lips as he took the first sip and set the cup back down. Another time, when she placed only one and a half spoons of sugar, she saw the purse of his lips as he tasted the liquid then watched as he added the exact amount she had left out, stirring carefully and proceeding to drink the rest of the cup.

Like her father, Farid gave her a household budget each month. Amra looked forward to organizing her finances and discovered that America offered multiple opportunities for saving. There were ongoing sales at the grocery store, coupons in the paper, and competing discounts if she went to more than one store. Farid was generous and told her she could use some of the money to buy clothes and makeup. But there was little that Amra needed. She preferred to stay with her simple outfits and purchased only a few things for dressier occasions. At first, she was able to scrape away a hundred dollars a month, but as she figured out the system of sales, her monthly savings increased. The money accumulated in a makeup pouch that she kept in her underwear drawer, never telling Farid. But it worried her to have so much money exposed at home. When a new bank opened only a few blocks away from their new house, she made her way there and inquired about opening an account.

"Will this account be only in your name?" asked the teller.

Amra's mother's words rang in her ears—"a woman should have her own money—plan for what is expected and unexpected."

"Yes," answered Amra, "just my name."

Amra walked home, suppressing the small joy she felt in the pit of her stomach. She knew the feeling, this sensation of guilty pleasure. She had felt it before as a child when she used to touch herself and experience the strange awareness that filled her body. Then again when she was nine and the boy who lived next door came over to play and enticed her to a shady corner in their yard, saying, "I'll show you if you show me," and they both pulled down their underwear, then the touch of his fingers sending the same pleasure through her until she heard her mother's voice calling. But this was only money, she thought, yet it called up a similar feeling in her. A pleasure she did not experience with Farid, who went about lovemaking as a task to be accomplished. He saw the act only as a means of conceiving a child, and she experienced nothing under his touch. As she made her way home, she caught sight of a man working on the roof of one of the houses. He had shoulder-length brown hair and a beard. Her eyes caught his, and, before she could turn away, he said "Good afternoon" and nodded. "Good afternoon," she responded, trying to keep her pace steady. She passed him quickly, but his face lingered in her vision. What would it be like to be married to a man like that, she wondered. What would such a life look like? Something of that thought defeated the pleasure she had been feeling. She felt betrayed by the promise of this America.

Amra knew she was pregnant as soon as Farid finished. As he rolled over, she could feel the movement in her body and knew that a child had begun to be created. She tried to convince herself that it was only her imagination, her fear. But the next morning, it was the first thought that entered her mind when she awoke, and as she stood in the shower, the water drowning her body, she knew with clarity that she was right. She went through the motions of her life over the next week, pushing back her thoughts and concentrating on her daily tasks. When her period did not arrive, she went and bought a pregnancy test. As she expected, it was positive. She wrapped the kit and the box in several paper towels, stuffed it in a plastic bag, and pushed it to the bottom of the garbage can. Her brain felt devoid of thought—neither anticipation nor anxiety entered her—only a sense of complete emptiness. Over the next few weeks, she began to feel the beginning symptoms—her breasts tender, a slight sense of nausea in the morning, a tiredness that made her want to lie down in the afternoon.

Sitting down for dinner with Farid one evening, she rearranged the food on her plate, as he gave himself a second helping of the chicken and rice. He gave a slight cough and said, "It looks like I'll be getting a promotion at work. It will make things easier. You should get pregnant soon," he added.

Amra looked up, her eyes drifting across Farid's thinning hair and tried to imagine a life of raising children with him. The child would combine their appearance, and the years would propel her forward. She would become a mother with expected duties. Another child would probably come, and her identity would mold into her children's lives. Was this the only choice, she wondered. She had been in America long enough to know that not everyone lived in this way—there were more possibilities here than in Egypt, although she had only caught glimpses of them in watching TV shows and movies and hearing stories from others. Some women never married; some married and chose not to have children. What would it be like? she thought, to never attach yourself to a man, to maintain only your singular identity. Was that a selfish life? Could there be some happiness without a husband and children? The option of being alone— what kind of life could be carved out by yourself? The only woman in her family who lived alone was a distant aunt whose husband had died unexpectedly only a year into their marriage before they had any children. After her husband's death, her aunt insisted on staying in the apartment by herself. She became a surrogate parent to all the children in the family, taking care of them, a kind of matriarch who offered her maternal services to others to compensate for her own lack of family. But Amra couldn't picture herself in that life.

Amra's trips to the bank had become more regular as each month she added to the account. The tellers came to know her, and she enjoyed the small conversations she had with them, realizing it was the only time she really spoke with an American. One day, as she made a deposit, the teller pointed out the growing amount in her account and asked if she were interested in a CD or money market. Amra's face registered her confusion, and the teller added that she could make more money. She suggested that Amra speak to the manager, and Amra nodded.

The manager was a young African-American man who shook her hand and gestured for her to sit down. Amra noted the particular shade of his skin and the fullness of his features. He could be from upper Egypt, she thought. As he began to explain the investment opportunities, Amra lost her shyness and followed his explanations diligently, adding the numbers on a piece of paper, comparing the possibilities he offered. An hour had passed before she realized it.

"Thank you," she said, "You've been very helpful."

"No problem." He smiled. "You have a knack for this. You should go into finance," he added as he stood to shake her hand.

On her way back from the bank, she found herself looking up at the rooftops for the same man who had greeted her. But when she came to the house where she had previously seen him, he wasn't there. She glanced up and saw other men on the roof, none of them looking in her direction.

Arriving home, she spent the afternoon preparing the evening meal. Farid had asked her to make stuffed cabbage and the process was time consuming. She set up the leaves and the stuffing on the kitchen table and began rolling each one. The house turned quietly around her, the silence humming steadily as she continued her work. Her mind filtered the images that intruded—her mother teaching her how to roll these leaves, how to select the produce in the market, how to keep her hands steady as she tipped over the pot of stuffed leaves once it was cooked. She sat in this kitchen, in this new country, repeating the motions she had so carefully learned. "This is not a life." Her voice spoke aloud and startled her. She looked at the half-filled pot and the remaining leaves and stuffing. Then she looked down at her own body, sensing the new heart that would be beating. "No," she said. Once she had finished rolling the cabbage, she pulled out the phone book and, after a few attempts of looking under different headings, she found what she wanted. She called and set the appointment for the end of the week.

When Farid came home on that day and found her in bed, he immediately asked, "Are you pregnant?"

"No Farid. I'm sorry," she answered. "It came today and the cramps are bad." She saw his face falter and added, "Your dinner is in the oven."

He nodded and made his way to the kitchen.

Within a few days, she felt well enough to get up and continue her routine, but something nagged at her. What she had done was irrevocable. While she cooked and cleaned, her thoughts plagued her. This country did not close doors like Egypt. Here people changed careers and went back to college when they were older, recreated their lives. She couldn't quite capture the reality of what she imagined, but she knew she wanted something that she could claim for herself.

When Farid returned home from a two-day business trip, he walked into the house and stood still holding his suitcase in the front entrance. The house pulled away from him, its walls expanding out to reveal the empty space. "Amra" he called, but there was no response. He went to the kitchen, but there was no sign of Amra's cooking. Nothing was on the stove or in the oven. The counters were cleanly wiped and everything neatly settled into its place, the way it looked every night after Amra finished cleaning up. He went up the stairs, hearing the slight creak on the wooden steps. Approaching the bedroom, a cool breeze swept by him as if someone was walking past. The bed was neatly made, the blanket tucked into the comers and the pillows leaning against the headboard. His eyes focused on the side where he slept. A few items were placed on the night table, and he went toward them cautiously—the shine of Amra's wedding band and the small diamond he had given her flashed a glimmer in his eye. The jewelry he had presented to her at their engagement sat in a swirl next to it. He looked up and the room exhaled its breath around him. He walked toward the closet and opened it. Her clothes were gone. Turning to her dresser, he noticed its cleanly wiped surface. Nothing of Amra was left.

AFTER THE FIRE

Vijay Lakshmi

YOUR WORDS ABOUT THE FIRE didn't make much sense to me at that hour. It was 5:40 A.M. My first concern was about our daughters. "Are the girls okay?" I asked.

"Of course, they are," you replied. "I'm calling you about a fire in the house."

"A fire?" I jolted upright and pressed the receiver to my ear. "What happened?"

"Faulty electric wiring. It began in the powder room and spread." Your voice fought to reach me against the noises in the background—of engines rumbling, men shouting, a dog barking.

"How bad—I mean the damage?"

"Quite bad." You took a deep breath, like a diver before taking a plunge. "Listen, I know you may not want to do it," you said, "and you don't have to if you don't want to do it, but could you come over?" That was the longest sentence you had spoken to me in years.

"Now?"

"Please."

"I'll try," I said, and put the receiver down.

I wanted to tell you that the house meant nothing to me. You meant nothing to me. Nothing meant anything to me. But my hands were already pulling on clothes. I dressed swiftly, grabbed my coat and car keys, stepped into the untrampled snow to clear the windshield, and drove away. The street I had lived on till a year ago, rose to meet me the moment I turned the corner. Then I braked. It was as if I were watching a fire on the TV. Two fire trucks and a police car flashing red and blue lights parked on the street.

The house was a dark silhouette against the smoke-gray sky. Pieces of broken glass icicles hanging from the smashed windows, electric wires dangling like tumbleweed and firemen running in and out of the gaping front door. One was spreading salt on the wet driveway. He looked up as I neared the driveway. "It's slippery," he cautioned me. "Watch your step."

Rubbing my hands to ward off the chill, I edged my way to where some figures were huddled under the leafless maple. They detached themselves from the shadows and surrounded me as a herd surrounds a dying calf. "So sorry. So very sorry," they whispered. I breathed in the acrid smoke that clung to their clothes, their hair, and their hands. Then your voice winged its way to me. "Ah, there she is!" Slowly, I turned around. I didn't know how an estranged husband and wife acted when they met in front of their burnt home.

"Thanks for coming," you said, relieving me from the necessity of thinking any further. Turning to the man by your side, you introduced him. "The fire chief. Uma, my . . . my . . ." you faltered. I wasn't your ex-wife—not legally yet—and I wasn't quite your wife either. We had been separated for a year.

"So sorry about the house," the fire chief rescued us from an awkward situation. Maybe he was familiar with cases like ours. Burnt out marriages. Burned down houses. I waited to feel a pang, a sense of loss. But nothing stirred inside me. No lump in the throat. No sorrow. No tears. Nothing. "It was a beautiful house," the fire chief said slowly.

Was?

I whipped around to look at the house again. The fire may have damaged it, but it hadn't destroyed it.

"Excuse me!" A long-limbed woman in jeans pushed her way past us, clicking her camera. I wondered if she was going to turn around and take a picture of you and me, a grim-faced couple standing in front of their burnt house—a parody of Woods' American Gothic. The firemen had begun to remove the ladders, take off their helmets, and roll up the hose. The fire chief wiped his chin with a grimy fist and handed you his card. "It's all under control now. Call me if there's anything—be careful when you go in. There might be some steam trapped under the carpet."

"Can we go in?" you asked.

"Of course. The house is all yours." I flinched at the unintended irony. I would have said something, something sharp, had Kathy, the next-door neighbor, not placed her hand on your shoulder and said softly, "Come now. You will stay with us. Patrick is getting your room ready."

She turned to me politely. "It's very cold out here. Please come with us."

I followed reluctantly.

"These faulty electric circuits can cause so much harm," Kathy mumbled. "Glad it wasn't any candles."

"I never burn candles," you said.

I checked an impulse to blurt out, "You did, once. Don't you remember?" It was you who had introduced me to the bewitching aroma of American candles. "So what is it going to be this evening," you would ask, when we were newlyweds. "Lilac? Vanilla? Cinnamon? Sea Breeze?" I would choose one. Every evening you lighted a new scent. Lying in the circle of your arms, I would inhale the aroma and with sleep-filled eyes watch the wax tears congeal. How could you have erased the fragrance of memory so casually?

Seating us in her family room filled with pictures of children and grandchildren, Kathy shuffled into the kitchen, filling the kettle, opening and shutting drawers and cabinets. Patrick, her husband, was already running the vacuum cleaner upstairs. Those were normal, everyday activities. Comforting and reassuring. We sat there without looking at each other, without saying a word till Kathy brought in a tray with tea, a bowl of nuts, and a couple of muffins. After hovering around for a while, she excused herself. I looked at you, then. Really looked at you. At your face, at your deep-set eyes behind thick glasses, at your high forehead. The sharp jaw line had begun to sag a bit, I noticed, and you had put on some weight. I pushed the bowl of nuts toward you. You picked up a handful and started munching.

Cocooned in our personal solitudes, we sat there—you staring at the wall, and I, trying to read the tea leaves in my tea mug till Patrick breezed in. I had always liked Patrick. Tall, sinewy, blue-eyed, patrician, he reminded me of my late father. He held out a sweater and a pair of jeans to you. "Put these on. Man, you must be cold." I realized that you were still dressed in your crumpled pajamas over which you had thrown an overcoat. Still wearing slippers. No wonder your face was gray from the cold. Later, when you were dressed in Patrick's clothes, you sat down with him to call the insurance company.

"I think I'll go and see the house," I said.

Without taking your eyes off the telephone directory, you said, "You shouldn't go in alone."

I didn't answer. I couldn't speak, for anger spread inside me like red wine spilled on a white tablecloth. Alone, huh? You shouldn't go in alone, you had said. As if you didn't know that I was alone, that I had been alone even when we were living together. Not eating together, not sitting together, not going out together, not watching TV together, we had given up on the daily rituals of living that bind a husband and wife together. Now, you had the nerve to tell me not to go in alone. Ramming the angry volley of words down my throat, I snatched my coat draped on the back of a chair and stepped out into the dead snow. Its guts spilled out, its eyes gouged, the house stood rooted like long-term grief. Along the driveway, mixed with snow were scattered half-burnt shirts, sweaters, coats, charred shoes, file folders, notebooks, books, and much more than my mind could register.

I had always feared sights of homes destroyed by floods or hurricanes on the TV. Had always wondered how people must feel about strangers gazing at their private lives scattered around. And now, it was a part of life—yours and mine—that had been tossed out on the driveway for every passerby to see, to feel sorry about. I swallowed my sorrow, just as I had suppressed my annoyance when the divorce lawyer had asked me to produce bank statements, letters, etc. "I don't want my private life put on display," I had told him. And he had smiled, as one smiles at a foolish child, saying, "In a divorce case, my dear, nothing remains private." I stomped into the barren backyard hoping to find birds singing in the trees, hopping on the grass, pecking at the feeders. There were no birds anywhere around, except for a lone pigeon watching me intently from Kathy's rooftop. When we had been together, the cardinals, blue jays, finches, and chickadees had flocked to the feeders filled with birdseed and the birdbath filled with fresh water. The feeders didn't seem to have been filled ever since I left.

Caught in a whirl of memories, I stood rooted in the cold, snow-covered backyard, till your voice hauled me back. You were beckoning me from the broken kitchen window. It seemed as if the kitchen were waiting for me to wipe the counters clean, to vacuum the soot carpeted floor, and to take charge. Memory swirled in again. "Something smells great," you used to say, the moment you entered the house. Then burying your nose in my hair, you would chuckle. "My wife is a house of spices." And the girls would giggle. "Ma is a house of spices." Snipping away the skeins of memory, I walked with you to inspect the debris. The house looked as empty as it was when we had bought it. But then emptiness had given us a license to dream. Now it left me with a feeling of emptiness—as if there were no past, no future, only a scorched present, crowded with blackened, broken wall plates and figurines—all collected over the years, stuffed in suitcases, lugged in carry-ons from India, each emblematic of a certain moment, a certain memory, a certain emotion in time. Then I remembered something.

"Can I ask for a favor?" You looked at me. "Please don't inform my mother," I said.

You drew in a sharp breath, as if I have said something preposterous. You had been a faithful accomplice in the bundle of lies I had been telling my mother, back home in India. She didn't know we had separated. She didn't know we were going to sell the house. She would never know about the fire. Without waiting for your response, I made for the door.

"I'll leave you a key under the doormat," you told me as I struggled with the clasp of my seatbelt. You spoke softly, as if we were in a room with a patient. "You might want to retrieve some of your things from this wreck."

"What's there to retrieve?" I sputtered, stepping on the gas pedal. The car leaped forward.

I didn't take the day off, for work provided a refuge. I worked furiously, without telling anyone what had happened. When I returned home in the evening, there were several messages from the twins. You had informed them, of course. As usual, you had stolen a march on me. As usual, you had proven to our daughters that you were the conscientious parent. I called them, seeing their faces clearly. Big dark eyes filled with a baffled concern as they tried to comfort me with the same youthful buoyancy with which they had assured me that things were going to turn out fine between us when you and I had separated. If they were near me, I would have clung to them as they had clung to me when they were small and had woken up from a bad dream. After I had hung up, I looked out of my apartment window on a cluster of pine trees feathered with snow that gleamed in the light of the new moon. I was filled with a longing for those years when the twins toddled in the snow and when you and I had pushed their plastic sledges. Images rose and fell like tiny villages nestling in the hollow of small valleys one sees while driving along a mountain road—one minute in clear sight, plummeting, in the next. I decided not to go back to the house. I ignored your messages left on my voice mail. Thoughts of what was gone would only hurt me.

But a week later, I couldn't sit in my office selling mortgages to new homebuyers anymore. I took the afternoon off and drove to the house. Picking up the key from under the doormat caked with soot, I unlocked the singed front door tacked with wooden planks. I was aware of Kathy peeping from behind a curtained window. She withdrew the moment I looked into her direction. She hadn't forgiven me for leaving you. When I had run into her at the grocery store a couple of times, she had passed by with a clipped hello. In a way it was better that way, for back in my hometown in India, a neighbor would have never let me slip by. She would have asked a hundred questions, cast doubts on your fidelity, whispered something about men being unfaithful, and even hinted at a woman in your life. With the help of a flashlight sitting at the bottom of the stairs, I staggered my way up, and into the blackened rooms with boarded windows. The pale circle of light fell on plaster hanging like the tattered shell of a firecracker. The girls' room was empty. You had boxed their stuff. I picked up a bottle of nail polish, a melted tube of lipstick, some cotton puffs and ribbons and placed them on the grime-covered dresser. I crept around like an intruder, watched by the shadows. The master bedroom had been damaged badly. The heat must have reached there sooner than the other rooms because of the double-doors opening on the landing. Shards of glass stabbed the soles of my shoes as I moved around, taking in the horror of destruction in its entirety for the first time. The flash light swept into view a surrealistic scene—walls streaked with charcoal stripes of wet smoke, curtains singed and lying on the floor, a mirror charred and smudged with shadows, and plastic bottles on the dressing table bent double like partners bowing to each other before a dance. The picture frames on the walls were empty, as if the people in them had walked out.

I stumbled into the walk-in closet, tripping over clothes strewn on the floor. The flashlight fell from my hand. In the violet gloom, I huddled into a corner, pulled the clothes around me, and closed my eyes. Where did we—I—go wrong? I asked myself. Was it my insistence of working? Or working long hours in the bank? Or asserting my independence? Or wanting to be like American women that made us go our different ways? Why didn't you shout? Smash dishes? Bang doors? Take me by the shoulders and rattle me like a rag doll? Why didn't I take your hand and ask you to sit down and talk? Open the windows to let the smoke out of the room? But all we did was to skirt around the widening gap, making polite formal remarks—cold and impersonal. We forgot that once we had recounted epics to each other. Now we were like two astronauts spinning in their different orbits in space. You started leaving messages on the message board in the kitchen. I did the same. One-way traffic it was. Just information. No response intended, none given. "I am going on a business trip. Will be back next week." "Water heater is dead." "Plumber will come at 4 P. M. today." "Your dentist called. Appointment at six, next Monday." We wrote not a word more than was needed. That's how we lived, scribbling inanities, till one day, I could bear it no more. "I am moving out," I wrote. "I can move out." "No. I will." "Okay. Take whatever you like." "I want nothing. Thanks." I had underscored the words with all the strength I could muster. I moved away. If you didn't have the sense to plead with me, to stop me, then that was it. Kathy and Patrick, who had been more like family than neighbors ever since we had moved next door to them, didn't ask any questions. I was glad I wasn't in India where I would have had to give a new explanation to everyone, and listen to each piece of advice that everyone would have given without a preamble. The break-up would have been a communal affair, therefore not easily broken. But here, in a strange land, there was no one to help us patch up our differences.

The girls didn't come home that Christmas. They decided to go away on a school trip to Mexico. That made things a little easier for all of us. I moved out quietly. You stayed away from home that day. Kathy and Patrick had looked at me from their porch, as I was getting into the car. If there was sadness in the old faces, I chose to ignore it. I was sure I was doing the right thing. I was convinced I could survive without you. And I did. I proved good at selling mortgage to people buying new homes. The bank was happy with my work. I had plaques on my office walls to prove that. The sound of wind moaning in the burnt rafters brought me back. Somewhere, a door closed. I heard footsteps climbing the stairs, coming up, and coming closer. Who was there? The house wasn't haunted. Had someone sneaked in to vandalize? I squeezed into a corner and waited.

A woman holding a candle in her hand glided in. She placed the candle on top of the singed bureau. I crouched into the corner. Was she a burglar? I watched her pick up the candle, hold it high like the Statue of Liberty, then laugh. She began torching the curtains, the pile of clothes on the bed. I tried to strangle the scream that erupted from my throat. The woman swung around. In the light of the leaping flames I saw her face. It was my face I was looking at. High cheekbones, pointed chin, dark eyes, a gash near the right eyebrow, and dark hair pushed back behind the ears. I felt the floor slipping under me. I went plunging down a dark shaft.

"Uma . . ." I opened my eyes to see you peering into my face. "You all right?"

I nodded. No words came out from my parched throat.

"What happened?" you asked.

I glanced above your shoulder, into the bedroom. It was dark. Empty. The curtain rods lay across the bed.

"There was a . . ." I began, then stopped. "What're you doing here?"

"I was driving by and saw your car parked on the street." Liar. Kathy must have called you. She had seen me. She and Patrick were your allies. They kept a watch on the house for you. "I'm glad I came," you said. "You must have been overcome by the toxicity in the house. Let's get out."

I didn't move. I couldn't.

After a moment's hesitation, you too settled down among the rumpled clothes, near me. The circle of light from the flashlight you had placed on its back on the floor flooded the ceiling and the wires snaking out of what had been a light fixture. Despite the proximity of the closet, we were separated by miles of recrimination on my side and a stubborn silence on yours. Unable to bear the void anymore, I asked, "What happened?" You said nothing, simply leaned against the wall, your eyes fixed on the pool of light on the ceiling. "Why don't you say something?"

After a long pause, you cleared your throat. "There were things," you said. "Small things that should have never been ignored."

"So much destroyed," I said. "So much lost. Wasn't your fault though," I consoled you.

"Faulty electric wiring has been known to cause many fires."

"I didn't know. I should have been more thoughtful, careful . . ."

"You were."

You crossed your arms across your chest. "... should've known that friction causes a spark and a spark can turn into a blaze. I didn't understand the fragility of ..."

"Of?"

"Of a home. Walls collapse like dreams and love ..."

I was no longer sure what we were talking about.

"One minute your life, your home is there around you, all safe and whole—and the next, it's gone," you whispered.

"It can be rebuilt."

"Can it?"

"Can't it?" I waited for you to say something. The circle of light from the flashlight was growing feeble. I waited for you to say that we must leave before the battery died out, before the evening grew colder and darker, before it started snowing again. But you said nothing. And my eyes began to sting. I had never cried. Not even when you had your gall bladder removed. Not even when I was in labor. Not even when the girls had come down with chicken pox. Not even when I walked out on you. Not even when I was lonely to my hair roots. But now something thawed inside me. I wrapped my arms around my knees and let out a sigh in splinters. You would have never known my tears had your fingers not brushed against my wet face.

INNOCENCE

Clarence Major

NYDIA AND I ARE WATCHING TELEVISION when a news
bulletin comes on saying that somebody just shot a government official in Los Angeles. The official was making a
speech. A "suspect" was seized on the spot. The suspect says he
is innocent despite the fact that cameras caught him in the act.
So many televised deaths lately, I am too numbed to react. A
further loss of spirit is what I feel.

I wake up in a sweat. It's one-fifteen and Nydia is still not home.
I get up and go to the kitchen for a glass of water. I check my
email. Nothing but unwanted crap!

In the living room I sit on the couch to drink the water.
While sipping water, I turn around and look out the window
at the dark city with its sprinkle of lights scattered across my
vision.

Then I glance down at the street. The cars, lined bumper to
bumper, are dark and silent. Then I notice the burning red tip
of a cigarette glowing in the car just below on the other side. I
stare at the red spot till I make out the figure of a man sitting
at the steering wheel. Beneath the glowing cigarette something

seems to be bobbing. I stare at the area till it becomes clear. It's somebody's head moving up and down.

I get the binoculars from the closet and, standing on my knees on the couch, focus them. This is perverse, but what the hell. I can now see the moving head clearly. It's a woman. When she lifts her face the streetlight catches it. My heart seems to come to a full rest and moves up into my throat. I refuse to believe what I am seeing.

At that moment the door on the driver's side opens. I had not seen him approach, but another man in shadows opens the door and I can see the streetlight glowing on the barrel of his silver pistol. He pulls the trigger. I am surprised by how faint the sound is. Then it comes again. Then two times more. He closes the door back, turns and—still a shadow—hurries down the street back toward Eighth.

Had the gunman not arrived, what would have happened?

Possibly this: I watch till the woman finishes. She kisses the man on the mouth. They talk for another five or seven minutes, then she climbs out of the car, checks the contents of her purse, glances up and down the street before crossing over to this side. While crossing she glances up at this window but obviously she can't see anything.

Then, I think, possibly it is Nydia. And she comes in and we have this conversation:

"I saw you," I tell her while she is taking off her clothes.

She looks shocked then tries to appear calm. "What did you see?"

"I saw what you were doing in the car."

She waves me away. "There you go again with your jealousy."

"I got the binoculars."

"How *low* can you stoop?"

But if it was Nydia then I had to be the gunman. I am not ready to be the gunman.

The morning TV news has the story: two bodies, a woman's and a man's, each shot through the head, found in a parked car in the Village off Eighth Street. What a relief! What sadness!

This is early Sunday morning. We're in the living room. I'm standing, looking down at Nydia.

"I'm leaving," I say. I'm surprised to hear myself say this. I realize at this moment how desperately unhappy I am, how desperately unhappy Nydia must be. I have no idea where I'm going.

She says nothing to my announcement. She is sitting slumped over on the couch. She begins to cry.

"You keep the apartment, if you want it." Apartments are hard to find in New York and I feel like I'm being very generous.

She stops sobbing and says, "Who gave you the right to judge?"

I'm in California. I answer the phone. It's Nydia. I don't remember giving her my new number. Could I have called her at a moment of weakness in the middle of the night? "Hi! Just want you to know I'm on my way to California," she says. " I'm not going to let you dump me." She hangs up.

Before I know it, Nydia is walking beside me on Fisherman's Wharf. Her request. We've had lunch and this morning I had my feet measured at the sandal shop. Now, at three, we should be able to pick up my sandals.

She looks different, better. I wonder why I left her. What was it about her that bothered me so? Oh, yes. I didn't love her. Or was it that I shot her and her lover and had to get out of town? Need I say anything about the quality of my memory?

The sandal shop is crowded so we have to wait a whole hour before the guy can go to the back to see if they are ready.

I have a little green convertible MG now. With the sandals in a plastic bag, we hop in and head for the hills. "I love it out here," says Nydia. "Let me drive."

I get out and walk around to the passenger side. She climbs over the stick. She blushes and giggles when she notices me watching.

I get her going in the right direction and once she's got it, she hits the gas; in fact, she scares me. The cops out here don't play that shit. Anybody black or in a sports car already has a highway patrol demerit—driving while black.

Sure enough we're pulled over and as the officer writes the ticket I keep my mouth shut. I figure it's the only way to stay alive when you're in this situation.

My new house is far back behind a swirl of palms.

We get out and while walking up the long flagstone path to the deck stairs, a stranger waves and calls out, "Hi! Didn't mean to startle you. I'm your neighbor. I'm Maxwell. My house is over the hill there. You can't see it from here." He's holding out his hand.

We shake. He's a healthy brown—that kind of brown California white men love to sport.

I tell him my name and say, "This is Nydia Wilson, from New York." He holds her hand a moment longer than is polite. I can see Nydia gets the message. Whether or not she wants it I can't tell.

I unlock the house. "Can I get you something, Maxwell, a drink?"

While I work in the morning, Nydia goes for long walks on the beach. This morning, two weeks after her arrival, I can't get anything started so I decide to go catch up with her, to walk with her.

I set out across the sand following the tracks of her tennis shoes. They seem unusually far back from the edge of the water, which isn't especially dangerous-looking this morning.

Then the prints cut back away from the ocean up a dune and over it. I follow. At the top I see what must be Maxwell's house, a modest one with bay windows and a wrap-around deck perched on stilts.

No Nydia yet in sight.

You already know what's coming. I walk on down the sand and up to the house. In the front yard I stop. All is silent except for the sound of sea gulls and the distant beat of the ocean. I shudder as I walk up onto the porch.

Just as I am about to knock I hear a loud gasp from inside.

I think oh well, why should I be surprised. Another gasp, a whimper, a moan, all punctuated by grunts.

I start to go back across the sand but once I'm in the yard I decide to make sure. I tip alongside the house and look into the first window. This is a crime, I know. A dining room. I walk around a pile of debris to the next window. A pantry. Then the kitchen. There! On the kitchen floor Maxwell and Nydia making those noises. Need I say more?

I refuse to watch.

I turn to leave but then a muffled scream pulls me back. I look again and I realize I am seeing a man killing a woman. I am witnessing a crime—murder! The woman is not Nydia. She's pink, not brown. But the man is Maxwell. He has a kitchen knife and he is driving it repeatedly into the woman's upper body. She is beginning to make fewer sounds.

Running back across the sand, I see Nydia strolling along the beach. I catch up. I know she has a cell phone. But I'm too out of breath by the time I reach her to tell her what I want. I want her to call the police but I can't get the words out.

They simply won't come. Nydia reacts to my distress by holding me in her arms. I weep with the pain of my distress. She begs me to tell her what's wrong but I can't.

Back at the house, feeling calmer, I call the police and spill my guts.

Nydia and I gaze out the window toward Maxwell's house, waiting.

Three hours later three policemen come to my door and say, "You imagined the whole thing. Mr. Maxwell is fine. No one was murdered. No blood is on his kitchen floor."

Before leaving they give me a warning about trespassing on my neighbor's property. "If it happens again, Maxwell will file charges."

Now that Nydia is back in New York, I am alone here again and winter is coming. But it is not as before when I was unaware that another house was just over the hill. Oh, I knew a house was over there but I didn't know about it. Now it is a sinister house of uncertainty. And anyway, how can I trust the police?

MOTHER, MOTHER, MOTHER, MOTHER EARTH

Donna Miscolta

A is for alone. "Leave me alone," the girl demands. "Don't let me be alone," she demands louder. The mother thinks how much easier the first is. But these are not either/or propositions, not stand-alone options. They're a package. Salt and vinegar.

The mother's mouth contorts with a bittersweet memory. Her girl is a toddler, climbing on her lap, declaring "I like you best, Mama." The mother smiles both at the truth and fickleness of this statement as the father sits nearby intent on the newspaper.

Just that afternoon, the mother had turned on a TV talk show while the girl napped. The guests were members of a support group whose teenage daughters had ceased speaking to them. The mother is sad for these women and, not daring to consider the question of *who* went wrong, wonders *what* went wrong.

Sometimes the mother thinks of the Chernobyl cloud that floated across the northern hemisphere when the girl was still in utero—a third-trimester fetus whose organs were still elaborating upon themselves readying her for life outside the mother's body. Just the thought of the menace was enough to unleash panic in the mother's body and thus the baby's.

B is for better. Be a better mother! There is no definition of *better mother* in the dictionary, despite its common usage in the lexicon of enraged daughters. Still, the mother wants to shout that she already is a better mother. Better than her own mother. The mother remembers her girlhood, the limitations, the confidence-crushing indifference to her existence.

When the mother learned she was pregnant, she hoped for a girl to whom she could say, *You are capable, you are strong, you are brave.* When she birthed a girl, she was relieved. She, from a family of few males, had no clue how to raise a boy. But she had been a girl once and at least knew what that was like, and she knew what not to do, having been raised by a mother who did not believe in herself and so did not believe in her own daughter. And now the mother has raised a daughter who is not afraid to say things to her mother. Like *be a better mother.*

She speaks her mind and that is a good thing, the mother reasons, though never would the mother have said such a thing to her own mother. Times change. The world turns and warms. Animals go extinct. As do the good old days.

C is for cat, the only one who truly loves her, the girl says. *Cats can't talk,* the mother wants to say, but doesn't. As if the girl reads the mother's mind, she says, "Scratches and bites are their love language." Maybe they're mine, too, the mother thinks. Figuratively speaking, of course. But there is the question of her daughter's love language. What of the literal scratches and bites, the kicks and punches? The name-calling. Where is the love in that? Somewhere deep inside, the mother assures herself.

"Here, draw a picture," the mother told the daughter when she was younger and her tantrums raged and raged. "Draw how you feel." It's what the parenting books said to do. The mother read many parenting books. The daughter threw the crayons across the room or stuffed them in her mouth, chewed them and spewed the pieces like a mad fountain. The father who read no parenting books said, "If we ignore her, she'll stop." The mother recognized this strategy as the same one men in power applied to climate change, their heads in the warming sand.

D is for doll. The mother says, "No, sorry, that is not an appropriate toy" when the girl asks for a Barbie. But the girl asks and asks, and so the mother thinks that denying her the Barbie will only make it more desirable. So she tells the girl she will buy the Barbie but first she wants to tell her some things about the doll. That it doesn't represent what real girls and women look like and that such dolls encourage an emphasis on looks over intellect, creativity, and compassion. See? The girl nods. The mother trails the girl as she walks up and down the aisle filled with Barbies of every profession—Doctor Barbie, Chef Barbie, Forest Ranger Barbie—each sheathed in tight-fitting fashions and stilettos. There's no Save-The-World-From-Its-Own-Folly Barbie. The girl chooses the trashiest Barbie, which the mother silently calls Slut Barbie. "Are you sure that's the one you want?" the mother asks. The girl narrows her eyes and juts her jaw.

When strangers used to stop the mother in the grocery store to say what a beautiful child she had, she wanted to cover the ears of the little girl. *She is not a doll to be admired for her looks*, she wanted to say, but never did. The mother learned from her mother that one receives compliments with grace, especially, she was told, when for *some* people they are rare as rainfall in the desert. And now rare in other parts of the world, the mother adds as she wonders about the value of looks in a world of scarcity.

E is for eat, which the mother takes care never to say, as in *eat your vegetables* or *clean your plate*. Food, not a foe, never a menace, is nothing to be forced. The mother tries to convey this by example. But the girl discovers the adolescent female's secret weapon of mass destruction. She reduces her mass to the bare minimum, just enough to support herself on flamingo legs. A diet of carrots dulls her face with an orange cast. "This is not sustainable," the mother says, borrowing a word from her job educating the public on the sensible use of resources to ward off their inevitable depletion and the end of the world.

The mother remembers her pride at how the baby girl had plumped up on breast milk in those early months. But at eleven and a half months old, on the anniversary of Earth Day, the baby girl refused the breast. Was the baby on to something? Was she rejecting the mother's body burden of chemicals accumulated over her life? Ah, the mother understood this was not

a rejection of herself per se. What an instinct for survival this
baby girl had!

F is for foot or fracture or face. All the Fs. The girl wants
fast-food for dinner. It's the only food she says she will eat. The
mother says, "Fine, get in the car." On the way back, the girl,
burritos steaming inside their foil wrappers on her lap, tenses
with something that is said or unsaid, done or yet to be done.
She rests her foot upon the dashboard in protest. The mother
does not reprimand her, choosing her fights, as the parenting
experts recommend. Suddenly, the girl shoves her foot hard into
the front window sending fracture lines to radiate like a mis-
shapen star. Fear floods the girl's face. Not fear of repercussions.
Fear of herself.

The mother had always feared other things. When alone she
slept with a light on, a chair against the door to block intrud-
ers, and public radio turned low. As a girl she feared the dark.
She still did, sure that monsters, ghosts, criminals, flying cock-
roaches, or right-wingers with guns lurked unseen. The mother
feared the unknown, which sometimes included her child.

G is for genetics. They learn that eating disorders can have a
genetic component. Mothers are blamed for everything, thinks
the mother, but on this she is clear: there are no eating disorders
on her side of the family. Myopia, diabetes, heart murmurs, those
yes. She holds open her hands as if to show she has nothing to
hide. She turns to the father. "Yes, alright," he says, an admission
of biology only. But *something* has to trigger it. They look at
each other until the girl interrupts the parents' staring contest to
scream, "I told you none of this is my fault." The father, though
there is shock in his eyes, says, "It's not that bad. Other families
go through this."

The mother considered the things she inherited from
her mother—wide shoulders and broad feet—and what she
developed from her mother's mothering of her—an indecisive
mind, a wobbly self-image. The mother was astonished when
the girl chastised her for a shrill voice when angry, an aloof-
ness when not.

The one with the shrill voice, the aloof one was the mother's mother. So unfair, thought the mother. Such a poverty of

understanding, she thought and then regretted the inapt use of *poverty*, as if it could invite misfortune and real-life privation in this gobble-down corporate economy.

H is for the hand that trembles from the medications, each with a purpose, each with its side effects, one to counteract the other. The girl is a stew of drugs. All aboil. She wears a petrified look on her face like makeup foundation. The mother wonders if she should take the girl's hand in her own or if it's better not to call attention to its small shudders. Leave her alone? Don't leave her alone? Will the girl pull her hand away? Or worse, strike something with it? It's just the one hand. Not both. Don't make a big deal out of it. And yet, the mother thinks, *Take a chance. Take her hand.* Too late though, the girl balls her fists and tucks them inside her armpits. As she tries to think what to do next, the mother stares at her own hands, at the hieroglyphs made by her wrinkles.

Somewhere the mother still has the girl's handprints from preschool. Green paint on blue construction paper. The hands pointing slightly toward each other, fingers spread, blank spots where the hands did not touch down on the paper. Those missing parts like little mysteries of the universe waiting to be solved.

I is for the invisible wall that separates them. Not a wall exactly. Not rigid, but capable of molding to their bodies. For instance when they hug, it's there to keep them from the clumsiness of their closeness. Protective, like the amniotic sac in the womb. Maybe the girl still shelters in that cytoplasmic shield for fear of what the world might inflict. How it might fail her. How the mother might fail her.

The mother recalls the recurring nightmare she had as a girl and into adulthood. She is separated by a low wall from her mother. As she readies herself to climb over to join her mother on the other side, the wall grows higher. Each time she tries to lift herself over, it grows more. Meanwhile her mother looks on passively. The wall grows until she can no longer see her mother. Sometimes her husband must shake her awake to silence her scream. She tells him the dream. It's that mother-daughter thing, he says, as if glad to be neither. Though he clucks with sympathy.

Later, the mother and daughter will spend a weekend together on the other side of the border. At the beach in Tijuana, together on the same side of the fence, they peer through its slats and feel the agony of the dispossessed.

J is for June, the month the girl was born—a month, according to the symbolism charts, that means sunshine and laughter, a month positive for improving relationships. In the early years, the mother relives the memory of the pregnancy, the birth, and the infancy, nostalgic for the mystery and miracle of it all. The mother accustoms the girl to be celebrated. Clowns, fairies, magicians, and other indispensables in the kids' entertainment pantheon appear at her birthday party over the years until the girl is too big for such things. But the expectation for magic remains and the day can never live up to the anticipation. Flaccid balloons, cheap party favors, a lopsided cake—all fodder for the filled-to-brimming landfill. Her birthday is all disappointment. Always the wrong presents. Is that all there is? Where is the love?

The mother has created a birthday monster, which she tries to appease with June pearls of wisdom. "Make your own happiness. Be your own happiness." She is a talking Hallmark card that secretly hates birthdays. The mother learned from her mother that if you don't expect too much, you won't be disappointed much.

K is for kiss my ass. It's not the first time the girl has said it. It's not the first time the mother feels the helpless rage, her heart clanging and banging with inadequacy. Be the mother. Be the grownup. Model good behavior. She hangs up the call, which enrages the daughter. How rude, how unforgivable. The daughter calls back and back and back. The mother doesn't answer. For weeks. The father shakes his head at this mother-daughter thing, this always simmering thing to which he is innocent bystander. You're right, he assures the mother. I understand, he winks to the daughter.

When the girl was eleven, she asked the mother how old you have to be to kiss a boy. "When you're thirty" is the first thing that came out of the mother's mouth. The quip exposed her as an amateur so she tried to pivot. "Older than you are now" was the best she could do. Quip upon quip. She blew it. There'll be other opportunities to practice good mothering, she told herself. But this seemed like a door closing on her ass.

L is for the lost years. The mother visits the daughter in the residential facility on the other side of the country. A staff person opens the door of the yellow farmhouse and invites her into the living room. The residents are in session and will be released momentarily, the mother is told. The mother judges the living room to be cozy—home-like. Still, it seems like a trespass to take a seat on the couch or any of the chairs. Though she's never been in one, she thinks this could be a sorority with its houseful of young women and shared spaces—a sort of sisterhood. Soon she hears a feral wail on top of rushing, stumbling feet and the thin specter of her daughter leaps out of the hallway—arms outstretched, hair flying, eyes wild. The daughter clings to the mother who pats her back and smooths her hair, closing her eyes to focus on the moment. When she opens them, she sees the gaunt look of her daughter multiplied in the other young women who have arranged themselves in a semi-circle, two deep—like a Greek chorus, except they're silent. They're weeping at the reunion, anticipating their own one day. Just when the mother has a moment of fright at the hunger in their eyes, the staff person comes in and ushers the sylphs back down the hallway.

When the girl was twelve, the mother, exhausted and defeated by the girl's volatility, proposed to the father that the girl see a therapist, a professional trained in the fits and furies of preteens indulged since birth by parents who were never on the same page regarding consequences for misconduct. Absolutely not, said the father. "She's in a phase. She'll outgrow it."

Ten years is not a phase, the mother thought. It's a lifestyle. So the mother instead took herself to therapy for the next ten years, which became her lifestyle. Meanwhile, the glaciers lost two percent of their volume, calving chunk after chunk, a term that suggests a birthing but in reality is a breaking apart.

M is for make-believe we are fine. The mother is visiting the daughter in her new city. A new start, a place to call her own. They eat out in restaurants and the mother silently applauds the daughter's appetite. When the daughter excuses herself to go to the restroom, the mother must trust. She sits and waits and peels the paper napkin on her plate into strips until she suddenly feels the press of all that wine and water she has drunk. She does not rush, but indeed her step is just quick enough to match her bladder's urge. When she opens the door, the daughter is at the sink washing her hands. They look at each other as if one does not suspect the other, as if there is nothing to suspect. The mother avoids the stall that has been newly flushed.

When the girl was small the mother was willing to encourage her imagination. But the girl seldom engaged in pretend play, quickly becoming suspicious of the tooth fairy's existence, and declaring Santa Claus to be nothing more than a cartoon. The only make-believe the girl engaged in was when the mother asked if she had crayoned the bad word on the wall, broke the hand-painted bowl, smashed the laptop with her foot. No, no, no, she did not. Prove it, the girl said. Make me believe, the mother said under her breath. A standoff as rigid as science vs. science denier. Nobody move and no one will get hurt is always a lie.

N is for needles. Let's get matching tattoos, the daughter says. The mother has never considered a tattoo. Tattoos are forever. The daughter persists and after a year, the mother consents. They live in different cities but they arrange to be tattooed together separately—same design, same time, different tattoo parlors. The mother closes her eyes as the needles buzz a sweet pea into the underside of her wrist, and she recalls that scent of summer that filled the house when the girl was born. When the buzzing stops, the mother examines the line drawing—no fill, no color. A simple, indelible line. She takes a picture of it and emails it to the daughter. The daughter does the same. A kind of pinky swear. Tattoos are forever.

When the mother's mother was old and her health was failing, the mother noticed the wrinkled skin on her mother's arms. When did it begin? Gradually, like the peel of old paint? Or overnight like the ripening of an avocado left on the sill? Now the mother's skin is aging with cracks and spots that texture her tattoo. Nothing is forever. Not even the eons-old Earth, its surface cracked from drought.

O is for objectives, a succession of them as the daughter must find her career after the lost years of illness. In her hurry to catch up, she tries on different dreamy dreams, walks out of the dressing room and into the world that is too big to notice her fashion designer forays or the fruits of her acting classes. She survives waiting tables. She is waiting to discover her calling, for doors of opportunity to open, for the object of her unnamed desire to tap her on the shoulder. There is a place for her at one of these tables. Where is the chair?

The mother knows this well, having shown up at the wrong table multiple times. The mother's mother had no choice of tables. Now the choices are as hard to reach as the world's water tables falling deeper into the earth from overdemand.

P is for the parachute that floats the daughter to earth. It's a college escapade. *Let's jump out of a plane* is someone's brilliant idea. The mother does not know this until much later. She thinks of the daughter's heart ricocheting in her chest, the sweat collecting in all the concave parts of her anatomy—the scoop of her clavicle, the armpits bristling with new hairs, the delicate depression of her belly button. She imagines her daughter's scream of fear and freedom. In those seconds of falling, then the minutes of floating, does the girl think of the past or future, or does she only experience the sensation of being? When her feet touch the earth, does she remember her mother and her mother's mother with pity that they have never been carried by the air?

When the girl was little, the mother would push her in the swing at the park. With each push forward, the girl's hair would lift off her shoulders with the breeze and flatten on the backswing. Forward and back, lift and flatten. The movement enchanted the girl and when the mother's arms tired and her mind went numb from the repetition, she removed the girl and carried her kicking and screaming to the car, her anger and indignation as raw and wild as if the world were coming to an end.

Q is for quota, as in how many times the daughter deems it necessary for the mother to call to prove her love. How many days per week? Every day. For how long? An hour. At least. The daughter waits for the mother to lead the conversation so the mother has learned to makes notes beforehand to avoid running out of things to say. The daughter's face is impassive on the screen, daring the mother to stop talking, ready to pass judgment on anything she says. Lose-lose. It's a game in which only one person knows the rules.

When the girl was young and the mother was trying to teach responsibility with chores, she added incentives. Extra allowance could be earned by unsolicited acts of help. She posted a chart as a visual for the good deeds. The girl took it upon herself to place a checkmark with each self-reported good deed until the mother had to set a quota at which point the girl lost interest. A misapplication of math and incentives, observed the father.

The mother does her own math. The mother called her mother once a week. The mother's mother never called her. An easy calculation: the mother 100 percent; the mother's mother zero. The daughter, for her part, is 1000 percent sure of her own calculations.

R is for race, as in life is not a race. Everyone on her own path on her own timeline the mother tells the daughter who is behind her peers in career years. They are walking together on a city street but the daughter races ahead to walk far in front alone.

The mother herself was a late bloomer, returning to school again and again to try out a new discipline, a new potential field of work. Finally, she fell into a job she could manage to show up for day in and day out, year after year to ensure a stable income. The daughter does not want a life like the mother's—of little excitement and barely any adventure. Suffering nothing more than boredom. If you don't count the fifteen or so years of depression that no one noticed. At least she avoided the mother's mother history of migraines. Everyone on her own path.

S is for said as in *you said that, yes, you did, don't try to gaslight me.* The daughter insists on her impeccable memory, which the mother knows to be less impeccable than her own. I have receipts, the daughter claims. The mother has those same receipts. She scrolls through the emails and Facebook messages and sees where a mind in search of fault will seize upon a word, a comma, a typo as proof.

When the girl was little, the mother more than once reverted to *because I said so* to end an argument. It was simple authority. The parent made the rules. The parent was the boss of the kid. But rules are made to be broken and power structures can be upset, except in a corporate capitalist society that creates homelessness and poor wages and blames the victims for their plight and now the daughter blames her baby-boomer mother for ruining the world as if it was the mother herself who invented the pretend theory of trickle-down economics.

T is for test. This is a test. This is a test. Is this a test, the daughter asks? Why me? What did I do to deserve this? It's not a test, the mother says. You could never handle what I'm going through, the daughter says. Don't be a drama queen, the mother thinks. It's not a contest. Everyone faces challenges in life. But what if it really is a test? Not just of the daughter but of the mother as well. And if it is a test, who is administering it and who decides if they pass or fail? But what if, in the words of the Emergency Broadcast System, it is ONLY a test. It's not the real thing. Just move on, the father says. Fine, the mother thinks, hold the baggage.

As a going-away-to-college present, the mother made a photo album, matching photos of the girl throughout the years with a quote by a famous woman. For instance, next to a picture of the girl chasing a soccer ball, the mother had glued the lines *Resolve to take fate by the throat and shake a living out of her* by Louisa May Alcott. The mother admired the boldly stated advice. The girl flipped through the pages of the album. What about the watch I wanted, she murmured like the wind that pushes forest fires across highways.

U is for the *un*-words the girl hoards in her vocabulary. Life is *un*fair. You can't *un*say it. That is so *un*cool. You just don't *un*derstand. That was *un*called for. I won't do it *un*less. Unless. Unless.

When the girl was little and learning the alphabet, she would say *u is for unicorn* and she would place her index finger to point outward from her bangs. The mythical and magical un-word. Wild woodland creature. Even then as the mother stroked the girl's hair, she feared the saying *rare as a unicorn* signaled the extinction to come for other creatures. Rare as a doe. Rare as a crow. Rare as a garter snake. You can't undo it. Unless. Unless.

V is for the view from then and now and tomorrow. The future is now and the girl is a woman, the anger less piercing, but the illness a faint footprint on every organ. Sometimes when the mother and daughter video chat, there is a stutter on the screen, a blink of pixels that fuzzes the daughter's face, a moment akin to the audio bleep-out of an obscenity on TV. Similarly, in real life encounters, a shadow passes like a speeded-up eclipse.

Once when the girl was younger, a preteen and still open to—even craving—alone time with the mother, it was the night of the Perseids. Wake me up to watch it, the girl said to the mother. The mother set her alarm and when it woke her from a dream she tiptoed upstairs. She anticipated difficulty in shaking the girl awake, but the girl was sitting on her bed waiting, a sixth sense having stirred her at the appointed hour. On the deck the mother lay out sleeping bags and they waited for the dark sky to erupt with shooting stars and remind them of their smallness on earth. We have the best view, the girl said.

W is for weathering the years, the wounds the mother and daughter have inflicted on each other, the words expelled like hard little BBs, some randomly, others deliberately aimed such as this one from the daughter that hits its target. "I'll be a better mother than you." The mother considers this declaration filled with scorn and hubris and promise. "Yes, probably," she answers.

The mother's mouth contorts with a bittersweet memory. Her girl is a toddler, climbing on her lap, declaring "I like you best, Mama." The mother smiles both at the truth and fickleness of this statement as the father sits nearby busy with the newspaper.

X is for the Xerox copy the mother makes of the crayon portrait the girl draws of her. The features are a bit exaggerated. Even so, the observational powers of her second grader are startlingly sharp. The girl has captured the mother's wide, big-lipped, stop-light-red smile, the round glasses, and unstylish bangs. Earrings dangle from the ears in mismatched colors. That is the daughter's artistic touch, making the mother more interesting, more daring. Better.

Will the daughter, who will be a better mother than the mother, have a child better than the daughter? Is it the progress that will guarantee the species? At least the family tree? Which like all trees are vulnerable to flames.

Y is for the years that pass while they're not looking or looking too long and hard for better days and happier times or when they're just not paying attention. When the girl wished she had a different mother. When the mother wished the girl was already away at college even though the girl was only twelve. When the world wished forest fires didn't always rage, glaciers didn't melt like popsicles, lakes didn't perform disappearing acts, guns didn't proliferate like flies, viruses could be curbed with politics.

Now the mother is old enough to be a grandmother and the daughter prepares to be a better mother than the mother has been to her. And so they wait, fingers crossed.

Z is for the zillions of uncountable stars in the sky yet to be wished upon.

A Fabricated Life

Pamela Painter

WHERE ON EARTH was Grace's email congratulating Trixie on getting a cat? She was certain she'd told her sister that she'd gotten a cat—probably wrote about a cat six or seven months ago when Grace pointedly asked if Trixie was still living alone. In fact, she needed to track down all her emails to Grace, emails about her life—or rather her fabricated life—since her niece, Grace's daughter, Bianca, would be arriving any day now expecting a cat, a boyfriend, and a sober Aunt Trixie with a paying job.

What had she said about a job?

She scrolled back through her emails to Grace in which she described a new apartment that allowed cats, the new job, her new friends. She paused at the one in which she had described "Nerd-boy," who *is always hanging around my desk at work, complimenting my new fluffy hairstyle. The guy has an enormous tie collection that he must pet and groom like a cat.* Now that was a coincidence—that she'd had grooming cats on her mind. Though he was no candidate for her usual in boyfriends. She resumed scrolling past the JOB email where she'd talked about her position as an executive assistant. *My boss said he didn't know what he'd done before he hired me.*

Yep, the subject line said CAT: *I went to the SPCA Shelter and adopted a two-year-old feline. Her name is Granite, for her elegant gray fur.*

Lordy, she must have been buzzed when she wrote "elegant gray fur." So, she would have to adopt a cat fast. A gray cat. It seemed the easiest thing to fake. How smart were ten-year-olds? Maybe Bianca was twelve? Did she like her Peruvian name?

When Trixie looked up cat houses—ha—she discovered a shelter in Boston's South End totally devoted to black cats. It seemed that numerous cat owners were superstitious about black cats. As a result, mewling black kittens arrived in boxes on the shelter's doorstep. She was tempted. But she'd told her sister gray. She couldn't remember ever having typed the word "elegant" before or since.

She put a different shelter's address into her GPS and got lost anyway. South meant beyond the Back Bay. Rain made it hard to see street signs. Her wiper blade was shredded. Weeping, she pulled in front of a dumpster. Feeling desolate, she wondered if she could get away with a story about the gray cat's demise. Fuck. Her flask only had a whiff of vodka left. For old times' sake, she breathed deeply, practicing: "Granite flashed out the door when—when UPS rang for a signature. No. When my neighbor showed up to complain about her late night Zumba. When Charlie's Liquors was delivering a case of vodka." She put her tongue in the neck of the flask and was rewarded with a heavenly drop.

But a cat would be good for a ten-year-old. Lord save her from a snarky preadolescent. Bianca had been snarky already when Trixie last saw her several years ago. Trixie remembered a long-legged, skinny kid whose nose was glued to her phone when her ear was not. And now, Bianca would be arriving on Trixie's doorstep and, as Grace had promised, staying for the fall, and "only the fall." Grace's husband, Drake, had tumbled into a test pit on his dig in Ecuador and broken both legs. He'd been moved to Quito, but he didn't want to leave the country. Tenure depended on this research, and he desperately needed Grace to keep the natives in line. Not quite Grace's words. Trixie had countered with, "Why can't you take Bianca? Homeschool

her?" Grace's voice was tight as she said that Bianca refused
to go. Then Trixie again: "What about Bianca's friends? Her
babysitter? Your sister-in-law?" She felt chastened when she
was told that they'd thought of those avenues, but they hadn't
worked out, and a prep school was way too expensive. "So, I'm
the last resort," Trixie had said. "You're her aunt," Grace said.
"And you're sober, right?"

"Right," Trixie said. "You want me to resend my email about
AA?" At least she hadn't lied about that. She said she'd been to
two meetings, which was true, and then quit because it was too
soaked in God stuff. Also true. She'd written, "Every time they
said the word 'God' I pictured being ushered into this black
hole with Stephen Hawking as MC." Not true, but she liked
the sound of it. He'd given the world only a hundred more years
before it killed itself with pollution, plastic, and new viruses.
She'd watched a YouTube interview with him when she was
looking up her astrology chart. Amazing what appeared for sale
in the right column of each screen. "I'm doing it without AA,"
she said.

There was a pause, and then Gracie said, "Besides, Bianca
loves cats, and Drake's allergic." The clincher.

"It has to be a gray cat?" the young man with a long,
almost-orange beard asked. The shelter was alive with mur-
murings and howls. Surely cats didn't howl? "How gray? I have
a cat in the third row that is partly white and partly gray. A
real sweetheart."

Trixie was tempted to take home "Sweetheart" but, remembering what she told her sister, conjured up another story
for the shelter volunteer. She told him about Greystoke, her
childhood cat, whose seven gray kittens had been—sure, why
not—gathered into a basmati rice sack and drowned by her
grandfather. "Ever since then . . ." She let her words trail off as
if grief-stricken by this memory rather than horrified at her
vilification of her beloved Grandpa.

The young man's beard quivered with sympathy. She imagined him petting it, or letting a cat nestle in its neck warmth.
She followed his orange beard out past rows and rows of stacked
silver cages filled with young cats with suspicious gazes and

hopeful twitching noses, older cats curled in on their sad and lonely past lives.

"A docile cat," she told him, describing her three-year-old terror of a niece who liked to pull tails.

He nodded and moved ahead more slowly, reading cat descriptions. "*Likes to dine on your table.*" "*Watches cat TV.*" "*A good mouser, but not a ratter.*" He peered into each cage for a docile cat that seemed as if it would only eat and sleep—preferably, Trixie thought, curled up and purring on Bianca's bed.

It was $100 for spaying and defleaing. A month ago she would have thought, *There go my next three bottles of gin.* But the cat was totally gray. Was she really going to call it "Granite"?

When the young man asked, "Name?" she said "Granite," then corrected herself when he said, "No, *your* name."

Cat food, a litter box, bags of litter, and a spiffy new cat carrier were nestled on the back seat, along with a gray cat that began meowing and panting the minute Trixie started the car. The panting surprised her. Huge lungfuls of air. At a red light she turned and aimed her empty flask at the cat carrier. The cat shut up. She hoped it would forget that little gesture later when she got out the catnip. She wouldn't mind a hit of something, a mind-embracing sweetheart of a line, maybe two, but she had sworn off that for sure.

The ten- or twelve-year-old Bianca was due in two weeks. Trixie was too embarrassed to ask her age.

The cat settled in. She liked the old radiator for naps, and people ambling by in the busy street below the window. Food disappeared—and reappeared, transformed into what she'd forgotten: piss and shit in the litter box. Trixie learned to sift the sand and smooth it out with fresh litter. Mornings there was a warm lump at the bottom of her bed, the first guest since a month ago, when she'd unadvisedly brought home a guy hanging onto the barstool next to her who designed tattoos. The next morning, she'd declined his offer of half a free tattoo. The other half he'd said he'd take out in trade, so to speak. She avoided that bar for weeks, grateful that she could remember which one it was. He certainly wasn't the imaginary boyfriend from work that she'd written Grace about four months earlier. *He's sweet.*

Has mom's sense of humor and Dad's lack of hair. He brings cookies to the office that I thought his mother must have baked, but no, he likes doing "pastries." Oh, how could she acquire the boyfriend she'd bragged about to Grace as easily as she'd acquired a cat? Did she want a boyfriend? She'd forgotten what a real boyfriend was like. Real breakfasts. Birthday presents. Real conversation. A shared addiction to reruns of *Seinfeld.* Someone sober.

She shopped for flowered sheets and a plush rug to put by Bianca's bed in the second bedroom, where she'd been hoarding liquor bottles, pizza boxes, and dry-cleaning hangers—those black wire ones that breed in the night. On the nightstand, she placed a spiffy new red diary with a tiny gold key. She bought a gift certificate for a place that sold posters of boy bands. They looked so young and callow in their torn jeans and mussed hair; not a one wore a tie.

That week at work, Trixie answered the phone, somewhat abashed at her coworkers' compliments on her new look—blouses and sweaters instead of her usual roadie T-shirts. *Southside Johnny and the Asbury Jukes. Big Head Todd. Queen.* Trixie's job was really that of a glorified receptionist rather than the executive assistant position she'd made it out to be. The boss didn't actually know her name, and barely greeted her when he strode past her desk, but at least it was a job with a regular paycheck to supplement Grace's grudging monthly dispensation from their parents' trust fund. She remembered sitting in the lawyer's office when the will was read after their father's slow dying and their mother's quick accident. Expecting a tidy sum, she'd been horrified at hearing the conditions of their will: that her sister was to write Trixie a monthly check on condition that she get sober and hold a job. How she would be monitored was not spelled out. It reminded her of Gracie doling out carrots and cookies when they played safari or explorers as kids. Hey, answering the phone at work— "Hello, Immortal Electronics"—*was* a job, though she sure as hell wasn't going to bring Bianca to work on Bring Your Child to Work Day.

Trixie's snoopy next-door neighbor had seen her arrive home with Granite. He showed up at her door two days later.

His tattooed right arm was waving—waving what? "It's a FURminator," he told her, after asking if she owned one. Her first thought was that he was coming on to her about some strange instrument of eros—had she ever used that word before?—then she remembered that he had three cats. "It is the Rolls Royce of cat combs," he told her as he captured Granite and brushed her till she was purring like a drum. Trixie squinted at him, taking in his old-fashioned mullet, his sleeveless undershirt, the cigar he'd parked on her porch railing. No, he wouldn't do.

She could make up another story. Jackson and I broke up last month; he didn't like cats. Or, *Fitzbag got a job offer from the dotcom crowd in San Francisco and no way was I going to be part of dismantling the entire Mission District.* No, a name like "Fitzbag" would give it away. Or, closer to the truth: *Joey's doing a bit of time in the penal system.* Nope, no need to go there. Besides, he was three men removed.

At work the next week, she found herself squinting at Nerd-boy. Once she could forget the sheer number of his ties, she actually liked his taste in patterns, fabrics, and knots. She imagined standing behind him, her arms around his waist as he tied a Windsor knot by rote, his gaze locked on hers in the mirror. She could imagine finding the small tug at the end of the exercise rather sexy, together with the downward stroke of smoothing the tie in place. Surely men must be aware of how all ties pointed south.

Two days later, when Nerd-boy came hanging around her desk again, she was ready for him. His tie was a march of spring petunias and hummingbirds. Almost a Windsor knot. Norm— his name was Norm, not Fixer, or Lefty—went into his spiel, asking her out for coffee for the millionth time—coffee!!!!—but she surprised him by suggesting that instead he should come over to her place for dinner. "Bring dessert," she told him. "One of those pastries you told me about." Little did he know that if he were going to be her boyfriend they'd have to move along fast. Grace would be leaving for Peru, her phrasebook in hand for saying "Dust every shard well" or "Nothing is too small to catalogue." Or, to Drake's doctor, "How much longer before the casts come off?"

Norm surprised her with a bouquet of forsythia, a taste for jazz, a mild allergy to alcohol, and a penchant for cats. Granite coated his pants legs with a layer of fur Norm didn't mind. Eyes narrowed, Trixie described the niece, soon to arrive for the entire fall. Turned out he had nieces of his own—"In the next town over. I take them to Red Sox games." The evening lingered along, though Trixie had imagined "limped."

A year later, after their engagement party guests left, and Bianca, who wailed when she said goodbye to Trixie and Granite, was safely on her way to her own home, they would look back at this dinner and Norman would tell her that he had known from the beginning that they were meant for each other: their cats and nieces were compatible, they both liked jazz, books, both were foodies, "and you liked my ties." She buried her face in his tie, also remembering that first dinner, when she hadn't planned a minute, never mind a life, past acquiring him for several dates so she could introduce a "boyfriend" to her niece. At that first meal, she hadn't known how to say good night. She'd been so used to falling into bed with anyone she met at a bar that she had forgotten how to act on a first date. Turns out the night of their first date was almost the same—falling into bed—though the morning after was totally different.

Portrait of Two Young Ladies in White and Green Robes

(Unidentified Artist, Circa Sixteenth Century)

Jane Pek

I.

A few hours ago your last descendant died. She held only a whisper of your essence—or, as one would say in this scientifically rigorous present, only a minuscule percentage of her genetic material was derived from yours—but, of them all, she was the one who reminded me most of you.

She was a documentary filmmaker, the third generation of your descendants to be born and raised in America. Her work examined ways in which the technologies of her era shaped people's lives. In her twenties and thirties she lived in China, where she made a series of films about the state's electronic surveillance system, the tools used by the government to monitor its population, the balance to be struck between security and personal freedom. Her documentaries were as fair as they could be, in my view, taking into account the inherent biases of her

Western upbringing and education. The Chinese government, which after all this time remains deficient at accepting criticism, disagreed. After they revoked her visa she returned to America and settled in San Francisco. You would have enjoyed San Francisco, I think. Its pastel hues and precipitous slopes, its anarchic spirit, the lapping glitter of water all around.

I befriended her later in her life, when it became clear she would have no children. I presented myself as an admirer of her work and a student of Chinese history; also, an immigrant from Hangzhou, where I knew her own family was originally from. We grew close. I made myself indispensable to her. At the end of her life, I was in the hospital room when the lines jagging up and down across the screen of the vital-signs monitor subsided. Humans have developed the custom of measuring the distance a person stands from the border between the living and the dead. They watch each step their loved ones take toward that one-way crossing, count down every last breath.

•

I suggested to your descendant once that the technologies highlighted in her films were really no different from what people living during the Ming dynasty or any other historical period of China would have called magic. Then, they had been watched by ghosts and demons and deities, their sins recorded, their actions influenced; now it was the turn of facial-recognition software, online-history tracking apps, predictive algorithms. She smiled and said that I was in the company of brilliant minds: a famous writer and futurist had proposed a similar idea many years ago.

I didn't tell her that I'd met this writer on a beach in Trincomalee, Sri Lanka, even more years ago, or that he and I had struck up a conversation while sipping lukewarm beers and waiting for the waves to settle. At one point he was describing his vision of the future to me, space elevators and communication satellites and personal devices that contained near-infinite reserves of information, and I said all that sounded much the same as the way things had always been, Chang-er floating to the moon, texts charmed to display whatever knowledge the reader sought, an enduring invisible world overlaid upon the physical one.

"Magic, you mean?" he said.

"That's one word for it," I said.

Mostly we had talked about what we were both there for, which was to go diving. He asked why I had chosen this relatively obscure beach. I told him I had heard that the remnants of a medieval Hindu temple lay submerged in the vicinity (the work of Portuguese colonial forces, which, after looting the complex and killing its priests and pilgrims, had gone above and beyond to lever it over the cliff edge into the bay). Later, when the sea had calmed, I swam between broken columns and poised bronze goddesses, over inscriptions of faith splintered across the rocks. Now and then I still search for such relics, even if I don't bother documenting them. Nostalgia, I suppose. In the green silence of the water I could sense the shimmer of the eternal. I hoped that when the writer found these ruins—I might as well have drawn him a map, with all the hints I provided—he would as well.

II.

The night before your wedding, the last night I would have with you, I surrendered my pride on the altar of desperation and asked you why in all eighteen hells you were doing this.

"I want to have a child," you said.

"Wait," I said, "seriously? Since when?"

"Since Xiangyang, maybe," you said. "It's hard to tell, these things."

Back then we didn't think in terms of time. Our references were geography and action, places we had been, things we had done. In Xiangyang we had talked a jilted, impoverished artist out of jumping into the Hanshui River, and spun a pretext to give him a hundred taels of silver: we would ask him to paint our portrait. We wore our best dresses for it, you in white and I in green, tinted our cheeks and lips, put pins in our hair. We never collected the painting from him. We prided ourselves on traveling light, and, anyway, we saw no use for it, a record of things that would never change.

Xiangyang was several Ming emperors past, a hundred stops ago in our travels through China. We looked for enchanted artifacts, analyzed and cataloged them, sought to understand the wondrous within the human realm. Until we stopped in at West Lake to follow up on rumors of a jade bracelet that could heal its wearer (a fake, it turned out) and you met the man you decided would do for a husband, I had never considered that we might not live like this always. For a moment I thought that I must not know you at all.

You had been hoping it would pass, you said, like a thunderstorm, or an inept dynasty. "Also, children frighten me. They need so much, and they are so easy to lose."

I placed my palm on your stomach, between the twin ridges of your hips. "All right," I said. "A child." I imagined your belly swelling the way those of human women did, the creature that would tear its way out. Yours; and not yours. "You don't have to marry him for that."

"It wouldn't be fair to him. Or to the child."

"What about to me?" This was why I hadn't wanted to ask. I'd known I would succumb to self-pity, and that it would make no difference.

You told me you had calculated the fate of the man who would be your husband based on the ten stems and twelve branches of his birth. He had a delicate constitution. He would pass in twenty-four years, before his fiftieth birthday.

I didn't say anything.

You said, "What is twenty-four years to you?"

I said, "What will twenty-four years be to *you?*" I wasn't thinking twenty-four. I was thinking fifty, sixty, your skin drying to parchment, your hair thinning and graying, your frame stooping ever closer to the ground in which you would—if you did this—someday rot.

You touched my face. I waited for you to ask if I would give up my own immortality, if I was willing to step with you out of the wilderness of myth and into the terraced rice fields and tiled roofs of history.

"You don't have to stay," you said.

I told some version of this story to a man I met in a tavern in rural Shandong. A spirit trading in her immortality to have a child with a human, asking her companion to wait twenty-four years until they could be together again. I was on my way north to Beijing, to bring your son back home following his placement as top scholar in the imperial examination; the boy might have excelled at composing eloquent Confucian nonsense, but he would have been picked apart by bandits the moment his horse trotted beyond the city walls. This man was traveling south, returning to Suzhou after visiting a friend. The tavern was empty except for the two of us. We ended up drinking together, probably for much longer than we should have, talking over the noise of the torn paper windows flapping in the wind.

When I was done, the man said, "But so . . . what happened? When the twenty-four years were up?"

I laughed. "Nothing." Seen in a certain light, now, I could appreciate the glinting, mocking edges of our story. The wine probably helped. It felt potent and tasted foul. "She died within two years. The birth was difficult for her and she never recovered." Neither of us had thought to calculate your fate, in addition to your husband's. After all, we had walked through fires and dived off waterfalls, dismembered demons, batted away the assorted Buddhist monks determined to save us by destroying us so we could reincarnate as lovely, pliant daughters and wives and mothers. What could possibly happen to you while ensconced in domesticity, running a medicine shop with your constitutionally challenged husband? It turned out you were fucking terrible at being a human.

My fellow traveler poured me another cup of wine from the jar we were sharing and told me a story as well, of a young man who had been in love with a prostitute but lacked the wealth to redeem her from the brothel. Instead, she was acquired by a textiles merchant and he took her away with him to another province. The young man expressed his sorrow through any number of histrionic poems. Twenty-four years later, no longer young, he was visiting a friend in a town in that province, and found out, by chance, that the no-longer prostitute lived close by, and also that the merchant had died and she was now a widow.

"Twenty-four years!" I said. "Really?"

He smiled. "Don't you think that's why we met today?"

"What did—," I almost said you, since it was obvious he was talking about himself—"he do?"

"Nothing."

I said, "He no longer loved her?"

"He did," said the man. "He chose his love over her."

Nine days after your son and I arrived back in Zhenjiang, your husband collapsed while in his shop. At the funeral I heard your voice beneath the drone of the Taoist priest reciting his interminable scriptures, asking: *What is twenty-four years to you?*

Quite a while later I read a story about two snake spirits in human guise. The white maiden and the green maiden, they were called. It's part of a collection of folktales by a late-Ming writer and poet from Suzhou. In this story the white maiden lives in the depths of West Lake and attains immortality from ingesting some magical pills that a human boy accidentally swallowed and then vomited out again. The green maiden's equally immortal state is never explained. The boy grows up to become the white maiden's husband, their early sharing of bodily fluids a portent of compatibility. A turtle spirit in the form of a Buddhist monk has it out for the white maiden—he was also in that lake, and wanted those pills for himself—and traps her in a pagoda. The green maiden, her faithful companion, hones her skills for twenty-four years and succeeds in breaking the white maiden out of her prison. After which, the white maiden returns to her husband and her son, their medicine shop, her bucolic life. Nothing further is said of the green maiden.

III.

At some point between your death and your husband's, I returned to Xiangyang to look for our artist. Age had petrified him; I barely recognized him beneath its encrustation. When he saw me he told me I bore a remarkable resemblance to someone he had met long ago.

"I painted their portrait," he said. "That girl and her sister." I imagined how you would have smirked at that, the notion of us as sisters, and for an instant it was like I was standing at the bottom of a very deep well, its lid skewed to expose a hallucinatory glimmer of sky. "That's so funny," I said, "because that's why I'm here." I explained that I worked for an art collector who had heard of the painting and was interested in acquiring it.

"You're sixty years too late," he said. "I gave it away. Couldn't stand to look at it."

I said, as calmly as I could, "Why?"

"I couldn't get it right." His arthritic hands curled open and then closed again. "There was something about the two of them. The way they were. I couldn't get that into the portrait." He stopped painting altogether shortly afterward.

"I'm so sorry," I said.

He shook his head. He told me his friend—the same one he had given the painting to—got him a position at a trading house, and within ten years he had made enough money for ten lifetimes. "Best decision I ever made," he said, "after not drowning myself over a whore."

•

It took me almost three hundred years to find that damn painting. From Xiangyang I followed the mercantile route that the cotton trader who had taken the painting would have, floating south and east on overladen barges down the Hanshui. By the time I located a branch of the man's family he had been dead for decades, his possessions scattered across his three concubines and fourteen children. Meanwhile, your son sold the medicine shop, returned to Beijing, rose to become a senior official in the Ministry of Justice, and—in what he must have thought of as a personal political coup, but with less-than-ideal timing—married your granddaughter into Ming nobility right before the Jurchens stampeded into the capital. I was in Changsha, checking on a lead from an art dealer, and I had to hustle to Beijing to extract her and her newborn from that shitshow. (I left her husband behind, which was better for all concerned.) I parked them in Hangzhou, the last place we had lived before I lost you, and there your family remained until the final act of the Qing dynasty, a modest clan of tea growers on the slopes surrounding West Lake, safely hidden in the undergrowth of history.

My search led me, eventually, to Guangzhou, the port city on the Pearl River where the Qing had consolidated all maritime trade. There I learned of an English missionary who fancied himself a guardian of Chinese culture and how he had convinced the painting's erstwhile owner, a recent convert to Christianity, to give it to him for safekeeping. In our great capital of London, he said, we have a special building that stores treasures from all over the world, to make sure they won't be lost, or ruined, or stolen. He had fled for England on the last clipper ship out of Guangzhou before the British navy began bombing the city during the Second Opium War.

And that's where our portrait is. Room 33 of the British Museum, in the company of a red lacquer box depicting a spring landscape and a commendable forgery of a Jingdezhen porcelain vase. The placard beneath the painting highlights the delicacy of its brushstrokes and the insights it provides into female friendship during the Ming era. Our artist was too harsh on himself. He might not have understood us, but he did manage to set down what he saw. You are smiling at me. It was something I said, I don't remember what. I used to think that as long as I could make you smile, the world would be a fine place. The colors of our dresses glow against the dun background and behind us the clouds swirl like at any moment they could lift us away.

There's something I must confess. When I finally saw the painting, I might have—sort of—cried. I never had, previously. They brought you away in the bridal sedan, and again in the coffin, and both times I watched you become the centerpiece of their human rituals, composed and costumed, almost unrecognizable to me. So then, three hundred years later, to be undone by patterns of ink on silk, swatches of white and green paint, a memory of an unmemorable day: it was quite alarming, actually. Thankfully, the man standing a few feet away from me in the gallery said, no doubt after observing me sniffle for far too long, "You seem like you could use a drink."

He could have suggested a dagger through my eye and I would have taken it. "Do you know a place?" I said.

He looked startled, which might have been for any number of reasons: my forwardness, my speaking English—I had picked it up from the sailors on the long voyage over—or the accent with which I was doing it, which must have made me sound as if I had grown up scuffling for survival on the docks of London. Then he laughed, and offered me both his arm and his handkerchief.

The establishment where he took me was gold trimmed and gaudy, with mirrored walls and fat, winged babies painted across the ceiling. He salvaged my opinion of him by ordering me an enchanting drink. It was a translucent green, as if lit by a hidden flame, and when I sipped it I could taste anise and fennel. After the first glass, he told me, I would see things as I wished they were; after the second glass, as they were not; and, finally, as they truly were.

As we drank he asked me what I had seen, looking at that painting. Beauty, I said, and how it passed.

"Young people are supposed to defer such dour thoughts to the old," he said.

"Oh," I said, "I just look young for my age."

"The ephemerality of beauty is indeed a tragedy," he said, "but surely not in art. The painting will preserve those women's beauty forever."

"While they grew old and died," I said. "That's even worse. It should have been the other way around."

He and I were both well past our third glasses by then, so I told him the story of the hermit on Taishi Mountain who would remain alive for as long as his portrait was intact. The version I told was the one you and I had followed from village to village throughout Henan Province, seeking to determine its authenticity: a scholar official, fallen out of favor with the first Ming court, who begged his portrait to assume the burden of aging for him so he could serve as a historian of the dynasty from its founding to its fall.

"Fascinating," said my drinking companion. "The Ming dynasty ended in . . . what was it, the seventeenth century? What happened to him then?"

"I don't know," I said. "The story doesn't get that far."

We had found him, this hermit, and you coaxed him into showing us the painting. The person depicted in it looked like some ill-tempered ancestor of his who at the time of the portrait sitting was still alive solely to spite all expectations to the contrary. Once he was done with this history of the Ming, the hermit told us, he would burn the portrait. He had no wish to live forever. On our way down from Taishi Mountain I said to you that I was sure he would come up with another reason for living before he laid down his ink brush. You don't think being eternal can start to feel tiring, after a while? you said. It hasn't yet, I said, and we have several hundred years on him. We made a wager: the loser would procure a water dragon's pearl for the winner. But then you died, long before the last Ming emperor did, and I never went back to Taishi to check.

I spent the rest of that day walking through London, admiring, despite myself, its gardens, its cathedrals, its prosperity, its purpose. It reminded me of the grandest days of the Ming, when lantern displays ignited entire mountainsides and Zheng He's treasure fleet measured the breadth of the oceans. In King's Cross Station I saw the twentieth century roaring toward us, all steel and smoke, insatiable, and I thought of how the Summer Palace had burned for days after British troops set it ablaze to punish the Qing government for outlawing the import of opium. When I returned to Hangzhou I put your great-great-grandson on a ship that landed in California shortly before the Chinese Exclusion Act was signed into law. He hated America, the vast and relentless otherness of it, but he never once tried to go back to China.

Quite a while later I read a story about an Englishman and a magical portrait, written by an author as noted for a controversial lifestyle as his literary skill. This Englishman's wish to remain young and beautiful is granted: his portrait will age in his place. He spends his days and nights seeking pleasures and indulging them. While his physical appearance remains unchanged, his painted likeness grows increasingly old and hideous. The Englishman believes this reflects a cosmic judgment being levied on his personal moral choices. He doesn't consider the possibility that the painting is simply showing him, as such a magical artifact does, what he would have become had he continued to age in typical mortal fashion, or that even his most callous acts are nothing out of the ordinary for a person of his breeding and his means, or that the cosmos has never noticed what humans do to themselves or to each other.

•

Imagine a *qilin*—you were always partial to those annoyingly pious creatures—which lives in an enchanted garden. The keepers mandated to care for this *qilin* feed it delicacies, brush its mane, polish its rainbowed scales, and all the while, these keepers, they're also secretly siphoning away the *qilin*'s magic for themselves, because they can. Visitors from beyond the garden are permitted in so they can gaze upon the splendor of the *qilin* and applaud the keepers for how well they are tending to their charge. The visitors bring stories of the *qilin* back with them, and that's how, over time, poachers come to learn about this remarkable animal, the grace of its antlers and its jeweled brilliance, an irresistible challenge.

When the first poachers scale the wall of the garden, the *qilin* is outraged. It puffs up its chest to scorch them with its righteous breath of fire, and . . . nothing. Nothing at all, except the emptiest, most embarrassing wheeze; and the rest of the poachers, waiting outside the walls, hear that sound as well, and they understand what it means. They overrun the garden, wound the *qilin* with their arrows, entangle it in their nets. The *qilin*'s keepers try to stop them and are either killed or persuaded to acquiesce. Once the *qilin* is on the ground the poachers carve away its ornamentation with their knives. There's something for each of them to take away and sell: the antlers, the mane, the dragon scales, the cloven hooves. They leave the *qilin* alive, though. This way the *qilin*'s ornamentation can grow back and they can return and cut it away again, and again, until this arrangement settles into normalcy, until the *qilin*'s purpose becomes, in the very first place, to bring the poachers wealth.

Now a horde of children crowd in. They see the garden as their playground, the *qilin* as their amusement. It will be fun, they think, to play at being keepers. They dress up in the uniforms they have stripped off the keepers' corpses and argue over what they should do with the *qilin*, flopping about in its own blood and excrement, until someone gets the idea of opening it up because who knows what treasures it might hold? The children rush to rip open the *qilin*'s belly and start grabbing at what's inside. The kidneys, the entrails, the liver, the heart. Because they can.

So you can see how what I did to your great-great-grandson, for him, seemed the obvious choice. Certain exile versus probable extinction. But I've come to suspect all I did was stretch the thread of your lineage tighter, and thinner, and in the end it broke anyway.

IV.
You know, I used to think about all the questions I would ask you if I could. Whether you had indeed run the numbers on your own fate but decided not to share, and if so whether it was to spare me or because you thought I would try to stop you. (Of course I would have.) Whether, if you could have seen how this would go down, one brief fuse of a human life lighting another until everything went dark, you would still think it was worth it. (You'd probably have said yes regardless of what you truly thought; you could never bear to be wrong.) Whether you didn't ask me to join you because you were afraid I would say no, or, maybe, that I would say yes. (I still don't know what I would have said. But you should have asked, you should have.)

This morning, though, I have no questions left. I leave the hospital and take a walk through the city. Up and down its hills, past the swaddled homeless on its sidewalks, along the reclaimed curve of its bay, under its gray-scale sky. The fog drifting in across the water is the Pacific Ocean's marine layer cooled to dew point, and also all the ghosts waiting to be remembered before the morning sun burns them away. You're gone now, six hundred years gone, but guess what: I did stay after all.

THE TOUCHES

Brenda Peynado

I'VE BEEN TOUCHED exactly four times in real life. The first was when my mother gave birth to me. I picked up her bacteria as I slid out of her womb, the good stuff as well as the bad. My father caught me, and his hands—covered in everything that lives on our skins—made contact. His bacteria, the yeast, shed viruses, and anything else from under his fingernails spread to my newborn epidermis. That was the second touch.

I was gooey and crying, and they both held me for a moment before the robot assigned to me snipped my cord, took me up in its basket, and delivered me to the cubicle where I would live the rest of my life. There it hooked me into the virtual reality mindset, the body-adapting and stimulating cradle station. Then Nan, what I eventually named my robot, turned on its caretaker mode and sent my mind into clean. Back in dirty, everything that came with me—the blanket my mother wrapped me in, the towel that wiped placenta from my face, the suction ball that pulled the goop from my nose and mouth, the basket—was incinerated. That was right after the first plague legislation, back when they were still allowing natural births and cohabitating marriage units.

I wish I remembered it. It wasn't the same, holding me in clean, my parents said. They'd tuck the blanket around me and sing me a song, and sometimes my mother would tell me what it felt like to actually touch me, to smell me. Then, my avatar still passed out back in my virtual reality bedroom, I'd pull out of clean and Nan would be above me, smiling with her LCD face screen, unhooking me from the wires and hugging me with her white plastic arms.

My parents are dead now. Their cubicle in dirty was incinerated. The only thing I have of the moment they held me is a video Nan recorded when she pulled me away from them and brought me here.

I've been thinking about them lately when Telo and I go to bed. I inherited the code for my parents' clean house, so the ephemera of their stuff is still there in the rooms, although I turned my childhood bedroom into the master bedroom and recoded the algorithm for how much space I could take up with the house. I've been thinking about which room would belong to the baby.

Since we elected to be assigned a baby, my avatar's belly has been growing. Most of the time I don't notice it, despite the code putting pressure feedback on my movement algorithms and my gait turning into a waddle. I'm getting stronger; that's what I mainly feel. But when I climb into bed, it's hard to get comfortable. Technically, Telo could have been the one to go through the pregnancy algorithm, since we don't believe in gender norming or any of those religious restrictions. He's the more nurturing of the two of us, and when I see him with his charges at the childcare center, surrounded by big-eyed, jumping kids that call him Mr. Telo, or more often with the younger ones, Mistelo, it melts me. But that's why I had to be the one to get pregnant. Supposedly going through all the algorithm motions of natural birth, even when you're getting the baby from a test tube, activates all those love centers and makes you feel more connected. I'm the one who needs the extra help.

Tonight, Telo pauses at the bedroom doorway, which tells me sex is on the horizon, and reaches for my hand. He scoops me up and I giggle at the rush upward. My face in his chest, he starts to rock me. It's the only thing that will turn me on. My therapist thinks I'm trying to get at whatever primal feeling would unleash in me if it were real touch. But since the pregnancy algorithm started showing, it's awkward and I don't fit right. He squeezes too hard on my belly and I can't lose myself like I used to. Telo can tell that I'm flinching. He sighs deeply, and then drops me on the bed.

"I'm sorry," I say. "Once the algorithm's run its course, things will get back to normal."

"It's not your fault," he says, and rolls over. "Good night, love."

And then we put our avatars to sleep, and I emerge into dirty.

There's Nan again, peering into my VR immersion ball. "Hi, sunshine," she says. She unhooks my headset, pulls me out of the ball so I don't start spinning it by getting up, and starts brightening lights slowly to get my eyes used to the idea that I'm in the real, dirty world again.

Not that I want to see much in dirty. Outside it's bald and diseased earth, trying to heal itself. All the superbugs—microbes and viruses that evolved immunity to antibiotics, that melted out of the polar ice caps and were released into the oceans, bugs we hadn't seen for a million years—they're all still out there, proliferating. Inside, the cubicle is a standard-issue sanitized room: only enough to feed yourself, hug your robot like you're supposed to, bathe when you need, and then plug right back in and sleep along with your avatar. Every crack is sealed, every intake and retake valve opened only once a vacuum is established in the rest of the system. Back before the toilets were vacuum sealed, they would spew all their bugs into the air, infecting everyone who used the same ventilation system, killing entire apartment complexes. It's revolting, knowing how even the bacteria we need is mutating on our very skins, inside us, just a roll of the dice before they turn into something deadly; knowing that if the seals around our doors were to give way, we'd probably be puking our guts out within the week, killed by any number of diseases, a bird flu or ancient mariner plague or limb-taking staph or airborne HIV. I'm itching to log back into clean where none of that matters.

"Time to eat," Nan announces brightly, a vacuum-sealed pre-cooked meal arriving down the chute. "Beef chili."

It's chicken and potatoes—even blinking against the light, I can see that. Nan's glitches have been getting worse, but I haven't gotten around to ordering spare parts. I know it's important. Without our personal robotics assistants that function as our doctors, our caretakers, our alarm systems, we wouldn't have survived the first sweep of plagues. Without the drones and army of specialty robots meant to take our place in the outer, dirty world, farming and manufacturing and construction, we would have to expose ourselves.

Best I can tell, Nan's power supply is part of the problem. It's shorting and restarting her modules at different times, and the desynchronization makes her go buggy.

"Remind me tomorrow to order a new power supply," I say.

"Yes," she says, "babycakes."

"Telo?" Telo, a pro at logging into the caretaker units while at work, often logs into Nan. I hate when he does that. I feel naked in dirty, my real self less attractive than my avatar, my hair matted and greasy because no one can smell me alone in my cubicle.

"Surprise," he says with Nan's voice.

He hugs me with her white plastic arms, the way Nan is programmed to do every night. The hugs are supposed to be soothing, meant to combat the developmental disorders of a lifetime of not being touched, but it's awkward. Nan runs cold, and there's no part of her that gives. I've thought of wrapping her in memory foam, but that would block her panels. At least in dirty, I'm not pregnant. My stomach is flat and my range of motion intact, and I can hug him back good and hard.

He holds up the soap and makes Nan's face a goofy grin, and I laugh and jump in the shower.

But then Nan glitches again, and she just stands there frozen with the soap in midair. Ten minutes later when she starts up again, she's only Nan and Telo has logged out.

When I wake up in clean, morning light is slicing in through the blinds and the birdsong I've programmed is playing on a loop from the window. Telo is next to me in the bed, dead to the world. My hand passes through his shoulder; his avatar is empty and he hasn't logged back into it. His avatar has been sleeping later and later these mornings. I wonder what he's doing over there in dirty. Eating, voiding, getting ready for the morning? He told me he looks almost the same as his avatar, except his dark hair is a lot curlier, and he lets it grow long. He has a scar on his shoulder where he fell on a sharp corner of his immersion rig when his robot wasn't looking, whereas his avatar's light skin is as smooth as glass.

"Remember to order a new power supply." I hear Nan's voice barely in range of my perception, her whispering into my headset back in dirty. I disabled her direct clean log-in after the last time hearing her voice loud above me made me jump out of my skin. This way, she's soft and distant, the way I like the dirty world.

I groan, stretch, try to remember where I left my tablet before I logged out last time. If clean was unregulated, I could simply wish the tablet into my hands. I get annoyed that part of the legislation to create clean required that everything be tied to a physical representation as close to real life as possible—so we don't become alien to ourselves, supposedly, none of this living exclusively in our heads. They wanted to pretend the world was back the way they dreamed it. I get it—nostalgia. Even though none of us can eat in clean, my parents left the kitchen in the digital representation of the house they used to have in real life, and I didn't code it out when I inherited because it was always there in my childhood. I use it as my meditation room, where I try to imagine the smell of coffee.

I find the tablet in the kitchen, blinking on a stool.

Things have been tight since paying for our test-tube baby, so before I order the part, I check our bank account. But there's more money in there than there should be, by at least five hundred bitcoins.

Telo yawns loudly behind me, walking stiffly into the kitchen.

"What's this?" I say, and I show him the tablet screen.

"Oh, I took on a few extra kids."

"More than a few."

"We talked about this, right? Wasn't it what you wanted?"

"Just be careful. If anything went wrong with a few of them at the same time . . ."

"Nah. I've got all the luck. You shouldn't worry about it. Off to work yet?" He leans against the doorframe, and I'm breathless, his avatar is that beautiful. His dirty self, of course, would look less perfect, less symmetrical, and his eyebrows droop downward. Still, the avatar is a cousin to him. Or at least that's what he says. I've never logged into his robot, and I don't want to. Even when he does it, it feels like he's looking into a secret self.

"Just as soon as I get this belly under control," I say, pulling on the dress I've recoded for maternity.

I ride the bus to the industry district. Avenue of the Giants features skyscrapers for the greatest minds in clean: the philosophers in the Commission for Digital Humanization, the engineers in the Commission for Stabilization, and the scientists in the Commission for Reentry, my building. There doesn't come a day when I'm not thankful that these are government task forces instead of corporate-run research, which would have guaranteed that only the rich would be able to reenter dirty once we figured out how to fight the diseases, with the rest of us remaining in tiny boxes. I flash my badge at the Reentry doors.

In the lab, Alicia is dancing behind the blood samples while they run. This lab is set up with a corresponding one over in dirty, manned by robots. Here, when Alicia puts in blood samples to run, robots put the real-life samples from humans or birds and set them spinning in the machine. It's seamless. It makes me wonder what would happen if clean were ever perfect, if we could eat and smell and taste here. Would we ever want to leave? Would we even care about that other world we ruined?

"Happy day, happy day," Alicia says.

I nod as Fermat walks in.

"How's reentry going?" Fermat says.

"Her robots have been breaking birds again," Alicia says brightly.

"Damn it." I turn around and something flutters in my corner of the lab, a reminder of the dirty world. Each TV screen on my wall is assigned to a drone feed or a robot following flocks of birds back in dirty. My tiny part of the reentry project is studying patterns of insect transmission of the avian flu. I'm working on a harmless version of the virus that spreads innocuously through mosquito transmission but prevents the worse one from taking hold in the host. We can't realistically vaccinate every bird on the planet, but if we inoculate a few and the harmless virus spreads . . . then we might gain traction. Of course, I'm always fighting with the research group on the top floor who thinks the answer is bringing mosquitoes to extinction altogether.

The bird flailing on the top right monitor has a broken wing. I can see the wavering outline of camouflaged robot hands holding it, one of my robots designed to sneak up on the birds and capture them for tagging, blood samples, and injections. Except some software glitch keeps making their hands too tight around the birds' bodies, killing my research subjects.

I log into the offending robot, bringing its tactile feed into my immersion ball back in dirty. In my hands is the bird. Every time I try to merely touch it, the plastic hands punch the bird's delicate body, jerking and missing its mark half the time.

Freeze, I instruct the robot. I log out and emerge back at the lab. I groan.

"Was that one of the incubators?" says Fermat.

The eighth bird in as many days, bringing my flock down to just the minimum for viral mutation conditions. I can't afford to send another robot and have the same thing happen. "I can't lose this grant," I say.

Alicia keeps pirouetting in front of the samples, her way of dealing with conflict. She must be having a bad day with her research, too.

Fermat, always the sensible one, glances down at my stomach, tabulates the cost against the pay of my grant. "You better get that sample some other way, then. I can't believe your data's almost wrecked."

Alicia stops her dancing, already knowing what I'm thinking. "No. You don't have to go out there."

I feel like a rock sinks through my torso. Leaving my container in dirty is one of my greatest nightmares. What if my bioball breaks? What if decontamination goes awry? At least I wouldn't be able to spread it to anyone else. "I think I have to," I say.

Fermat shudders. Alicia starts dancing again, taking one giant leap in the air. At the apex, she gets stuck and her avatar goes transparent, shimmering and splayed midjump. She's logged out of her avatar.

"We had work to do!" Fermat yells. He throws a lab notebook at her avatar, but the notebook goes right through her. For the rest of the day, with her avatar floating up there, we'll be distracted, waiting for her to drop from the air when she logs back in.

And that brings me to the third touch. An hour later back in dirty, I'm looking for my flock. I'm pushing the joystick, rolling my containment bioball forward near the waterfront, where both mosquitoes and birds are plentiful. I only see one other bioball out, likely another researcher since few people are approved for them. My bioball is clear plastic all around, and the bottom of it gives me a window through puddles and waste canals. It makes me gag, all that muck swirling around underneath me, filled with bugs that are compelled to feed off and destroy me. Inside, though, I'm safe.

The birds flutter around me as I roll down the old boardwalk. I turn my camouflage mode on, and they stop seeing me. One of the rocks ripples, and I know that's my glitching robot, in camouflage mode, too. The bird is dead in its hands, although the robot's skin is reflecting the sky behind him, so it looks like an upside-down dead bird is stuck in the gray air. At times I think dirty is just as virtual as clean.

I push my hands through the sealed glove openings and unclench the robot's invisible hands. The bird spills into my gloves. A drone whirs overhead, delivering a sample kit. I pull out a needle from the kit and draw thick blood from the necrotizing bird. I pack the bird in a plastic bag and place it into the drone's trunk. Maybe something that can be used later to track how decomposing tissue spreads and nurtures the virus. "Name the sample Decomposing Subject 932," I say, looking at the code tag on the bird's ankle. The drone's light blinks once in affirmation.

I keep seeing ripples out of the corner of my eye back inland, but I don't see any wildlife and the rest of my robots are dispatched to follow other control and experiment flocks. It must be vertigo from moving around in real life instead of the controlled movements of clean.

I carefully roll my ball into the flock, the starlings preening and eating mites off each other. I pick them up gently for my samples, crooning their own birdsong at them through my speakers, holding their warm bodies in my hands—almost my hands, except separated by the rubber of the gloves. What would it feel like to run a bare fingertip along a feather?

I chose starlings for my research because of how invasive they are. Someone let them loose in New York's Central Park centuries ago out of nostalgia—they wanted to release all the birds from Shakespeare's plays—and within a hundred years they were all over the continent, taking over other birds' nests. If you wanted to track spread, what better species? Not much different from humans, in that respect. Germs were nature's population control, but we refuse to give up our freedom. We're another kind of germ, spreading unchecked.

I let the last bird go, dispatch the drone to our lab's twin in dirty. "Return to the lab for repairs," I tell the robot, but it appears to be glitching, frozen. "Reboot," I say.

Nothing.

Fine. I roll back down the boardwalk, cross past the barricade holding back the rising sea. The ripples in the air start up again, this time accelerating down the street toward me. A camouflage's slight delay. It's on a collision course.

I pull the joystick hard left, and whatever it is glances off my ball, throwing me. I smash into the closest wall, my seat belt throttling my chest, and I plunge into darkness.

My ball's emergency lights flash in my face. There's a hissing air leak somewhere. The lights show me I'm inside the wreckage of what used to be an ancient restaurant, one of those places where people in dirty used to congregate and infect each other. My chest throbs against the seat harness, but other than that, I'm not hurt. The air smells like rotten fish and mold. I want to cry; if I can smell dirty that means it's in here with me. I roll the ball out of the crunching mess and emerge into the gray light.

"Are you okay?" I hear a female voice over crackling speakers.

I want to scream at her for not seeing me, but then I realize I left my camouflage mode on, too. We couldn't see each other. "The ball's breached," I say. Center left, where the air is hissing out. I hold my hand up to the hole, trying to plug the air.

"Mine, too," she says. She drops the camouflage. She's holding her arm. Her hair is everywhere, come loose from the crash. She looks like Alicia, almost, except her eyes are black instead of violet, her nose more hooked.

"Alicia?"

She grimaces.

"What are you doing out here?"

"I was trying to help," she says. "We have to get back to filtered air."

Panic surges up in me. I turn my bioball, message Nan to prepare a decontamination entry.

"Wait!" Alicia says. She pushes her ball up to mine, lining up our breaches.

"Do you have a patch?" I say. "What are you doing?"

She puts a finger through, her fingertip suddenly on my palm.

At first, I'm revolted. All the microbes from her hands, from everything she's ever touched, cultured underneath her fingernails and attaching to me. Then the soft rub, the heat of her fingertip, the prickle of the virgin sensation. It feels like joy and pain at once, everything forbidden.

Mosquitoes hover around us. Are they my mosquitoes, harmless? Or wild ones, carrying death?

"I have to go," I say, yanking my ball away, rushing back to decontamination with my palm pressed against the breach.

My hand burns the whole way back, and I keep telling myself it's not flesh-eating bacteria, it's not a mosquito bite, it's just touch. My third touch. The only one I remember.

Nan gasses me, burns the ball, and opens the inner door back into my cubicle with a roar. "You are now class five contaminated. Your permit to leave your cubicle is rescinded," she says cheerily.

"It was just my hand." But I know that's a lie. I know how bugs spread and cross-contaminate, and even the breeze of my breath can push bugs farther than the initial contact area.

"Permit rescinded," Nan says, and leans in to hug me, wrapping me in cold plastic. Then she freezes around me, glitching.

In a week or two, all that infected me should manifest itself, and if it kills me, Nan will be incinerated along with my body. I want to smash her into pieces already, this broken world along with her. Shouldn't we just bury it all? Instead, I hold her hand, mold it around mine where it burns. Her hand cools mine. I breathe deeply, the plastic smell of her.

"Everything will be okay, Nan. Reboot."

"Welcome home, sunshine," she says, as she reactivates and releases me.

When I get back to clean, Alicia is still hanging up by the ceiling. Fermat is coding DNA and squinting his eyes. I drop heavily into my chair and start composing a message to Telo about what happened. My eyes keep glancing up to Alicia's hovering form, her translucent hands, the whorls of her fingertips. I want to talk to her about what just happened. We touched. I touched her real skin, traded microbiomes, contaminated myself. Surely, I'm infected. I take deep breaths and try to calm down.

Trembling, I message Telo from my console. *Something happened to me. I had to go into dirty. Video me?* But I get his logged-out autoresponse. I realize he's in dirty. All of us are, but I'm used to thinking of everyone as somewhere else, *out there,* or nonexistent until they log into clean. But Telo could live in the dirty cubicle right next to me. I could have passed feet from his body. I could have touched him instead of Alicia.

I wrench myself from that line of thinking. It's forbidden for good reason, dangerous even without the superbugs out there, each of our microbiomes completely unused to the other's. Microbiome shock alone could kill. Would I inflict that on someone I loved, just to feel their skin in real life? Before today, I would have said no.

When I was in high school, I saw someone who was infected. She didn't catch it from anywhere; it was her own bacteria that had mutated. It wasn't killing her, exactly, but it was eating her slowly. Her avatar was unaffected and perfect: clothes ironed, black hair sleek, eyes bright. But she kept closing them and putting her head on the desk, and her breaths sounded like she was gasping for air. None of us wanted to be around her, and come lunchtime we scattered away from her. We knew, logically, we couldn't catch anything in clean, but that didn't stop our instincts from kicking in, the part of us that wanted to burn her up in her cubicle so that whatever she had went down with her. Even the teachers asked her to stay at her home in clean from then on.

I get a message from Telo. *Sorry, trouble at work. One of the kids had a problem and then her robot wouldn't respond to me. I'm heading home now. Tell me all about it when I see you?*

Above me, Alicia's avatar turns solid and the gravity algorithm kicks in, her hair flying up around her until she lands on the floor. She catches my eye, and her leg taps to a rhythm. Her dancing means her heart is racing as much as mine. Her avatar's long hair is flat and sleek, but I know back in dirty, her hair is wild as a halo. Back in dirty, has she been infected?

"Salipa." She calls my name, holding out her hand from behind the lab equipment.

I see Fermat, hunched over his screen. "Not here," I say.

I lead her outside into the hallway. Down the elevator, where we stand next to each other. She slips her hand into mine. It's the same hand she touched before, and I don't pull back. She's nearly dancing again as we go out the glass doors to the fountain at the center of the Avenue of the Giants. The fountain trickles in a rhythmic, programmed loop. The water smells like nothing. Completely clean. Children are playing in the arcs of water, but back in dirty, they aren't actually wet. They don't have to worry about water being a petri dish full of killer bugs.

Alicia's hand slides up my arm. But it doesn't feel like it did earlier, our hands finally naked atop each other. It feels dull, muted, her small hands feathers that have been covered in wax. I move away, breaking contact. "Are you okay?"

She shrugs. "It might be a few weeks before we would get symptoms, Sal."

"What were you doing out there, anyway?" I walk toward the children, a little girl perching atop a ledge. Nothing here can hurt her. Be careful, I want to warn anyway. We've already lost so much.

"I go outside sometimes, and I didn't want you to be alone. Plus, I'm a scientist. I was curious."

"You knew I was out there. Why weren't you more careful?"

"Please," she says, touching me with that dull hand again, resting it on the hump of my stomach. She leans in, looking at my eyes, and then grabs me and kisses me. I don't pull away. She feels just like Telo, the same algorithm.

"Wait," I say, gasping.

She's going to cry as she pulls back. Then she logs out, her hands frozen still reaching for me.

When I get home, Telo has programmed our living room the way I like, the light frozen in the fierce orange of sunset, the sound of waves hitting shore somewhere nearby, a double Brazilian hammock strung up in the center of the room underneath the chandeliers. He's glowing in the light.

"Bad day at work?" he asks.

I shed all my clothes. I'm naked and I need him, so I jump into the hammock, ignoring the pressure of my giant belly, and wave him in. Once he's wrapped around me, I tell him what happened in dirty. I don't tell him that it was like nothing I'd ever felt before, because the comparison would mean that I'd never felt it with him. I don't tell him about Alicia's kiss.

"So now we just wait for the incubation period to end," he says. "Maybe you get lucky."

"Lucky?" I say. "Everything around our cubicles in clean is devastated."

"Lots of people get lucky. Let's hope for the best and cross that bridge when we come to it."

His response makes no sense. Lots of people? "You're so calm about this," I say.

He shrugs into me. "Nothing else to do."

Something kicks me in the stomach hard. I gasp.

He freezes like he's the one that's done something. "What?"

"Just the baby." The simulated kicks punch me a few times in the stomach, then they're gone. I know that to increase bonding when they finally assign us the child, I should stop thinking of it as a simulation and start thinking of it as our child. I wish I had Telo's gift, but I see how it runs him ragged, trying to fulfill everyone, all those children crying, hungry, not yet able to find the words for what they need. But then I imagine Telo smiling above a baby startled with wonder, both of them without me. I can't help but wonder, "If I got infected and you lose me, would you keep the baby?"

"Stop," Telo says. "Trust me, you'll be fine."

"Even if I'm not infected, I'm not fine. If I can't pick up robot slack, I might lose my research. But now I'm quarantined and I can't go out again."

"I could go for you." He puts his face in my neck, and he's tangled around me. Back in my immersion ball in dirty, tiny electrical impulses prick my nerves, simulating his weight on my skin. Just like Alicia.

"Telo, no. Look what happened to me. That's just a hypothetical permission you have. *If* one of your kids is in danger and *if* their robot fails or glitches too bad for you to log in. And that hasn't happened yet. I would never ask you to risk yourself. Forget it; it's just data. I can start again when the robots stop glitching."

"And redo two years of work? Lose your grant? Could we still afford the baby? I guess . . . I'll have to take on more kids."

"Telo," I say, now the strong one, and I put my finger cross-wise against his lips, shushing him. It's the hand with the palm that has felt another person. The waves soundtrack washes over us. I close my eyes and wish with all my being that it felt the same, that the same electricity would flow through me as when Alicia's fingertip jolted me awake.

"Don't you want more from life?" I ask, even though every-thing around us is designed as a paradise: the waves, the light of sunset licking our skin, the hammocks and the slow rocking sensation.

"Every single day I want more," he says, and he grips me hard, like a secret is being dragged out of him, like he's strug-gling to breathe.

I awake from Nan shaking me. "Hello, sunshine," she says. "Time for food and voiding."

"Excellent," I say.

My arm has pinprick marks nestled in the crook. She's been taking samples. I look toward the door, the decontamination chamber that lies just beyond. The lock screen is activated with a new code that says permanent. What she does while I'm in clean.

"My new power supply has arrived," she says.

It's unpackaged, carefully placed on the floor by my immer-sion ball. "That's great, Nan. Want to bend over so I can install it?"

"Yes," she says, and complies.

I open up her back, pull out the old supply. I can hear it sparking. I click in the new one.

"Reboot," I tell Nan. But nothing. She stays bent over like that. When I ran her debug, it didn't throw up any other hard-ware flags. Could the problem be something else? Are Nan's glitches connected with the other robots' errors?

She looks broken in half. Suddenly my ten-by-ten cubicle in dirty feels empty and crushing. I wolf down my meal, log back into clean.

In clean, I'm still in the hammock, Telo asleep and logged

out next to me. I can't tell what time it is because the blinds are still programmed to leak out sunset.

If there is ever a time to log into his robot, it's now. He gave me the passcode when I gave him the digital key to my house, and never once had I been tempted to use it. But is he okay? Do I need to warn him about the robot glitches? Do I need to see him in real life even if I'd be embodied in a plastic humanoid? Do I need to tell him about the kiss, about my numbness, about my hunger?

I say his cubicle number into the air, then the passcode.

"Accept log-in?" I hear.

"Accept."

His cubicle looks exactly like mine, but his robot seems to be working fine. My hands, the robot's hands, aim and squeeze correctly.

"Telo?" I say, and the bright robot voice saying my words startles me.

He's probably asleep in his immersion ball, but when I open the padded door, he's not in there. He's not anywhere in his cubicle. He's gone out into the dirty world. I open and close my robot hands, grasping air.

In the morning, the news has figured it all out, about the glitching robots having all contracted a code virus. Usually the sick ones are robots that have been repeatedly logged into. They're working on a fix.

Telo still hasn't come back by the time I leave for work.

At work, Alicia is there, but she is translucent with her head on her desk, the polite way to log out.

"She said she was feeling sick," Fermat says.

"Feeling sick?" I ask.

He shrugs. "I don't need her for this part anyway."

If she's sick, is it something I contracted?

And of course, on the monitors, I see my robot gathering samples is still frozen in place. It's like dirty is infecting clean, spiraling out of control.

Telo, are you okay?

Yeah, just at work. I slept in this morning.

Late night?

The usual.

When Fermat logs out to use the bathroom back in dirty, something comes over me and I hug Alicia, of course falling through her empty avatar, landing headfirst on her desk inside her. Through her translucent form, I see that she's written something on a notebook. My name, over and over. Then at the end, a phone number.

I pick up the notebook through the haze of her empty avatar. I call the contact, one trembling number at a time.

"Have you used us before?" says the person who picks up.

"Who is this?" I ask.

The woman sighs. "Okay, new customer." A moment's pause. "Alright, I have your details and your account. Ten P.M. tonight. Just be sure that your robot is disabled and that your cubicle door can be accessed from the outside."

"In dirty?" I say, terrified.

"Are you kidding me?" she says, and she hangs up.

For the rest of the day, I watch my flocks on the drone monitors. The robots with useful digits are all glitching, not to be trusted near the test subjects. But not even I am to be trusted, apparently—not in dirty, not in clean.

When I think about the phone call, my heart skips a beat.

I try to call the number back, cancel what I might have just signed up for, but the number is now disconnected. The baby kicks again, and I grip the lab desk until it passes.

What was coming for me at my cubicle? A delivery? A replacement robot? A person? And despite myself, despite knowing what it would cost them, me being class five contaminated, I want it to be a person. I'm willing to ruin them.

When I get home, Telo is waiting for me. No hammocks this time, or sunset. Just the regular couches and afternoon light. He's left the waves programming, which he usually does before he brings up something sure to cause an argument, meant to calm me in advance. His avatar doesn't register any of the visible effects of tiredness; he looks as perfect and unruffled as ever. But he yawns.

My anger eclipses everything else. "Where were you last night?"

"What do you mean?"

"You weren't in your cubicle."

"You logged into my robot?"

"You hypocrite. You log into mine all the time."

"I mean, I don't mind, it's just you never have before. Of course you can log in. But why last night?"

I shrug. "Why aren't you answering the question?"

"Just the kids, obviously. With the robots down I had to help with some of the babies. What is wrong with you?"

"You weren't trying to help me with my research, were you?"

"No, I was definitely not trying to help you." He's amused, smirking.

I snort. I don't know why I'm so angry. "I'm sorry," I say. "It's just—I needed you and you weren't there. It's a glitch, I know. But anything could have happened to you." I don't mention my own guilt.

"I'm here now."

He hugs me. I let myself be swept up, but I can barely feel it. The projection clock on the mantel says nine o'clock.

He yawns again. "Maybe we should go to sleep early tonight," he says, draping me over the bed. "Since we were both up late."

I shrug, trying to remain calm. "If you're tired."

"You know *you* are, babycakes," he says, nestling himself behind me. He spoons me, and we both close our eyes before we log out, our avatars back in clean locked together and shimmering.

In dirty, Nan is stuck folded over and motionless. Just in case, I point her camera toward the corner. My cubicle still says that it's permanently locked, but it's always been accessible from the outside, in case the government, scientists, or caretaker robots need to come in beyond the delivery chute. Some people are so paranoid about the bugs outside that they smash the screen, blowtorch the entrance shut. The occasion anyone would have to use it is so rare as to be ridiculous, but once, a cubicle row caught on fire and the drones couldn't put it out. The people who had sealed themselves in burned in there, everyone else rolling their bioballs toward their new cubicle row. All of these people rolling through the smog-filled, devastated world with their own frail, impoverished selves, and now they could see each other: uglier, greasier, weaker than their avatars.

I feel nauseous and hold my head over the toilet just in case. A symptom of a disease? Nerves? Then it passes.

Still an hour to go. It's been a few days since I showered, and I can smell myself. I pull the curtains in the corner opposite Nan around myself, turn on the vacuum-sealed drain. I soap myself carefully. If I slip and fall, no one will come running. Not even Nan can save me now. As I pass the soap over my skin, I tremble. Here, my stomach is flat. In a month, if I'm not dead from superbugs, a baby will be placed into my arms. Which version is the lie? I think of Alicia, her fingertip, my palm, and let the water touch me clean.

At ten o'clock, nothing happens. My door stays shut, and I am alone. I want to confess to Telo right away, nudge him awake and tell him what I hoped for, how much this world is not enough, how this cubicle that I might never leave feels like a trap and all I am able to do is run in the fields of the virtual world. Would he be enough? Would the baby be enough? Would all of our research for reentry be enough?

The decontamination chamber outer door opens. A man rolls in, then steps out of his bioball and lifts his arms to be scrubbed by gas. The door to my cubicle opens.

He moves quickly to wedge the inner door open with one of Nan's arms. He freezes when he looks up, as if he's as surprised to see me as I am him. Then he relaxes and grins.

"Hi," he says. "We have ten minutes."

I don't say anything. My hair is dripping down my back, moisture immediately absorbed by the floor's dehumidifier. I keep glancing toward the door that should be shut, that should be the second barrier protecting me.

"Here I am," he says.

"I'm contaminated," I warn. "Class five."

"I guess that's the risk," he says, like he's not surprised. He's much shorter than Telo, balding even though he's about my age, skinny like all of us in real life, much darker skin, green eyes to Telo's startling black eyes. He has a scar on his shoulder. His palms are stretched out to me.

"Here I am," I say, but I don't move.

When he walks toward me, I flinch. He surrounds me with his arms. I can smell him, his underarms, my breath on his skin. I drown in the tidal wave of him. I put my arm around his neck, and his squeeze lifts me to my tiptoes. I am floating on someone else's skin. In a few weeks, we could both be gone, dead from infection, nothing left of us—not our cubicles or robots, incinerated; not our ephemera, wiped from clean.

"Babycakes." He breathes into my hair. He is crying.

I realize. The extra money, the late nights, his nonchalance about the risks of touch. Telo has touched many people before me. I'll be angry later, confess my own, but there's no time for that now.

"You look nothing like your avatar," I say, but I don't let go. Telo is alien, uncanny, the resemblance only slight. Who are we? How can we raise a human child and teach it who we are without lying, without shame?

"That's what you have to say to me?" He grabs my hair, puts his other arm underneath my legs, and lifts. He trembles with the weight of me, something he doesn't do in clean. How little we are, for how much we can ruin.

"Take me," I say.

"Take you where?" he asks. "This is how we live."

We're snotting in each other's necks, licking the salt from our wet faces, smelling each other down to the feet. I run my fingers in the curves of his ear. If we hurry, this touch could last a lifetime.

And this is what we can tell the baby assigned to us, if we survive: We can pass on our ruin through love. This box that you wake up in is evidence of how dangerous you are with need. We will give you what we can. We will offer up the world to your hunger.

ELECTION

Maurice Carlos Ruffin

I READ THE SCRIPT VERBATIM, always starting with the line, "My name is Simone Winters and I'm calling because Roland Chereau cares about our town and you." I'd make twenty calls each hour, thirty if I had a lot of hang-ups. Roland wore crisp banker's suits with wingtips. One morning, he came to the campaign office with a vase of flowers, flowers not specifically for me, and yet flowers he placed right in front of me. As if the others wouldn't notice.

He made me one of his special assistants. I'd go with him to debates and fundraisers. Afterwards, I'd stand next to him trying not to make eye contact, my arms stiff against my sides. His tangy cologne in my nose. Each morning, I awaited his call. He'd rented an apartment on the outskirts and that's where he'd call for me to meet him at.

The last time I went to the apartment was the day after Roland won the election. We lay in bed. He was happy. So was I, of course. I knew better, but a part of me believed he would leave his wife and kids due to his newfound strength. He wouldn't care about the media questions. I was twenty-one years old and raindrops tapped against the window as if they were trying to get my attention.

The night before, during his victory speech, Roland's supporters hung on to his words for dear life. He spoke about how together they would solve all their problems once and for all. I asked him if he believed everything he said.

"No," he said. "But it makes folks feel better when I say those things. Part of the job description is to make people believe."

"Should I believe you love me?" I asked. Immediately, I regretted myself.

Roland was quiet for a few seconds, staring at shadows on the ceiling. He turned my way and I knew he was about to say something, so I put a finger over his lip.

THE GOOD, GOOD MEN

Shannon Sanders

⁂

THEO HAD COME ALL THE WAY from New York with no luggage. From the parking lot Miles watched him spring from the train and weave past the other travelers, sidestepping their children and suitcases with practiced finesse, first of anyone to make it across the steaming platform. His hair was shaved close on the sides, one thick strip left to grow skyward from the crown of his head. In his dark, lean clothing, hands shoved deep in his pockets, he was a long streak of black against the brightly colored crowd. He alone had reached their father's full height.

He made no eye contact with Miles as he strode to the car and yanked at the door handle, as he folded himself in half and dropped heavily into the passenger seat, releasing a long breath. "Fucking hot," he said, pulling the door shut.

Miles threw the car into drive and steered out of the parking lot, out of the knot of station traffic. "Summertime," he said by way of assent.

These words, the first the brothers had spoken aloud to each other in over a year, hung in the air between them until the car reached the mouth of the highway. Their mother, Lee, had finally moved back out to the suburbs, to the end house in a single-family neighborhood Miles had seen often from the road, all crisscrossed with telephone wires. He was grateful for its proximity, only a four-mile drive from the train station. Last time around, searching for her dumpy apartment deep in the District, he and Theo had lost precious time to gridlock and confounding one-way streets and been beaten there by their sisters, turning the whole operation to chaos. A mess of shifted allegiances and hand-wringing, tears, hysteria. Later, in the relative quiet of Miles's living room, Theo had complained of his ears ringing.

"No bag, nothing?" asked Miles now, nodding down toward Theo's empty hands. "We need to stop for a toothbrush?"

"No," said Theo. "I'm good. I'm out tonight, right after Safeway."

Miles thought of Lauren back home, washing the guest linens and googling vegan dinner recipes since morning. "Okay," he said. "Quick trip, though."

"Just to keep it simple," said Theo. "We dragged it out last time. A task like that always expands to fill whatever time you allocate for it. You know? We gave it two days, and it took two days. We were inefficient." He reached for the dashboard and gave the AC knob a hard crank, calling up a blast of chilled air. "This time, two hours. We'll give it two hours, and we'll get it done in two hours."

Miles suppressed a shiver. Stealing a glance at his brother's outstretched arm, he saw an arc of freshly inked letters at the biceps, disappearing beneath a fitted sleeve. Lauren, who kept aggressive Facebook surveillance of all her in-laws, had kept Miles apprised of each of Theo's new tattoos for years, undeterred by Miles's disinterest. Only this last had caught his attention.

"Bad stakeholder analysis, is what it was," Theo was muttering. "Last time, I mean."

"What's the new tattoo?" asked Miles. "The words on your arm?"

Theo blinked at the graceless transition, then obligingly pushed up his sleeve. "Got it in Los Angeles, on a work trip. A girl I was with talked me into it. I had been thinking about this one for years." He traced his finger around the lettered circle, four words rendered to look like they'd been scrawled on by hand in a familiar chicken scratch. *"Miles, Thelonious, Mariolive, Caprice.* For us, obviously."

"But where did you get Daddy's handwriting to show the tattoo artist?"

Theo let the sleeve drop and folded his arms across his chest. "From a check he sent to the old house for us, with our names in the memo line. I found it in a stack of Lee's work papers with a bunch of other ones and took it when I went to New York. It was in my wallet when I went on the Los Angeles trip."

Miles felt a swell of heat despite the frigid air. "You took a check from her and never gave it back?"

"Did you not hear me? It was with a bunch of other ones, and it was about eight years old. All the checks were years and years old, some of them reissues of older ones—he would write that in the memo line. He would send them, and she would put them someplace idiotic like tucked in the finished crossword puzzles or a pile of old magazines. And then I guess lose them, so he had to write new ones. She was always doing that kind of shit with checks. I found this one, and the others, all mixed in with the girls' old coloring books. I took *one* and left the others there for her to find never. Is that okay with you?"

Theo's posture, now, was rigid, his face turned squarely in the direction of Miles's. Miles took his eyes off the road long enough to stare back, but like a traveler gone too long from his hometown, forgetting its habits and idioms, he had lost his fluency in the quirks of his brother's face. At one time he had been able to tell, from the slightest twitch of an eyelid, that Theo had been teased past his threshold and was about to burst into tears; to hear an impending temper tantrum in the sharpness of his inhalation. All of that was years ago, when any impulse would buzz between them like a current, felt by one brother even before the other acted on it, when a germ passed to either would invade the other in the blink of an eye. A faraway, definitively ended time. The composition of Theo's face was the same as always, brooding features assembled slickly under a strong brow. But now it was like their father's face in the pictures:

impassive, all traces of his thoughts as strange and unreadable as hieroglyphics.

Lee had a new man, again, this one a fellow patron at the karaoke bar where she'd been throwing away money every week for months. It was known that he mixed good homemade cocktails and spoke a little French, which was probably what had done her in, because he wasn't particularly good-looking and didn't seem like anyone's genius. He had a dog as big as a wolf, supposedly, and for some reason wore too much purple and a signet ring on his little finger.

Miles's spotty intel had come from Mariolive and Caprice, who, working innocently but in tandem, were only a bit less ineffective than either of them was separately. Lauren, for all her expert stalking efforts, couldn't find even a single Facebook reference to supplement what little was known about her mother-in-law's new relationship. It was not known where the new man came from, what he did for a living, or what wives and children lay crumbled in his wake. Nor what in God's name he was doing making regular appearances at karaoke bars, if not trolling for naifs like Lee.

But without question he had established himself as a regular at Lee's new house out in the suburbs, as evidenced by his car's presence there on each of four spot checks Miles had conducted upon receipt of the intelligence. It was there on a Sunday afternoon, a black sedan parked casually in the carport behind Lee's dented Ford Explorer. There again the following Thursday as Miles inched homeward past the wire-crossed neighborhood in rush-hour traffic. There on a Friday after dark, the lights on in the little house behind it, a hint of movement within. And then, confirming Miles's nauseated suspicions, there again the next morning at sunup, the house still and silent.

Mariolive had said, *At least this one has a car.* Which was more than could be said of certain previous ones, like the one who'd needed Lee to drive him up to Philadelphia once a week to try to see his estranged son. Or the one who'd put the dents in the Ford Explorer driving down 95 in the dark after cocktails.

But still: a grown man, well past any definition of middle age, living unashamedly off a woman with air between her ears. Who lived by the word of her daily horoscope and always kept a tambourine handy to punctuate moments of spontaneous group laughter.

And also: a karaoke bar. An unforgivable fall from grace into the soulless and vulgar. Lee had met their father at a District jazz lounge that no longer existed, a place Miles had long imagined as dark and deliciously moody like the man himself, with threads of light piano melody curling through the air between sets. Their father was the MacHale third of the regular Tuesday-night trio Somebody, Somebody & MacHale (Miles thought he would never forgive Lee for this offense alone, her willful forgetting of the group's full name, which no amount of internet searching could recover), the long-fingered bassist who looked a little like Gil Scott-Heron and stood almost as tall as his instrument. MacHale never talked between sets, but he had a smile like a swallow of top-shelf whiskey. Lee had learned from him about melody and improvisation, about modality, how bebop could lift you, how the blues could crush you.

From that she had found her way, albeit over some thirty-five years, into the drunken sump of some suburban karaoke bar. A place where, by very expectation, the music was shit.

Mariolive estimated she'd been hearing consistent mentions of Mr. Signet Ring for two months. Caprice, marginally more reliable in temporal matters, thought it had been four. In his email to Theo, Miles had taken liberties: *Bro. Hope you are well. Yet another motherfucker living up in Lee's house for the past six months. You have time to go to Safeway?*

Theo, perpetually glued to his devices for work purposes, had written back within a minute: *I'll make time. When?*

He was explaining again about the stakeholder grid. "It's about maximizing your tools to push your agenda forward," he said, drawing squares in the air with long fingers. "You look for the intersection of interest and influence—the people who want what you want and have some power toward achieving it—and you mobilize them. High interest, high influence: that's your first quadrant. That's who you need on your side. They can help you mobilize the folks in the other quadrants. As long as you keep your first quadrant happy, you'll always have some muscle behind your agenda." "Got it," said Miles.

"My mistake last time," said Theo, "was thinking the girls were in the first quadrant. I thought they were with us and that I could use them that way."

"When really . . . ?"

"*Low* interest, high influence. Not actually on the same page as us, not actually ready to go to goddamn Safeway, but influential. You know? Noisy. They have Lee's ear and she listens to them, wrong as they are. They're third quadrant. You keep third quadrant as far away from the task as possible, because otherwise they'll destroy it."

"Ah."

"Which is why, this time, no girls."

This had been their mistake the last time: inviting their sisters. Mariolive and Caprice were a storm of emotion, almost as changeable and ridiculous as their mother. The last time, when things came to light fisticuffs between Theo and the squatter who had infiltrated Lee's shoebox apartment in the District, both girls had simultaneously burst into hysterical tears. *No, Theo, stop,* they wailed, each one clutching one of Lee's shaking hands. *It's fine, it's fine, just let him stay.* When only days earlier, they'd agreed that the non-rent-paying leech of a boyfriend needed to be escorted out of the too-small apartment. When only minutes earlier, they'd been helping Miles gather the boyfriend's belongings—tattered books, crusted-over cookware— and toss them unscrupulously into the cardboard boxes brought for this purpose. Mariolive had thrown herself in front of the boxes, her thick black braid darting from side to side with each shake of her hair. *Let him stay with Mommy.* Which was why it had taken a total of two days, two trips back to the apartment, two separate escalations of physical contact, to get the lowlife to leave, believably for good.

The time before that: uneventful. The brothers working alone, both of their sisters away at college, had sent the motherfucker packing for Philadelphia within twenty minutes of focused intimidation. Then, as now, Theo had been wearing head-to-toe black, and incidentally Miles had too (he had come straight from coaching football practice), and to the infiltrator they had appeared a powerful and unified posse; the infiltrator—a foot shorter than Theo, who had just reached his full MacHale height at that point—had actually cowered and promised he would never again take advantage of Lee's generosity. Lee herself, crying and wringing her hands in the corner of the room, had been easy to ignore; each brother had a lifetime's practice.

Once, MacHale had sent Miles a letter. The letter, etched out in blue ballpoint and in MacHale's erratic, challenging script, confirmed Lee's memory of their first meeting at the long-gone jazz lounge. She had been the girl who turned up to all his gigs in halter dresses she'd made by hand from colorful see-through scarves, swaying her considerable hips at front and center as though they'd hired her as a dancer. Perfect rhythm, and stacked as all hell; but too pretty, an almost unbearable distraction. And too silly to be bothered by the fact that everyone—including MacHale, losing notes on his bass—was watching her. He had never seen anything like her, a black girl with glowing cinnamon skin and hair the color of a well-traveled penny. Sometimes she wore an Afro with a shiny turquoise pick in it, even though by now it was the 1980s and people weren't doing that so much in the District anymore, and on those days he couldn't look at anything but her.

She claimed not to know anything about jazz but somehow could hum all the staple melodies after hearing them once. Often, she brought her own tambourine and accompanied the trio from the lounge floor. The black men and even some of the white ones stared greedily at her, hollering their approval, and even then she didn't stop, her craving for attention apparently bottomless.

I'm sure you know the feeling, read the letter in MacHale's faint handwriting. And even at his first read, Miles *had* known the feeling, having experienced Lee's oblivious attention-seeking many times over, and having also experienced the misery of watching girls he wanted flirt with other men. By instinct he understood why his father had seen no choice but to set aside his bass one day and leave the lounge with her, thirty minutes before the gig was scheduled to end, or to marry her six months later and quit the gig altogether. He certainly didn't need her, the someday mother of his children, swaying and twirling her hips into a future of infinite Tuesday nights.

Belatedly, something dawned on Miles. "Wait," he said. "So you think *I'm* in *your* first quadrant."

Theo, thumbing through emails on his phone, grunted by reply. "If this is done in two hours," he said, "I can get the 7:05 back to New York. There's a gin-tasting event in Brooklyn that I want to get to by midnight."

"Gin at midnight is worth rushing back for?"

"Networking. There's these guys who'll be there that I need to maximize face time with to kick off some new stuff I'm doing in the coding space, and if I hit them up while they're a little bit loose, I might be able to—" He faltered audibly, looked at his brother, and reconsidered. "Anyway, yeah," he concluded finally. "I definitely want to get back for that."

Miles's hand twitched toward the phone in his pocket but instead tightened around the steering wheel. Lauren called this, the type of work people like Theo did in places like Brooklyn, which no amount of description could clarify to outsiders, *alternawork*.

"Unlike Lee," Theo continued, "I can't just leave money on the table. I think about those checks she never cashed, and I just—man." He whistled, a low, pensive sound.

Miles sensed, in the shifts of Theo's upper body, that some familiar, troubled presence had joined them in the car. The mishandling of money had always offended Theo deeply; as a boy, he'd been brought to tears many times by Lee's fretful comments about bills. And from amid the high-piled detritus of the many chintzy apartments Lee had occupied over the years, Theo had somehow sniffed out, and pilfered, MacHale's forgotten child-support checks. There was something so pathetic in it that Miles was almost, *almost* moved to touch his brother's shoulder and to apologize for it, for all of it, on Lee's behalf.

For years the brothers had been inseparable everywhere but at school, where they were two grades apart. Living the other two-thirds of their lives in symbiotic closeness, Miles the mouthpiece for both of them. From playing like the best of friends to fighting savagely at the drop of a hat, their feet and elbows always in each other's face, a constant bodily closeness like nothing Miles would ever experience again. Like a first marriage.

Among other things, MacHale and his wife had argued about this, whether brothers should be together so much, immersing themselves so fully in their two-person games. Lee had discouraged it, having gotten it into her mind that Miles's engineer's brain was stifling Theo's fanciful imagination, or that they were conspiring daily to rearrange the carefully curated array of crystals and candles on her dresser into an unintelligible mess. She wanted them to be apart sometimes, at least long enough for Miles to complete his early homework assignments without Theo's scribbles winding up all over them. She lived by the importance of occasional aloneness, shutting herself into the bedroom with the crystals for twenty-minute stretches while both boys pawed at the door, indignant.

But in those days she had left them to their own devices for hours while she worked—sometimes impossibly long shifts at the Macy's makeup counter, other times sorting garments at the consignment shop in Northeast, using her pretty face and her honeyed words to sell them to their second owners. Each day, when she was out the door, her long skirts trailing behind her like plumage, MacHale had gathered both boys, not giving a fuck about their aloneness, and sat them before the bass in his practice room to listen while he did his finger warm-ups, his spiderlike scales and arpeggios.

He would play a song or two at a time, then go fix himself a Sazerac, and then do another few songs, delighting the boys by weaving made-up lyrics about Lee into the classics. Into "I Cover the Waterfront" he worked lines about how Lee left her men all home alone too much; "So What" became a song about her big butt and how she wore those skirts to show it off to the men at Macy's.

MacHale gave the boys little nips of his Sazeracs (nasty, and then gradually less nasty) and told them jokes he'd heard at the clubs where sometimes he still played jazz. He disliked television but every so often let them watch episodes of *The Cosby Show*, he sneaked them out to two Spike Lee movies in the space of a year. He said no to buying them a Nintendo, no and no and no again, each of thirty thousand times they asked; but in the afternoons before his gigs, he let them sit on his back to watch cartoons while he snoozed on the couch.

And yes, sometimes he sent them into the master bedroom to swap any two of Lee's crystals, laughing riotously and giving them double high fives when they returned triumphant.

And then Lee, returning late at night from doing inventory at the consignment shop, was a wildcard who often shattered the consistent peace of daytime. She might be happy and pull out her tambourine, shaking it and her hips when the whole family was laughing. But she might just as readily make a beeline for the stove and wordlessly slam a pan onto it, storm clouds nearly visible over her slick copper-colored bun as she began to stir-fry chicken and peppers. MacHale making the boys laugh by mimicking her cooking posture with exaggerated flourishes, or pretending to bite the nape of her bare neck like a vampire.

Her high drama, her hysterical turns of phrase. *Tell it to the devil, you piece of shit,* Miles once heard her scream on the front porch under his bedroom window, the words slicing their way into his dream. Her idea of a welcome-home as MacHale returned from one of the many gigs that didn't end till well past midnight. She ranted with wild passion, her words otherwise shrill and indistinct, while MacHale responded at a blessedly normal volume, his low, moody murmur so comforting that before he knew it Miles had drifted back to sleep. In the morning it was as though nothing had happened; she served the boys their eggs and toast with a wide artificial smile, pretty as ever with a purple ribbon braided into her hair.

At one of these gigs, MacHale broke his left tibia and fibula and landed himself in the hospital for a stay that dragged on like a prison sentence, forcing Lee to quit the Macy's job and surrender several of her shifts at the consignment shop. (*Are we going to be poor?* Theo asked, practically in tears; and Lee laughed one of her untamed, destabilizing laughs. *You thought we were rich before this?*)

After that MacHale was on the couch, suffering the television he so disliked with his leg stretched stiff before him, eating half of what Lee offered him and rejecting the other half, irritable each time she reminded him he could not drink whiskey—not even in cocktail form—on meds as strong as the ones he'd been prescribed.

She was moving more slowly than usual, in the first bloom of visible pregnancy with the girls, and she complained often about her aching back and feet in a way that seemed to Miles to be wildly insensitive, considering. MacHale called the boys to him on a Saturday morning. *We need eggs and sausage and green onions,* he said, making eye contact first with Miles, then with Theo, looking back and forth between them; nothing he had ever told them had seemed so important. *But I don't like your mama swishing around in the streets like she does. You boys go with Lee to Safeway and you don't let nothing happen to her. Nobody looking funny at her, nothing. You understand?*

The boys, with their small chests puffed out, gangly Theo actually walking on tiptoe to appear taller, flanked her dutifully on the walk to Safeway.

The eggs were found easily, but in an aisle full of loitering men, so Theo stayed behind with Lee while Miles darted ahead and grabbed a carton, checking the contents for cracks as he'd been shown to do.

Aren't you helpful, said Lee.

She forgot her purse in the aisle with the sausage but didn't realize it till they'd reached the green onions five aisles over; Miles, able to see in his memory's eye the maroon felt satchel slung over one of the shelves, deployed Theo back to that aisle, holding Lee in place with produce-related questions until his brother returned triumphant with the purse.

In the checkout line they stood behind Lee, shoulder to shoulder between her and the other customers, because she was wearing one of those skirts and it just seemed like the thing to do.

At home, their chests puffed out ever farther, they each received praise and a kiss to the forehead from MacHale, and the pride that hummed between them nearly overpowered Miles's eight-year-old body.

A week later, wobbling a bit on his new crutches, MacHale took his sons to the toy store and led them straight up to the checkout counter, behind which was kept all the costliest merchandise. With each hand palming one of his sons' flocked heads, MacHale got the cashier's attention and nodded up to the top shelf.

A—what do you call it, Miles? A Super Nintendo Entertainment System, please. We'll take one of those for these good, good boys.

Happiness hummed between Miles and Theo, their feelings in perfect alignment, one of the last moments in which this would ever occur.

Some weeks after that, MacHale recovered the ability to walk without crutches, and then he was gone, driven away finally by Lee's whims and her nattering.

Thirteen years later, Miles would break his left tibia and fibula playing college football and find himself bedridden for too long and slowed by a cast for even longer, a total of six idle weeks during which he thought he might scratch out his own eyeballs from boredom. When the cast came off, he would feel as though he'd been fired from a cannon, an unstoppable projectile who ran instead of walked whenever possible, and through this experience come to understand finally why after surviving all those years with Lee his father nonetheless could not survive a single solitary second with her post-crutches.

And sometime thereafter, when MacHale's letter, five dense handwritten pages addressed "To my firstborn on his twenty-first birthday"—only a few weeks late—arrived to confirm the projectile theory, Miles would find that he felt satisfied with this explanation. Not that he had ever felt particularly otherwise.

But in the immediate, MacHale's abrupt exit ripped a hole in their little house in Northeast, all its inhabitants left at Lee's mercy. What outcome could MacHale possibly have foreseen but pandemonium? Before anything else, there was Lee's unilaterally scrapping Ella and Pearl, the very good names MacHale had chosen for his daughters-to-be, replacing them with absurdities she'd dreamed up through God only knew what nutty arithmancy. There was an intolerable glut of visitors, relatives of Lee's come out of the woodwork to rock the babies and distract Miles and Theo from their grief with nonsensical questions about school. There were foods served that MacHale never would have tolerated, the delicious staples replaced with eggplant and tofu and loaves of bread with pea-size seeds in them.

There was the unceremonious discarding of the double bass, which MacHale had said he would come back for but which instead became the property of a disadvantaged District high school's music department. MacHale's left-behind shirts and pants, the ones he wore to gigs, a spare collection of twenty or so all-black garments, were swept from the master closet and sent to the Salvation Army. MacHale's Copper Pony went down the toilet and the bottles into the trash can, leaving the bar cart empty. For a short time they lived as in a sanitarium, every word anyone spoke echoing disconcertingly off the bare walls.

It did not last. Soon enough Lee filled the closet with more clothes of her own; the extra space seemed to give her the feeling that she could now acquire as many impractical garments as she wanted, new things from department stores and all the leftover inventory from the consignment shop. Bolts of cloth found all over the place, wrapped around her body in ridiculous ways but still drawing street whistles that burned her sons' ears. She began wearing her turquoise Afro pick again, sometimes in her hair, sometimes tied to a length of cord and worn above her cleavage as a statement necklace. She spray-painted the bar cart magenta and gold and filled the top half with the priciest of each kind of spirit, the bottom with bottles of wine brought to the house by her consignment-shop employees and other friends when they visited.

She collected stacks of papers that nearly reached the ceilings. Recipes torn from health magazines; drawings the girls did that she could not bear to throw away; Miles's and Theo's schoolwork, which miraculously had not lapsed. When mail arrived bearing MacHale's name, she quickly spirited it away, envelopes and all, to places unseen, sometimes returning the most boring contents—old invoices, typewritten correspondence from the city—to her stacks of papers. Lee's treatment of MacHale's more personal mail infuriated Miles: sometimes he'd see the scraps of ripped-up letters in the trash can and want to explode.

Once she opened a check from MacHale and laughed aloud as she crumpled it into a ball before Miles's horrified eyes.

If I threw this on the ground, it would bounce right through the ceiling, she said with a cackle, dropping it into the pocket of her carnelian skirt.

There was no more jazz; she played terrible music on the tape player and then on the CD player, and cheered the children through their homework with that imbecilic tambourine.

Look what I found! she crowed one day, and to Miles's horror she pulled from her satchel two sets of hand cymbals to give her daughters. Their small hands barely fit into the straps, but they screamed with happiness anyway, filling the room with noise.

She gave MacHale's entire vinyl collection to a man she met at work, and for the first time in a while Miles and Theo had something to talk about.

She gave Daddy's records to that guy, said Miles, barging into Theo's room and finding him there with his head in a textbook. *I think they might be dating or something.*

Theo lifted his head, looking sick. *Oh, that's nasty,* he said.

A silence hung between them. After a time, Miles cleared his throat. *Do you ever,* he asked carefully, *think about that one time when Daddy sent us with her to Safeway?*

And then bought us the Nintendo.

Yeah.
Yeah.

Miles had decided immediately upon receipt of MacHale's only letter to him that he would neither mention nor show it to Theo. It went on for five pages and did not once mention MacHale's younger son, nor either of his daughters. The return address, to which Miles sent multiple overeager replies, had turned over to another renter mere days earlier, with no hints as to where MacHale might have gone. Anyway, the letter itself was more than good enough, even the revelation of seeing MacHale's quirky handwriting up close an unexpected joy. Whatever unease he had felt seeing it inked on Theo's arm was repaired by knowing its less-than-honorable origins.

Their exit loomed. "Will Lauren and I see you again soon, then?" asked Miles, flicking on his turn signal.

"Don't know," said Theo.

Miles thought of Mariolive, who by Lauren's report was holding on to her shithead college boyfriend even though she should know better by now, all those letters after her name. Maybe they'd be hitting Safeway again soon, for her.

Into the shabby, wire-crossed neighborhood, he steered the car. Beside him, Theo was silent but alert, scanning the boxy little houses of Lee's neighbors, his phone inert in his pocket.

The grass was freshly cut, a touch that struck Miles as the work of a much craftier adversary than all the sloppy past boyfriends. A dog, chained to Lee's wrought-iron fence and unsurprisingly not wolf-size, slept under Mr. Signet Ring's black sedan. Its collar was turquoise and spattered with glitter and seemed to have sprouted a number of multicolored feathers.

They retrieved the cardboard boxes from the trunk and walked shoulder to shoulder up the walkway, Theo hunching just the tiniest, barely perceptible bit, which Miles appreciated. A hideous summer foliage wreath hung from the front door, and the faintest four-on-the-floor seemed to pulse through a downstairs window.

Both brothers lifted their fists. Theo dropped his, and Miles knocked.

Lee herself opened the door, a fuchsia scarf tied around her silver-and-copper hair. The synthesized sounds of disco music flooded out into the front yard, rousing the dog. Shades of excitement and then concern passed over her expressive face in an instant. "Boys?"

Behind her, sitting on the couch in veritable purple jeans, the *Post* spread out before him, his ringed little finger keeping time against the edge of the newspaper, sat Mr. Signet Ring himself, looking at the brothers with only mild curiosity.

"You," said Theo, maintaining eye contact with the boyfriend as he stepped around his mother, while Miles began the work of containing her in the foyer. "We need to talk to you."

STICKS

George Saunders

EVERY YEAR Thanksgiving night we flocked out behind
Dad as he dragged the Santa suit to the road and draped
it over a kind of crucifix he'd built out of a metal pole in the
yard. Super Bowl week the pole was dressed in a jersey and
Rod's helmet and Rod had to clear it with Dad if he wanted
to take the helmet off. On the Fourth of July the pole was
Uncle Sam, on Veteran's Day a soldier, on Halloween a ghost.
The pole was Dad's only concession to glee. We were allowed
a single Crayola from the box at a time. One Christmas Eve
he shrieked at Kimmie for wasting an apple slice. He hovered over us as we poured ketchup saying: good enough good
enough good enough. Birthday parties consisted of cupcakes,
no ice cream. The first time I brought a date over she said:
what's with your dad and that pole? and I sat there blinking.

We left home, married, had children of our own, found
the seeds of meanness blooming also within us. Dad began
dressing the pole with more complexity and less discernible
logic. He draped some kind of fur over it on Groundhog
Day and lugged out a floodlight to ensure a shadow. When
an earthquake struck Chile, he lay the pole on its side and
spray painted a rift in the earth. Mom died and he dressed the

pole as Death and hung from the crossbar photos of Mom as a baby. We'd stop by and find odd talismans from his youth arranged around the base: army medals, theater tickets, old sweatshirts, tubes of Mom's makeup. One autumn he painted the pole bright yellow. He covered it with cotton swabs that winter for warmth and provided offspring by hammering in six crossed sticks around the yard. He ran lengths of string between the pole and the sticks, and taped to the string letters of apology, admissions of error, pleas for understanding, all written in a frantic hand on index cards. He painted a sign saying love and hung it from the pole and another that said forgive? and then he died in the hall with the radio on and we sold the house to a young couple who yanked out the pole and the sticks and left them by the road on garbage day.

TEARDROP

Joanna Scott

H E CAME TO THE DOOR wearing Bermuda shorts and a Jockey undershirt, gripping a ribbed tumbler I assumed was full of water. Only after he stumbled over the weather strip and I accepted his damp hand to shake did I put two and two together: the liquid in his glass was his beloved Smirnoff, poured from a bottle I knew he kept in the freezer because I had seen him reach for it at parties when he was mixing up a round of screwdrivers.

We were all drinkers in our extended family, but my brother-in-law had emerged over the past year as the only full-fledged drunk among us. I congratulated myself on foreseeing his decline. I had always thought he was a loser.

I did not say aloud, *My sister had a dozen better men vying for her love, and she made the mistake of choosing you.* Instead, I asked him, "How are you?"

"Hanging in there," he said, pulling his hand from my grip and covering his mouth in a failed attempt to muffle himself as he cleared his throat.

As I stood there awkwardly, waiting for him to invite me inside, his vaguely wearied expression suddenly lit with interest. I turned to see what he was looking at just as Bob, the family cat, crept from behind the trunk of an old hemlock in the front yard, stalking an invisible prey in the pine needles.

"Is Jody ready?"

My question stirred my brother-in-law to action. "Jo!" he howled into the house. "Jo, your aunt is here!"

I heard a distant thud, and Jody's voice yelling in reply. "Be there in a sec!"

"What do you hear from Ellie?" I asked. Ellie, my sister, was in the hospital, recovering from a double mastectomy.

"She's coming home tomorrow morning," he said, which I already knew, since I had visited her the previous day, and every day before that. Today was the only day I would not visit my sister in the hospital, for I had agreed to her request to concentrate on her daughter, who might need, my sister suggested, a little extra attention.

"I would pick Sis up myself, but I have to go into the office early," I said, while with my eyes I reminded my brother-in-law that he was a lazy pig who had lost his job back in December and had settled contentedly into dependence upon his wife, an overworked high school social studies teacher. And now that my sister had cancer, my brother-in-law could think of nothing else to do but fill his glass with booze.

"No problem, were all set. Whoa there!" He staggered, causing his morning aperitif to slosh over the rim, as Jody, dressed in a polka-dot T-shirt and denim overalls with grass stains on both knees, squeezed between her father and the doorway and leaped into my arms.

"My little lady!"

"My bestest auntie!"

"I'm your only auntie." I spit on my fingers and rubbed the dirt smudge off her cheek.

"And you're my bestest papa!" she said, leaning out of my arms in an appeal toward her father, grabbing him by his unkempt goatee and pulling his face close in order to cover it with kisses.

"You're my bestest girl!" her father chimed, beaming, reeking of that particular spirit he preferred because of his idiotic belief that it couldn't be detected by a Breathalyzer. "Now you be good today, no shenanigans, eh."

"I'll have her home by—"I began as Jody wriggled out of my arms. She landed on her bottom before I could catch her.

"Ow!"

"Oh, baby, are you okay?"

Her assurance that she was just fine took the form of crazy giggles and a manic lunge for the cat, which she caught up in her arms and squeezed so hard that any other cat would have scratched in fury, while Bob just settled into the embrace with a loud rattle of a purr.

"Take care of Papa," Jody ordered Bob. As she lowered him to the ground headfirst, the cat righted himself with a maneuver that looked very much like a backflip.

"Love you," called her father as I took Jody's hand and led her to the car.

"Love you back!" Jody shouted, for all the neighborhood to hear.

The year was 1965. Lucky Debonair had just won the Derby and an earthquake had rattled Seattle.

"Did you hear about the earthquake in Seattle?" I asked Jody, turning the page of the newspaper to follow the story.

"Is everyone okay?"

"Yes," I lied, deciding at the last minute that my little niece was not ready for a tale of death and destruction.

"That's good." She put the finishing touches on the smiley face she had been tracing in the dust on the train window. "What are we going to do today?" she asked, forgetting the plans we had made over the phone the previous evening.

"Don't you want to go to the zoo?"

"Yeah," she said, then added, upon consideration, "No."

As the train pulled out of the station, we were joined by two new passengers, who ignored the other empty seats in the car and chose the bench across from us, forcing me to change my position and point my knees at an uncomfortable diagonal. The woman was pale, with gray hair and fuzzy eyebrows the color of dried cornstalks. The boy, who looked to be slightly younger than Jody, was Black. He wore a baseball cap backward on his head, and for some reason he wore mittens though it was summer. His features were bunched in an expression of pure rage, as if he were just looking for someone to provoke him into a fight.

"Did you know a brontosaurus weighed like seventy-seven thousand pounds?" Jody announced out of the blue. Instead of addressing me, she spoke directly to the boy across from her, who only glared in response.

"Really?" I tried to make up for the boy's icy manner with my own enthusiasm. "That's incredible!"

"Yep. And it only ate vegetables!"

"You mean it was a vegetarian?"

"It loved to eat. It ate all day." She was still talking to the boy, who, in his quiet seething, appeared to take every word as a direct offense. I crinkled my newspaper in an attempt to distract Jody, but she kept chatting. "It just ate and ate and ate and ate." She made tearing and chewing motions with her mouth. "It mostly hung out in the water near the shore. Wanna know why? Because it was too fat to stand up on land. What a fatso! Except not for its brain. Its brain weighed, get this, just one pound."

"Just one pound!" I echoed.

She bounced on the cushion and in her excitement kicked the woman, who glanced coldly at me to register her indignation.

"Jody," I whispered, taking her wrist. "Please."

She fell back into her seat, and I released her and returned to the newspaper. The train was rolling slowly, grinding along the track past repairmen. Jody waved at them as we passed. One of the men waved back. The train inched along. I absorbed myself for a few minutes in an article about the rising prices of real estate. When we came to a full halt, I looked through the circle on the window. We had stopped in an underpass; on the concrete wall someone had spelled out the word HERO in dripping orange paint.

My attention moved to Jody, and I noticed only then what was happening. Jody was staring at the boy across from her, and the boy was staring back, the children locked in a contest that I worried could only end badly, the two of them barely breathing, the woman in charge of the boy making notations in her notebook, oblivious to the children as each tried to make the other blink, both of them set on nothing less than a victory that could only be humiliating to the loser.

"Jody," I said in a low voice. "Jody, if you don't want to go to the zoo, where do you want to go?"

The woman across from me busily scratched away with her pencil; the train started moving again with a jerk; the two children went on staring, rigid as statues.

"Jody!" I hissed.

She refused to acknowledge me. I watched in dismay as she filled her mouth with a gradual intake of breath, bloating her cheeks and forcing her pupils together in cross-eyed concentration. She held the pose for so long that she grew red in the face. I feared that she would cause herself to faint, and I was about to offer a friendly poke in her cheek to deflate her when the boy suddenly erupted, throwing himself backward against the seat and squealing with uncontrollable laughter. And then Jody was laughing, too, wiggling and bouncing and laughing. The sight of two small children laughing hysterically caused the woman across from me to giggle, and then I couldn't help it, I was laughing too, and then the couple across the aisle from us started laughing, and then the conductor passing through to collect our ticket stubs joined in the laughter. The whole train car was shaking with glee as we pulled into a tunnel, the darkness forming a backdrop behind the window, the interior light illuminating the dust lines of the smiling face on the glass.

By the end of the journey, my ribs ached from all the hilarity. I composed myself, folding the newspaper and checking my purse to make sure it was snapped shut. I gave a friendly nod to the woman across from me to indicate that she and the boy could enter the aisle ahead of us. She reached for the boy's hand and inadvertently pulled off his mitten. I looked quickly away, but a glance had been enough to see that the boy's skin was badly scarred with swollen raw-pink crescents, most likely from some terrible burn. The boy was too happy to care about his injury right then, too carefree to be self-conscious. He was wobbling his head and sticking out his tongue at Jody as the woman tucked his hand back in the mitten. Jody laughed again, and the boy laughed. He was still laughing as the woman tugged him along the platform, and they disappeared into the crowd.

"If you don't want to go to the zoo, where do you want to go? Jody? Hello, Jody, earth to Jody."

We were strolling aimlessly on the sidewalk, surrounded by women carrying shopping bags, packs of teenagers all wearing embroidered bell-bottoms, couples holding hands. It was a holiday weekend, and the stores were advertising sales. A horse-drawn carriage shared the street with taxis. There was cigar smoke, exhaust, and the smell of manure in the air.

We stopped to buy a hot pretzel, and I convinced the vendor to sell it to us for a quarter instead of the thirty cents he tried to charge us. I wanted to show Jody how business transpired in the city, to teach her to be savvy and prepare her for the tough competition in life.

We had just crossed a side street when Jody stopped. I thought she was bending down to tie her sneaker. No, she was leaning toward a homeless man propped up against the wall of the building. The two stumps of his legs, amputated at the knees, extended in front of him. Draped in an army overcoat, he was holding a sign: HUNGRY. His upturned baseball cap on the sidewalk was already full of coins.

Back then I was working as an editorial assistant and during the week commuted into the city. I kept loose change in my purse just so I wouldn't have to fumble with my wallet when I wanted to help out a panhandler. Usually I would make some paltry contribution and move on as quickly as possible to avoid contemplating humanity's inequities. But that day with Jody, it didn't occur to me to reach for change, because I was too appalled by what Jody was doing. Before I could stop her, Jody offered her half-eaten pretzel to the man, a gesture that I was sure would be registered as insulting and provoke, I predicted, a barrage of obscenities, or worse. I grabbed her arm and led her away.

I was as wrong about the man as I'd been about the boy on the train. The man held the half loop of the pretzel high, as if in victory. "Bless you, child!" he called to Jody. With his free hand, he blew Jody a kiss. Jody stretched out her arm as if holding a baseball mitt, then made a show of tucking the kiss she'd caught safely in the pocket of her overalls.

It was Jody who decided she wanted to visit the Cloisters that day. I was surprised that a little girl would choose the Cloisters over the Children's Zoo, but I didn't try to talk her out of it. We took the M4 uptown, and we were inside the museum by noon, sitting at a table in a stone corridor, eating self-service cheese sandwiches and looking over a map of the galleries.

We started out in one of the gardens, where Jody spent a long time sniffing the different herbs growing below the quince trees and comparing their fragrances, trying to decide which she liked best. She admired the wild creatures that were carved into pink stone capitals. In the Glass Gallery, she wondered about the roundel depicting a king perched atop a patchwork horse. She thought it funny that the king was pointing at something ahead of him while his two servants were looking in the opposite direction.

In a small gallery adjacent to a chapel, we found ourselves surrounded by members of a large tour. The docent was speaking loudly, lecturing about the paintings in the room, and we stuck around long enough to learn from her why in one of the paintings, a saint was holding a cittern, and in another painting, a saint was holding a book. We learned that backgrounds were painted gold to make them visible in candlelight. We heard stories of martyrs and prophets and were encouraged to look closely to see secret symbols.

Jody seemed in no hurry to leave the gallery, even after the tour group moved on. There was one painting in particular, hung low on the wall, that caught her attention. It was an oil portrait on wood. Inside the heavy gilt frame was a portrait of a woman, her almond eyes outlined in black, her dark brows curved, her nose exceptionally long and narrow. The face was stiff and unnaturally elongated, making it look mask-like. I wouldn't have thought the painting would be of any interest to a six-year-old girl, until Jody called my attention to the one detail that I had to agree was quite striking: a teardrop, perfectly realistic, on the woman's cheek.

Jody's finger reached precariously close to the portrait. Remember that back then there were no electronic motion detectors protecting paintings. There wasn't even a dedicated museum guard in that particular gallery. The nearest guard was stationed inside the doorway leading into the adjacent chapel. I pulled Jody's arm away from the painting and encouraged her to take a step back. At a safe distance, we stood side by side, examining the teardrop. I wondered how a tiny drop of paint, a visible bump on the wood, could so convincingly render the transparency of a tear. I was fascinated and yet, for some reason I can't explain, troubled by its illusion. The effect of the tear was like a clock's quiet ticking in a dark room, and the longer I stood there, the more unsettled I felt.

"How about we go to the gift shop?" I suggested. "You can pick out something for yourself. My treat." Without waiting for Jody to respond, I took her hand and led her from the gallery.

We stopped in a nearby restroom, and when Jody finished drying her hands ahead of me I asked her to wait out in the corridor. I took an extra minute to reapply my lipstick, and then went out, expecting to find Jody beside the door. But Jody wasn't there. I looked up and down the crowded corridor, then returned into the restroom and called her name. She did not answer. A toilet flushed, and from a stall emerged an elderly woman in a pillbox hat. I went back out into the corridor, my panic growing as I called for my niece, my voice rising loud enough to cause strangers to turn around in search of the disruption.

I thought Jody might have misunderstood my instruction to wait out in the corridor and had gone on her own to the gift shop. But she didn't know where the gift shop was. I considered how easily distracted she was. Maybe she had followed another docent's tour, or gone outside to smell the herbs again. Could someone have lured her away? She was a little girl who lacked the ability to recognize danger. No, I corrected myself—she may have been overly friendly, but she wasn't stupid. Most likely, a security guard had spotted her and recognized that she was too young to be on her own. Where was the room where they brought lost children?

One thought pounded out the next as I rushed across the

Chapter House, down a corridor and through the chapel and into the garden. I could hear the honking of impatient drivers on the street beyond the walls, and, further in the distance, the whine of a siren. I ran back through a corridor, stopping to check every gallery. I tried to be reasonable, telling myself that Jody must be nearby even as I feared the worst. I had lost my sister's daughter. My bestest niece. Dear, sweet Jody.

"Jody, there you are!"

If I had been thinking clearly, I would have known exactly where I would find her—back in the last gallery where we had lingered to gaze at the dot of a teardrop.

"You gave me a scare!" I said, even as I became aware that the elderly woman in the pillbox hat was staring at us from across the room, as if we were the ones on exhibit. I lowered my voice to a whisper. "Don't ever disappear like that again, Jody!"

"Sorry." Her attention was now on her hands, perhaps so she wouldn't have to meet my reproachful gaze. Her lower lip was curled in a pout, and with her thumbnail she picked at dirt underneath the nail of her index finger. I decided to give her an extra minute to feel remorseful and bided time by looking back at the painting, taking in the entirety of the portrait, thinking again that the face was like a mask, unreal except for that very real teardrop that was no more than a pimple of silver paint.

No, not even a pimple. In place of the teardrop was a flat, scratched blankness. A fuzzy nothing that reminded me of the shadow left behind when a candy button is peeled off its paper ribbon.

I looked at Jody, who was working at her fingernail, trying to pry free a fleck of dirt. I understood in an instant what she'd done. Beneath her sharp fingernail was a minuscule silver chip of bone-dry, ancient paint—a pimple of paint.

Jody, I didn't say aloud, we better get out of here! I just grabbed the little hand containing that six-hundred-year-old teardrop, and I led my niece from the gallery, past the woman in the pillbox hat and into the crowded corridor, down the marble stairs, and out onto the street.

•

I used to be assiduous at keeping a personal journal. The record of my life consisted of a daily paragraph or two written in my sloppy handwriting, sometimes in pencil, more often in pen, in one of the spiral notebooks that are now gathering dust in my attic. I don't know why I even keep them around. Rarely do I bother to read what I wrote, for I am apprehensive about what I may learn. I don't like to be reminded of unfulfilled dreams, love affairs that ended badly, tests I failed, job interviews that came to nothing. I don't want to see that the entries written in pencil have faded so much they are largely illegible. Regarding that day in June of 1965 when I treated my little niece to a trip to the city while her mother was in the hospital, I would rather forget how hard I was on my brother-in-law. Perusing words committed to paper fifty years ago, I wince at my vindictive charge that my sister's illness was her husband's fault. I am embarrassed at how oblivious I was to my own shortcomings. I read with disbelief about my indignation, my impatience and false assumptions.

My sister, in fact, would heal and go on to live a good life in remission for another twenty years, happily married to Jody's father, who, shortly after his wife came home from the hospital, would get himself to an AA meeting and spend the rest of his life sober. Jody was destined to grow up and have two daughters of her own and work as a psychologist before succumbing at the age of sixty-three to the same cancer that afflicted her mother. At a New Year's Eve party shortly before her death, she would ask me, "Auntie, do you remember that day you took me to the Cloisters when Mom was in the hospital?"

How could I forget! In fact, it turned out to be too easy for each of us to forget in our selective ways. I would gather from Jody that while she remembered the staring contest with the boy on the train, along with certain other details of the day, she had no recollection of her act of vandalism, and I was not inclined to remind her. Concerning that particular incident, my memory is infallible. Other events of that day, however—my success at reducing the cost of a pretzel, for instance—would be lost to oblivion if I had not provided an account in my journal—luckily, in pen.

•

On the train home that day in 1965, I didn't bother to impress upon Jody the magnitude of her crime. I resolved to keep it a secret for the child's sake, and for the sake of her beleaguered parents. On a subsequent visit to the Cloisters the following month, I discreetly returned to the gallery to check on the painting, but it had been removed from the wall and replaced with a coat of arms. As far as I know, the painting of the weeping woman was never exhibited again.

Jody, meanwhile, would continue to be driven by an insatiable desire to relieve other people of the burden of their sorrows. To the end of her life, her inability to tolerate sadness was as much a fixed trait as the color of her hair, and it accounted for both her cheerful, loving spirit and an impulsiveness she never fully learned to restrain.

Let me, though, take full responsibility for the damaged painting. I was the one who brought Jody to the Cloisters, and I was the one who lost track of her. I chose to protect her with my silence. Only in her absence, after we buried her next to her mother, was I ready to make a full confession. And so, last month, I put my testimony in a letter addressed to the director of the museum, and then I sat back and waited for my punishment.

You can imagine my surprise when I received no reply. I had confessed to covering up an act of outrageous vandalism; I was ready to endure the consequences. At the very least, I expected that the museum would demand compensation for the damaged painting. Perhaps my letter had never reached the director. I picked up the phone and called his office. I told my story to an assistant, who, after hearing me out, put me on hold while she checked the catalogue. Back on the line, she reported the museum had no listing of any work of art in their collection that matched the painting I described.

"Ma'am, you must be mistaken," she blithely insisted.

I asked to speak to her boss. Oddly, the assistant put me through to the Department of External Affairs. What did my story have to do with External Affairs? They wondered the same thing and put me on hold. I was referred from one staff member to another, until I reached someone in a curatorial department, who confirmed once and for all that the painting I described had never existed.

"Really!" I couldn't contain my irritation. "Do you think I just made up this whole story? How about I put it in print and we let the public decide?"

Which brings me to my current predicament. Unable to verify this story but determined to publish it, I have been instructed by legal experts to pretend that any resemblance to real persons is entirely coincidental. Gone is the truth, along with that dried-up drop of paint. Believe what you will. I'll just say that it is not the first time a museum has lost track of an item in its collection. Maybe the damaged painting was destroyed, or it was stolen, or it was discreetly used to repay a debt. My guess is that in one of the unused bedrooms of some mansion hidden at the end of a long, gated drive is a portrait of a weeping woman who sheds no tears.

A Beautiful Wedding
in Nantucket

Anna Sequoia

LAWRENCE WAS THE YOUNGEST SON, the favorite. He was finishing his long residency in thoracic surgery and had already been offered the chance to join a practice in Boston. Now he had met "the girl," the one for him. His parents, who had divorced after 24 years of marriage, were ecstatic. The girl, Alana, had started a dating service with a friend. When she saw his application, she didn't let her friend see it. She kept Lawrence for herself.

"He could not do better," his mother, Barbara said. "She's Jewish. Her father's an attorney. The *grandmother* graduated from Mount Holyoke. Lovely people. Here, look."

Barbara handed the photograph to Margaret, her niece by marriage. They were sitting in the bright kitchen of Barbara's small condo.

"She's tall," Margaret said. The girl in the photo was dark-haired, slender and pretty, with an obvious nose job. She had her arm wrapped possessively around Lawrence's shoulders. Lawrence looked very happy to be held.

"They have a vacation home in Nantucket. I was just up there," Barbara said.

"Have they met Gene yet?" Gene was Margaret's favorite uncle, Barbara's ex-husband.

"No, they have not," Barbara said, annoyed.

Margaret wasn't clear how she had inherited Barbara after the divorce. There was no deep affection between the two of them. She'd always had the impression that Barbara made an effort to be nice to her simply to placate Gene.

"He told me right away that you were special," Barbara had told Margaret. "He said you were curious, smarter than the other nieces, talented. He'd struggled for the kind of opportunities he had, coming from that awful family, and he wanted to make sure that didn't happen to you. You were the first one I invited to our apartment after we married."

Barbara had not been well received by most of Gene's family. For one thing, she was small, barely five feet tall and very slim, in a family of women who generally gained thirty to fifty pounds while pregnant, sometimes more, and never took it off. Gene's sister, Sylvia, a six-foot-tall broad-shouldered woman with massive, rigidly corseted breasts, was particularly disdainful of Barbara.

Barbara's background was modest, but she had style; she had that in common with Gene, and that of itself seemed to irritate the family. She did not look like them, and she did not dress like them. She had grown up in Brooklyn, the daughter of emigrants from Poland, and graduated from City College. Barbara was intelligent, well informed and, to the family's way of thinking, too religious.

"The thing is," Barbara said to Margaret, "for twenty-four years I entertained those people at my house, holiday after holiday. Every Passover, every Rosh Hashonah. I bought gifts for them. I was attentive. I was polite. And believe me, it wasn't easy—any of it. Then the minute Gene and I separate the only ones I hear from are you and your mother. Unbelievable."

"He's their family," Margaret said.

"They're welcome to him. All those years when he was drinking, pissing away his practice, they wanted nothing to do with him. Now all of a sudden he's so popular. I know Gene; he's probably buying crazy expensive gifts for them, buying their affection. You know how he does it, he did it with you."

Margaret bristled. Gene had always been generous with her, but that wasn't what her relationship with him was about. Margaret and Gene had been unusually close most of her life. They would speak several times a week. They would meet near his office uptown and go to lunch or dinner together, or to museum or gallery openings. Gene was lively, amusing and generous. To her way of thinking, he was the only one in her family who was any fun. She missed him.

"Believe me, if those close-minded ignoramuses knew the things I know about Gene they wouldn't be so lovey-dovey toward him," Barbara said. She had finished her tea and with her thumb and forefinger was slowly, systematically biting the edges of the thinly sliced lemon.

For years, Barbara had said nothing to the family about Gene's drinking. She'd said nothing about his pattern of getting drunk and hitting Lawrence's older brother. And it was the first time Margaret had ever heard Barbara even hint at what Margaret had long assumed was Gene's double life.

Margaret had intuited it years before she knew what any of it might mean—her mother mockingly referring to Gene's childhood friend Max as his "girlfriend." The effete publicity stills he had taken as a young man when he was looking for work in the theater, before he finally gave up and went to dental school. Margaret kept one of those shots on the wall of her studio: Gene in profile, looking young and pretentious, his hair in exaggerated waves. Plus, more than once she'd seen him interacting with his producer friend, Severn Crowley: the jokes, the innuendoes, the extravagance and crazy drinking.

"I can't tell you how hurt I am," Barbara said when she telephoned Margaret. "*No one* is going to the wedding. I'm not kidding. *No one.* They sent invitations to all your delightful aunts and uncles, and to all those cousins of yours and *not one* person has accepted. How do you think that makes Lawrence feel? How does that make Lawrence *look*? Not even your *mother* accepted."

"Barbara, it's a wedding on the beach. My father is in a wheelchair. He can't do it. She's not going to leave him behind."

"Oh, I'm not talking about them. But not one of those low-lifes is willing to travel to Nantucket for my son's wedding? What's wrong with them? I thought they all love Gene so much all of a sudden."

"Maybe they're intimidated. Maybe they're intimidated by the fact that it's in Nantucket. Maybe they think it's too high-falutin'."

"Oh come on, that cousin of yours with the rich husband can't come? What about him? With all their fancy friends and their house in Bridgehampton?"

"Barbara, she wears her initials in rhinestones on the lenses of her eyeglasses. You really want her there? In one of her flowered muumuus?"

"Well thank God I have some decent friends. Anita and Jeffrey are coming. They rented a cottage for us. I saw a photo. Charming. At least I won't be alone. But it doesn't look right. What is Alana's family going to think? They have *dozens* of people flying in from all over. It's going to be all *their* friends, *their* family."

"Where is Gene staying?"

"I don't know. It'll be someplace that costs too much money, you can bet on that. All I care about is that he behaves, that he restrains himself for the three nights of parties. That's all I want. A modicum of dignity."

"Three nights?" Margaret's invitation was for a reception given by the parents of the groom on one evening, then the wedding at a beach the next day, followed by a reception on the grounds of the bride's parents' home.

Margaret must have shown her surprise. "I know," Barbara said, "yours is for two nights. The first night is the immediate family."

"Immediate family." That hurt. And it wasn't the only thing. Growing up, Margaret and Gene had always regarded each other as immediate family. It was the two of them versus the rest of the family. And there was more: Margaret's partner, Ruth, had not been invited. Under normal circumstances, Margaret was positive Gene would have made sure the invitation would also have included Ruth.

The whole wedding was not sitting well with Margaret. Her invitation felt more like a command performance: she was being manipulated, and she was annoyed with herself for allowing it. Gene had told her more than once that he and Barbara considered her the "most presentable" of the nieces. Obviously, in this case, part of being "presentable" to Lawrence's new family meant hiding the fact that she was gay. And the truth was that she had almost no relationship with Lawrence. When she would go to Gene and Barbara's house for dinner, Lawrence would sit at the table and barely say a word, then disappear upstairs to play with his cameras or his microscope. He was just a brainy kid with thick eyeglasses, chronic asthma and allergies to nuts, fish, chocolate and peas. The only time she could remember ever having had an actual conversation with him was when her father was in the hospital and Gene urged her to call doctor Lawrence to discuss her father's condition; Lawrence had never called back to see how her father was doing.

"Don't think I'm not dreading Gene being there."

"I don't think he would do anything to embarrass Lawrence."

"I'm not so sure. You don't know how angry he is."

"I think I have an inkling," Margaret said. "Does Gene have anyone coming? Max?"

"Thank God, no."

"I thought you liked Max."

"No Max," she said. "I don't know what Gene said to him. Whatever it was, it had to be something unforgivable. All those years. Even he won't talk to him."

Margaret knew only too well how horrible Gene could be when he was drunk, the kinds of things he could say. She'd put up with that part of him for years, the late night complaints about Barbara, that she was frigid, a cold, conniving bitch, that she was ruining his life. And then one night Gene had called at 1 A.M., his speech slurred, and started berating Margaret's mother. "She's an interfering piece of shit," he said. "Why is she taking Barbara's side in this? She's a ball-buster, she always has been. I don't know how your father can stand her. She's a disgusting fat pig. Who the fuck does she think she is, she's a real bitch . . ."

Margaret asked him to stop, but he continued. She hung up. After that, he cut her off entirely; he refused to speak to her.

"What about his pal Severn Crowley?" Margaret asked.

"He's not coming either. I don't know why. Besides, all he does is bring out the worst in Gene. Who needs him."

"So he's going to be alone at his son's wedding?"

"Yes. That's the way he's made it happen. He's fallen into bed with those cousins of yours and even they won't support him. And you should see the engagement gifts they sent. They'd have been better off sending nothing. Alana told me she returned one of the 'silver' cake servers your darling rich cousin sent. Who in their right mind gives an engaged couple a cake server anyway? You know how many they received? Six. At least most of them were real. Alana took this one back to Macy's. She said she was mortified. It was a clearance item. $12.99. That's what they think of your uncle."

"At least it wasn't inscribed. Alana and Lawrence would have had to keep it."

"Very funny. That would have cost more."

Something had happened the previous evening. Something to do with Gene, but no one would tell Margaret what it was. Barbara seemed even more tense than usual when Margaret arrived at the welcome party. She barely had a chance to sit down at one of the wooden benches when a tall, elegant woman with ramrod posture approached her.

"You're the cousin, Margaret," the woman said, "the artist."

"Yes."

"I'm Alana's grandmother. I am delighted to meet you. I wonder if you wouldn't mind taking a walk with me."

"Of course," Margaret said.

"I'm so glad to meet someone else from Lawrence's family. Barbara mentioned you. She said you and Lawrence spent a good deal of time together when he was young.

That was not exactly the truth.

"I understand your people are from Poland."

"Russo-Poland. The borders kept changing. Our grandfather was from Vitebsk. More likely from some shtetl outside Vitebsk. I really don't know much more than that."

The grandmother pulled herself even more erect. "We're not *that* kind of Jewish," she said, pausing for emphasis. "Our people have always lived in Berlin. Alana's great great grandfather was a judge at the Bundesgerichtshof, the Federal Court of Justice."

They walked a bit toward the water. Then she said, casually, "I'm wondering if anyone in your family enjoys alcohol?"

Oh, here it comes, Margaret thought. Gene. Barbara had said they were "such lovely people," this new family. And here was this grandmother, this elegantly dressed woman with the patrician accent plying her for information, basically telling her that her granddaughter was marrying down by marrying Lawrence, and not being particularly subtle about it. These are not such lovely people, Margaret thought. And then something she hadn't expected welled up in Margaret: a lifetime of hurt and resentment toward her own extended family. That was the moment she decided to just lay it all out.

"My grandmother, Gene's mom, used to have a little glass of 'medicine' before she went to bed," she said, smiling, all innocence. "My mother used to joke about it."

"Is your father a drinker?"

"Not at all. I think I saw him tipsy once in my entire life, on a New Year's Eve. On New Year's Eve he and my mother used to have a couple of highballs. Seagram's Seven Crown with Seven-Up."

"What about the sister? Sylvia, correct?"

"Yes," Margaret said. The grandmother must have made a list with everyone's name and family relationship on it, she thought. Margaret particularly disliked Sylvia, who had taunted her from the time she was a child.

"I think she probably drinks quite a lot when they go on those cruises," Margaret said.

"What about Gene's other brother? Jacob, isn't it?"

"Uncle Jake," Margaret said. He was the one in that family she most despised, the one who used to sneer "Here comes the geeeen-yus," every time he saw her.

"Well, Jake drinks when his Mafia clients come over. It's part of doing business with them."

"His Mafia clients?" the grandmother said, trying to control her voice. She stopped walking.

"Sure. He's an accountant. That's most of his practice. He handles a lot of the Lucchese family's 'legitimate' business people: plumbing suppliers, road contractors, stonemasons, restaurant suppliers, that sort of thing. Usually they do business over a few whiskies. I've known most of those guys since I was a kid."

The grandmother visibly collected herself and they turned back toward the tables.

"You have a brother, don't you?"

"Yes."

"Does he drink?"

"He likes beer. He's an athlete, those guys all drink beer when they finish a game."

"Does he drink a lot of beer?"

"Sometimes. Then he catches himself and pulls back."

"What about you?"

"I like good wine," she said. But she certainly had not had much of that since the break with Gene.

When they got back to the area where guests were sitting on picnic benches, people had already started eating. There was no sign of Gene. Margaret went over to the bar and ordered a gin and tonic. She really didn't care if the grandmother saw it. Then she spotted him: Gene was standing at the top of the flight of wooden steps that led down to the deck. He was holding onto the railing that ran down the center of the staircase, but he looked as though he wasn't seeing anyone. He was blind drunk. Then he began a kind of dance routine, skipping down three steps at a time, as though to music, doing a little twirl, stopping, and then another three steps. By the time he reached the bottom step all conversation had stopped and all eyes were on him.

Margaret felt sick. She turned and saw Barbara, who looked as angry as she had ever seen her. Then Barbara turned away from him, put on her false smile and sat down with her friends Anita and Jeffrey.

Gene walked over to the area where the waiters were serving food, then took his plate and sat down at the only empty table. Margaret couldn't stand it. She went over to him and sat down. He barely acknowledged her. She sat there while he finished his meal, knowing that Barbara would never forgive her.

The next day, a horse-drawn carriage stopped in front of the inn where Margaret and another wedding guest were staying, to take them to the assembly point. There, they climbed into one of the small white buses that were going to take them to the beach.

The bus stopped at the top of a bluff. Several other buses had already arrived and guests were slowly making their way down the path toward the beach. It was perfect weather, sunny and warm but not hot, with high wispy clouds and a slight breeze. Sailboats bobbed off the coast. Margaret looked down at the antique lace chuppah, and the rabbi and Lawrence standing waiting. Barbara was dressed in a pastel chiffon shift that fluttered around her slim legs. She looked deliriously happy. The bride's mother was standing with her.

"It looks like a movie," Gene said. "A beautiful movie." He had walked up beside her from somewhere. He hadn't been with the crowd in the buses. Margaret assumed he must have arrived by cab.

"Gene," Margaret said, and reached out to him, running her hand down the arm of his perfectly tailored jacket. The material was so soft, so obviously expensive. Vicuna, she thought. Of course.

Gene said, "You know, I did miss you."

"I missed you, too, Gene," she said.

"I know that," he said.

Then he took her arm and they walked together down the path toward the wedding on the beach.

ECHOLOCATION

Asako Serizawa

Vision and hearing are close cousins in that they both process reflected waves of energy. Vision processes light waves as they travel from their source, bounce off surfaces and enter the eyes. Similarly, the auditory system processes sound waves as they travel from their source, bounce off surfaces and enter the ears. Both systems extract a great deal of information about the environment by interpreting the complex patterns of reflected energy they receive. In the case of sound, these waves of reflected energy are called "echoes."

—*Wikipedia*

W E—Erin, Mother, and I—are visiting (Aunt) Katy, Aunt in parentheses because she won't stand for it, the stupid title, she told us (though she doesn't mind Doctor, we observed), her pointy glare shriveling our tongues so they learned to disobey us before disobeying her again. We're here in Boston because it's summer, and Mother is giving a lecture at a university (2024: *{Re-}visioning the Refugee Crisis*), and Dad's going to a pharmaceutical rep conference despite the global travel alert. Dad's plane is a 787 Dreamliner. It has a cruising altitude of 43,000 feet. Erin says Dad's at least at 30,000 feet by now, but I'm not supposed to think about that.

Erin is three point two five years older than me, which makes him Responsible, but he's plugged into his laptop, unlikely to notice where I am or what I'm getting into, which at the moment is Katy's bedroom closet. Katy's jumble is magnificent. All soft silver like liquid pearls, but I don't touch anything. Not even her gorgeous clutter of shoes, which are stampeding her milky button-downs puddled on the floor. In back, something glitters. When I reach for it, the closet blurs. I rub my eyes; the button-downs float and multiply. I shut my eyes and step back, step all the way back into Katy's room. Breathe. Centeredness is the only way to clarity. Even here, 2,691 miles from Studio Oneness, I hear Kirsten's voice guiding Mother and me and the neighborhood ladies through her breathing meditation. What do you see? Kirsten says. I see a blue smudge and a beige rectangle that morphs into a plastic fold-down table, a packet of peanuts rattling on a napkin. Intention is the gateway to manifestation, Kirsten says. I intend Dad's 787 to fly steady.

·

Okay, I lined up the shoes. Katy will notice, but Katy's a busy person; she might appreciate the organization. Erin's busy too. He's busy going through Puberty. Puberty makes him irritable in a way he can't explain. I'm supposed to stay three point eight feet minimum away from him. But that can't stop my eyes from traveling.

Erin Before vs. Erin After. There are pros and cons to both.

- Cons: Voice Change. When he laughs, an alien heehaws out of his face. Freaky. Also, he accuses people of thinking things about him they never thought to think about. Very freaky.

- Pros: Greater Intelligence. Which he shows off, but I don't care. Knowledge is a form of Power, and knowledges must be gathered from many different sources. Mother says it's one of the most important things to remember.

"Erin?" My eyes touch his face. "Can unco-surgeons fix things besides cancer?" My voice joins my eyes, and I rub them all over his face; three point eight feet means nothing to sound and light waves.

"*Unco*-surgeon" Heehaw heehaw. "Did you just say *unco-surgeon?*" Heehaw heehaw.

Sarcasm is a Con. I click my pen and write on my hand to Ask Katy Later.

•

Dinosaurs first appeared 230 *million years ago.* 65 *million years ago, a catastrophic extinction event ended their dominance. One group is known to have survived to the present. According to taxonomists, modern birds are direct descendants of theropod dinosaurs.*

—*Wikipedia*

Why were dinosaurs dominant?
Did theropods survive because they turned into birds?
When did humans appear?
Are we dominant now?
Like what's a catastrophic extinction event?
Erin returns to his Code and refuses to google more.

•

"Stop it. What's wrong with them?"
My eyes, Erin means. I turn my back and rub them some more.
"I'm warning you, Mai," he says.
I retreat from the living room and rub my eyes In Private.

•

Once upon a time, people thought robots would take over the earth or take people's jobs. So far there are still poor people to manufacture things, but Jacki our neighbor back home says we should prepare for when the earth turns barren and everyone will have to live like people who still can't afford things like air conditioners, even though they themselves assemble them in boiling factories that squeeze every drop of their sweat before tossing them out like bug husks. *Think* of the inhumanity, she always says. And they don't even get Minimum Wage, which is required by Law, I always say. And Jacki's eyes shine. Oh, honey, forget minimum wage; they get nothing, nada is what they get paid, and who can live on that, or buy air conditioners, with or without an employee discount? Jacki abhors air conditioners. They make the rich richer and the earth hotter and give her a special chill: the Chill of Monstrous Irony. She makes it a point to boycott them.

Dad doesn't approve of Jacki. He says he and Jacki don't see eye to eye, which Jacki says is because they exist on different eye levels. Dad and Mother also exist on different eye levels, but they make it a point to look at each other. Dad says, Nobody should ruin anybody's life, but people need jobs, and companies offer them. What does Jacki do for people besides boycott air conditioners?

Mother doesn't disapprove of Jacki, *per se*. She tells Dad it's the exploitation Jacki objects to. Besides, she says, we have to start somewhere, and every bit counts. Like Jacki, Mother believes today's real war is with the Climate. And she says "we" to spread the responsibility. We, we, I think, like a French person. But Mother also tells me not to hang on to Jacki's every word; hearts can be in the right place but don't always lead to the best results. What Mother doesn't know is that Jacki's connected to The Universe. People like Jacki are burdened by Knowledge, which they feel so clearly they can no longer live like they don't see it. Such people are often shunned by Society, which is set up to encourage Blind Complacency. One day The Truth will prevail and reorder the world as we know it, but Jacki's skeptical if one day will be soon enough. Even Erin, who avoids Jacki, can't deny it could happen. The End, I mean.

•

2:43 P.M. Birds are chirping in the gutters, squirrels are making brown waves in the grass. Sunset is not until 7:47 P.M. Which means five hours four minutes of daylight left. I make my way to the center of Katy's living room and breathe.

•

Explosive decompression: *A steep drop in cabin pressure, causing disten-tion, blistering, even popping of air-filled materials*—such as maybe the eardrums and lungs, we think. Erin says the statistics are low, only ten passenger planes since 1954, which was seventy years ago. But low doesn't mean never. Does it?

•

"What the heck?"
Japanese suicide torpedo "kaiten" found. *Thursday, volunteer divers still searching for Malaysian Airlines Flight 370 nine years after its disappearance found what they believe is an intact Japanese World War Two-era manned torpedo known as the "Kaiten"*. . . *{To read the full story, subscribe or sign in}*

Kaiten 回転, *literally "Turn the Heaven," were suicide crafts used by the Imperial Japanese Navy at the end of World War II. Manned by the Special Attack Unit, the first Kaiten was a Type 93 torpedo engine attached to a cylinder that became the pilot's compartment. Early designs allowed the pilot to escape after final acceleration toward the target, but this was later dropped so that, once inside, the pilot could not unlock the hatch. The Kaiten was fitted with a self-destruct control in case the attack or vehicle failed.*
—Wikipedia

"So someone's in this thing?" Erin says, peering at the news article's greenish underwater image. "Is he, like, vacu-um-sealed—like *preserved?*"

Effectiveness {edit}: Despite the advantages of a manned craft, US sources claim only two sinkings were achieved, while some Japanese sources claim a higher number.
—Wikipedia

"This is insane," Erin says. "When *was* World War Two anyway?"

•

"Erin, can we check on Dad's plane?"

•

Katy has six windows: one in the kitchen, one in the bathroom, two in the bedroom, two in the living room. My favorites are the ones in the living room overlooking a courtyard with one fountain and one oak tree that scatters light in the summer and pelts the windowpanes in the fall until the first snow brings out the notice Courtyard Now Closed For Your Safety. Erin wonders why they even bother; nobody ever goes out there. When I asked why not, he said it's because the courtyard's an idea, something to look at and be reassured by, like a museum. Look at this brownstone, five stories high and shaped like a U, hoarding that patch of grass and those twittering birds splashing in that fountain that's only pretending to be ancient, like something that's been there and will be there forever and ever—

—but won't? I guessed.

Erin rolled his eyes. What we need to ask is who's the beneficiary? Who is it reassuring?

Not Jacki, I guessed again, filing away the word: beh-neh-fishery.

Exactly, he said, prouder of himself than of my Educated Guess.

Is that why Katy bought the apartment?

Erin frowned. Erin has a crush on Katy, even though he's in love with Anja, who is a better programmer than him and draws in a notebook and is complicated. You have zero clue, he said.

I clicked my pen and wrote on my hand to Ask Katy If Fountain Is Fake.

•

4:12 P.M. I kneel on the couch and push my face into the living room window screen. Four floors down, the cherubs on the fountain look sketched. "I bet Anja would love that fountain. She'd adore the naked cherubs," I say.

Erin, who is also on the couch, pulls me from the screen. "You're going to rip it," he says.

I stop for a minute, then push in again, more carefully. "Was Anja born deaf? Is it weird that she doesn't know your voice?"

Erin turns a page in his book.

"What does Anja draw, anyway? Does she draw you?" He turns another page.

"Anja said she saw you signing. She knows you practice. Do you sign to her, Erin?"

Erin plunks down his book and plods to the bathroom. If Katy were here, he'd close the door, but Katy's at work, so I listen to him pee. He pees a long time, then flushes and blasts the tap. When he returns he has two spots on his jeans where he dried his hands.

"Mindfulness is the way to save water," I say.

Erin picks up his book. He's in hardcore Do Not Disturb mode. But this means he can't tell me to scooch three point eight feet away, so I scooch closer.

"Does Anja draw because she misses sound?"

Erin doesn't even twitch. Puberty is powerful. In the window, a fly materializes. It taps and taps the glass, then drops and buzzes along the sill. "I bet Anja would let you make out with her in that courtyard," I say.

Erin slaps his book. He's glowering, but at the fly, which just hopped from the window to the coffee table. Erin's a fly killer. Mother hates it when he uses a book, but books are his weapon of choice, and he's about to bring it down. In my mind, I picture a giant hand plucking the book and frisbeeing it across the floor. But if I'm good, Erin might speak to me, so I say, "Nice! People will pay you big money when flies take over the earth."

Erin's eyes flick toward me, then he slams down the book and inspects The Damage.

•

"Mai, you cow! What'd you do that for?" Erin snatches his book sprawled on the floor and glares at me. He's a master glarer. Which makes me think I'll miss it if I never saw it again.

•

Whales are descendants of land-living mammals. They are the closest living relatives of hippos. The two evolved from a common ancestor around 54 million years ago. Whales entered the water roughly 50 million years ago.

—*Wikipedia*

Why did whales enter water and not hippos?
Will one outsurvive the other?
What happened 54 million years ago?

•

The 787 is two point two five times as long as the biggest known whale. It holds the Guinness World Record for the longest passenger jet. Seven is a lucky number in many cultures, and so is eight. At over 40,000 feet, even the 787 is like a fly squeezed inside a giant fist of air.

Also, Malaysian Airlines Flight 370 was bigger than the biggest known whale, and it vanished like it never existed.

•

"Erin, do you think they'll open the torpedo?"

•

Katy's courtyard ends at a wall, on the other side of which is a lawn, overgrown with thickets preparing to ambush the stone house with the faded patio, two lawn chairs sunning on it. Erin says he's seen people lounging there, but I think what he saw were ghosts.

Can you see ghosts during the day? I asked Katy when she got home last night.

You mean me, personally? Or do you mean can you see them because they exist during the day? she asked back.

Both, I said, impressed by her fine distinction, up there with Spock and Sherlock Holmes, the Greatest Descendants of the Age of Reason and Enlightenment.

Well, I've never seen ghosts, day or night. But that doesn't mean they don't exist, she said.

Can you always see things that exist?
You'd at least see the evidence, I'd think.
Can you *only* see things that exist?
Katy thought about this. I hope so. But sometimes people see what nobody else does.
Like Sherlock Holmes, I said.
Heehaw heehaw. Mai's in love with Sherlock Holmes.
I'm *not* in love with Sherlock Holmes.
Katy snatched my hand. Don't, she said.
She's been rubbing them like crazy, Erin told her.
Do they hurt? She peeled back my eyelids. It doesn't look like conjunctivitis, but it doesn't mean it won't be. I'll see if I can get some drops.
Katy's Enlightened; she looks and also sees. But that doesn't mean she always knows. Seeing is not always knowing, and seeing cannot always solve all problems. Humans often see only what they want to see or believe they're seeing. Dad said that, believe it or not. Does that mean if nobody wants to see you, you don't exist? What about if you want to see but you can't? Or if you can hear but not see? I decided not to ask in front of Erin.

•

"Great, Katy's going to kill you."
Erin's in the kitchen, jabbing me with his toe. I'm evacuating Katy's below-the-sink cabinet: cleaner (chemical); dishwashing pods (chemical); recycling bag with twenty-three take-out containers plastic #6. "Did you have a good chat with Anja?"
Erin stops jabbing. He plods to the fridge and clatters out an ice cube. He leans on the counter, crunching it. The sound makes me shiver. "You're a weirdo, did you know that?"
"You're Prejudiced, did you know that?"
Erin walks away, and I lean into the cabinet. Then I close my eyes and open my pores and feel the cold peeling off the U-shaped pipe. The cabinet itself is warm and scratchy and smells like mold. I run my fingers over the braille of the wood, the nicks and chips like secret dimples, the damp patches like half-peeled scabs, then I touch something: a spongy nest. My fingers shriek, but I don't let them shrink. Darkness is not the

enemy; Fear's the enemy—it's the number one enemy of the human species. Jacki does not support Fear. Think what'd happen if you always reacted or made decisions only out of Fear. Jacki chooses to prepare by (a) doing what she can to prevent The Worst, and failing that (b) doing what she can to survive with Integrity.

•

Dad pooh-poohs The Worst. Next thing you know, I'm doomed because I was born on a Friday the thirteenth, he says.

Dad believes in Reason; he believes it will prevail. Mother wishes he were right, but it's humans she doesn't trust. Look where Reason and technology and science got us, she says.

•

"I want to see the plane. I want to *see* it."

•

Katy's a doctor; she believes in all possibilities, fundamentally. Still, she lives like she doesn't believe in The Worst. Yesterday, she had one tube of tomato paste, three apples, and one tub of organic hummus in her fridge. Katy doesn't plan for Eventualities. When she sees a Lack, like in her fridge, she seeks Abundance, like in the supermarket. Katy fixes things. Which is how we ended up at the supermarket after she got home from work last night. And because it's summer, it was still light out, the gray streetlights holding their breath, and Katy said, Look. I looked up and saw a shadow blip across the sky. When I blinked, the shadow lurched and swallowed the clouds. When I rubbed my eyes, the shadow smudged and strobed like distant lightning before breaking into pinpricks of light that fused into one pair of eyes belonging to one crow perched on the telephone wire, watching the passage of our groceries.

•

"Mai?"

"What?"

"You know what."

And I do. Erin's my brother; he doesn't need to be in the same room to know what I'm doing. Jacki calls it the Mind's Eye, which is a knowing that's independent of seeing and that beats seeing because seeing doesn't always add up to knowing. Feel that tingling on the forehead? That's how you know you *know.*

I sit firmly on my hands and draw my awareness away from my eyes to my forehead and concentrate.

•

The term "human" refers to the genus Homo *(H.). Scientists estimate that humans branched off from their common ancestor, the chimpanzee, about 5-7 million years ago and evolved into several species and subspecies now extinct. Debate continues as to whether a "revolution" led to modern humans ("the big bang of human consciousness"), or a more gradual evolution. According to the Out-of-Africa model, modern H. sapiens evolved in Africa 200,000 years ago and began migrating 70,000 to 50,000 years ago, replacing H. erectus, inhabitant of Asia, and H. sapiens neanderthalensis, inhabitant of Europe. Out-of-Africa has gained support from mitochondrial DNA research which concluded that all modern humans descended from a woman from Africa, dubbed Mitochondrial Eve. Both human and chimpanzee DNA, to which human DNA is approximately 96% identical, are undergoing unusually rapid changes compared with other mammals. These changes involve classes of genes related to perception of sound, transmission of nerve signals, and sperm production.*

—Wikipedia

Why did humans split off from chimpanzees?
How come some humans survived and not others?
Why are we changing like no other mammals?
Are we all changing, or only some?
How rapid is rapid?

Who was Mitochondrial Eve?
Where was Adam?

•

"Do you think we'll ever know who's in the torpedo?"

•

5:45 P. M. Two hours two minutes left. Out there in the world, there are gorillas who have learned to sign, and humans who have learned to see like bats and whales. Daniel Kish is such a human. And so is Ben Underwood. Ms. Alvarez-Johnson called it human echolocation.

•

Human Echolocation: A learned skill whereby humans use sound, such as palate clicks, to navigate the environment.

Clicks (mouth): Clicking sounds made by placing the tongue on the palate and snapping it back. Mouth clicks are used most often by the blind to determine the distance, size, and shape of objects and locate them, but they may also be valuable to rescue workers, such as firefighters.

—*Wikipedia*

But *how* do you stop the earth and sky and sea and people from erupting like a sudden sun blinding the bluest sky, leaving an endless archipelago of beached fountains leaking algae, a verdant hieroglyph of a lost civilization, fluorescing in the permanent dark.

•

"Erin? just at first, will you read to me if I go blind?"

Erin looks up. At first his eyes are blank. Then they widen, tadpoles of fear darting across them. He wakes his phone: Mother won't be home for another hour, and Katy even later. He drums the table. Drums and drums. Then he looks at me, pulls a chair next to his own, lifts the three point eight feet rule, and I know he *knows*, and he's going to tell Mother.

·

The Sun is approximately halfway through its main-sequence evolution. In 5-6 billion years, it will enter the red giant phase, during which its outer layers will heat up and expand to eventually reach Earth's current position. Recent research suggests that the Sun's decreased gravity will have moved the Earth out, away from the danger of engulfment, but it will not prevent Earth's water from boiling and its atmosphere from escaping into space. Long before that, however, as early as 900 million years from now, Earth's surface will already be too hot for the survival of life as know it. In another billion years, the surface water will have disappeared.

—*Wikipedia*

Will whales shrink to the size of moles and enter the earth?
Will they have learned to see underearth by then?
Where will humans be?
Will they have learned to see underearth too?
Why do we exist, Erin?
Is anyone else out there?
How will they find us?
Will they tell our story?
What's going to happen to us, Erin? Are we going to bring about The End?
Are we, Erin?
Are we?
Are we?

OFFICE BREAK

Sharyn Skeeter

JD CALLED JUST IN TIME. I was walking back to my office door after quitting when I had an urge to ask "Boss Susan" to tear up my resignation letter. So, yeah, good thing his call stopped me. I knew I had savings—enough for, maybe, three months—and I was depending on my accounting degree to get a new job. It was unlikely that Martin and I would be starving on the street. No. I knew I couldn't—wouldn't—do that to my son.

So, JD's out-of-the-blue invitation to dinner distracted me from that whim to stay trapped in the stack of forms on my desk. That would've been a disaster, though, as I saw it, JD's and my relationship had been itself almost a disaster. But on his brief call, he sounded upbeat, like his usual jokester self, as if he'd forgotten what I did to him. So, I figured, this dinner— even with my ex JD—would be a well-deserved celebration for my new life, whatever that might be.

But do you know what Susan had me doing? When the system crashed in our human resources office, she told me to tally up the "Race" boxes applicants had checked on forms. I had to do this by hand!

Two things . . . One, Mom didn't slave over filing cabinets for decades to send me to college to do this! And two, I had a problem with reducing a whole application to race. Too many assumptions about people in those tiny boxes. But I don't know. I might've gotten my job because I checked a box. But look where they put me—in human resources, not the accounting job I wanted. Did Susan bother to read my resume or did she just count my box?

Anyway, when the system got patched up—well enough to scan all those forms—she said since I'd started it manually, it would be easy for me to finish. So, Diana, the new assistant, did the applicant interview that I'd set up, while I counted "Race" boxes. Since most were checked "Other," to me, that assignment amounted to eight hours of useless, unenlightened tedium. That's what put me over the top.

But by end of work at five, after saying a few perfunctory goodbyes and cleaning out my desk, I loaded my tote bag with my personal belongings. Then, as I closed the office door, the reality of actually seeing JD—having dinner with him—hit me. Was I really *that* desperate? Was that why I'd agreed to have dinner with him at a midtown bistro? I figured if things got too heated, I'd tell JD that I'd have to get home to Martin. JD would understand that.

Instead of taking a taxi, I felt compelled to walk the ten blocks from the office to the bistro to have time to think without listening to a cabbie's jabbers about midtown traffic. While I waited on a corner for the walk sign, I had a minute to text Martin. "Working late. Have leftovers. Do homework. Love you."

I felt guilty. I hated lying to Martin. (Maybe it reminded me too much of how his father, Ty, had lied to me about "late work nights.") So far, he was a good 12-year-old. He was the beautiful human being who I lived for. The New York City streets hadn't corrupted him yet. But what would I say if he found out the truth about tonight? He liked JD. Why, I don't know. But he might've wanted to see the man himself. My tote bag's straps dug deeper in my shoulder with each block I walked. No, I couldn't tell Martin that I said "yes" to dinner with JD.

Even Martin knew no other men ever called me. He was such a perceptive kid that last Saturday, as I was sipping a glass of Bordeaux in my lacy robe, he told me I looked lonely. I couldn't wait for him to go to bed so I could let out the tears. Yes, if I'd told him about JD, Martin actually might've encouraged me to see him.

Workers were streaming out of office buildings onto packed sidewalks, rushing to bus stops and subway stations to get home or to have a drink. I was ten minutes early when I saw the red and white sign for Chez Josie on the next block. I didn't have a mirror so I hoped that my hastily applied lipstick hadn't left red smudges on my teeth. When I was in high school, my mother had warned me not to wear Fire Engine Red on my espresso skin. She warned that it would just call attention to my color and full lips. Mom said, "I figured if those tan-skinned girls could call themselves café au lait, then you, Agatha, are rich, black espresso." But I figured if those white girls were spending big bucks to plump up their lips with Botox or whatever, I should flaunt what I was naturally graced with at birth.

Anyway, I wanted to look good. But I dreaded JD seeing how life was wearing on me these past six months. I just hoped that my comfortable black pumps, chipped nail polish, and basic navy shirtdress wouldn't give away my precarious situation. When I felt the sweat spot on my back, I panicked and thought in hindsight that I should've taken a taxi. I felt, too, that steamy, humid midtown Manhattan gave my face a sweaty shine.

Inside, in the shock of cool air conditioning, I scanned the room and went up to the hostess stand. I didn't see JD. Chez Josie servers were rushing to place dinner settings on red and white tablecloths. Would he show up at all? I felt flush, suddenly wanted to make a fast getaway before he arrived.

"Can I help you?" The woman's meticulous smile was painted on in purple gloss. I sensed her black-outlined eyes looked past me.

"JD Smith has a reservation."

She glanced at the reservation book. "This way."

The hostess led me past empty tables, some with dirty dishes, to one in the back near the kitchen. I wondered why, the few times I dined out in this neighborhood, I was always seated at back tables. Was it how I looked? I wanted to believe it was just the hostess looking for a clean table. I passed dim wall lights, wooden chairs, and a few booths butting the wall. I was surprised that there weren't many patrons of the after-work crowd here. Sure, it was Wednesday. But this was New York. No evening was too early in the week for a night out. Just a few boisterous men were complaining of bosses—something I knew too well—and a lone graying woman with a tan Coach tote, identical to mine, at the bar with a half-empty glass of white wine, nibbling *pommes frites*. Good. It would be quiet and dark. He wouldn't see my new wrinkles and puffy eyes from too many sleepless nights.

The hostess placed two menus on the table. "Can I get you something to drink?"

As I began to sit, the sight of a man at the hostess stand caught me in the throat. I could barely say, "That's him." Even at that distance I'd recognize his habitual fidgeting as he picked up a menu from the stand and put it back without opening it, twice. He always seemed shy and well-suited for working with computers. Sometimes I was shy, too.

Last fall, he tried submitting a project proposal at my, now old, company. He didn't get the contract, but when he saw me at the pound adopting a kitten for Martin from the same litter that he was, he started a conversation. That led to a date, many dates. After long work days, JD had a way of cheering me and our mutual shyness made me comfortable with him. I didn't feel like I was expected to perform, as I did with some men, like some unnatural, to me, fantasy woman. Some of my cousins could play that role well. I couldn't. But during our trip, he hit a nerve I'd long ignored and I had to end things.

The hostess glanced at him, picked up the menus, and led me toward the front. JD turned to us, half-smiled, and half-waved. I didn't respond. He'd gained a few pounds but this was no doubt JD, the man who I left at a resort in Anguilla in January. He was still oddly attractive at 36, like a nerdy Prince William when the prince had hair.

We were both silent as the hostess sashayed us toward a booth. I wanted to ask flat out why we were seated near the front. Was it because he was white? But before I could say anything, she pointed to his overnight bag and said, "You should have more room here."

Yes, we did need more space. But an overnight bag? What was he thinking would happen tonight?

JD's blue eyes penetrated me for a few seconds and he said, "You're beautiful."

Before I could respond, he turned to the hostess. "Would you tell our server we'd like *fromages?*"

OK. That's it. My head was already bursting. *Just because he doesn't drink, why would he assume I want cheese?*

"And *I'd* like a glass of white Bordeaux," I said in my most properly businesslike voice.

The hostess nodded and disappeared. For a moment we stared at each other like ex-lovers with nothing else to say.

Finally, JD said, "So . . . how's Marty? He was such fun to play ball with."

"His name's Martin. And he's fine, just getting to that worrisome adolescent stage."

The server brought the cheese plate and Bordeaux. With a sip of chilled wine, I was becoming more refreshed after that walk.

"Oh, we all go through that teen awkwardness, don't we?"

"It's not the same for boys like Martin."

He nodded. I remembered how he'd held me during my tearful rants about Trayvon Martin, about how that could've been my own boy. He comforted me then, though, like now, he was silent. At the time, I thought that was because he realized how much he didn't know about me. I sipped more wine to fortify myself against any show of weakness, a skill I developed when Ty left me.

He questioned me again, "And, you? Your job . . . ?"

He was fishing for conversation as he munched on cheese.

I sipped Bordeaux, hesitated, then said, "It goes on. We had some cuts. I was lucky that I wasn't let go last month. I got a minor exec title—with a teeny raise. And I quit today." I tried to sound neutral. Before Anguilla, I'd told him how excited I was about my job. I really wasn't. So now, I was afraid I gave him too much information.

"Hey, why? You told me you always wanted to be an executive."

"Yes, but I was still under the unpredictable HR director." I thought of the untallied "Race" surveys I'd left on my desk.

"If you weren't happy with your job, I'm glad you quit. But why did you stay so long?"

He was annoying me. I didn't know if it was his interrogation or his heavy tweed sports jacket in June, his IT guy all-year dress-up outfit. But whatever it was, I knew he didn't invite me to dinner for small talk and this wasn't the happy "new life" celebration that I'd hoped for.

"Why? What do you think? I have to work. For a few years I challenged myself to stay on that job, yes. But, look, I needed the paycheck. What about you?"

He got that nerdy, thoughtful look that last year I found endearing. Now it bordered on irritating.

"I left my job a few weeks ago . . ."

I put down my wine and leaned back, eyes squinched. "Oh, wait . . . Now I get it! John David wanted to see me to ask for a job? And now I tell you I quit? Ha!"

"Agatha, I'm not here for a job."

"Then what do you want?"

He closed his eyes and breathed deeply.

"My mother died today . . ."

I put down the wine glass and looked at his face for any trace of deception. His mother died, really? But when he opened his eyes, they were glistening, watery. He seemed sincere.

He whispered, "She died this morning in Florida."

His hands were folded, shaking on the table. I pushed aside the cheese plate to touch his hands. They were cold. Mine were warm. For a second, I wanted to close my hands over his to comfort him, but I retreated when seeing my dark fingers on his pale hands jabbed my memory of his slight to me in Anguilla.

But that memory was dulled. Even though the incident was traumatic, the memory of it at this moment—though I didn't like admitting it—seemed trivial and self-indulgent when I looked at the tight face of the grieving man across the table. I covered his hands with mine.

"I'm sorry, JD, I really am."

"You're the only one I've told. I thought you'd understand."

I watched him as he tried to compose himself. He had no tie and his collar was unbuttoned. I sensed how my fingers would feel stroking his neck, twirling the hair on his chest.

"I do want to ask you for something."

I let go of his hands and sat up straight. Yes. I figured he had something more than grief to lay on me. Suddenly, I wanted to get this dinner over with. I wondered if Martin was OK at home alone, when the server with the pulled back hair hovered around the table.

"Before we get involved with whatever you want to ask, I'd like to order *steak-frites*."

I thought eating while I listened to him would curb hunger and anxiety. Then I'd have Martin as an excuse to leave quickly. The server took our order for two of the same. JD's voice was stronger when he ordered, unlike the grieving man he was a moment ago.

When the server headed for the kitchen, JD, with the same tone, blurted out, "Agatha, I need to ask for a loan . . ."

I paused, watched a party of four get seated in the back, counted to ten with one deep breath, stared at JD, and said, slowly, "What? Are you kidding?"

"I'll pay you back in a few weeks."

"How? Even before I quit my job, I was almost living paycheck-to-paycheck and you just told me you're not working."

"This is an emergency. I need a one-way plane fare to Florida tonight to deal with my mother's business."

"OK . . . and . . ."

I tried to deaden the appeal of his earnest look by sitting up rigid, straighter. The sweat spot in my dress back felt drier.

"I have a dream job lined up in Orlando. When my mother got sick, I wanted to be closer to help her. But suddenly she's gone and the new job isn't paying my moving expenses until a few weeks from now."

"Where is this new job?"

"Disneyworld."

"Oh . . ."

He always did like to joke. But even at that I couldn't imagine a job at Disneyworld would be his dream. We'd visited art museums together, discussed Modernists, and the latest storms due to climate change. I couldn't see JD with Mickey Mouse. But he had wanted to help his mother and, with his new position, he would have changed his life to be near to her.

"So, no, Agatha, I don't need a job from you. Only a loan so I can get there now to take care of my mother's affairs."

"So why me? Why come to me for help?"

He looked directly in my eyes. "You know why. Because you owe me."

"I owe *you*? For what?"

"Maybe you forgot Anguilla." He leaned back.

Oh, he would bring up *that*! "Of course, not. How could I?"

The server brought our *steak-frites*. I ordered a glass of Cabernet-Sauvignon. As this conversation was going, I thought I might need the blurring effect of the wine more than the steak. JD's staring was making me nervous.

"You must've forgotten, otherwise you wouldn't ask why you owe me."

"I certainly can remember our trip last winter, but I have no idea what you're talking about."

"OK. Let me remind you."

He sounded like my old high school algebra teacher when half the class "forgot" their homework.

After a pause, he said, "Right after new year's, I took you to one of the best resorts in the Caribbean. You were so beautiful. I wanted to take you to a beautiful place. I'd felt that about you last fall. I felt good about how our friendship . . . and more . . . developed. When, finally, we planned the long weekend together, I had dreams of walking with you on the beach. Spending that time with you would've meant a lot to me. I wanted to ask you to . . ."

I thought, *Why didn't he say it?* but I was afraid to ask, afraid to hear what I might've lost. I said instead, "It was a lovely place. Great beach and food ..."

"Are you listening to me?" he asked, exasperated.

I looked at my *steak-frites*, picked up my fork, and, with a sudden loss of appetite, put it down.

He continued, eyes downcast, as if to himself, "Yes, that's what I hoped for us. But you said something happened."

I was relieved that the red wine arrived. I took a long sip to free my words.

"Yes. We just got there. But after I unpacked and showered, I got a call that my cousin Pearl had died. You know, I had to get back to the City."

"Uh-huh ..." He looked up at me.

"And I got the next flight back."

"You think that was so easy for me?"

"I assumed you ..."

"What? Had lots of cash just for you? I won't even tell you how much it was to change the ticket for you and the hit I took on the vacation package ... and the ..."

I slouched, felt defensive. "I didn't think ..."

"Right! You didn't ..."

He was getting louder. The man being seated in the next booth asked for another table.

"I thought you'd understand that it was an emergency."

"Yes, such an emergency that you didn't want me to go back with you to support you as best as I could ..."

He quieted his voice. To control his anger?

"My family gets very private when a relative dies. They'd never met you. I honestly didn't know how they'd feel about you and me ..."

But I did know. If I'd have allowed him to be supportive of me on such a wrenching trip, they would have respected his compassion. But ...

"Why didn't you? Because I'm —?"

"No." I was getting queasy. I was reminded of what I disliked about those checked boxes on the forms. I quit my job partly because of those, but now I had trouble getting out of the boxes

that we were in. We talked in assumptions that were circular
and easy.

"Look! It was great—no problem—for me to meet Martin."

"Yes. But he's just a kid who loved to play ball with you when
you took him to the park. You don't know my parents . . ."

I was a grown woman. Why was I blaming my parents?
Because I couldn't look at myself hard enough to admit what
I'd done?

"We hadn't even been there a full day and you left."

"I had to."

"How was the funeral?" He leaned back, taut, as if ready to
pounce.

"Sad . . ."

"Sure. And you never called me. No thanks from you,
nothing!"

"I was too upset to think."

I felt like a victim—no, a witness—on the stand in my own
court. The few *pommes-frites* that I'd nibbled on were leaping in
my stomach.

"Yeah, so was I. You know, after you left, I went down to the
bar and drank rum punch until I could hardly stagger out to
the beach. The best I could do was sit in the sand and watch the
sunset. I felt so sorry for myself. Slept it off the next day and,
when I didn't hear from you, got drunk again the next night."

"But you don't drink . . ."

"No, I don't. And I didn't the next night, after I realized what
a fool I'd been."

"A fool? What do you mean?"

"Listen, Agatha, I have a *real* emergency. My mother *really*
died. I have to get to Florida. What I'm asking for is only a
fraction of what I paid for you."

"What do you mean 'real emergency'?"

"Oh, come off it!"

I believe I asked for that rebuff with my goading. I lowered
my eyes, gulped down a few cold *frites* to keep from talking.

He went on, "I was concerned about you—and very lonesome
when you left. Since you didn't pick up my calls to you, that
third day I called everywhere around New York—the church

where you said the service would be, and even your sister who had Martin for the weekend. I tried to reach whoever I could. I wanted to send flowers to let you know I was thinking of you and your family. And nothing! No one knew what I was talking about. They'd never even heard of any Cousin Pearl!"

His face was turning red. I couldn't look at him. I put down my fork and folded my hands tightly in my lap. I tried to control my breathing.

He leaned forward, put his hands flat on the table, and said, "Yeah, I know all about it. You lied! Don't you have anything to say?"

He was right. I lied because I was afraid to show him my pain. That's it! So, now seeing him—JD, ex-lover—across the table, staring at me, waiting, I felt I'd already screwed up. Ha! Him and my job in one day! I had to come clean.

I released a muffled shout, "You don't know how you hurt me."

"*Hurt* you?"

"This is hard for me to talk about. OK?" I had to breathe. His face went blank.

I said quietly and deliberately, "After I unpacked my things, I went to take a shower. I wanted to explore the resort with you in fresh clothes. I remember clearly that, as I wrapped myself in a white towel, you asked . . . you asked me if the black would wash off my skin."

He looked puzzled. "I said that? If I did it was a silly joke. You know me. I like to joke. You said yourself that it made you feel better when you've had a hard day."

"My color is not a joke! *That's* why I left."

"Wait a minute! A joke blew the weekend? Are you serious? I assumed you . . ."

"You assumed what about me?"

He was unsettled. "I thought you would laugh . . . OK, I'm listening."

I ignored him. I was stuck in the recurring memory of how I ran into the bathroom and turned on the shower so he wouldn't hear me crying. My feelings were too raw to talk to him then. When I got myself together and walked out of the shower, I said nothing about his "joke." I only knew I had to leave. I was too upset to tell him what wound he'd picked at.

Now, six months later, sitting in a bistro across a table—a safe distance—from him, I said, "I'll try to explain, if you'll listen." "OK . . ." The rigidity in his shoulders softened. I was beginning to feel safe with him again.

"When I was a high school freshman, I thought I was friends with some girls—white girls—in biology class. I liked science and did well in that class. One day when I went into the restroom, four of them were there giggling. Before I could say 'hey,' they grabbed me and squirted water from the sinks all over me. I couldn't pull away from them. They were laughing and saying I was an experiment. They were trying to wash off my color. When I screamed, they laughed more. Two of them held me down, while the others poured water on me. Some black and Latina girls came in, saw what was happening, and quickly turned around and left. I don't know why they didn't help me. Maybe they were afraid those girls would turn on them, too. When I was totally drenched, they left me sitting in a puddle on the tile floor. I was shivering. By the time a teacher found me, I was sobbing. She called my mother to bring an outfit change. When we got home, my mother told me to hide myself in modest clothes and minimal, if any, makeup. I began to notice that's how she dressed, too. But, me, I was so ashamed that I sat at a back desk for the rest of the year and almost failed bio, while those girls acted as if nothing had happened. They should've been suspended."

As I spoke, his brow grew tight and wrinkled. His lips moved as if he wanted to speak, but couldn't. I felt drained, but strangely relieved—as if, by talking it out, years of pain had begun to float away. Not completely—I still felt the humiliation, viscerally— but it was a start.

I continued, "After that, I couldn't trust anyone. I was afraid to make friends for the rest of my high school years and I was mostly a loner in college."

He whispered, "I'm so . . . so sorry. I didn't know."

"You couldn't have known. All these years, I've kept this to myself. I didn't even tell my sister. I was so embarrassed and traumatized. But I also knew she'd be at that high school the next year. She was a good student and I didn't want her to be afraid to go."

"But what about Martin's father?"

"Ty? Well . . . That was just after college. I couldn't tell him. We never really talked. All I want to say is that he was a nice-looking guy who knew I was flattered by his attention . . . He's never seen Martin . . . I really don't know why I'm telling you all this. I really shouldn't."

He got up to sit on my side of the booth, folded his hands on the table. I couldn't look at him. I was flustered by the warmth of his body next to me.

"I'm sorry. I'm sorry for both of us." He seemed to be talking to himself.

He lifted his arm to hug me but I pulled away, looked at him contrite as he was, and fished my tablet out of my tote. I needed to put things in balance. Maybe it was my training as an accountant.

"What are you doing?"

"Googling. You need to fly to Orlando. tonight I'm looking for the next flight."

"Oh, I . . . But you don't have to do that."

"I want to."

"Are you sure you and Martin will be OK, financially?" For a moment, he held my wrist from the keyboard.

"You need this. I'll manage." I calculated that my leftover vacation pay would cover his fare.

"You're sure?"

"What's your address?"

He handed me a business card. "This is my new address in Orlando."

He watched me type his info to buy the ticket. He turned away from me. I think he was crying.

He whispered to himself, "I wish my mother had known you. I wish *I* had then as I do now."

I wasn't ready to respond to that, so I just said, "I emailed the reservation info to you."

When I started to return his card, he waved my hand away and said, "Keep it . . . so you can find me . . . to collect the debt." I put it in my tote.

When the server leaned over the booth behind my shoulder, I realized that we'd barely touched our food. "How are we doing here? Would you like that packaged up?"

I became aware of the line of waiting diners at the door, the after-work crowd.

"Yes," and I thought *It'll be tomorrow's dinner.*

"Take mine, too. I didn't touch it. Martin can have it."

By reflex I almost yelled at him, *I don't need your charity*, but instead I nodded in acceptance. Then, too late, I knew I'd have to tell Martin the truth that it was from JD. That JD thought kindly of him might make Martin happy.

"Agatha, I'd like for you to visit me in Florida. Would you?"

I couldn't think of anything to say. The server brought the bill. We split the cost, I took my tote and the shopping bag with the warm boxed meals, and we quietly, thoughtfully walked out into the frantic, hot New York City rush hour.

"When you come down, you could bring Martin. He'd love Disneyworld. Since I'll have some spare time in the next few weeks, before my work starts, I'll check out accounting jobs for you, too."

Was he making assumptions again? Maybe. But this was different. I felt he really cared about me. I didn't respond, just looked at him. He held out his hand. I took it, squeezed it, let go, wanted to hug him but patted his arm instead.

Finally, I said, "Martin—and I—might like that. I'll think about it. I'm sorry about your mother."

He kissed my forehead. "Thank you."

I half-smiled and walked toward the subway. When I got to the entrance, I thought I felt him standing under the bistro sign, watching me. I turned to wave and, yes, he was still there.

THE SPECIAL WORLD

Tiphanie Yanique

i. The Ordinary World

Fly was alone. When his parents had dropped him off, they hadn't come in like the other parents had done. He'd asked them not to, felt grown asking. Didn't need their help with his one suitcase, half his weight, or with the backpack strapped to his body. He hugged his mom at the building door. Her eyes were furiously red, like she was witnessing the end of the world. Fly shook his father's hand. His father held on and shook and shook, until Fly lurched away. His own palm sweaty and shaky. His father's hand made a fist—nonthreatening to Fly, but embarrassing all the same.

Yes, it was good to leave his folks at the door. Fly walked in the dorm like he was from the place. Never looked back.

He knew his room number by heart, but he again pulled out the piece of paper that had come in the mail: 504, it still said. He took the stairs, passing other freshmen hiking with their parents—book boxes and mini fridges between them. On the door to 504, Fly's government name was written in bubble letters on kindergarten paper. He took it off, crumpled it to a jagged ball. He wanted to eat it. Chew it down to paste and then crap it out. Instead he let it fall to the floor, roll sadly under the extra-long twin bed.

There was only one extra-long twin bed. Sitting on that one bed in his new college home, Fly felt just like he had the night before. Nervous, and alone in that feeling. Wondering what his roommate would be like. If they would be cool with each other. Fly left the door open. Just in case. He wondered where the other guy would sleep. He guessed they'd have to roll in a cot.

Within the hour the floor got loud and then louder. The parents who had stayed were leaving. The students were losing their minds with glee. Three girls tumbled out of the room from across the hall. They smiled at Fly with manic smiles—like they were laughing at him. "He was cute," he heard one say as they went, but she sounded hesitant. Like she was surprised. And maybe it wasn't even Fly she was talking about. But no, Fly was sure it was him. That was something he had. The good looks.

In this fashion Fly missed orientation that afternoon. Missed convocation that evening.

His mom had packed him industrial amounts of pork-rind chips and beef jerky. They hadn't been Fly's favorite in years, maybe had never been his favorite. But there he was, lying on a quilt his grandmother had made for him, munching on a jerky stick, and staring at the ceiling. He was imagining his body floating five stories up, imagining that there wasn't a bed or floor or five floors beneath him, because there wasn't, not really; everything was connected, which meant that nothing really was keeping him from slamming to the ground but his own awareness of the bed and the floor and the five floors below him. He felt smart thinking metaphysical things like this.

Then a freckled guy with hair so blond it was white leaned slowly into Fly's doorway. The man floated there, at a slant, and then smiled. Fly froze, the jerky a sad flaccid meat hanging out of his mouth.

'You must be . . . ?" The man asked this with his smile and his white eyebrows slanted up.

But Fly didn't answer. The man righted himself and stepped into the threshold. His legs were short and thick and Fly wondered if he was a dwarf.

'You got the single," the man said, and he said it so casually and happily that Fly realized that the man was young—maybe not even a man-man. Though the guy, Fly now took in, had a full bushy blond beard.

"So what are your allergies?" the other said. "Sorry, forgot my clipboard."

Fly felt his mouth open, but nothing came out.

"Dude. I'm your RA," the other said now, almost sternly. Cautiously.

"What's an RA?" asked Fly.

"Oh, shit!" said the RA, regaining his smile. "It means I'm your dude. I'm like your big, uh, brother, or maybe *brother* is the wrong word, or whatever. But anyway. Resident assistant." He high-fived the space on the door where Fly's name had been. "Your name got lost. But anyway, I'm Clive. Look, we'll figure out the allergies later. No worries. But we have a meeting downstairs, like now." His grin went wonky for a second, but reset. He used his whole arm to wave Fly toward him.

Fly spit the jerky out and followed.

"Remind me your name?" Clive asked as they walked down the hallway.

"Fly," said Fly.

At the meeting there was an actual adult. A grown-up. A white woman who also had a hint of beard. What was up with the hair on these people? She introduced all the RAs. Half of the RAs were black—one of those was a guy who seemed girlie . . . but one was an actual girl. Dark-skinned and pretty. When introduced, the girl kept her arms at her sides but waved her hand like a shiver. Fly wished he was on that girl's floor. But when she started talking there was no blackness in her speech to speak of—nothing southern even. Just all "you know" and "like" and even a "yay!" at the end. Fly looked around to see if anyone else sensed her fraud. But no one met his eye.

He was not going to survive freshman year. He was going to end up back home in Ellenwood before the week was out.

But he didn't. He got registered for classes. He started classes. Intro everything: American History, World Religions, World Music. Bare min. credits, because he still wasn't sure he would stick, so why stretch. He started having lunch with the students from Introduction to World Religions, because the class ended right around lunchtime, so why not. They would talk Judaism. Fly didn't think he'd ever met a Jew in his life—except for maybe his dad, who identified as black Jewish every now and then. But now there were a bunch of actual Jews. And they were saying things like "We're not really white," though they sure looked white to Fly. And also: "God as a concept is real. But God as a divine—well, that is a social construction."

Fly started really reading; before he'd read books just for the sex scenes. But now there was still no roommate, so plenty of time. At the World Religion lunches, he would add things like "but for the black man, religion is the only safe route to masculinity. The secular black man as a man is too dangerous." He'd never known, he thought things like this before. It was his father who first spoke these narratives—out loud during dinner, instead of dinner conversation. Now, when Fly spoke, the others would nod or shake their heads. Even the shaking heads were an agreement—like "ain't that something."

Walking out of the dining hall, Fly would pass a whole section of the cafeteria where the black and brown kids hung out. He longed for them. But how did those kids of color all know each other already in week two? There were only like one or two brown kids in his classes. Where were they all and how could he get in?

2. Call to Adventure

Fly didn't actually have any allergies, but Clive kept asking. Clive would do his crazy lean in the doorway, and Fly would offer: "Strawberries?"

"Nah," Clive might say. "Can't be strawberries. They don't give a freshman his own room for that. They would just put you with someone else with a strawberry allergy."

"Peanut butter?" Fly tried again.

"Nah. Same. It's got to be epic. Like music gives you epilepsy or some shit." Clive righted himself. His short legs now in the threshold. "You epileptic?"

"I don't think so."

"Yeah, I don't think so either." Clive had his clipboard; he looked at it and sighed. "So, classes good?" he asked Fly.

"Uh, yeah."

Clive looked up from the clipboard. "I mean, *are* you allergic to strawberries?"

"No."

"Oh, fuck," said Clive, which felt like an overreaction to Fly. Cursing always felt that way. But Clive wasn't looking at Fly anymore. Clive was looking down the hallway. He stared at whatever it was, then looked at Fly and took a deep breath. "Okay, man," he said. "Be good."

With Clive now gone Fly could hear what was coming. His door was open, as always, and he could hear the knocking, the cheery chatting, the hesitation, the sweet rejection. He knew they were making their way down to his room. And when they did, Fly was ready for them. Had been preparing for the fifteen minutes it took the pair to make it to his doorway. They didn't do the Clive lean-in. They stood together side by side, filling Fly's threshold, like his parents might have if he let them come visit. Fly didn't even let them get their spiel out.

"Come on in," he said, just as he'd been practicing in his head.

The girl had dark curly hair, and he'd only seen clearer skin on babies. Smooth and white as milk. A Jew, Fly figured. The boy was wearing glasses that he kept pushing back up his nose. The girl did most of the talking. The boy watched her through his slippy glasses and nodded like that was all he was ever going to do.

"And so we hope you can come to church this Sunday. It's just off campus. Can we count on you?"

"I'm there," Fly said. The guy was Arthur; the girl went by Suzie.

3. *Refusal of the Call*

Fly, finally getting some social life, went to a house party off campus. He went with the World Religion students, though at the party they all gathered on the couch like zoo animals around the one tree in the cage. The tree in this case was marijuana. The sophomore who had brought it called it "Mary Jane," like it was his girlfriend. The house was dark, but still no one was dancing, and Fly didn't make out another black kid in the whole place. An actual girl got up on a table and started gyrating, like a stripper. Fly felt gross for her, about her. But he still tilted forward to look up her skirt. Her white thighs were in shadows. He sucked Mary Jane and leaned back into the conversation: "Judeo-Christianity is a way for straight men to admit their attraction to other men," someone was saying. "Like God is the man you can love without being accused of homoeroticism." Fly put on his serious thinking face and listened. Getting high in college was definitely better than getting high by himself.

The next morning, Sunday, passed with Fly in bed—sleeping. Waking up to eat the last of the beef jerky sticks. Reading a homework essay by Bates on Turkish music, another by Pollard on reggae. He used a highlighter as he read, instead of taking notes. Highlighted most all of the page.

Fly had forgotten all about the two evangelical kids. Forgotten about church, and the Church, and who needed it? Right? Who needed Jesus when you had Peter Tosh? Christianity had been stabilizing when he lived with his faith-crazy parents, but now—now, who knew, maybe he didn't even need stable. He thought on all the ways to become a man—music maybe?

But then Arthur and Suzie showed up. Right in the middle of Fly's midday nap. This time they were a surprise. They came straight to his room, where his door was forever ajar. "I really missed you in church," Suzie said. Which was the first time anyone had claimed to miss Fly besides his mother, who was always claiming it. *I miss you, come visit, I'll wash your clothes, I'll cook a meatloaf.* It was nice of this girl to say she missed him. And then the girl kept saying more things, like, "Should I come meet you here next Sunday before service?" And, 'You can walk me to church. Wouldn't that be nice?"

The boy, Arthur, nodded at her, his glasses still slipping down his nose. "I'll be alone," Suzie said, turning her body more clearly away from Arthur. "Arthur is giving a junior sermon next week, so he's got to be there before everyone else." Arthur looked down at the ground; his glasses teetered. He took them off and cleaned them on his shirt.

"Sounds like a plan," said Fly, who was sitting on his bed in pajamas his mother had bought him, thankful that he had something on besides his boxers. When Suzie and Arthur left, Fly wished he'd said "congratulations" to Arthur. Fly felt bad about this failure for hours. Must be a big deal to give a sermon, he thought, even a junior one.

4. Traversing the Threshold

Clive leaned into the threshold. "I get it," the RA said, smiling. "I totally get it." He pulled his body back up and stood in the doorway. His still surprisingly short legs. 'You're not allergic to anything, man. I mean, could it be that you . . He looked at his clipboard and shook his head. "Sorry, it's just I'm trying to find a reason."

Fly was lying on his bed, in boxers only this time. "It's okay," he said.

"But you have your own room, dude. I didn't get my own room until I was a junior."

Fly didn't know what to say. "Sorry?" he said.

"Thanks, man. I guess you just got lucky. Right?"

"I guess?" said Fly, feeling something musty enter the room. Though Clive never did. Never did enter.

Fly woke up that Sunday to the knocking. He opened the door and there was the girl. Suzie. The churchy Christian Jewish girl, whatever that meant, with the milky skin and curly night-black hair. Fly was only in his pajama pants. His chest bare.

He still had that muscle, left over from basketball, that lean teenage-boy body that can hold a vestigial tautness for years. Suzie pulled her breath in and then shot her eyes to his. Kept them there like her soul depended on it.

"I'm too early," she said.

"Uh, sorry. What time is church again?"

"No, I'm early. But you don't have a cell phone. I mean, why don't you have a cell phone?" She smiled, though the smile seemed mean. "It's just that I'm singing in the choir, so I like to get there on time."

"Yeah," Fly said. He wanted to look down at his crotch. See if there was a stain there from sleep. But he didn't.

"Should I wait out here?" she asked.

"Uh, no. Go ahead. You know. I'll catch up."

She nodded. Something was off with her. It was his body, he knew. His body had made her nervous. Had a girl ever seen his bare chest? He couldn't remember. His mother didn't count. Couldn't count.

"Sorry I was too early," she said. "I really hope you come."

At the elevators she turned to look back at him, and he realized that he was, stupidly, just standing there on his own threshold. He flung himself back into the room.

No, he wasn't going to go to some white people's church with that white girl. No way. His mother would never, ever let him bring her home, anyway. No point. Instead he closed his door, pulled his pajama pants down, and jerked off. He imagined the cum splashing onto her milky face. Imagined her smiling, like a porn star, her enjoying his pleasure through the whole thing.

He got up to go shower down the hall in the communal bathroom. He took long showers. Good way to break up the day. Shower caddy in hand, slippers on his feet, he turned out of his dorm room door, and there was Clive. Clive had a stack of papers in his hand. "Was about to slip this under your door, man," Clive said. He slapped one sheet of paper to Fly's chest.

Fly walked with it to the showers. Read the list through again and again. Campus cults. No matter how many times he read it, Suzie and Arthur's church was still the first one on the list.

After his shower Fly couldn't find his one pair of Stacy Adams. Thought, *Well, that's that.* But then found them. Put on a collared shirt and slacks.

When he opened the doors to the church, the choir was going, and the place was packed with students clapping and smiling and shouting and dancing, and it was a real party up in there. Real gospel music, stuff Fly was familiar with. The young people at the end of the rows noticed Fly come in and smiled bigger. These strangers were so happy he'd come. He smiled back. He could hear tambourines clanging. And one of those steel pans a guest professor had lectured about in World Music. The light was way bright. And there were more Asian people in this one place than Fly knew even existed on the whole campus.

Arthur found him. "Oh, man, so glad you're here!" Arthur looked crazed. He'd also just said the most words he'd ever said to Fly. "Come here, brother!" There was, indeed a space right next to Arthur for Fly. Like everyone had been waiting for Fly. Like Fly was special.

"Did I miss you?" Fly said, feeling weird about it.

"You're here now!" Arthur shouted gleefully. "You're right on time!"

Fly found his place, between Arthur and an Asian kid so tall that even tall Fly had to look up to him. This guy gave Fly a fist bump. Then the place went hushed. Everyone looked ahead to the altar. The choir was up there. Robed like a real black choir. In fact, all the members of the choir were brown or black, except for Suzie, who was there now stepping forward to a single standing mic.

"Suzanna," Arthur whispered to Fly. The whisper had all the lunacy of someone shouting from a mountaintop.

She tipped her face to the microphone and shut her eyes tight. "I," she started. And she held it. The *I*. Held it there with her eyes so tight. "I been buked, and I been scorned." There was no music at all holding her up. She opened her eyes and sang the line again a cappella. This time straight all the way through. "I've been buked, and I've been scorned." She put her arms out with her hands like she was welcoming them all. And then Fly leaned in to look more closely at her, leaned in even though she was so many pews away.

By the time Suzanna was on "trying to make this journey all alone" Fly knew. Suzanna was no white girl. Not one bit. Not a Jewish nonwhite girl, even. Suzanna was a girl raised in the Church, singing since she was a toddler. A black church. This was a Negro spiritual she was singing. Suzanna was a straight-up black girl. It was evident now that she was singing. Of course, Fly could even see it in her face now that he knew. The full lips, the curly hair. The lightest-skinned black girl Fly had ever seen, but now he could see the color rising to her face. She was getting browner by the octave. She was a black girl named Suzanna who could sing spirituals. And Fly knew she was the girl he was destined to love.

In fact, Suzanna was, right now, looking at him. Right at him. Which meant that she knew it too. He stared back at her. Everyone around him started sitting; the song was over. But Fly stayed standing. He stayed standing, and she stayed standing. Until the pastor started talking and Suzie backed up, back into the choir. An all African American and Latino gospel choir, though the senior pastor, it turned out, was regular white. Actually white, with waxy blond hair to settle it. Fly sat down. But he stayed staring at Suzie until she looked away from him. Then he looked up at the ceiling. He could feel that his back was wet. That he was sweating through his clothes. There was probably a wet spot at the back of his shirt. But he looked up at the plain white ceiling and imagined that there was no ceiling. That he was out there in the sky because he was the sky. When the pastor said *Amen* and everyone else said it too, Fly returned from the sky and looked over at Arthur, and Arthur was looking at him. Arthur's eyes were hooded, like he had something very serious to say. But then Fly realized that was just how Arthur's eyes were. Arthur was some kind of Asian. Clear now that he wasn't wearing his glasses.

What was this craziness? Fly thought. What did it all mean? All the people of color were camouflaged. Maybe they had been around Fly all the time, and he'd been too self-absorbed to notice. Maybe he was camouflaged too.

After that service Fly started to feel exhausted practically all the time. In the one extra-long twin bed, he would stare at the ceiling and think about kissing Suzie. Practice it in his mind until he fell asleep. Then he would dream about Suzie, Suzanna, letting him touch her. Even after weeks of walking her to church and watching her from the pews, he'd never even touched her through her clothes. Fly didn't think of his father, Gary Lovett, meeting his first love at church. Of that girl winning Gary's heart over the Bible. Fly had never heard that story, though he'd lived in its wake. Fly just slept a whole lot. Masturbated like it was a job. Practice, he told himself. Then Fly slept some more. He'd heard somewhere that sleeping a lot meant you were in love.

5. *Tests, Allies, and Enemies*

The Jewish kids from World Religions weren't camouflaging; they were doing the opposite. They were posing as people of color—when for all Fly could gather they were really just white. He couldn't be bothered with their lack of authenticity. Fly lunched now with Arthur and the other ethnically jumbled Christian kids. Arthur was from the Midwest. Didn't speak Chinese or Korean. Though he wore what Fly knew was a Buddhist bracelet around his left wrist. Fly's father had worn four or five of them on the same wrist for years. Fly never said anything about it to Arthur, but it surely meant that Arthur wasn't totally devoted to the cult, if the church was a cult. Though it turned out Fly himself was feeling less nuanced. Actually *felt* it. He felt solid, manly, sure of his faith now. Like how he'd been as a boy, with Pastor John. No more experimenting intellectually around thoughts. Now Fly would have an unbending thought and then feel real good about it. Fly had been all A's, but his World Religions grade slouched at the midterm. He couldn't muster a nuanced thought about Bahaullah or Krishna. He was all in for Jesus these days. Felt good. Felt grown.

But music was still Fly and fly. The World Music class was in a lecture hall, but the teacher was some kind of famous person who had been on tour for the whole first half of the semester. Every week there had been a new lecturer, delivering what was some kind of straight genius take on K-pop or Vude. Each teacher gave homework, but Fly never did it. Homework was a dumbing down that was for the actually dumb students, not for him. Instead after each class session Fly would go to the library. Look up the guest professor. Check out the book or books they'd written. Then he and Suzanna—he liked to call her by her full name now—would sit in his room and read. Just read. He his music books, she the Bible or maybe an education textbook. Though maybe she was the only one reading, because it was impossible for Fly to read with her sitting at his dorm desk with her naked feet propped on his bed. Him lying in his bed, sometimes napping, sometimes not; their feet sometimes touching.

Too often Clive would lean into the doorway, smile—"just checking on my chickadees"—and lean back out.

6. *Approach to the Innermost Cave, or, The Meeting with the Goddess*

Thinking about Fly getting saved by the Lord started to make Suzanna slutty. It got so that whenever they talked about it, she would unbuckle his pants and then close the dorm-room door—there was always that awkward thrilling moment with his dick straight up and the door wide open. She would kneel to him and say something deflating like, "I really want to be sitting next to you when you receive Christ. I just want to watch Jesus come on you!" But Fly was nineteen, the horniest he was ever going to be, so he could hold the stiffness, despite. Then she would lick and suck until he said he was cumming. She would use her hands that last minute or so to get him there, and after she would climb into his sore sensitive lap. All her clothes still on, she would make him hold her. Then she would say something bananas like, "When you become a man of God there isn't anything I won't submit to you for." Then sometimes she would cry.

Boy, did Fly want to be a man of God. But to be honest he felt like he was already, had been since he was a child. But

Suzanna needed to witness it. Women were like that, Fly figured. So he drove home one Saturday. Picked up his dark blue
suit, which was newly snug around his shoulders.

"A suit," his father said. 'You drove over an hour just for a
suit? You going weird on us, boy?" Which was ridiculous coming from his crazy father.

"Don't mind that grumpy man," his mother said, all eagerness
and gratitude. She was losing it with joy at Fly's just being home.
Her face was so stretched with the smile Fly thought it looked
scary. "Are you staying for dinner?" she asked. "Meatloaf?" and
then she added quickly, chirpily, "my special meatloaf."

He stayed for dinner but drove back to school that night. The
next morning Fly walked up to the altar when the white pastor
opened his arms. Got himself saved for Suzanna, though he'd
been saved before. Pastor John had saved him from the back of
a van.

But now it was a whole production. More than Fly had
realized. Anyone saved was invited, beseeched, to an ice cream
social after church with the "Prayer Warriors." Arthur was
there, and Arthur took over as Fly's personal warrior of prayer.
Arthur's prayers were loud and urgent and he went on and on,
and Fly could see how Arthur might be a pastor, a senior one,
someday. Then other young men hugged Fly—sincere bear hugs
that were more male affection than he'd ever received. But the
young women hugged Fly too, and that was stranger than the
men. Because the girls hugged and held on, seemed suddenly
to find him, what was it? Not just cute. Sexy; they found him
sexy. They hugged him, met his eyes, gripped him with their
fingers. Offered to bring him ice cream—"What is your favorite
flavor?"—then buzzed around him with what he could feel was
a lusty adoration. "Vanilla could be my favorite," he said, testing
out his theory to a white girl. She looked down at her shoes and
then back up at him, took a gulp of breath, and he saw that her
eyes were watering like she might cry.

Suzanna came up, held Fly's hand until the other girl
blushed and ran off with the ice cream order. He felt Suzanna's
middle finger loosen in his hand; this middle finger's knuckle
rubbed gently across his palm, again and again. He felt his

crotch tingle in anticipation But there were more prayers and congratulations and welcomings to Christ. And then he had to eat the ice cream.

When they got back to his dorm Fly pulled Suzanna through the door. "Leave the light on," she said, even though he hadn't given light or its absence any thought. "I want you to see me." And then she took her clothes off with a drama of someone who'd been practicing, which Fly so appreciated. Her underwear dark with wetness when she finally peeled them off. Then she flung herself onto the bed, face first, raised her hips so he could see all God had given her through the soft plump lobes of her backside. When he put his hand to her there at the center, she pressed herself hard against him, but she was slick. It made him think of candy gone sticky in the sun.

"I want to submit," she said, facing the wall, away from him. "But do it so I don't lose my virginity." Fly feared she might mean in her bum, which he wasn't prepared for. He used his fingers on her, while he stroked himself, trying to figure it out. Then, oh goodness, Suzanna started singing. Humming really, but not like a girl in a porno. Like actual singing. All harmony and lovely. Wow, did he love her. He twisted his fingers in her a little; she raised her voice up an octave. He pushed his fingers in more; she trilled.

"Let me know," he said; "this is my first time too. Let me know, okay?" She didn't answer, but when he slipped it in, not her ass after all, it was so easy, smooth, wet, sticky. He remembered what she'd asked, so he held his pelvis tight and went slow, slow. She sang sweet, so sweetly. He went a little deeper. "No," she said, talk now, no music. He felt her clench tight on him like a fist. He pulled back, slowly, and she released him, but even that was . . . well . . . "Jesus, this is good," he said. Her singing started again. He went in a little, but never all in. He had the idea of what she wanted now. Just a little bit of him, the tip; maybe half of him. No more. Until the too-soon end.

"Was it good?" she asked, facing him now, her arms and legs wrapped around him.

"It was you," Fly said. "It was perfect."

7. The Ordeal

Clive leaned into the doorway. Then he righted himself. Fly was lying alone in his bed, but a little alone time was okay these days—he was exhausted with classes and church. Clive put one hand to his chest and the other out like a stop sign. "I'm not saying you're gay," Clive started inexplicably. "I'm just, man. I just want you to know that it would be okay if you are. And it would make sense why you'd want your own room, you know. No temptation and no weirding anyone out. I get it. It's just. That religious cult group . . ." Clive's hands were still in the same strange position. Hand to chest, other hand out—Fly recognized the gesture. It was like: stop in the name of love, before you break my heart. "But dude," Clive went on, "they could mess you up, you know. I mean, as far as I can tell, God loves the queers as much as he loves the, um, not queers. I just want you to know that that is how I feel." Clive dropped his hands.

"Thanks," said Fly. Clive nodded and then turned around. He stood in the doorway for a minute with his back to Fly. Fly was trying to get some reading done; Suzanna would be over soon. And sex with her, holding back the way she needed him to, was tiring but thrilling, and afterward he would collapse and sleep like, well, like a teenager who'd just had sex. But Clive was still standing in the doorway, and now he turned back around. "Listen. Look." Clive looked at the chair at Fly's desk longingly, as if he wanted to sit down. "I didn't make myself clear just now." Fly felt bad for the guy; he'd made himself clear enough. "It's just . . ." Clive seemed distraught. "Dude, listen. I've seen this before." He stared at Fly pointedly until Fly realized he was supposed to ask something.

"Seen what before?"

"This group. This girl. Specifically, this girl."

Fly wanted to sit up, wanted to face Clive, punch Clive's face, face off in some way. But instead the tension gathered inside Fly's body. Quietly, it gathered. He felt the sweat trickling down his neck.

"I've seen her with other guys. Other freshmen. Gay guys mostly. She turns them straight. Or tries to. Or something.

Breaks their hearts. Because a man still has a heart. You know. Straight or . . ." Clive made his hand wiggle like a fish, "still a man. A human being."

Fly had the question ready for Suzanna: *Do you love me or are you missioning to me for the love of God? Is our sex lovemaking? Or is it conversion therapy? Just because I was lonely doesn't mean I was gay.* And was lonely what gay people were anyway? Fly, again, didn't think he'd ever spoken to a gay guy. Though Fly was pretty sure he'd been lonely his whole life. But then Fly didn't ask Suzanna anything when she came that night. Wanted to. Really did. Couldn't.

8. Atonement with the Father

Instead he dropped Sue off at her dorm room. Then he got in his car and drove home. Did it fast, under an hour. It was late, and the house was dark. He went to his bedroom, straight. He quietly opened his childhood closet, which had been his only closet until just a few months ago. He was looking for the porno video he'd had all these years. The one he'd kept and treasured, the one that had taught him what sex could be. He pulled the video out from beneath the magazines of white girls, which were stacked beneath the magazines of black girls. He cracked the video case. Then he carefully cracked the video itself. Unspooled the film. Sliced it to pieces with a knife from his mother's kitchen drawer. Left the house with the slaughtered tape, dumped the scraps of it before he got back to campus. Never even woke his parents.

That was a Friday. The next day his mother called to cry that his father was leaving her. Fly drove home again that Saturday. He went to his father's little office in the house. The older man was crowded in there, and Fly could tell that he'd been sleeping there at least a few days, maybe weeks—hell, maybe since Fly had left for college. Fly scowled silently at his father boxing things up. All the ridiculous goggles and respirator masks. All the rat-repelling handbooks. Fly wanted to curse or punch, but he couldn't tell what was his place. His father spoke up first. "She wasn't with us in the pictures," he said. "She was separate. Alone on the mantel. And that made all the difference." Which

Fly didn't understand then, and never fully understood either, though after a few slow seconds he realized the "she" was his dad's ex-girlfriend, the same one from the videotape Fly had dumped the day before.

But the elder man didn't seem to be talking to Fly at all, hadn't looked at him yet. He had a book in his hand and was placing it in a box. Instead he looked at the book. Then he finally looked at Fly. He passed the book to Fly wordlessly—*Invisible Man*, by Ralph Ellison. Fly's first copy. It should have been a *thing*. An occasion, religious-like. But it wasn't.

Fly walked away. Walked down the hallway to his own bedroom. His mother was in the kitchen cooking chicken and rice and a baked ziti and a lasagna and whatever else she could fit onto the stove and into the oven. Fly couldn't face her, was humiliated for her. Was for himself too. Divorce was an embarrassing admission, either of failure or of a deeply consequential mistake. Either way, awful. Fly was trying to be a man about it.

He felt exhausted but went back down the hallway again. His father was taping the boxes now. The tape made a loud screeching noise when pulled across the box, was ripped with a violence at its jagged cutting edge. Fly took a deep breath and started in on his father: "I mean, really. Mom put up with you. Clenching your fists every time you heard the voices. And you doing your stupid Hindu meditation chants, or praying to Allah or worshipping anything that anyone else had ever worshipped. Because you couldn't stand yourself. I mean, for years Mom has put up with you. The least you could do was stay by her." Fly's hands were shaking, his arms were glistening with an anxious sweat.

Fly's father looked up at him. But then Fly had to turn away, head back down the hallway, because his father was crying. And so was Fly.

9. *The Road, Back*

Fly headed back down the hallway. He had never seen his father cry before. This was a vexing thing to realize, because Fly had always thought his father was weak, the mental illness and all.

But his father, he realized, had never cried in front of him. Was Dad off his pills? Or was he also devastated by his own leaving? Fly was too devastated himself to consider this much, so Fly drove back to campus, his own tears obscuring his vision. He imagined getting pulled over, getting handcuffed unfairly by a police officer; he imagined spitting in the cop's face, getting so brave and angry he could use his own head to smash the cop's head in. But Fly felt tired just thinking about it. The steering wheel was slick, and he realized it was his own hands sweating. He drove so slowly.

The pain clamped onto his chest as soon as he hit the bed. It hurt so badly he was sure he'd fallen on something hard, but only his soft pillow was there beneath him. The pain was on the left side, where his heart was—it was broken, his heart was.

The next day when Suzanna came to walk with him to church he was still in bed, sweating and in agony. Who knew divorce could feel like this? Suzanna held back at the door, looking at him in horror. "Divorce?" she said, snarling like it was contagious.

"My heart is breaking," he said. The fatigue was in Fly's bones, in his skin—his teeth felt tired. He didn't notice the exact moment when Suzanna left. Had she made it to church?

Later Clive leaned into the threshold, but almost fell over. "Oh, shit," he said. When health services came, they came with a stretcher.

"Mono," the nurse practitioner made clear.

"A sexually transmitted disease?" Arthur said when he and Suzie passed by Fly's dorm room that night. Fly was less sweaty now, but still beat.

"Sorry I didn't come earlier," Suzie said. "A girl got saved so I had to stay and pray for her. You don't have a cell phone, so . . ."

"It wasn't my heart," Fly explained, though Suzie's eyes were so big and he was so tired. "It was my spleen. Swollen. But I'll be fine."

But of course he wasn't fine. His mother had to come get him. His teachers had to get a formal letter excusing him from exams. His final grades would be the grades he'd earned so far, which was good, because he'd barely read a thing since he and

Suzanna had started having sex. Fly slept until Christmas, it felt like. Didn't feel rested until New Year's. His father came once to visit him.

When the spring semester started, Fly was pretty much better. Suzie came to his dorm room the first day back. She came to tell him before he heard it elsewhere. "I was saving myself for the man God created for me," she said, looking Fly in the face with the authority of a grown woman. Arthur had actually given Suzanna a real engagement ring; it gleamed like a miracle on her finger.

.

So Fly was alone again. Four classes this semester. Another music, an English, and an algebra for the gen-ed requirement, plus an African drumming class for his soul. The English teacher was uninspiring, assigned them stupid stuff, like Harry Potter, which Fly felt was beneath him. For the midterm they had to memorize the various stages of "The Hero's Journey," a form the teacher professed was the basis for all Great Narratives. This seemed like such a stupid thing to say that Fly lost all respect for the professor immediately.

But Fly could memorize a list. Critical thinking was beyond him these days; the mono had addled his brain. Or maybe it was the actual heartbreak this time. But he could do the basics (reproduce the algebraic formulas, plug them in), though he never understood the mathematical meaning. What did it matter? Anything that followed a formula was useless anyhow. Still, alone in his room lonely Fly started charting his own life in his notebook—applying the hero's quest to the life he'd lived thus far. But no matter where he started the story he couldn't find his way to a resurrection. So he plugged in his father's life, what he knew of it. There must be a complete narrative in there—dad had lived long enough. But no, there was no heroic return for Fly's father. There never would be.

ANCHOR BABY

Ye Chun

Actually, there's something I want to ask you," he says after bringing the groceries to the living room. "Have you heard of the term *anchor baby? Anchor.* Do you know what it means?"

She can't interpret that look of his, nor the tone of his voice. He may suddenly burst into laughter and say something like *Look at your face; I'm joking.* That seems to be the logical conclusion to such a question, which she senses is meant to insult, as it is unfathomable for a man who has been polite to her to suddenly talk like that. This is the second time he helped her carry groceries upstairs. He also knocked on her door once, telling her she'd left her key in the lock.

He shakes his head, his face settling into a semi-grin, like he is recognizing something deeply ironic in the situation. He sits down on the couch without being asked to, his eyes now level with her belly, which is in her thirty-eighth week of pregnancy, fourteen days before she's due.

She has only vaguely heard of the term before, maybe in the articles she read on the internet while preparing to come here— about raids on the West Coast where this kind of birth service is more developed but also more prone to disasters: women with bursting bellies or suckling newborns taken to police stations for visa fraud or money laundering. Mrs. Liang told her that she was not running a business—she was merely renting out her condo and providing pregnancy and postpartum assistance to her, which was perfectly legal. And what you're doing—coming here on a tourist visa and giving birth to a child—is perfectly legal too. Just relax and enjoy the rest of your pregnancy and bring home a U.S.-citizen baby, she told her after picking her up at the airport, before leaving her alone in this small condo, which was described as "spacious and luxurious" in the ad and had indeed looked so in the photos.

Now the man sits in the living room that she has decked up a little with a vase of lilies, a bamboo plant, and a few stuffed animals for the baby. He looks at her with a glint in his eyes, as if he's stimulated by the fact that he has said what he said, and that now there is nothing to stop him from saying more. Or as if he is equally curious to see how she will respond and what he will do next.

But she has not let the term stick. It doesn't matter what they will call her baby. All that matters is that she will be born a U.S. citizen, not a bastard, as she would have been if she were born in China. But you can go to Hong Kong or Singapore, Lao Li had said. Why does it have to be America? Because, she'd said, I only want the best for our child.

The man is about Lao Li's age, tall, skinny, with big feet; his floor creaks in the evenings when he moves about in the upstairs condo. Fleetingly, she has imagined what he might be like in bed, how he would be different from Lao Li—as she lay alone, among IKEA furniture you see often in China, her body expansive, her skin aglow, with nothing but her own hands to quell her hunger. Besides hunger, there has been a vague trepidation that lurks in the back of her head, the pit of her stomach. Only a couple nights ago, she dreamt of a chicken claw sticking out of her belly, the rest of the chick, or baby, about to spill out.

"I don't know," she says to the man. She must feign ignorance, pretend nothing wrong is going on. Intuition tells her she must not confront. She must look as if she doesn't get it. She is a foreigner, a Chinese—the cultural gap makes his words and behaviors untranslatable.

"I'll look it up for you. You know how to read English, right?" He takes out his cell phone from his pants pocket and starts scrolling and typing on the screen.

She has taken mandatory English from middle school through college, and after finding out she was pregnant, she enrolled at an adult education center to refresh her language skills. If her baby's future is in America, her future will be here too. At least that was what she thought then.

"Why?" she says. "Why do you ask me about this?"

He ignores her question, holding up his cell phone for her to see. "This is what *anchor* means. Take a look."

She reads the first definition:

Anchor —noun

1. any of various devices dropped by a chain, cable, or rope to the bottom of a body of water for preventing or restricting the motion of a vessel or other floating object, typically having broad, hook-like arms that bury themselves in the bottom to provide a firm hold.

Her daughter, who grows bigger in her belly every day, does not have "broad, hook-like arms." On the sonogram, they look rather short and thin, more like fish fins that help her float than metal arms that "provide a firm hold."

"Why?" she asks again. "Why do you ask?"

"Isn't the baby you're carrying going to be an anchor baby? No offense, but am I wrong?"

If her baby who is due in fourteen days is an anchor, then she is a boat. She does feel like a boat with full-winded sails sometimes, ample, unmoored, navigating unknown waters. Why did she decide to sail all the way and drop her anchor here? To give her child the best. But now America is this real place, just like Lao Li, who used to stand for something— maturity, wealth, confidence, success—all the things that she did not have herself, in the end was revealed to be this real, aged person with large pores and a quick temper. The man sitting in front of her was also an idea before—a well-mannered gentleman who has helped her with groceries and told her she'd forgotten her key—but has now suddenly turned real, sinister.

"I don't know what you mean. I need to cook dinner. I'm eating for two, you know." She tries to smile, to be amiable. There is the saying *yi rou fee gang,* to conquer the hard with the soft. That is what she's got—the soft and yielding, which may appear to be a weakness, but she draws power from it. She has done that with Lao Li, never confronting him, giving him what he wants, in exchange for what she wants. What did she want then? A condo, a savings account, a monthly allowance, an easier life than the working one in which you start as an assistant and climb and climb, not ever able to save enough and buy a one-bedroom. At least she knows what Lao Li wants. What does this man want?

He remains seated, looking at her as though she has said nothing. She glances at the door, which is partially closed. Two people are talking and walking down the stairs—her next-door neighbors, who make either tumultuous love or loud arguments across the wall. If she yells now, they may still be able to hear her.

"That Chinese lady who comes here from time to time. Are you related?"

Maybe he is secret police, here to arrest her. And before he does it, showing all his cards, he will torment her first.

"Yes, she is my aunt." To visit my aunt in Maryland, she had told the customs officer when asked the purpose of her visit. Mrs. Liang lives in a house in the suburbs with her postman husband and three children and is always busy. She will chat during the car ride to and from the doctor's office and drop her off outside the condo despite an invitation to come up and have some tea. According to their agreement, Mrs. Liang will *zuo yuezi* for her after the baby is born, sleeping on the couch where the man is sitting right now and cooking for her for a month before she takes the baby back to Shenzhen.

"What about the girl before you? Is she your sister?"

"Who? I don't know."

"A woman about your age who was also pregnant. When she had the baby, she disappeared. And the one before her? Your aunt must have lots of nieces."

To conquer the hard with the soft. But how? *What do you want?* Can she simply ask? Is it too hard a question? *Don't hurt me.* Is it too hard a request?

Or should she try the door? Head over to it, open it up, and cry out. But he will outpace her. He will sprint and shut the door before she reaches it. He will clasp her face, push her to the floor, knock her out, rape her, kill the baby. Is there murder in his eyes? She is not sure. She is still hoping he will turn this all into a joke. Just say, *Sorry, I'm pulling your legs. I'm just kidding. I'm* . . . all those English expressions for humor that Americans are so known for.

She is still being hopeful. That's all she can be. She had hoped Lao Li would divorce his wife, and when that did not happen, she hoped she would give him a son, and when it turned out to be a girl, she hoped she would get this done quickly, smoothly, go back and try again to have a son. Or try something else. She will hope for something else. If there is nothing else, she will at least have a daughter. "At least you won't be lonely anymore," Lao Li said on the phone after she'd told him the baby's sex, which doctors in China would not let you know. That was all he had to say, and it is true: at least she won't be lonely anymore when her daughter is born. Now the question is how to get her daughter safely born.

The man watches her, waiting for her to make a move. That must be his strategy. She needs to pee. She feels a wet patch on her panty. She has been feeling it sporadically, just a drip, which can't mean that her water has broken. For the water to break, she thinks, there has to be more than a drip or two. If it is not pouring, it is squirting. Water where the baby swims. No anchor there, just a tiny, warm lake for her daughter to live. Who is listening right now, kicking, waiting for her to make a decision, a favorable one to alter the situation, to bring safety back to her, let her mature fourteen more days, until she's ready to come out.

Then they will deal with the term *anchor baby*, a name already given to her.

"Do you want some water?" she asks. What's softer than water? She will get out of this spot, pinched between the couch and the TV stand, the man's big feet and long arms reachable to her belly. She will disturb the inevitability in the air. She can see a visible change in the man's eyes. He is taken by surprise. The mockery in his face is loosening its claws, its "hook-like arms."

"Yes, water would be good."

She turns toward the kitchen. He may follow her, corner her, wave the kitchen knife and slice her open, or turn on the stove and burn her belly. There is no lock in the kitchen. And she needs to pee. She pauses by the kitchen door for just a second, walks on to the bathroom, and locks the door from inside. She sits down on the toilet and strokes her belly. She is alone with her baby here, at least. No intruder in this little room. She might need to give birth to the baby all by herself in this bathroom. She misses her mother. She wants to go back inside her, shut her eyes and dream, even though her mother would be just like her, not knowing what to do. Her mother has never quite known what to do, wearing the look of a lost child that she wants never to wear herself. How far she has come, from that dingy little town to Shenzhen, to America, but what difference does it make—to end up being cornered by a man, to be raped, her baby butchered. She will not let that happen to her. She has gone too far to let that happen. But here she is: the water sliding down her thighs, the warm, pinkish water her baby needs to swim in is abandoning her world. She bends over. It is happening: the water breaking, the cramps, the pain, while she is nowhere near a hospital, separated from her cell phone by a door and a man with contempt on his face.

But she needs to go to the hospital. She cannot imagine giving birth here all by herself. She will pay them cash. Where is her cash? The man could be ransacking her cash right now. Why did she let him in? She has no one but herself to blame if something goes wrong. Everything is already going wrong. Baby in distress. Is the baby still alive? It is still moving, agitated and unsure like herself. She wants to see her gynecologist, the

Chinese-American woman who carries herself with ease and confidence. She wants her daughter to be just like her one day, at home with her environment.

"Are you okay?" the man asks outside the bathroom door.

"I'm in labor," she cries. "I need to go to the hospital."

"I can help you," the man says after a pause, "I can take you to the hospital."

But she cannot trust him, cannot open the door and let chance decide her fate. She will have to do it all by herself. She is howling in pain now, making those awful sounds she does not believe she can make. "Go away. Leave me alone," she yells at the door in between moans. She will have to make it all by herself

"I'll help you," he says again through the door.

But she will not trust him. She is all on her own now, depending on nothing but this one body that's splitting into two.

•

Does he mean it? Will he really help? He wants to help. He has helped her with her groceries, has told her she'd forgotten her key. He has no intention to hurt her. He just wanted a chat, about something that was bothering him, to get something off his chest. He is not a criminal. He has never hurt anyone intentionally. He has done nothing except ask a sensitive question so that she will tell him the truth. The truth— that is all he wants, a slight confession, when everyone keeps their secret to themselves. He wants some truth. Maybe he will give her a piece of truth too, if she gives him one first. An exchange of truth between a man and a woman who would otherwise be total strangers. Nothing personal. Just the truth for once. But what is the point? No point maybe, just this final need to be mean, to be open. Is the only way for him to be open to be mean?

"Listen, I'm sorry I said those things to you. I want to help. Please trust me. I want to help you."

•

The pain is all there is. The rest ceases to matter. She is squatting on the floor now, which is wet, sleek with the same pinkish water that was inside her. The child is in there, with her big dreamy head: cry if she can, cry with her. She is moaning so loud she's deaf to it. She is unreachable. She is locked in her pain. No one can hurt her. She is protected by her pain. Her body feels nothing but the pain. That's all she is, the pain. She, the pain, and the baby who knocks her head on her life's edge, this thin edge.

·

What's he going to do? Leaning against the door that's locked from the inside, listening to a woman's horrible sound of giving birth, the sound you choose to forget the moment you come into the world. A mother's sound. His mother, dead for thirty years. You had a big head, your big head wouldn't come out, too big for me, they had to cut me open. I thought I was going to die. His mother who would say anything out loud, who pinned her suffering like a gold brooch on her chest, who talked and talked until he was gone, shipped to the war, no more on the receiving end of those verbal spits. You must not die. You must learn to stay alive. You can't be so selfish as to die on me. I've got no one else. Did she really say that? A mother to her only child whom she claimed to love so much she had to hurt. She just couldn't help it. It was not personal. It's not that I'm angry at you. It's only that I love you too much. If I didn't, I wouldn't have said all those things. It's your life, you know, no one else's. If you lose a limb, it's you who will live without a limb for the rest of your life. That's why I'm mad. I'm not going to be there to live with your lost limb for you. She is dead. He is here, with no lost limbs, but with something else missing, something harder to see. His mother knew but she pretended not to know. She would only see her own suffering reflected back to her, which made her angrier, at herself, at him, the extension of her suffering life. Let's die together. Let's drink this trembling glass of pain till it's over. Cheers.

Another birth. Another woman who has no idea what she is doing. Another child coming into the world pre-burdened with pain.

.

She must stay awake to this pain, not overcome by it, not slipping under. She must trust that her body knows what it is doing. Her body has outsmarted her again and again—conceived a child weeks before she even knew, made her throw up and then eat this and that so that the baby could grow, made her laugh and cry so that the baby could learn to feel, made her reckless and afraid so that the baby could have a will. The baby must be pushing too, with her little arms and legs and blind fists, beating, flailing, reaching for the light. She must follow her body, which is breaking itself.

.

Is the weeping from inside him? His mother had kept her last breath until she saw him. She had waited, with such a will, holding that tenuous, tenacious breath, to touch his hand, to tell him that she had loved him more than anything else in this world, despite everything, and he said, I know. He forgave her. Or maybe she didn't say anything, just looked at him, with those embittered eyes, so accustomed to bitterness that bitterness was in everything they saw. Eyes that looked at him, and then suddenly were looking at nothing. I've done my best, he read in her eyes. I wish I could have done better, but I've tried.

He slips to the floor against the door. His mother had pushed and pushed, and his head was caught in the narrow canal. He could have died, but was kept alive, brought to this moment to be a door apart from a birth taking place. "You can do it," he says to the door. "Breathe, breathe."

He feels as if he is once again crawling in the birth canal, the strangling tunnel toward life, his mother's heart pumping blood, her moans drowning his own. He will make it out somehow, as there is no turning back.

.

She sees the crown, the creamy black moss. She takes loud, shuddering breaths as her body continues to push and break. She sees the earthy head, the close-eyed face, blood-streaked, stunned, wrinkly. The baby is skidding out, mouth agape, gasping for air.

From beneath her body, she takes hold of this red child, who tenses, gathering her might into a howl. An announcement or protest? For hunger or fear? She palms her lopsided head and puts her to her breast. The baby smells her, groping for her nipple, and latches on. She holds her there, rocking lightly. Their voyage has just begun.

CONTRIBUTORS

Claire Boyles (she/her) is a writer, mom, and former farmer who lives and writes in Colorado. A 2022 Whiting Award winner in fiction, she is the author of *Site Fidelity*, which was longlisted for the PEN/Robert W. Bingham Award, the Colorado Book Award, and the High Plains Book Award. Her writing has appeared in *VQR*, *Kenyon Review*, *Boulevard*, and *Masters Review*, among others. She has been a Peter Taylor Fellow for the Kenyon Review Writing Workshops and has received support from the Kimmel Harding Nelson Foundation, the Bread Loaf Orion Environmental Writers Workshop, and the Community of Writers. She teaches in Eastern Oregon University's low-residency MFA program in Creative and Environmental Writing.

Joseph Bruchac, an enrolled member of the Nulhegan Abenaki Nation, is a traditional storyteller, musician, and a writer. For over fifty years he has been creating literature and music that reflect his indigenous heritage and traditions and has been a featured storyteller at the National Storytelling Festival and the British Storytelling Festival. Author of over 170 books for children and adults, his poems, stories, and essays have been published in hundreds of magazines and anthologies, ranging from *Parabola* and *The Paris Review* to *National Geographic* and *Smithsonian Magazine*. His many honors include a National Endowment for the Arts Writing Fellowship, a Rockefeller

Humanities Fellowship, an American Book Award, and the Lifetime Achievement Award from the Native Writers Circle of the Americas. A graduate of Cornell University where he was the varsity heavyweight wrestler and editor of the student literary magazine, *The Trojan Horse*, he also has a Master's degree from Syracuse University and a Ph.D. from the Union Institute of Ohio. His experiences include three years of teaching in Ghana, West Africa, eight years running a college program in a maximum security prison, and five decades of martial arts training, with black belts in Brazilian jiu-jitsu and Pentjak-silat where he holds the rank of Master. His most recent books include *Rez Dogs* (Dial)—a novel in verse, *Peacemaker* (Dial)—a story based in the time of the founding of the Haudenosaunee (Iroquois) League, and *One Real American* (Abrams)—a biography of Ely Parker, Seneca Chief and Civil War general.

Chitra Banerjee Divakaruni is the award-winning author of 18 books. Her themes include the Indian experience, contemporary America, women, immigration, history, myth, and the joys and challenges of living in a multicultural world. Her work has been published in over 100 magazines and anthologies and translated into 29 languages, including Dutch, Hebrew, Hindi, and Japanese. She has won numerous awards, including an American Book Award and the international Premio Scanno Prize. Divakaruni also writes for children and young adults.

Her latest novels include *Oleander Girl* and *Before We Visit the Goddess*. Two of her books, *The Mistress of Spices* and *Sister of My Heart*, have been made into movies. Her novels *One Amazing Thing* and *Palace of Illusions* have been optioned. Her collection of stories, *Arranged Marriage*, has been made into a play.

She was born in India and came to the United States to continue her education, receiving a Master's degree from Wright State University in Dayton, Ohio and a Ph.D. from the University of California, Berkeley.

She currently teaches in the nationally ranked Creative Writing program at the University of Houston. She serves on the advisory board of Maitri in the San Francisco Bay Area and Daya in Houston, organizations that help South Asian or South Asian American women in abusive situations. She is also closely involved with Pratham, an organization that helps educate children (especially those living in urban slums) in India.

She has judged several prestigious awards, such as the National Book Award and the PEN Faulkner Award.

Toiya Kristen Finley, Ph.D., Nashville native, has been a freelancing writer and editor her entire adult life. She earned a doctorate in literature and creative writing from Binghamton University. Over her career, she has published more than 80 works of fiction, nonfiction, comics/manga, and games, and has over 20 years of experience writing in a range of genres, tones, styles, and voices. She gained editorial experience interning at Henry Holt's imprint, Owl Books. At Binghamton, she founded the literary journal *Harpur Palate* and served as its managing/fiction editor.

In 2011, she cofounded the Game Writing Tutorial at GDC Online with Tobias Heussner and served as an instructor in 2011 and 2012. In videogames, she has worked as a game designer, narrative designer, game writer, editor, and diversity/narrative consultant (or some combination of the five) on everything from AAA titles to mobile games to games for children to small indie projects. Recent work includes writing visual novel Siren Song (Stardust Works), copyediting for *Destiny 2* (Bungie), and developmental editing on *Insecure: The Come Up Game* (Glow Up Games).

A presenter at conferences throughout the year, she has lectured on freelancing and storytelling and led workshops on narrative design and game design. She is a member of the IGDA Game Writing Special Interest Group's Executive Board. *The Game Narrative Toolbox* (CRC Press), a book on narrative design she coauthored with Jennifer Brandes Hepler, Ann Lemay, and Tobias Heussner, was published in 2015. *Narrative Tactics for Mobile and Social Games: Pocket-Sized Storytelling* (CRC Press), which she edited and contributed to, was published in 2019. Her latest books are *Freelance Video Game Writing: The Life & Business of Digital Mercenary for Hire* (2022) and *Branching Story, Unlocked Dialogue: Designing and Writing Visual Novels* (2023) both from CRC Press. Of late, she has been working on her own visual novel series, beginning with *Incarnō: Everything Is Written.*

Tom Gammarino is author of the novels *King of the Worlds* and *Big in Japan*, and the novella *Jellyfish Dreams.* His short stories and essays have appeared in *American Short Fiction, The Writer, Entropy, The New York Review of Science Fiction, The Tahoma Literary Review, Cleaver Magazine, The New York Tyrant, Bamboo Ridge, Hawai'i Pacific*

Review, The Hawai'i Review, and *Interzone,* among others. He is the co-editor of *Snaring New Suns: Speculative Works from Hawai'i and Beyond.* He holds an MFA in Creative Writing from The New School and a Ph.D. in English from the University of Hawai'i, and has received a Fulbright fellowship in creative writing and the Elliot Cades Award for Literature, Hawai'i's highest literary honor. In 2021, two of his short stories, "What We Yield" and "Interface," were nominated for the Pushcart Prize. Originally from Philadelphia, he lives on O'ahu, where he teaches Creative Writing, Science Fiction, Magical Realism, and Jazz Lit to some highly awesome high school students. You can find him at www.tomgammarino.com.

Amina Gautier is the author of three short story collections: *At-Risk, Now We Will Be Happy,* and *The Loss of All Lost Things. At-Risk* was awarded the Flannery O'Connor Award and the Eric Hoffer Legacy Award and a First Horizon Award. *Now We Will Be Happy* was awarded the Prairie Schooner Book Prize in Fiction, the International Latino Book Award, the Royal Palm Literary Award, and was a Finalist for the William Saroyan International Prize. *The Loss of All Lost Things* was awarded the Elixir Press Award in Fiction, the Phillis Wheatley Award, and was a Finalist for the Hurston/Wright Award, the Paterson Prize, the John Gardner Award, and shortlisted for the SFC Literary Prize. Gautier's work has been supported by the Bogliasco Foundation, the Breadloaf Writers Conference, Callaloo, the Camargo Foundation, the Chateau de Lavigny, Dora Maar House/Brown Foundation, the Flamboyán Foundation, Hawthornden Castle, Kimbilio, the Kimmel Harding Nelson Center, the MacDowell Colony, the Mellon Foundation, the Ragdale Foundation, the Sewanee Writers Conference, the Vermont Studio Center, and the Virginia Center for the Creative Arts. More than one hundred and forty of her short stories have been published, appearing in *AGNI, American Short Fiction, Boston Review, Callaloo, Latino Book Review, Los Angeles Review, Oxford American, Southern Review,* and *TriQuarterly* among other places. For her body of work, Gautier has received the Blackwell Prize, the Chicago Public Library Foundation's 21st Century Award, and the Pen/Malamud Award for Excellence in The Short Story. Gautier is Associate Professor of English at the University of Miami, where she is the 2021-2024 Gabelli Senior Scholar.

Before running away from home, **Anthony Lee Head** was a trial lawyer, history teacher, and martial arts instructor living in San Francisco. In a fit of middle-aged madness, Tony and his wife Cheri drove 3,500 miles to begin a new life in Playa del Carmen, Mexico. There they bought a run-down hostel near the Caribbean Sea, which they transformed into an award-winning hotel and bar. Living in a white sand and blue water paradise, they rented rooms, poured drinks, ate tacos, blogged about their unconventional life, practiced their Spanglish, and navigated the endless challenges of living and working in a foreign land. After a decade of inhabiting the wonderfully strange world of expats, they returned to California, bringing with them a pack of rescue animals—four dogs and six cats. After settling just north of the Golden Gate Bridge, Tony began formal practice as an ordained lay Zen Buddhist, while beginning to indulge his inner storyteller. *Driftwood: Stories from the Margarita Road*, which has been named to the *Kirkus Reviews* Best Books of 2020, is his first book. He is currently working on both a new novel and a memoir based on his adventures in Mexico. Connect with him at www.anthonyleehead.com.

Meng Jin is a novelist whose stories explore the ways in which the self fractures and attempts to cohere in times of hallucinatory social, political, economic, environmental, and technological change. Jin is obsessed with form and how the novel can bend, break, and expand to realize the stories writers need to tell today. Her first novel *Little Gods* was published by Custom House. The *New York Times* wrote that it "expands the future of the immigrant novel" and NPR's Gabino Iglesias called it "one of the most complex character studies I've ever read." Jin is a Kundiman fellow, a David TK Wong Fellow, Elizabeth George Foundation Grantee, and Steinbeck Fellow. Her short prose appears in *Best American Short Stories* 2020, *Pushcart Prize XLV*, *The Threepenny Review*, *Guernica*, *Ploughshares*, *Vogue*, and elsewhere.

Charles Johnson, Ph.D. (Philosophy), University of Washington (Seattle) professor emeritus and the author of 26 books, is a novelist, philosopher, essayist, literary scholar, short-story writer, cartoonist and illustrator, an author of children's literature, and a screen-and-teleplay writer. A MacArthur fellow, Johnson has received a 2002 American Academy of Arts and Letters Award for Literature, a 1990 National Book Award for his novel *Middle Passage*, a 1985 Writers Guild award for his PBS teleplay "Booker," the 2016 W.E.B.

Du Bois Award at the National Black Writers Conference, and many other awards. The Charles Johnson Society at the American Literature Association was founded in 2003. In February 2020, Lifeline Theater in Chicago debuted its play adaptation of *Middle Passage*. Dr. Johnson's most recent publications are *The Way of the Writer: Reflections on the Art and Craft of Storytelling*, his fourth short story collection, *Night Hawks*, which was nominated for a 2019 Washington State Book Award, and *GRAND: A Grandparent's Wisdom for a Happy Life*. With Steven Barnes, he is co-author of the graphic novel, *The Eightfold Path*. Johnson is one of five people on posters created in 2019 by the American Philosophical Association (APA) to encourage diversity in the field of philosophy. His forthcoming book in November 2022 is *All Your Racial Problems Will Soon End: The Cartoons of Charles Johnson*.

Pauline Kaldas is the author of *The Measure of Distance* (novel), **Looking Both Ways** (essays), *The Time Between Places* (stories), *Letters from Cairo* (memoir), *Egyptian Compass* (poetry), and the textbook, *Writing the Multicultural Experience*. She also co-edited *Dinarzad's Children: An Anthology of Contemporary Arab American Fiction* and *Beyond Memory: An Anthology of Contemporary Arab American Creative Nonfiction*. She was awarded a fellowship in fiction from the Virginia Commission for the Arts and has been in residency at MacDowell, the Virginia Center for the Creative Arts, the Writers Colony at Dairy Hollow, and Green Olive Arts in Morocco. She is Professor of English and Creative Writing at Hollins University. Visit www.paulinekaldas.com.

Vijay Lakshmi (Chauhan), born and educated in India, came to the U.S. as a Senior Fulbright Fellow to do her post-doctoral work at Yale University. She had already published *Virginia Woolf as Literary Critic* (Heinemann), and nearly two dozen scholarly articles in various journals. Lakshmi took to fiction writing after emigrating to the America. Her first short story collection, *Pomegranate Dreams and Other Stories* was published by Indialog in 2002 and 2004. Her short fiction has been published in several journals, including *Wasafiri* (London), *Orbis* (London), *Paris Transcontinental* (Paris); *Amelia* (US), and *Asiatic* (Malaysia). Her stories have have been collected in several anthologies—*In Search of Sita* (Penguin, India); *A Rainbow Feast: New Asian Short Stories* (Marshal Cavendish); *Bridges: A Global Anthology of Short Stories* (Temenos Publishing) and *Where We*

Started (Paris). *My Dogly Days* (Austin and MaCauley 2019) is her first book for young adults.

Clarence Major's recent novels include *Dirty Bird Blues* (reissued as a Penguin Classic, 2022), *Thunderclouds in the Forecast,* (2022), *The Lurking Place,* (2022), and forthcoming *The Glint of Light,* (2023). He has recently contributed to *The New Yorker, The Harvard Review, American Scholar,* and other periodicals. His poetry was selected for inclusion in *The Best American Poetry,* (2019). Winner of a National Book Award Bronze Medal (1999), a Fulbright-Hays Exchange Award (1981), the Congressional Black Caucus Foundation Award in 2015 for "Lifetime Achievement for Excellence in the Fine Arts," the PEN-Oakland Reginald Lockett Lifetime Achievement Award for Excellence in Literature (2016), and many other awards and grants. In 2021, he was elected to the Georgia Writers Hall of Fame, and in 2022 he was selected writer of the year by the Georgia Writers Association. He is Distinguished Professor Emeritus in the English Department, University of California, Davis. Major travelled extensively in Europe and Africa, and lived for extended periods in France and Italy. His papers (manuscripts and correspondence) are in the Given Collection at the Anderson Library, University of Minnesota, Minneapolis, Minnesota. Clarence Major lives in northern California.

Donna Miscolta's third book of fiction *Living Color: Angie Rubio Stories* was named to the 2020 Latino Books of the Year list by the Las Comadres and Friends National Latino Book Club. It won the Next Generation Indie Book Award for Multicultural Fiction and an International Latino Book Award for Best Collection of Short Stories. Her story collection *Hola and Goodbye: Una Familia in Stories,* winner of the Doris Bakwin Award for Writing by a Woman, won a 2017 Independent Publishers award for Best Regional Fiction and an International Latino Book Award for Best Latino Focused Fiction. She's also the author of the novel *When the de la Cruz Family Danced,* which poet Rick Barot called "intricate, tender, and elegantly writ-ten—a necessary novel for our times." Her work has also appeared in literary journals and anthologies. Raised in National City, California, she has long resided in Seattle where she worked in local government for thirty years. Find her at www.donnamiscolta.com.

Pamela Painter is the award-winning author of five story col-lections, and co-author, with Anne Bernays, of *What If? Writing*

Exercises for Fiction Writers. Her stories have appeared in *The Atlantic, Harper's, Five Points, Ploughshares, SmokeLong Quarterly, New Flash Fiction Review,* and *FlashBoulevard,* among others, and in numerous anthologies such as *Sudden Fiction, Flash Fiction, From Blues to Bop: A Collection of Jazz Fiction, Four Minute Fictions, Flash Fiction, Micro Fiction,* and *New Micro.* She has received grants from The Massachusetts Artists Foundation and the National Endowment of the Arts, has won three Pushcart Prizes and *Agni Review's* John Cheever Award for Fiction. Painter's flash stories have been presented on National Public Radio, and on the YouTube channel, CRONOGEO, and her work has been staged by WordTheatre in Los Angeles, London, and New York. Painter's newest collection of stories is *Fabrications: New and Selected Stories* from Johns Hopkins University Press.

Jane Pek was born and grew up in Singapore. Her debut novel *The Verifiers* was published by Vintage/Knopf in February 2022. *The Verifiers* was a New York Times Editors' Choice, an Indie Next and LibraryReads pick, a Good Morning America recommendation, and a Phenomenal Book Club selection. Her short fiction has appeared in the 2020 and 2021 editions of *The Best American Short Stories.* She currently lives in New York, where she works as a lawyer at a global investment company

Brenda Peynado's genre-bending short story collection, *The Rock Eaters*—featuring alien arrivals, angels falling from rooftops, virtual reality, and sorrows manifesting as tumorous stones—has garnered starred reviews from *Publisher's Weekly* and *Kirkus Reviews.* Her stories have won an O. Henry Prize, a Pushcart Prize, the *Chicago Tribune's* Nelson Algren Award, and inclusion in *The Best American Science Fiction and Fantasy.* She's currently writing a novel about the 1965 civil war in the Dominican Republic and a girl who can tell all possible futures, and she teaches creative writing at the University of Houston.

Maurice Carlos Ruffin is the author of *The Ones Who Don't Say They Love You,* which was published by One World Random House in August 2021. It is a *New York Times* Editor's Choice and a finalist for the Ernest J. Gaines Award for Literary Excellence. His first book, *We Cast a Shadow,* was a finalist for the PEN/Faulkner Award, the Dayton Literary Peace Prize, and the PEN America Open Book

Prize. It was longlisted for the 2021 Dublin Literary Award, the Center for Fiction Prize and the Aspen Words Literary Prize. The novel was also a *New York Times* Editor's Choice. Ruffin is the winner of several literary prizes, including the Iowa Review Award in fiction and the William Faulkner–William Wisdom Creative Writing Competition Award for Novel-in-Progress. His work has appeared in the *New York Times, The LA Times, The Oxford American, Garden & Gun, Kenyon Review,* and *Four Hundred Souls: A Community History of African America.* A New Orleans native, Ruffin is a professor of Creative Writing at Louisiana State University, and the 2020-2021 John and Renee Grisham Writer-in-Residence at the University of Mississippi.

Shannon Sanders is a Black attorney and writer. Her debut short story collection, *Company,* is forthcoming from Graywolf Press. Her short story "The Good, Good Men" was a 2020 winner of the PEN/ Robert J. Dau Short Story Prize for Emerging Writers. Her fiction appears in *One Story, Electric Literature, TriQuarterly, Joyland,* and elsewhere. She lives near Washington, D.C. with her husband and three sons.

George Saunders is #1 *New York Times* bestselling author of eleven books, including *Lincoln in the Bardo,* which won the 2017 Man Booker Prize for best work of fiction in English and was a finalist for the Golden Man Booker, in which one Booker winner was selected to represent each decade, from the fifty years since the prize's inception. His most recent book is *A Swim in a Pond in the Rain,* an exploration of the Russian short story. The audiobook for *Lincoln in the Bardo,* which featured a cast of 166 actors, was the 2018 Audie Award for best audiobook. The story collection *Tenth of December* was a finalist for the National Book Award, and won the inaugural Folio Prize in 2013 (for the best work of fiction in English) and the Story Prize (best short story collection). His forthcoming collection is *Liberation Day: Stories.* He has received MacArthur and Guggenheim Fellowships, and the PEN/Malamud Prize for excellence in the short story. In 2013, he was named one of the world's 100 most influential people by *Time* magazine. He has taught in the Creative Writing Program at Syracuse University since 1996.

Joanna Scott is the author of ten novels, including *Arrogance,* a PEN-Faulkner finalist, *The Manikin,* a finalist for the Pulitzer Prize, and *Follow Me,* a *New York Times* Notable Book. She has also published two collections of short fiction, *Various Antidotes* and *Everybody Loves Somebody.* Awards include a MacArthur Fellowship, a Lannan Literary Award, a Guggenheim Fellowship, the Ambassador Book Award from the English-Speaking Union, and the Rosenthal Award from the American Academy of Arts and Letters. Scott is the Roswell Smith Burrows Professor of English at the University of Rochester.

Anna Sequoia is the author of ten non-fiction books, including the best-selling humor book, *The Official J.A.P. Handbook* (N.A.L.), and the animal rights classic *67 Ways to Save the Animals* (Harper Perennial), which was endorsed by philosopher/activist Peter Singer. Anna has served as Co-Chair of the Publishing Triangle, was a charter member of the National Book Critics Circle, and was on the Editorial Board of Upper Hand Press. Anna's current writing project is a series of interconnected short stories about a Mafia-connected, blue collar Jewish family. Anna has appeared on more than one-hundred radio and TV programs.

Asako Serizawa was born in Japan and raised in Singapore, Jakarta, and Tokyo. Her debut book of fiction, *Inheritors,* won the PEN/Open Book Award and The Story Prize Spotlight Award, was a Massachusetts Book Awards Honors Book, and was longlisted for the PEN/Robert W. Bingham Prize. A recipient of grants from the National Endowment for the Arts and the Mass Cultural Council, her work has also been awarded two O. Henry Prizes, a Pushcart Prize, a Rona Jaffe Foundation Writers' Award, and fellowships from the Fine Arts Work Center in Provincetown, MacDowell, Civitella Ranieri Foundation, and elsewhere. She currently lives in Boston.

Sharyn Skeeter was fiction, poetry, book review editor at *Essence* magazine and editor in chief at *Black Elegance* magazine. She taught journalism, writing, and black American literature at Emerson College, the University of Bridgeport, and Three Rivers, Norwalk, and Gateway community colleges. Sharyn Skeeter's poetry and articles have been published in magazines, journals, and anthologies, including *Hypertext Magazine, Hawai'i Pacific Review, Monkeybicycle, Poet Lore, Connecticut River Review, Obsidian II, Fiction, Chicago Quarterly Review, Re-Markings, Callaloo, In Search of Color Everywhere* (ed. Ethelbert Miller) and *Our Black Sons Matter* (ed. George Yancy). Her debut novel *Dancing with Langston* received the 2019 Gold Foreword

Reviews INDIES Book of the Year Award (multicultural adult fiction). She has given readings and participated in literary events in the United States, India, and Singapore. She's on the boards of Hugo House (school and community for writers) and Earth Creative (international platform for artists who care about sustainability and climate justice), and is a former trustee at ACT Theatre. Her archive is at Washington University. She's from New York and now lives in Seattle.

Tiphanie Yanique is a novelist, poet, essayist, and short story writer. She is the author of the poetry collection, *Wife*, which won the 2016 Bocas Prize in Caribbean poetry and the United Kingdom's 2016 Forward/Felix Dennis Prize for a First Collection. Tiphanie is also the author of the novel, *Land of Love and Drowning*, which won the 2014 Flaherty-Dunnan First Novel Award from the Center for Fiction, the Phillis Wheatley Award for Pan-African Literature, and the American Academy of Arts and Letters Rosenthal Family Foundation Award, and was listed by NPR as one of the Best Books of 2014. *Land of Love and Drowning* was also a finalist for the Orion Award in Environmental Literature and the Hurston-Wright Legacy Award. She is the author of a collection of stories, *How to Escape from a Leper Colony*, which won her a listing as one of the National Book Foundation's *5Under35*. Her writing has won the Bocas Award for Caribbean Fiction, the Boston Review Prize in Fiction, a Rona Jaffe Foundation Writers Award, a Pushcart Prize, a Fulbright Scholarship and an Academy of American Poet's Prize. She has been listed by the *Boston Globe* as one of the sixteen cultural figures to watch out for and her writing has been published in the *New York Times*, *Best African American Fiction*, *The Wall Street Journal*, *American Short Fiction* and other places. Her latest novel is *Monster in the Middle*.

Ye Chun (surname: Ye) is a bilingual Chinese American writer and literary translator. Her collection of stories, *Hao* (Catapult, 2021), was an Indie Next Selection and was longlisted for 2022 Andrew Carnegie Medal for Excellence in Fiction. She has also published two books of poetry, *Travel Over Water* and *Lantern Puzzle*, a novel in Chinese, 海上的桃树 (*Peach Tree in the Sea*), and four volumes of translations. A recipient of an NEA Literature Fellowship, a Sustainable Arts Foundation Award, and three Pushcart Prizes, she teaches at Providence College and lives in Providence, Rhode Island. Visit her at www.yechunauthor.com.

PERMISSIONS

About the Editor

Sharyn Skeeter was fiction, poetry, book review editor at *Essence* magazine and editor in chief at *Black Elegance* magazine. She taught journalism, writing, and literature at colleges and universities. Her poetry and articles have been published in magazines, journals, and anthologies. *Dancing with Langston*, her debut novel, received the 2019 Gold Foreword Reviews INDIES Book of the Year Award (Multicultural Adult Fiction). She has given readings and participated in literary events in the United States, India, and Singapore. She's on the boards of Hugo House and Earth Creative, and is a former trustee at ACT Theatre in Seattle.